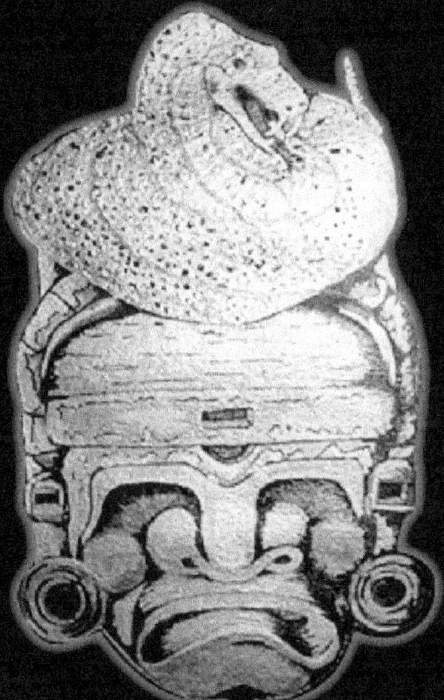

MYSTERY FROM THE TRAIL OF TEARS

"We consider Kitty Sutton's novels a tantalizing hook to reel young readers into the magic and enjoyment of our nation's history." -Kathleen and Michael Gear

WHEEZER
AND THE
GOLDEN SERPENT

KITTY SUTTON

"In *WHEEZER AND THE PAINTED FROG* Kitty Sutton has   penned the first of a delightful series of novels set against the Cherokee removal. Orphaned and exploited in a new land, a young Cherokee girl seeks justice for the murder of her brother-and to her aid comes Wheezer, a small white dog with the charm and sensibility to both ferret out the bad guys and bring a sparkling cast of characters together .

We consider Kitty Sutton 's novels a tantalizing hook to reel young readers into the magic and enjoyment of our nation 's history ."

-W. Michael Gear and Kathleen O'Neal Gear - New York Times bestselling authors of People of the Morning Star.

"Once again Kitty Sutton has spun a magical tale in *WHEEZER AND THE SHY COYOTE*. New villains are preying on the Native peoples' struggling to build new homes in Oklahoma. Wheezer's beloved 'People' are drawn inexorably into a dangerous web of intrigue as they struggle to stop the insidious whiskey trade. With 'his 'people 's' lives on the line, it's up to Whee zer and his curious new friend 'Yellow Eyes, a shy coyote, to break the case open.Steeped in Native American history and lore, WHEEZER AND THE SHY COYOTE is a worthy successor in the 'Mystery from the Trail of Tears' series."

-Kathleen O'Neal Gear and W. Michael Gear - New York Times bestselling authors of *PEOPLE OF THE SONGTRAIL.*

"Wheezer and the Painted Frog is at once joyous and heartbreaking. You will ache for the suffering, be outraged by the wrongs fascinated by the way of life, identify with Sasa and above all you will love Wheezer. You will look for his spirit in every dog you meet!

Good luck and all best wishes Anne"

-Anne Perry, Author of *Acceptable Loss*

Wheezer and the Golden Serpent
by
Kitty Sutton
Illustrated by Kitty Sutton
Published by Little Buffalo Arts Publishing

© 2018

Cover art: Kitty Sutton
© 2018 Kitty Sutton and Little Buffalo Arts Publishing
ISBN-13: 978-1-7321496-4-9
ISBN-10: 173214964X

Kitty Sutton

Acknowledgments

A grateful acknowledgement to the following people who supported, and assisted in the research for this book.

Christine Case-Leng
Pico Triano
Denise Sinn
Susan Welker
Sanja Koteska
Hanna Asfour

Also, I wish to extend my gratitude and admiration for the artists which contributed illustrations for this book.

Sanja Koteska
Hanna Asfour
Rich Truong
Natasa Berec

Dedication

This book is dedicated to my three wonderful Jack Russells, Wheezer, Bridget and Happy, who keep me on my toes and watch over me while I research and write. Without them I would not be able to put pen to paper or digits to keyboard.

Letter to my readers:

In writing this story about the great 1843 International Peace Council, I endeavored to give you the reader all of the information that I could. To accomplish my goal, I was forced to take some literary license. The recorded history of this event is somewhat sketchy. There was a second council, hosted by the Creeks, though not as well attended. We know that Pierce M Butler, the Cherokee Agent, had been asked to transcribe the speeches for both the 1843 and the 1845 councils. I was able to locate the actual transcription of the speeches at the 1845 council, but not for the 1843 one. So to give you the best picture of the magnificence of such a meeting, I combined the two. You may read more about these councils by checking out the files at Oklahoma Chronicles online.

It was a necessity to use the famous personages who actually attended these councils, however again I was forced to take license and create conversations. All of the conversations, other than the speeches at the council itself, are a product of my own imagination, trying to deduce the most likely occurrence, such as the meeting called by Ross when he found that a Cherokee was helping the Mexicans. Historically, Chief Ross was told about such a man and his reaction was to hold the conference. Since the Cherokee mode of government is closer to a democracy than a dictatorship, I surmised that he would call a meeting of his head men to discuss a course of action. Again, those conversations were fiction. All of the non-famous characters were composites of the people of the tribes that I know and are therefore fictitious. I tried to be as authentic as possible in their speech and actions.

I found it very difficult to stick close to the historical references when there were wide gaps of information. I try very hard to make my books heavy on the historical and light on the fiction. As one of my readers once told me, "Your books are actual history that you have told as a mystery and where the fiction in no way interferes with its historical value." Much historical fiction is actually fictitious stories placed in historical places or times and are light on the history.

I hope you come away from my books with some knowledge of the events of that bygone time. And, I hope if you are Cherokee or any of the tribes that attended the councils, you will remember this information and pass it along to your children.

One fact I would like you to come away with after reading this book is that Chief John Ross saved the Republic of Texas from a full scale invasion by Mexico. He did it using statesmanship. Words, not bullets. He effectively took the weapon of starting a civil war in Indian Territory away from the invaders and crippled their plan. He never received any commendation of his very skillful handling of a bad situation; one that could have cost the tribes their newly found homes and land. History would record Sam Houston as the hero of the day. At the time, Indians were not thought to have those types of skills.

So now you know, the rest of the story!

Kitty Sutton, Author

Sasa As A Young Lady

Prologue

In the warm glow of a lowering sun, Fernan picked his way over the bodies strewn on the ground in every direction and pose. The stench of burned flesh clotted his nostrils and choked his throat. Flies covered wounds and the pools of life's liquid seeping into the dry ground. The devastation was enormous: everywhere he looked, there were burned buildings, ruined statues, broken bodies and silence, except for the relentless buzzing of the flies. That silence was so thick, Fernan wanted to scream just to break up the deafening non-sound, but he did not feel like screaming. He had screamed enough over the days and weeks it took to destroy this city. Somehow, a scream now seemed inadequate for the ruined new world city he saw before him. A land desolated after months of fighting.

Was it not only a few months ago that Moctezuma was giving Cortez and his men a feast in their honor? Had we not all been relaxed and friendly with these new people, he thought? He walked on, taking care to show respect for these defeated people, not actually having a place to go. Cortez and all of the other men–those still alive–had moved on, presumably to the next of Moctezuma's cities, looking for more gold, and they had probably given him up for dead. Gold was what glowed in their eyes and ran in their veins now.

Within the vast stone room, Moctezuma had lovingly revealed the art of his people. Not just gold, but also a beautiful blue gem-stone of some kind which adorned masks and ornaments of all description. For some of them, their use could only be guessed at. Moctezuma had described for Cortez the mines in faraway places which had yielded those blue stones, their color as turquoise as the blue-green oceans that surrounded the islands off the eastern coast of these lands. He had also shown Cortez a red stone that was no stone at all, but a breed of lovely coral divers risked their lives to harvest. There were also pearls and polished shells, the beauty of which he had never seen before, but Cortez had eyes only for the yellow metal, and he became blind to anything else. As a show of friendship, they were allowed to go into Moctezuma's palace and within a week, Cortez had his men kidnap Moctezuma, holding him for months. Once they had glimpsed the vast wealth that adorned every surface and wall of the king's inner chambers, their plans had changed. Instead of diplomacy and treaties, they began to rain down terror on the city. He doubted that Cortez had ever seen that much wealth in all his life, in spite of his comings and goings to the royal palaces of Spain.

It seemed most of the *conquistadores*, except for himself, Fernan Agustin Lorencio D'Villanueva, had no reservations about slaughtering hundreds of the inhabitants of this great city, by the command of their leader. Tenochtitlan had been the greatest city of the Aztecs and Fernan had been forced to participate in the slaughter of a people and their culture. The memory was like bile in his mouth.

The sun was getting lower, but he had no will left to think of his own needs. Who was left to bury the dead? Cortez had not paused in his headlong rush for more to even give his own fallen men, more than 700 of them, a Christian burial. Fernan knew that by midday tomorrow, the bodies would begin to bloat and give off an unbearable putrid smell, and it would be impossible to stay. He also knew that Cortez would come back to make sure they had gotten all the gold before melting it all down, forming it into ingots and sending it back to Spain.

Where was he to go? No matter what the cost, he had no intention of following Cortez and take part in another slaughter like the one he had witnessed. No, better he take a different route, fade into this land and never see another Spanish face evermore.

A sound, small and barely audible, broke the overburdening silence. Whatever it was, it was close. Maybe there was at least one soul left to help, one person to plead forgiveness from. It would make all the difference. He hurried around a stone monument and found a door standing open. The sound came again, it was coming from inside the monument. Fernan placed his hand on the stone wall outside the door, but something rough and sharp stung it and made him draw away quickly. Gazing up, he could see there had been some kind of ornament on the outside, but someone had taken a knife to pry it off, leaving the wall rough and naked.

A soft moan erupted from inside, and Fernan hurriedly crossed the threshold, opening the door wide. The lowering sun was shining directly into the previously concealed room. On the floor, leaning against a rock wall, was his friend Adalberto with an arrow sticking out from his chest.

Fernan bent down quickly. Adalberto was saying something.

"Yes, my friend, I am here. I am afraid I have no medical supplies to help you, but I have water," said Fernan.

Adalberto nodded. After a small sip from Fernan's water skin he motioned his friend to come closer.

"Fernan, my friend. This was my last day of fighting. I am going to my ancestors today, but before I go I need to make amends for this terrible thing we have done to these people," whispered Adalberto.

"Ah, I too wish for absolution, my brother, but there is no priest here. The soldiers have followed Cortez to the next town, looking for more gold, as if they did not find a lifetime's treasure here, purchased with blood. I am afraid we will have to approach God without it," Fernan sadly replied.

"Let me do one small act of penance with you as my witness, dear *compadre*," Adalberto replied.

"My friend, you are dying, what can you do for penance in the time you have left? Do you not think that I am not a fit one to be your witness, for I too have much to ask forgiveness for from our Savior?" asked Fernan.

"But you must do this, for us both. I know I will be gone soon, and who knows how long you have, yourself. If you did not follow Cortez, you are already a marked man. Is this not so, *compadre*? Look Fernan, look where my finger points. Before I was shot, I covered it with my cloak. It is a beautiful thing, is it not?" said Adalberto.

Fernan had not noticed the cloak covering something protruding from the inside wall of the small room. He quickly whisked the cloak away and for a moment his eyes were blinded by the glinting sun rays reflecting off the object. Fernan had never seen anything so exotic and strange. Indeed, it was better than any of the items Cortez had stolen from the King's chamber. His quick gasp of breath betrayed his appreciation. It was a large sculpture of a golden serpent atop a green mottled golden Aztec head. It was attached to the wall, but was also sitting on a ledge. It was at least as tall as the distance from his elbow to the tips of his fingers. And it was a beautiful thing.

"Yes, you see it," whimpered Adalberto. "I heard what Cortez planned to do months ago, and I could find no way out of it. Then today I could not stand to kill one more woman, or one more child. So when the slaughter started again, I looked for a place to conceal myself. I do not want to burn in hell for what has been done here my friend. I threw my cloak over it, so that none of the men would see it. But, before I could close the door, I was wounded. Now, my friend, you must pry it from the wall, wrap it in my cloak and take it far away from here. Do not let Cortez take it from this place. It is my only way to show God where my heart is. Not with riches and glory," pleaded Adalberto, as his breath began to fail him.

"It is so big, where could I take such a thing? But, I too see what you are saying. This may be the only thing you and I are allowed to do, for these people will be no more and there will be no one to say who they were or how they lived. Yes, I will take it," agreed Fernan.

Quickly Fernan pried the large golden serpent and the head from the wall and wrapped it all up in the cloak. He was surprised to find how heavy it was, but then, it was gold. He turned to see if his friend needed more water, but it was too late.

"Poor Adalberto. Alas, I cannot stay to bury you either. If you wanted me to take this away so that Cortez cannot find it, then my friend I must leave now, for he will come back, and I do not intend on being here when he does. Goodbye my friend. You could not prevent what happened, no more that I could have, but preserving the Golden Serpent will be our penance, which I will do for the both of us, yes," finished Fernan.

And so, Fernan began to walk north since he knew Cortez had gone west, and as he went, whenever he encountered any tribal nations, he would show them the Golden Serpent, and they would immediately allow him passage, food, shelter and whatever else he needed on his journey. And the Golden Serpent disappeared, except for the stories women told their children, at night, and the rumors of the beautiful Golden Serpent of the Aztecs. And a story began to form that whoever possessed it, would have wealth and good fortune, but that if anyone gained it by stealing, as Cortez had done, their fate would be death. And the legend continued to grow. No one knew how far Fernan had walked or where he had hidden the Golden Serpent. Over the years, people thought they knew where it was. Some of them walked into the forests never to be seen again, and some came back empty handed, but this never stopped the story from growing and spreading until it became the thing of legends and myth.

Tremont Hotel

Chapter 1
Life as a Young Lady

Sasa rode wide eyed and alert to all the new sites before her. Boston was enormous, with so many people all in one place and with buildings made of stone and bricks, not a log house to be seen anywhere. At least, not in the main part of the city. Some of the buildings were breathtakingly high. One of them, called the Custom House, was not finished yet, but would be soon; people stood around its perimeter just to watch the construction. Sasa had no idea of its exact height, but Jackson Halley, her guardian, told her he believed it to be the tallest building in Boston. It even had a dome being built over the top, partly made of glass to let in natural light. It was a wonder to behold.

She rode in a fine white open topped carriage drawn by four speckled grays with purple red plums attached to their bobbing heads. The seats were red velvet, with gold buttoned tufts along the back. There were smells, too, which she did not recognize, but made her mouth water all the same. She noticed little places where to eat, with tables and chairs sitting outside on the sidewalks. People sat and ate while passers-by waved to them. Everything was bright, busy and exciting. She had waited for this promised trip for the last four years, and now the promise had been honored. She relished her reward for passing all the final exams. Now, her education was finished, and she could begin the real work of helping the Cherokee people.

Anna and Jackson sat on the opposite seat, while Wheezer sat anxiously next to her, which would be natural for any Jack Russell Terrier. Jackson had found that out personally when Wheezer, then named Jack, had been sent to him as a gift from the Rev. John Russell, the breeder, who lived in England and who had invented the breed. That meant Wheezer was the first Jack Russell Terrier to come across the ocean to America. There seemed to be no end of new things Jackson, Anna and Sasa were learning on a daily basis. Wheezer was just as delighted with the trip, so much so that Sasa found she had to keep a good hold on his collar, for he was apt to jump out to chase a small animal seen across the street or up in a tree. He loved to run and bark, his favorite activities, but he also loved people too.

Wheezer had been with her since soon after the Trail of Tears; she was then at the point of despair when she found him close to death in the forest, and he needed someone to care for him after a snake bite. Wheezer had been the one to help her solve the murder of her little brother, Usti Yansa, or Little Buffalo in English. They had had many adventures since then, and he always stayed true to her, but in a city as large as this one, he could easily get lost. The year after Sasa met Wheezer, Rev. John Russell sent them another specimen of that unusual breed. This time it was a female. They named her Penny. She was back in Van Buren, Arkansas on the mule breeding ranch the Halley's owned. Penny had just had puppies when they had to leave, so they left her to do her motherly duty while they were gone. The ranch hands and Jackson's partner would look after Penny and the pups.

The air was warm and fresh with the smell of cherry blossoms from the trees lining the streets on the large thoroughfares; it filled her with sheer joy. Many people waved to the party in the carriage with her, but at the same time they took a good, long look at the dark skinned beauty dressed in fashionable clothes riding with Jackson and Anna Halley. Sasa smiled back at them, her excitement bubbling over so much that Anna placed a calming hand on her slender arm.

As a small child, Sasa had spent her early years in the Cherokee homeland near New Echota, Georgia. Her family had farmed tribal land, and raised stock to sell at the market in the town nearest their home. Remembering those times was difficult, it felt a world away. New Echota had seemed a big city to her then, even if it was a Cherokee town. Now she was a young woman, seventeen, tutored by the finest money could buy, regardless of the fact that she was a full blooded Cherokee who only a few years before had walked the Trail of Tears. She had done her duty, studied hard learning the white man's law, always knowing that effort and money were being spent so that she could be of some practical help to her people, and maybe to all of Indian Territory.

It was funny, her reaction to the pictures of Boston she had seen in a book at home, were nothing near her reaction to the impact of the real thing. Now she was realizing she had not known the half of it.

"I see you are enjoying your trip, Sasa," observed Anna, with a slight grin.

"It is much more than I could have ever imagined. So much bigger than the pictures we studied in class. I did not think I would be so impressed. One day my people will hopefully have nice cities as well," said Sasa.

"I rather like the towns of the Cherokee, only it's a different style of living. I don't think you can really compare it. You must admit your people lived many millenniums without the finery you see here. Don't be fooled, Sasa. This wealth is an illusion," replied Anna, who then leaned forward to whisper into Sasa's ear, "All of this land you see, once belonged to many different tribes and was taken in a similar way as your own was taken." Sasa's eyes grew large, her face solemn, knowing firsthand the pain and loss of upheaval and war.

Anna was like a mother to Sasa, and she had been her first teacher. Since Sasa had lost her own mother after the Trail of Tears, Anna had helped to guide her, educate her and give her the benefit of her womanly wisdom. She also had several elders of the Cherokee who took an interest in her education, and she was encouraged by Anna and Jackson to learn all she could from the Cherokee and the whites. They felt it would make a difference to helping her people someday.

Jackson had taken Sasa's education seriously. When Sasa came to live with him in 1839, however, Van Buren,

Arkansas had no teachers. Jackson asked his father, Andrew Halley to help him find a suitable tutor to move to Van Buren until her education was as complete as it could be. Jackson was adamant that she learn as much about the white man's law as possible, so Andrew hired Professor Enger from Boston, a law professor, to tutor her as if she were attending a first rate college back east. It was evident that Professor Enger was not so pleased to be there.

It had only been three and a half years since she had walked the now famous Trial of Tears with her family. Sasa had been thirteen, almost fourteen years old. She had lost her parents and her brother, but that same year she met Jackson Halley, who would become her guardian, and his dog, Wheezer, would be her best friend. It was true that Jackson was a white man, but he had many friends among the Cherokee and his business partner was Archibald Flint, a Cherokee who brought his family to Van Buren, Arkansas before the dreaded march from their homeland. They all had a share in Jackson's mule breading ranch.

Sasa looked down to make sure her silk walking gown was not wrinkling. She spread out some of the folds with her snow white kid gloved hands. It had been difficult to fashion her hair as white women did. Her hair was long, board straight, and thick. But with a curling iron and patience, Anna succeeded in getting it up and into the newest mode for a young lady of high social circles. Sasa was seventeen and therefore younger than normal for what Anna had set in motion, but she did it because Sasa was so much more mature than most of the white young ladies who were even three years her senior.

Anna had plans of introducing Sasa to all of society, as well as her own social circles, for not only Sasa was her student, but Anna was also married to her guardian, and had therefore decided to make Sasa her protégé. Sasa remembered the discussion they had had about what to do if her reception to Boston society was not well received. It had taken place one night in the State Room on the steamer they took up the coast. They sat on the bed while Anna brushed Sasa's hair.

"Sasa, are you nervous about meeting so many white ladies of society?" she asked.

"I have been trying not to think of it, Anna. I truly want them to like me, but I must confess that maybe I should prepare somewhat, in case it does not go well," replied Sasa.

"Remember that you have had the training of a lady. Always keep your deportment with slight interest, and if anyone tries to goad you into a heated response, just become imperious, look down your nose at them and sniff. Just sniff and look away, as if they had not spoken. If some society lady says something snippy, show total disinterest to their jabs. As long as you act every inch a lady, you will win the admiration of those looking on, and the aggressor will end up looking a fool. However, if you are the one to get heated and give a smart remark back, it may sting them a bit, but they will have won the day. Then they will say, behind their hands, 'see, she is only a red Indian, just as I said she was'," explained Anna.

"I see what you mean, but it is hard to know what to expect. I have no real experience in white society. For example, the Cherokee people do not say cutting remarks to anyone, it is considered in bad taste and it would make our elders ashamed," observed Sasa.

"Oh, it is just as much in bad taste in society as well, but that does not stop some superior society matron from trying. She may even be someone from whom everyone expects to hear sour notes, so it is best for you to plug your ears up and clamp your mouth shut, nod and . . . ?" Anna prompted her.

"Sniff, and then sniff again," laughed Sasa, then she turned to silently take in the daunting view that seemed like the fairy tales Anna read to her sometimes. She wondered... if she closed her eyes and opened them again, would she be back close to her own people in Indian Territory?

Abruptly, Sasa was jolted out of her reverie by Wheezer, who had placed his rough paw on her arm. He gave her a quick warm lick on her cheek. She noticed that the carriage was slowing to a stop in front of a large stone building that occupied a long area down the road which, as Jackson had explained, was called 'an entire city block'. The front door had two huge tall white pillars in front, as if guarding the front entrance. It looked formidable and cold, not welcoming at all.

Jackson saw the puzzled look on her face and smiled with wry humor, while his eyes quickly glanced over to meet Anna's equally humorous expression.

"This is The Tremont House Hotel, Sasa. It is relatively new and boasts modern amenities. They say it has the first indoor toilets. I myself have been looking forward to seeing this modern wonder of architecture. It was designed by Isaiah Rogers in 1829, and since then he has designed many large and wonderful buildings in New York. We are almost ready to disembark. There's nothing to fear." Jackson gently patted her hand. "Once we stop, the carriage driver will dismount and open your door to hand you down to the sidewalk. He will have our luggage brought in, so you needn't worry about anything. Just follow me into the building, we will check in and receive the number of the suite of rooms we will be occupying," he explained, just as the carriage came to a halt.

It happened just as Jackson had said it would. She held onto Wheezer's leash while he obediently trotted next to her as if he had done this before, many times. The front of the building was impressive and presented four tall stone pillars. They came through the entry, and the room widened out into a huge foyer with a high ceiling, brightly lit by gleaming chandeliers. A plush red patterned carpet greeted her feet, and she smelled fresh lemon polish and candle wax. The entry also boasted large comfortable furniture in plush velvets and side tables in dark walnut. The lamps on the tables carried shades of glass from which dangled many prisms, cut crystal jewels sending rainbows of color around the room. She felt she could sit in this room alone and be happy doing nothing at all except looking.

Jackson had received their allotted room numbers and the party swept up a grand marble staircase which curved elegantly up to the second floor. It was wide enough to allow the entire party to climb the stairs abreast; instead, a porter led the way, then Jackson Anna and Sasa with Wheezer followed. The porter kept looking back at Wheezer with puzzlement and apprehension, but Wheezer paid no mind. Sasa found herself holding her breath and had to remind herself to breath naturally, but it was difficult because she found it all too exciting.

On their way up they encountered two young gentlemen, both in gray striped pants and black cut-away coats. Just as one young man placed his black beaver felt top hat on his sandy haired head, he saw Sasa. Briefly, she glanced at them, but he had stopped on the stairs to watch her in obvious awe. At the top of the stairs, surreptitiously she looked again to find him still staring while his friend tugged at his sleeve, trying to get him to hurry. She felt a curious, pleasant feeling. She would have to remember to talk to Anna about it later.

The porter paused in front of large, dark double doors. He opened them, allowing them to enter. At once, they were bathed in soft muted light filtered through sheer cream curtain panels, framed by heavier dark maroon silk drapes. The room looked like a sitting room, with several doors leading off from it.

"I think this should be your room, Sasa," said Anna, standing by an open door. "This room faces the main street and has the most light. Plus the decor is not as dark as in the other rooms, more feminine I think."

Sasa walked into the large bedroom, but stopped midway inside.

"Anna, my bags are here already. How did they do that so fast?" she asked.

"Oh, they have back ways and unknown passages to help them get around without being obvious. Now, don't you go and unpack. There will be a maid up in a moment to do that for you," announced Anna, from her own bedroom.

"What?" Sasa exclaimed, as she rushed over to Anna and Jackson's bedroom. Stopping at the bedroom door, she was flush with indignation. "I have been putting my own clothes away since I can remember, Anna. I would be embarrassed to just stand there and let someone else do it for me. I mean, I am not disabled, nor am I lazy. It is just ridiculous, I can do it."

"Oh, but you must not, Sasa," pleaded Anna. "This is what is acceptable among the ladies of society, and if you want to be welcomed by them, you must learn their ways. If you try to do things like you did back home, why, you will alienate them. They will think you are a backward hick. You have not studied for so long, at such an expense and with such dedication, to allow that, now have you? This is the way to effect some change in the way that the whites and the United States government perceive any of our Native tribes. Right now, they have been convinced that no-one can learn and be civilized as they are. It was the excuse they used to settle all the tribes on designated lands, away from their own homelands. It is your job to prove them wrong, Sasa. Only you can do that."

"But, something as silly as letting a white girl put away my clothes like I was the Queen of Sheba, I don't know if I can bear it," insisted Sasa.

"I know it will take some getting used to, but there are two sides to that coin. You see, you are also providing a job for that young maid. She is probably feeding her entire family on what she makes here. If you deny her the ability to do her job, you might cause a problem with her employment. The management may even think she offended you in some way. Right now, the hotel management is not looking at you as a Cherokee Indian. You are dressed as a perfect lady, and conducting yourself as a lady should; you are accompanied by your guardians, who are white and of some influence, so no matter what their personal thoughts on the matter may be, it would be unthinkable to deny you the same amenities that other ladies are afforded. You must learn to be gracious, but not haughty or overbearing. After all, Sasa, you are the one who wanted to help her people. At the moment, this is the best way for you to do so," said Anna.

Sasa subsided and walked back into her room, not knowing what to do, so she just stood at the window while Wheezer tried out the top of the bed. Soon, a soft knock at the entry door revealed the young maid they had been discussing. Sasa smiled at her and invited her into her room.

"Hello Miss. Me name is Sarah. I am to be your maid for your stay, so you must call on me whenever you need help. You just ring that bell pull, here in your room by your bed, Miss, and that will alert me that I am wanted. I am happy to unpack your things, and also to help with your toilet. People say I have a good hand at dressing hair, Miss, and I must say you have a fine, thick head of it, too," said Sarah.

When Sasa just stood staring at her in astonishment, Sarah became worried.

"Oh, Miss. Did I overstep me bounds? You are right. It is not me place to comment about your person. I am rightly ashamed, Miss."

"Uh, no, Sarah. There is no problem. I thank you and I shall be, uh, glad of your help," Sasa hurriedly replied. Then, seeing how young the girl looked, she added, "When do they let you go home Sarah?"

"Oh Lordy me, no, Miss. I live here. I have me own little room downstairs with the other servants. I gets one afternoon off a week, when I go and sees me mother, but I am available to you night or day. Just ring and I'll be up here in a snap, you wait and see," answered Sarah, with a pleasant smile and a wink.

"I am amazed that you don't get more time to yourself, Sarah," said Sasa.

"Nah, it's all right, Miss. This is the best job I ever had, and glad of it I am. Me and me family, we came here about ten year ago from Ireland and jobs are not that many that I can go apickin and achoosin. My Ma is at home with the little ones, my Da works at the shipyards and I work here. That way, me Ma don't have to feed nor clothe me, ya see. All in all, I am fairly happy so far," explained Sarah, as she finished handing up Sasa's fine new gowns in the large chifferobe standing tall against the far wall.

Her room featured a fine four poster bed in the middle, and a vanity table with a chair for preparing her toilet.

There were oil lamps by the bed, and two plush, comfy looking overstuffed chairs by the windows as a small sitting room arrangement with a small tea table in front. Sarah saw Sasa looking at the sitting area and table.

"Miss, would you like some tea? There is no problem at all, I can get it for you at any time of day or night. You can also have cookies or cakes. Even some small sandwiches, if you like. I can imagine you might be a mite peckish from your trip," said Sarah.

"You know, Sarah, I think that might be very nice. But, please bring it for all three of us." replied Sasa.

Just then, Wheezer crawled out from under the bed and in so doing, he startled Sarah, who let out a stifled squeak.

"Don't be afraid," laughed Sasa. "This is Wheezer. He is a Jack Russell Terrier and new breed to the United States. He is very smart, and you can talk to him like you would a person. I think he understands most of it, but he is a bit rambunctious and loves to play."

Sarah's eyes sparkled with enjoyment, "Oh, Miss I love dogs. If you need anything for him, I would bust me buttons to get it."

"Well, now that you mention it, if you have some chicken downstairs, I think he would be most pleased with something to eat," nodded Sasa, her tan skin flushing with pleasure that someone would take notice of Wheezer in this very foreign feeling city.

Wheezer barked his agreement, so Sarah scuttled out of the room to fetch the tea and Wheezer's treat.

Chapter 2
Not All That Glitters

Sasa paced the floor, anxiety, coming from every pore. She had been waiting for Anna to come back from a lunch engagement which Sasa had declined to attend. Anna swept into the room, a smile transforming her features. Meeting old acquaintances, friends, and even some not so friendly was a special joy of her visit. She removed the demi-cape which matched her powder blue day suit, whose matching long, full skirt which was supported by crinolines so stiff they could almost stand on their own. One of the crinolines contained varying sizes of hoops to encourage the full skirt to stay at its fullest. Anna's face was rosy and aglow with smiles and she stopped at her bedroom door to deposit her gloves, parasol, demi-cape and bonnet atop her bed.

It was obvious she had a wonderful time, but then immediately she sensed the distress that seemed to fill the suite. She hurried into Sasa's bed chamber to witness Sasa's anxious pacing.

"Sasa, what in the world has happened? When I left you were fine, now you are falling apart. Did someone force themselves into the room? I can call the concierge and I am sure he will find the culprit. I just can't imagine that happening in the finest hotel in Boston," exclaimed Anna, as she rushed in to take hold of Sasa's arms in an effort to calm her.

Sasa held several notes in her hands, each penned on expensive stationary and smelling of fragrance. She held them out as if they contained a disease.

"Anna, I can't do all this. I just can't," she wailed.

Anna suddenly could see the frightened child that Sasa had been when faced with tragedy, death and starvation back in 1839. She had forgotten how vulnerable Sasa might still be, especially since this was her first visit among Boston society. Sasa stood there in her polished white cotton morning dress with little red roses all over it, and she was on the verge of tears.

"What is it? I can't imagine anyone being hateful; we really have only just arrived," Anna murmured.

"No, you don't understand. Read these...these letters. These people don't even know me. I can't imagine them all wanting to meet me. Do they want to make a fool of me?" whined Sasa.

Anna took the notes from Sasa's shaking hands. Sinking down on the comfortable feather bed, she began to read through them while Sasa watched, expecting to see Anna jump up in indignation as well. Instead, Anna began to smile as she read each note in turn. Finally, she raised her head with a sigh and a dreamy look in her eyes.

"You don't have to be upset, dear. These notes are from the mothers and daughters of Boston society who are giving balls and teas. You have been invited to attend, and it is exactly what we hoped would happen," she calmly explained.

"What? These people don't even know me, Anna. How can they want a full blood Cherokee Indian to come to their parties and balls? I will be a laughing stock and I won't go," Sasa declared, with a temperamental stamp of her foot.

"Dearest, don't you remember what I told you about what a young girl does in society when she ceases being a child and is ready to take her place as a woman? It is called 'coming out' and it is always done beginning in the spring and going through the summer. I have been grooming you for this very thing, Sasa, you mustn't be afraid of it. These ladies would not bother to invite you, unless they really wanted you to come. Believe me, the last thing they want at their event is to have a scene. They would avoid it like the plague. You are just letting your own fears get the better of you," replied Anna.

"But Anna, I don't understand why I would get so many. I know you wrote ahead and told them of my lineage. Can clothes and manners change me that much that they would all of a sudden admit me into their circles?" pouted Sasa.

"I believe that you are confusing a different type of society than Boston. Boston is a refined place. We have many learned men here, some even helped make our constitution. We are not in the south, Sasa. The white people in Georgia, South Carolina and Tennessee have had slavery for so long they don't know what it is like to treat people as equals. They have put their own kind so far above all the other races that they would never be able to do what these ladies are doing today. The ladies of Boston know what you have been through and how hard you have worked. Their fathers and husbands have heard the Professor's report of how bright a student you were, plus they know that I would never bring you to begin your season if you were not ready. They truly want to meet you. Now all you have to do is enjoy the attention, take pride in dressing nice and having people want to speak to you, not to mention the young men who have already taken notice of you. This trip is not just a gift to you, it is also to give you the needed experience, so that you will know how to behave in polite society. And why do you think we want you to have this experience?" asked Anna.

Sasa bowed her head, knowing the answer, but reluctant to admit it.

"So that I can help my people bridge the gap between the whites and the tribes in Indian Territory. I know that, but I guess it is so hard for me to take this risk. Remember, Anna, I was there when men, white men who were charged with getting my people to Indian Territory safely, murdered those who were slow, or too sick, or just killed on a whim. It was that way with every group. I realize that this is a totally different context, and I guess I can't hide if I want to accomplish good results. I was just overwhelmed by the number of invitations, I guess," she replied.

"Oh, well, that's because everyone who is having a party, or ball, or tea wants to get their invitations out early, so they can be sure to get the best of society to attend their event. It is common to get this many every day for a few days now, so just be prepared. We will need to go through them all and make a decision as to which ones you will attend. That is something I can help you with. You see Sasa, most young ladies are looking to snag a rich husband. That is what coming out is all about, but your purpose is a little more abstract than that, and we will need to be more subtle. We will choose the invitations that promise to have the most influential attendees. Making the acquaintance of people of power and influence is what you are about Sasa, not necessarily looking to find an advantageous match as well. If ever you feel the time has come for that, we will be happy to help you through that as well, if that is what you wish," said Anna.

"Oh please Anna," countered Sasa, with a sudden shudder, "I am not ready to even talk about marriage. Those men may admire all they like from afar, but that is something I am not wanting in my life right now. I will be pleasant, I will mind my manners, but I want to get started in helping the people in Indian Territory before I settle down and have to raise a family. Besides, I doubt that I would want to marry a white man anyway. It is not that I am not attracted to them, I just know that it would take a fairly extraordinary white man who would work side by side with me to accomplish the goals already set out before me. I don't think there is a man out there like that. I know Jackson is extraordinary. Most white men believe that women are to keep their home and raise children. I am not against such things, in fact, I think that kind of life would be pleasant in the extreme, however, since the year when all of my family died after walking the Trail of Tears, I have known that I must do something more. So, don't worry, Anna. I will not be seeking masculine companionship for some time to come."

So Anna and Sasa settled at the writing desk to sort through the invitations Sasa had already received. As they opened each missive, Anna instructed Sasa on what types of criteria she should consider when making a decision as to what event to patronize.

Within about thirty minutes, they had the invitations separated into stacks according to the calendar of days in the month. Then on a sheet of paper they drew columns separating them as to time of day and labeling the top of each column, for example: Breakfast, Lunch, Tea, Dinner and lastly, Evening.

The knock on the suite door announced the maid. Anna had tea delivered up to the room and now prepared to serve it. Sasa shook her head, declining the repast for now, so Anna prepared her own cup and sat in a blue silk brocade covered chair to take her tea, but continued instructing her.

"You will not receive very many invitations to breakfast except for the mornings when they plan to "run to hounds". It is a little early for a hunt just yet, but I am sure you will receive an invite. Breakfast is always served at the hunt party. We are both excellent horsewomen, so I would advise you to accept at least one of those invitations, when the time comes. Lunch can span quite a large period of the day. It could be a brunch starting about ten in the morning and can go as late as early afternoon. In fact it could butt right up to tea, that is, if one plans to take tea. Tea time is usually handled in the form of a social call, but you can also be invited to a "Tea" which is like an early mini party and has nothing to do with social calls," chuckled Anna, then she continued. "Dinner is usually around seven in the evening, no earlier, but can also be as late as nine; in London, it can even be as late as ten. A society dance, or a ball, usually begins at nine or ten in the evening, and can last from at least midnight to one in the morning."

"How can that be? Back in Van Buren, the parties I attended started no later than seven and broke up by ten. One of my town friends said it would be a scandal if a young lady were out at midnight; she would be considered a loose woman," objected Sasa, a tiny frown on her young face.

"Well, what can I say? This is not Van Buren, this is Boston, and it is like being on a different planet, at least I think so, since I have never been on a different planet, but you know what I mean. Boston society has its own rules on what is proper, and you will learn those as we go along; they are too numerous to mention all at once," replied Anna.

Sasa thought, Oh fine, with rules too numerous to mention all at one time, how on earth am I going to know if I am breaking a rule she has not told me about yet? I have never heard of a people that have more rules than they do days in the year. But if this is what I must learn in order to be in their social sphere, then I must.

"All right, now what do we do?" she asked.

"Well, now we will list each invitation we received in the column it should be in for the day we have been requested."

"Why can't I just pick the ones I want to go to and throw the rest away?"

"You could do that, but it would be a serious breach of protocol," explained Anna, watching the puzzled look creep onto her protégé's face. "You see, Sasa, we will need to send acceptance notes to the ones we accept, and a kind decline to attend note to the others. If you tossed them in the trash, we would not know who to send the notes to or where. Also, since we are putting it in the column in an organized list, if for some reason we change our minds, we can choose a different event to accept on the spur of the moment." Anna absent-mindedly twirled a tendril of blond hair that had come loose from her tidy bun.

"It seems like a very time consuming way of doing things. No wonder the government gets so mixed up," pouted Sasa.

Anna paused to consider the complaint. Quietly, she rose and stepped to the desk, pulling up a chair next to Sasa and taking her small young hands into hers.

"Oh, sweetie, this is not the government now. This is society and how it works, and yes, most women spend the majority of their time arranging their affairs for the season. However, there is a grand pay off for the men who attend these events and who court the women. This is where business is agreed upon, where big ideas start and money is made. The men would not in any way admit that they make their fortunes on the arrangements of women, but it is so, so true. That is the reason you, of all people, need to know how this is done. This is the white man's world and it is completely foreign to your life with the Cherokee. These men think that being civilized is this type of life," Anna spread her arms wide to include all of Boston, "logical and ordered, and very few of them have ever had to worry about their next meal or having enough money to do anything they wanted. If any one of them had been forced to walk the trail with your people, they would have never made it to Indian Territory. They have no way of understanding what they have put you through. It is an abstract thought in their minds, but nothing on which to base your experiences. It was logical to them, even good for your people.

"See, Sasa, that is why there needs to be someone of your people who knows both worlds, who can bring the sides together in ways that the government can never do. There are men who know both worlds, but they lack a woman's view. For hundreds of years your people were a matrilineal people, where family followed the woman, not the man. Women had power and status, even in your government. I heard that you even had a council of women who discussed decisions about the tribe, and that the men needed their support before they could be undertaken. Our people have never had that in our background, but women do play an important role in society all the same, and on the whole, men with social wives do much better than men with none.

"It may take years, even lifetimes, and I have no idea if you will succeed, but you can be the one to start, to show the way for others who will come later. Jackson and I want you to have the knowledge and wisdom, and this is just one way to help. There are others who are helping in ways that you could never do, so it won't be you alone. You are just part of a larger picture," explained Anna.

Sasa sat at the desk, thinking of what Anna had just said. She could see the sunlight beam into the room. Dust motes floated, moved by an invisible current, each particle and piece of fluff going with the flow as if swept up in a swirl of river water, yet there was no wind. All was silent, except for the large wooden clock sitting on the mantle, ticking, ticking. Anna waited silently as well. Sasa thought, *I suppose I am like these particles and fluff, moving in the current. I am alone, yet I am with a multitude of others, each having its own destination. We momentarily meet, and then are swept away to join with a different circle of particles. Who knows who is making the current, pushing the stream. I am beginning to see how tenuous the opportunities are. Maybe I can help bring about change, maybe not, but this is the stream I am in and I must go where it wills.* She shook herself a little, and said, "I am beginning to see. Wado, Anna."

"I have every confidence in you, Sasa. I believe that, eventually, you will see clearly what your people and my people can only partially see. There is no way to eliminate greed, lies, or evil, but even though those things exist, not all are greedy, not all are liars and evil is not everywhere and exists among both white and red peoples. The people of the tribes are not all good or all bad, just as the white man is not all good or bad. If by learning the ways of our white society you will help your people eventually, only God can know that, but nothing can be gained if we don't try. As it stands now, most white people are very ignorant of how civilized your people are. You can help them understand if you find those who will listen," said Anna, as she straightened in her chair. "But, first things first, we must make out our schedule, send our acceptance and declining notes."

So, Sasa spent the better part of two days with Anna, writing notes to people Sasa did not know, although she felt she soon would be able to put new faces to these new names.

Periodically, Jackson would appear to take Wheezer out for a walk in the nearby park. Wheezer was learning new things as well. He was having to learn to not automatically jump up on people. Boston had never seen such a breed of dog before. Once Wheezer got a chance to show his intelligence, though, he fast became the center of attention wherever he happened to go. He had no time to miss his playtime with Sasa, he occasionally thought of Penny, whom he had left back in Van Buren with their latest litter of five strong pups. He would have a lot to tell her when they got back.

Sasa was anxious, attending her first tea, but the attendees were such a small group that it did not overwhelm her. It felt odd to not have Wheezer with her, since they always did new things together. However, Anna said that Boston society would not look kindly on it, plus Wheezer would be confused when everyone did not respond happily to his playful antics.

She now sat in the home of Mr. and Mrs. Steven Standish. Caroline, the young socialite who had invited her to her tea party, had married into the well-known Standish family. She had come from a small town in New Hampshire. Sasa sat demurely on the edge of one of the parlor chairs, in a room that was fairly large, with a high ceiling and chandeliers that could hold at least twenty candles. Sasa wondered briefly how long it would take to light that many for just one fixture. The walls were covered in a light beige, floral patterned wallpaper, with the curtains made to match, and the chairs were covered in a costly slightly shiny, darker beige material. Her chair was high backed and armless, and where the wood was exposed, the legs and wherever it was not upholstered, showed the dark deep warm glow of cherry wood. More casual pieces of furniture that were placed around the room, were large, comfortable chairs and couches with fringe around the bottoms. They had matching antimacassars at the arms and back. It was the most elegant room Sasa had ever seen, which left her awestruck.

She calmly held her tea cup in her right hand and the saucer in her left with a white linen napkin draped over her knees. She hoped most devoutly that she would not spill a drop onto her shot silk, water blue taffeta day gown, for it would never come out. Sasa had acquired a new wardrobe soon after arriving in Boston, in latest styles and colors. She hardly recognized herself in the mirror these days.

She listened carefully as Caroline talked of Boston life since her marriage.

"I am sure the weather is going to be just fine for our little picnic next week. I am so looking forward to it. Do you enjoy picnics, Sasa?" asked Caroline.

"Why, yes, I am very fond of anything that happens out of doors. I love the fresh, clean air and all the colors. I am most obliged that you invited me," answered Sasa, with a sweet smile.

Today Sasa had taken great care with her wardrobe and grooming. Her hair was in the latest fashion, her dress was conservative yet very flattering, its trim and accents of a dusty darker shade of blue, also shot silk. She had added a woven silk floral shawl with fringe, ecru pigskin gloves and a demure bonnet. She was the epitome of a lady.

Then another young lady from across the room perked her raven head up and inserted herself into their conversation.

"Oh Caroline, I think you have forgotten yourself, dear. I am sure that Miss Halley is not acquainted with our kind of picnic. I mean, she grew up eating out of rough pottery over a campfire on a daily basis, didn't you, my dear?" asked Miss Abigail Cole, with a wicked grin.

Caroline stopped her speech in midstream to look back at Abigail with a searing stare. Sasa saw the trap and was ready to defuse the mischievous intent of Miss Cole. First, as planned, she looked bored and then sniffed, acting as if she were talking to a child.

"Why, yes, Miss Cole, you are correct in that I have eaten out of doors many times in my life. However, at my home in Georgia, we lived in a very nice double log cabin, much like the log cabins many of your grandfathers likely lived in when they homesteaded this land. We ate at our own maple wood table and I seem to remember the Blue Dutch china my mother used for special occasions, and the very nice silverware we used. As for picnics, I have had the pleasure of being invited to a few and enjoyed them very much," she replied, satisfied. "The most pleasant one I can remember was with Captain Nathan Boone and a couple of his men. Do you know him? He is the son of Daniel Boone, and a regular visitor at our ranch" Here she paused, so that everyone in the room could see Abigail's answer was a quiet "no", then she went on, "The Boone family joined my guardians and I for a lovely repast on a hill overlooking the Arkansas River. Below, we could see Fort Smith. It was a lovely day.

"Then, of course, for the last few years I have lived with the Halley's in their mansion and ranch, just outside of Van Buren, Arkansas. It is the frontier, but his home is one of the most modern in the area."

Miss Cole had turned pale, but not to be outdone, she countered, "I am sure you are not aware that my family goes all the way back to the original colony. They came over on the Mayflower. We were among the very first settlers."

Sasa, in a calm, clear voice commented, "Oh how nice. I can trace my family back much further; they did not come here on the Mayflower, though, because they were already here and had been for a few thousand years. I believe that some of my ancestors were there to greet yours. In fact, I seem to remember a story about that colony; that the local tribe had to teach them how to live off the land. It seems over half of that colony had died from disease and starvation, yet there had been natural food all around them. I suppose your ancestors must have been some that had been saved by the Indians. What a small world we live in, don't you think?"

Miss Cole, who had no comeback for that, quickly looked away and began a new conversation with whomever was at hand. Caroline daintily put the back of her fingers up to her mouth to barely conceal the giggle she could not hold back. She quickly flashed an appreciative smile back to Sasa, a job well done indeed.

Then she leaned over in a conspiratorial way. "I am afraid, Sasa, that you may have some unfortunate moments with that one. Her father is Col. William Cole, and is known for being an Indian fighter. I suppose she will have a hard time seeing you as the lady you are," she murmured, trying hard not to overstep her new found friendship.

"She can have no harder time than I at imagining me a lady, but just the same I will keep on the watch," replied Sasa.

"If you ever have a question, or need my help, do not hesitate to ask. I am already an admirer of your accomplishments," said Caroline, sincerely.

"Thank you, Caroline. I will do that," answered Sasa.

"You must say you will attend the ball.

Sasa nodded her head slightly, acquiescing to the unavoidable. Better to face what must be faced, or be doomed to failure and always asking yourself, 'What if?' And so far her stay in Boston was showing her that, though the surroundings were foreign to her, the nature of people were basically the same. She was finding it to be true that, no matter what color they were or walk of life they came from, everyone needed, they loved, often sorrowed, sometimes believed, hated, planned, succeeded and failed. She meditated on that for some time during her stay. Hopefully, she would always find it true, no matter who she might meet.

While the women chatted in different circles, Sasa listened to the noise of 'Society'. *Yes, it is noisy*, she thought, and as she appeared to just be content to listen to the conversations all around her, she began to slide back... back to the sounds of her people. The drums, the chanting and dancers. Noisy, but in a different way. The drum was like the heartbeat of the People, bump-bump, bump-bump. With each downbeat the drum was hit harder and the dancers knew exactly where their feet should be. The women were not in the costly gowns of Boston society, but in the traditional costumes, the designs handed down through millennia. The singers sitting around the big drum sang chants passed from father to son, father to son. Women too would join in the songs that lent another layer to the music. Then, the sound of the drum began to fade and the chatting women came into focus once again.

The time to return to her rooms at the hotel was fast approaching, and the other women at the tea seemed to be winding down their conversations. Sasa heard a sound from the hall and then the closing of a heavy door. Presently a young man appeared in the doorway. As he strode into the room, Sasa noticed his sandy hair, fair skin and perfectly cut gray tailcoat with a waistcoat in off white satin brocade. He removed his gray top hat when coming into the room.

"I do apologize. I had no idea your tea would still be occupying this room," the young man said, as he scanned it, noticing each and every young lady present. Then his eyes came to rest on Sasa, and she suddenly realized that he was one of the young men that had passed her on the stairs from the lobby of her hotel, a few days past. She looked quizzically up to meet his searching eyes with her own direct stare.

"Oh, there you are, Caroline," he went on, as his eyes moved to the young woman next to Sasa. "I am sorry that I came sweeping in and disturbing all of your friends. I was looking for Steven," he said, once again raking Sasa with his keen blue-gray eyes.

Finally, Caroline recovered herself and exclaimed, "Oh, Albert, there is no problem at all. You know most of the ladies here today, I dare say."

"But, sister-in-law, I have not had the pleasure of meeting the young lady sitting next to you," he objected, as he made a slight bow from the waist.

"Sasa," began Caroline, "This is my brother by marriage, and of many talents, Albert Standish, "Steven's younger brother."

"How do you do, Mr. Standish?" said Sasa, putting out her hand for Albert to grasp in his fingertips, which he did; he then brought her fingers up to his lips, lingering a little longer than necessary.

"He is my one and only brother-in-law. And Albert, this is my new friend, Sasa Halley of Van Buren, Arkansas, on the frontier. She is here for a visit with her guardians, the Halleys, and while she is here I expect you to be on your very best behavior," demanded Caroline.

"Your wish is my command, dear Caroline," replied Albert. Then turning to Sasa, he added, "I really am not as bad as most brothers. I imagine you have a few too, Miss Halley."

Sasa suddenly felt the room sway and her body go cold, although outwardly she stood as calmly as she had before. Only the blinking of her eyes gave any indication of the distress she suddenly felt. Albert noticed immediately, "Miss Halley, I hope I have not blundered so soon in our acquaintance. Are you ill?" he asked, as he pulled her arm through his and he slowly walked her past what was left of the chattering women. They glided through a set of double doors leading into a garden just touched with the new spring. Albert looked genuinely concerned.

Sasa took a deep breath of the fine, crisp, fresh air, then nodded to Albert. "I think I am fine now. Thank you for your kindness. I just had a quick spell, nothing to be concerned about."

But Albert would not be put off, "I feel I have said something that caused you distress. Please tell me what it was so that I do not do it again."

Sasa sat down on a stone bench under a budding Cherry tree. She could feel Albert's eyes upon her, and felt she must give him some kind of explanation.

"You could not have known. I lost my own brother only a few years ago, he died in my arms when we were children," she said.

"How incredibly awful, Miss Halley. I cannot imagine what a hard memory that must be for you. I do hope you will let me make it up to you sometime in the future. Might I ask, what he died of?" asked Albert.

Sasa's expression froze on her face; the amiable countenance she displayed when first they met was replaced with bitter regret.

"He was murdered. Poisoned. Which is an all too often occurrence in Indian Territory these days. But I really don't want to talk about it now. Being here in Boston is a special gift to me from my guardians, and I don't want to spoil it for them, or myself."

"Quite right, quite right, Miss Halley. We shall not speak of it again unless you want to. Uh, I understand you will be with us for the entire season, is that right?" asked Albert.

"Well, I guess that you already know something about me, Mr. Standish," countered Sasa.

"I confess, and I beg your forgiveness, Miss Halley. When we passed each other on the stairs of the hotel, I was so curious that I asked the hotel manager. We are old acquaintances, and I don't think he told me anything that would be considered private. I also confess to coming home early in the hope of getting a formal introduction to you," admitted Albert, as he lowered his sandy haired head, tilting it enough that he could still see her expression. It gave him a mis-chievous boy appearance.

Sasa had never met anyone like Albert, but then how could she? Her experience with white men had been limited to Jackson Halley, his associates and the rough white soldiers at Fort Smith, whom she avoided at any cost. So meeting a young white gentleman, so charming and disarming, was not what she expected, but dreaded all the same. She felt she could relax just a tad, as long as he remained a gentleman.

Sasa could hear the faint staccato of horse hooves as they hit the bricks that paved the road at the front of the Standish's house. Suddenly, she was reminded that her carriage would be waiting to take her back to the hotel, and she should not make the coach driver wait in the cool air.

"Well, it really was nice to meet you, Mr. Standish. The coach driver is sitting outside waiting for me, and I don't want to take up too much of his day," she said.

"What?" Albert chuckled. "You mean, you are worried about displeasing the coach driver? Are you, really? I have never heard of anything so refreshing in my life. However, I feel I must tell you that no one worries about what their hired help thinks. They are there to do a job and not complain. You really must put that out of your mind. After all, if he were to quit in a pique over waiting for you, there are twenty other 'down and outers' waiting and ready to take his job. I doubt very seriously that he would voice anything of the sort," he concluded, with a slight smirk on his face that Sasa did not think well of.

"Mr. Standish, if I worry about someone's feelings, it is because it is the Christian thing to do. Have you never heard of the Golden Rule, 'do unto others as you would have them do unto you'? It does not take anything out of one's day to be kind, Mr. Standish, especially if you happen to be better off than they. You should be thankful you are not a coach driver, or a beggar, or even worse, an Indian," she countered, with a bit of heat building behind her temper.

"Whoa, now, wait a minute. I had no intentions of offending in any way. I just wanted to make you… uh… help you to be more familiar with the way things are done in Boston. Maybe on the frontier things are different. I humbly do apologize, please say you will forgive me," pleaded Albert.

Sasa thought for a moment. Had she been judgmental? She very well may have jumped to conclusions. His meaning may be a far cry from the words he said, the implied snobbery.

"Of course. I am always ready to forgive, especially if the person is repentant," she nodded with a faint smile that barely touched her lips, but came through her eyes.

"I really must be getting back to the hotel, I would not want to worry Mrs. Halley. She will be watching for my return," she finally told him.

She began to turn, but he held her elbow just enough to stop her from taking a step, then withdrew his hand, as if scalded.

"I… I know we shall see each other from time to time, I hope you will allow me to escort you to the park some afternoon, after all your obligations and calls have been made?" asked Albert, as he turned his gray beaver felt top hat in his hands nervously.

"I don't have any objections, if the time permits, Mr. Standish. I do have a very full schedule," answered Sasa. She turned and walked back through the house, her head and visage erect and graceful, said her goodbyes to Caroline, then out of the door, leaving Albert to gaze in wonder after her. When she had quite gone, he muttered, "What a firebrand. Exciting as well as different."

Later that night, Sasa lay abed with Wheezer by her side. She gently stroked his head, then with loving, honey tan hued fingers, she rubbed him behind his ears, which was one of his favorite petting spots. Her day had been full of confusion and uncertainty; self-doubt crept through her thoughts. While Anna deemed it a great success, Sasa felt her day at the tea party had been fraught with unvoiced hostility. Not all, but definitely some of the young ladies at the tea were decidedly cool to her, and that Abigail Cole showed her feelings quite well.

She had put on her most comfy nightgown, made of flannel for the nights were still cold, and she did not want to light a fire which would require Sarah to get out of her bed and come up to lay the wood, make sure the ash had been collected and the grate blackened. No one should have to pry themselves out of a warm bed, just to do a small service, and then pay for that lack of sleep through the entire next day.

She looked at Wheezer. He was always by her side, whenever possible. Awake and alert, smiling that silly smile he did and probably thinking of what mischief he could get into next.

"Wheezer, I had a very odd day today. I am not at all sure that I did well. Caroline Standish was very gracious, I cannot fault her one bit, but I think she will suffer the hidden enmity that is bound to rear its ugly head eventually. I would hate to be the cause of any embarrassment to such a nice lady.

"I don't know what to think about her brother-in-law, Mr. Albert Standish. He seemed very much smitten with me, and he was a perfect gentleman while we were in the garden, but there was something about him that I am worried about," she said, as she pulled her fingers through her thick black hair in a nervous gesture.

Wheezer perked up his ears as if to say, "I am ready to listen to what is bothering you". He had an uncanny way of looking a person directly in the eyes which made Sasa feel like he understood every word. In the past, he had shown that he was very capable of understanding what was going on around him, but did he actually understand all the words she said? There was no way to tell for sure, so she just continued to pour out her true feelings.

"To tell you the truth, Wheezer, I am not interested in any white man. I don't think they are bad, because lots of Indian women have been marrying those white Irishmen that have come over from their country. It is called Ireland, and the people have lots of trouble there, plus a terrible famine because their food, especially potatoes, become rotten in their fields. I hear that the Cherokee in council has adopted the Irish and have offered any help they can, which is really not much. Poison Woman told me that the Cherokee have lost so many to starvation that when they heard of the starvation in Ireland, they could empathize with their sorrow and the pain of it. There have been many marriages, especially of Cherokee women and Irish men. But these men don't try to put on airs like they are better than the Indians. At least not the ones I have met.

"I am not so sure, when it comes to these society whites. They automatically think they are better, just be-cause they have the money to live well. I am not sure I can trust them to not turn on me once the novelty of my being a Cherokee who has been made into a lady is past. I wish you could go with me to some of these tea parties. Then maybe they would focus on you instead of me. Anna says that it would be a big mistake to allow you to go. So, for now I will just have to tell you what happens when I come home to you," Sasa went on, as Wheezer wagged his tail, then gave a loud sigh as he settled down beside her.

"Don't worry, Wheezer, you are still my 'White Black Whiskers' boy. Remember, boy, that is my secret name for you. Only you, me and the Creator know what that means," added Sasa.

Wheezer tilted his head with his ears perked and the tops of them flopped over. It was like he was asking a question.

"Maybe it has been a while since I called you that secret name. Well, you might not be able to see it, Wheezer, with it being so close to your eyes and all. It's because of your snout," giggled Sasa, quietly. 'Your snout is dark on one side and white on the other. But, your long whiskers are white on the side that is dark, and black on the side that is white. It is so unusual that I gave you that secret name, like getting a Cherokee name. That was back when I only had you for family," she reminded him.

Wheezer belly-crawled across the cover a little so that he could snuggle his muzzle in Sasa's neck. Then, after giving her a good night lick on the cheek, he settled down for a good all night sleep.

Sasa thought it would be so nice to not have the worries she had; then maybe she would sleep better than she did. Soon, however, she drifted off to sleep with her trusted Wheezer sleeping next to her, and it made them both feel more secure.

Chapter 3
Heart to Heart

Finally, Sasa and Wheezer were sound asleep in her room with the door closed. Anna felt hopeful; if they were extremely quiet, she might have some personal time with her husband, Jackson. Loving and being loved by a man like Jackson was almost like a dream come true for her. She had been raised in luxury and pretty much took it for granted, until she made that remarkable decision to spend the spring and summer of 1839 with her father, who was a temporary Indian Agent at the Cherokee's last removal camp within Indian Territory. She had been so naive then. She had missed the many years away from her father, thinking of him in some heroic role as if in a play. Unfortunately for her, Anna's mother had not confided to her that the reason why he was never home was that he was told in no uncertain terms to leave off visiting them. After his being involved in some shady dealings when they lived in the frontier town of St. Louis, her mother, Clarissa Edwards, had packed both herself and Anna up and left for Boston, so that Anna could be raised in society. At twelve, she was sent to Miss Dorothy Cadwell's Finishing School, until the time when she would be introduced into society.

She walked around the room, putting things in order; picking up the items belonging to Sasa, Wheezer or Jackson, she put them next to their bedroom doors for them to find in the morning. She doused the lamps as she finished her tidying.

She hesitated at the window that looked out over the park across the street, gazing but not really looking, and thought. Those were heady days, being admired by young men, but they all seemed to lack heart. I found their constant condescension of other races and women appalling. I could not bear to see others, no matter the race, treated like animals, and it seemed that all the young men of my acquaintance were hopeless bigots. I knew, though, that I am the exception to the rule, not them. But, then I met Jackson Halley when he came looking for his dog Jack, renamed Wheezer by Sasa, and I found in him a godly heart. A man of truth and justice, besides being brave, fearless, and tender to women. It sure took him long enough to propose.

Anna had taken a house in town. It had belonged to a missionary and was located behind the fort, at Fort Smith, in Arkansas. She agreed to tutor Sasa, but her real reason for staying was to wait for Jackson to make the first move. He never did. As it turned out, he had decided, without asking her, that since she was so high in society, she would not want to stay on a mule breeding ranch. After proving him incorrect by showing him how well she could handle the mules and how much she could help at the ranch as a true partner, he got the message and they became engaged.

They were married at the end of 1840 and she never looked back. She was as much in love with Jackson as she ever was, and having Sasa as their ward felt like having her little sister to live with them. It was a joy to see Sasa blossom into a fine lady. On this trip, Anna noticed how Sasa turned heads. She was a beautiful young lady, and Anna felt proud of having had a hand in bringing that about. But, it was not until Jackson's father, Andrew, brought Professor Enger from Boston, that Sasa's mind was greatly opened. Now, almost two and a half years later, Sasa was the most accomplished young lady. Even if Sasa had been white, she would never have had the benefit of an education that almost no white woman would ever be afforded. Thus, that made Sasa very unique to her people and white people alike.

Tonight, however, I want some time with my husband, Anna thought. She carefully opened their bedroom door and slipped in. Jackson had left the oil lamp burning low. He was breathing evenly and did not stir, so he must be asleep. No matter, she would undress and take care of her necessary night time rituals. After unbuttoning the many buttons down her dress front, she hung it up on a peg in the wardrobe closet, then she quietly donned her baby blue silk night dress with the pink tiny ribbons and sat to brush her long blond hair one hundred strokes, as she did every night. Before she was done, a form appeared behind her and placed a hand on her shoulder.

"I see you are still up, my love. I have been waiting for you so long, I thought you would never come in. Twice

I almost fell asleep, but, just watching you prepare for bed brought me awake with renewed interest. I could watch that a million times, and never tire of it," Jackson told her in a low, confidential voice.

"Oh dear, you say the nicest things, darling. I bet you say that to all the girls," Anna giggled.

"Now, Anna, you know I don't have eyes for any other females except for my Mollies, those wonderful female mules of mine," answered Jackson.

"And don't I know it. I may not have married you if I had known how much time you gave to those girls. No, I believe you, darling. I am so happy. I love our ranch, and I love all our friends, the Cherokee families around us. I could not think of a better life," said Anna.

Jackson momentarily frowned, then faintly smiled at her.

"What? What was that look for? Is something wrong with our lives, Jackson? Don't tell me you have gotten tired of me already," asked Anna.

"No, my dear, nothing like that will ever happen. No, I was just thinking of some of the reports I have received from Nathan Boone, at Fort Gibson. He has been there for a few weeks. It was just a small worry, nothing to bother you with now," he replied, as he stroked her long hair.

"I want to know, Jackson. If it is something to worry about, then maybe two of us worrying will get it over with faster," she smiled.

"Now, that is not the way I heard it. In fact, it is the opposite. I have never heard of two people worrying to get it over quicker," he chuckled.

"It is a saying uniquely my own, dear. Now, what are these reports that weigh on your mind? And don't give me that nonsense that a woman needs not know these things.

Are we not partners, in every sense of the word?" said Anna, seriously.

"How did I end up with such a woman? Sometimes, I think you are as stubborn as my mules. All right, but I won't have you fretting about this day in and day out. I may as well tell you, since it may become common knowledge eventually, anyway.

"We have been getting reports of raids along the Indian Territory border. It seems to be old grievances between the tribes in the territory, but Nathan feels that there are some odd facets to the attacks, even if he can't put his finger on it just yet. His last letter told me he thought something big was brewing in Indian Territory. What is odd is that none of the tribes will own up to the attacks, which is extremely unusual since they would normally be open and proud of reaping retribution against an enemy.

"Nathan can't seem to pin down the individuals doing the raiding. And it is not just one tribe. Reports will come in that the Choctaw are on the warpath, and then the settlers are saying it is the Cherokee. The settlers in Arkansas are getting a little antsy, and they don't know what to make of it. When soldiers arrive at a village that is said to have done the raid, there cannot be found anyone who had participated in it. No hot and tired ponies, no buzz in the town. In fact, they can't even find a reason for the raid. I am not sure what is happening, but it is beginning to have a lot of people agitated in and around the territory," explained Jackson, as Anna led him over to the bed.

They climbed in and snuggled together for a bit. Anna stroked Jackson's face, then traced the contours of his ear. She found him very handsome, especially since he did not hide his face behind a bushy beard, as most men did. She loved to see his strong jawline and watch the muscles work there. She had threatened once to shear him like a sheep, in the middle of the night, if he ever took to growing a beard. She pondered his worry.

"Darling, I know that there has been much fighting just below the territory, in the Republic of Texas, since the war with Mexico. I heard that Mexico is still launching armed warfare along their new border. Perhaps it has something to do with what is going on there," answered Anna.

"I don't see how it can. I mean, what does Mexico's fight for Texas have anything to do with Indian Territory? As far as I am aware, the Mexicans have not recently fought for control of that northern Texas border, and the raids are not happening in any sort of pattern. There is no rhyme nor reason to them. Nathan said that he has been approached by representatives of several of the tribes, who are just as baffled and worried as the settlers, who swear an Indian war is about to erupt at any time now, and that they will all be slaughtered in their beds. There seems to be no cause for such a view. But, that has not stopped them from writing to Washington City for the Army to send troops. However, Nathan told me that he has sent the facts to Washington, advising them that no such action is needed at this time until they sort out what is really happening," said Jackson, yawning as he finished his explanation.

Anna knew she had kept him up too late. It did not matter. It was important to be there for him when he needed her. That, too, was an important part of their marriage.

"Well, we will think on it tomorrow, sweet heart. You are tired, and we don't need you to be sleepy eyed in the morning. Good night my love. Please turn out the lamp, dear," she said with a kiss.

He dutifully turned out the lamp and then turned toward the wife he so fondly loved and took her in an ardent embrace.

"I thought you were too sleepy for romance," giggled Anna in the dark.

"Whoever said that is a rascal, a cad and a liar, my dear. The night belongs to us," said Jackson.

Chapter 4
Wheezer on Patrol

It had only been a few days into their stay, but Wheezer was getting restless. He was not getting the exercise he was used to, and being cooped up in a hotel room was getting very old. His humans were going to and fro, not considering him, for they had so much to attend to and schedules to keep.

Wheezer sat in the middle of the main room, on the red Turkey carpet, watching each one in the family go in and out of the doors to their bedrooms, or leaving their room to venture to the basement where the new water closet and indoor plumbing were located. Then they would return, while Wheezer still sat in the same spot, not moving so much as an inch. Finally, he got tired of all the frenzied activity, and just as all of the family went into their own bedrooms, he leaned back using his tail to balance his posterior like a three legged stool, and sat up. His front paws pumping up and down in unison as he began to howl and bark as if he were about to be shot.

They all came running and converged on Wheezer, who still had not moved. When he finally had their attention, he fairly skipped over to the entry and leaping atop the Windsor chair where his leash was laid across an arm, he grabbed the end, trotted over to the group, dropped it on the floor and looked all around with expectant eyes and a furiously wagging tail.

Jackson tried to remain stern, but Anna had to cover her mouth to muffle the chuckles that erupted.

"Jackson, the U.S. Army should hire Wheezer to plan their strategy of attack. He has done a wonderful job of figuring out just what would bring us all here to do his bidding, and executed it with perfect precision. Wouldn't you say so, Sasa?" she commented.

Sasa knew better than to answer, for fear of humiliating Jackson that he had been manipulated by his own dog. However, she was also having a hard time concealing her smile.

When Jackson reached down to pick up the leash, Wheezer began turning in circles as fast as he could go without catching up to his own tail, barking as he twirled.

"Okay, boy, I will take you for a walk," surrendered Jackson.

But Wheezer stopped and looked in turn to Anna, then Sasa. It was obvious he expected the entire family to go.

"You are right Wheezer. We need to do more things together while we are here. So ladies, grab your shawls and parasols, we are going out for a stroll in the park," decided Jackson, as he smiled back at Wheezer, who was displaying all of his fine white front teeth in what he thought was a smile.

Sasa and Anna made for their rooms to change for a stroll in the park. Sasa chose a tan suede skirt, with a tweed jacket over a ruffled front cotton blouse. Once she donned her black riding boots, she only had her small, demure hat to place securely on her head. Anna, for her part, decided on a one piece full length dress in hunter green wool. With that she put on her high topped boots, then a floral shawl and her matching bonnet and parasol. Now, she was also ready.

When the women emerged from their rooms, basically at the same time, Wheezer briskly trotted over to a small basket beside the writing desk, reached in with his head and pulled out a small horsehide ball. He deposited it into Sasa's hand, and then he was also ready to go.

Quickly they came down the curved staircase with Wheezer pulling them the entire way, so much so that Jackson had to be careful not to trip. Jack Russells, it seemed, could be stronger than they looked. They barely had time to wave to the front desk as Wheezer whisked them out of the front entry and then narrowly missed being run over by a rolling wagon wheel.

Soon they were in the park across the street from their hotel. There were fine trees, some with flowering buds on them, a lawn already deep green this early in the season, and manicured patches of flowers dispersed throughout the park, with daffodils and hyacinth blooming in profusion. This was a nice strolling garden with winding paths for leisurely walks arm in arm with your beau. Unfortunately, there was not much room for Wheezer to run, nor a place for Sasa to throw his ball. So, Wheezer had to settle for a walk down the path.

Without warning, Wheezer dashed away as the leash broke from his collar, leaving Jackson's fingers holding a limp piece of leather. In a flash Wheezer was nowhere to be seen, but they had not lost him since they could clearly hear his barking. Quickly they ran towards the frenzied barks, arriving at a clearing bordered by tall mature trees. Sasa kept looking around for Wheezer, behind bushes and around the few monuments to someone or other. She finally noticed the looks of consternation on the faces of the other walkers in the area. When she followed their gazes, she found Wheezer. An older man with a tweed riding cap, ran up, panting, to Anna and Jackson.

"Did you all see that? I mean, I have never seen the like in all my born days. That dog came tearing out of the bushes, chasing a gray squirrel, and as that critter ran up the tree, why, so did that dog. I am not lying, for there he is. Just look up folks." said the man to all the onlookers.

Wheezer's family stared, wondering how they would get him down from that height. One wrong move and the fall would kill him. On his part, Wheezer did not seem worried in the slightest: in fact, he would have been happy to climb even higher if the limbs had provided him with the means to do so. Evidently, the squirrel was long gone. Wheezer suddenly quit his barking and stared intently out beyond the tall bushes at something only he could see. His tail stood out straight in line with his spine, then began to quiver and just as suddenly he exploded down the tree, almost in a free fall, only having to touch the tree two times. When he was on the ground he took off in the direction he had been looking. Naturally, Jackson, Anna and Sasa gave chase.

When the trio caught up with Wheezer, he had a man down on the ground, his jaw wrapped around the man's wrist, growling a warning not to move.

"Hey buddy, get this mutt off of me, ya hear? Come on, give me a hand. Dad blamed mongrel ought to be shot, he is a danger to society," yelled the man on the ground.

Wheezer held him fast, though, and refused to let go. Just then the gathered crowd heard a small squeal.

"It is gone. Oh my, it is gone. My money is gone. I just took it out of the bank a few minutes ago and now it is gone," cried an elderly little woman in black bombazine, a prim little hat and a black silk purse which she waved around as she cried.

She came into the clearing where everyone had gathered, "Isn't anyone going to help me? I had it in my right pocket. I tell you I was robbed just now. It was all the money I had, please, please help me."

Before anyone could utter a word, she noticed the vignette of the dog and the bazaar scene, which caused her to forget, for a moment, her complaint. Wheezer had not been distracted by the screaming of the old woman, however, and continued to give warning growls while holding the man fast.

When the man on the ground spied the little old woman, he began to thrash around, trying to get loose of Wheezer's iron clamp on his wrist. In the meanwhile, Sasa seemed to understand the particulars of the situation. Still holding the man's wrist and standing on top of the man's chest, Wheezer gazed up at her. She gave him a slight nod, and Wheezer then began to whip the man's arm around. Like a magician in a magic act, a small flat bundle fell from the man's sleeve onto the ground. Everyone could see what lay there, and the stunned silence was deafening. Just as quickly, angry sounds erupted from the crowd as the men advanced on the thief still on the ground. As they grabbed him by the collar, lifting him up on his own two legs, Wheezer finally let him go, having accomplished his aim.

Sasa bent down, took his fine head into her hands to look Wheezer directly in the eyes and said, "You have done a wonderful thing, Wheezer. It shows me that your heart is good. Now, you might want to take this bundle over to the little woman you helped. It belongs to her."

Wheezer looked intently at Sasa's face in order to work out the meaning of her words, then he looked down at the bundle of money on the ground, and Sasa nodded her head once again. Finally, he picked the bundle up in his mouth, trotted over to where the old lady was standing as she watched the constables take the thief away, and sat down in front of her to await her attention. Patience, is something Jack Russells are not very good at. Thankfully, the woman looked down and saw her money in Wheezer's mouth.

"Oh, I am so happy to have this back," she exclaimed, as she patted Wheezer on the head. After securing the bills this time into her silk purse, she approached the Halley family.

"My name is Mrs. Herbert Wise. I am a widow, and you can call me Nellie. I would like to thank you for apprehending this foul thief. I have no idea what I would have done had I not received this money back," she said to Jackson, with tears brimming in her eyes.

Once Jackson realized what Nellie had said, he quickly tried to disavow the praise she had heaped on him.

"My dear Mrs. Wise, I truly do apologize, but I am not the hero of the day that you have supposed me to be," he demurred, while Mrs. Wise looked puzzled.

"It was our dog, Wheezer, who saw what was happening to you and rushed to your defense," continued Jackson.

"Saw me? Sir, I do not understand. How could he have seen me when I was behind that wall of bushes just over there?" asked Mrs Wise.

Just then she looked down and noticed the wagging tail that belonged to Wheezer. He stood in front of her with a wide smile on his face.

"Well, I know this will be hard for you to believe, however, if you ask any of the people who witnessed what happened, they would tell you that Wheezer climbed that tall tree a few yards away, and was perched up there looking over the bushes from above. It was he who saw your distress, and it was he who jumped the thief and wrestled him to the ground, pinning him there until the constable could arrive. He must have seen the man take your money. He is your hero Mrs. Wise. My family and I only stood here, watching, like everyone else. But, let me introduce you," said Jackson.

"Introduce me? To a dog? I don't think I quite understand, sir," she said.

Wheezer answered her questions by coming to her and gently lifting up his paw for her to shake for an introduction.

"My, this is an extraordinary day. I have never heard of a dog climbing a tree, but if you say that is what he did, then I count myself lucky to be the recipient of his attention," declared Mrs. Wise.

Noticing Wheezer's bright, happy face, she then knelt down to Wheezer's level to say, "Uh, Wheez…er… Wheezer, I will write you down in two places today. The first will be in my diary, and the second will be in the front of our family Bible. It will say, 'This is the day that Nellie was saved from an uncertain future when an extraordinary dog named Wheezer, climbed a tree, spied a thief who was

making off with her money, and came to her rescue.' Generations will see that in my family Bible and be proud of
you," Mrs. Wise told him; then, after taking more than a
few moments to write herself to a standing position again,
with Jackson's help, of course, she did a small curtsy and
walked home with every dollar of her money intact.

Chapter 5
Treachery in Indian Territory

The sound of the screams deafened her ears as Tsi-ya struggled to find a place to hide from the attack that had come out of the dark night. Torches held high, the marauding warriors with their heavy clubs, were galloping through the screaming crowds, stopping only to swing at a target. Women and children were fleeing blindly on the paths which served as early streets for the small Choctaw settlement. Usti Tsi-ya, or Little Otter, did not know where her mother and older sister had run to, but she knew she was not safe where she was.

She had been fetching some ears of dried corn for her mother, so that they might have it ready for the morning meal. It had been hot during the day. Her mother had always said it was easier to do the hand grinding to make corn meal on their stone mortar at night in front of their small fire, than working hard in the heat of the day. Little Otter enjoyed helping her mother with this task before bedtime. Listening to her uncle tell stories of their homeland, before they were forced out of their homes to live in this wild land they called Indian Territory, was a special treat.

Little Otter had only been gone a short while. She had picked up an armful of ears of dried corn, as much as a seven year old could carry at one time, and was on her way back to their little log lodge when she first heard the screams. By the time she reached the lodge, everyone was gone and the frenzied battle going on around her caused her to run back to the corn crib, her long black hair flying behind her. The crib stood on four sturdy poles like a giant box on stilts. She had to scramble back up the tree limb ladder and throw herself up on top of the dry corn to get all the way inside. But this was not a good place to be. *Oh, why did I choose to hide in here?* she thought. Food would typically be one of the first things they would raid, so she was frantically looking for any hole she could squeeze through and then try to run into the woods.

"Otter, Otter, where are you girl," she could hear her Uncle calling for her. She peeked out the door of the crib. Her uncle was a big, husky man whom she and her family depended on since her tribe was matrilineal, meaning that descent and family name were carried through the female line. Fathers did not raise their children. That task fell to the wife's brother. Otter saw him now. He was on his black and white pony, looking all around for her.

"I am here Uncle, up here with the corn," she yelled.

Her uncle looked up, then urged his pony over to stand just below and as he raised his arms to her, she confidently jumped out of the corn crib door. He enveloped her in his big muscular arms and she felt safe. Suddenly she felt her uncle kick the pony hard. A screaming warrior was bearing down on them fast, there was no time to lose.

"Otter, grab the mane and hold on, I need my hands," her uncle yelled.

Quickly she grabbed onto the pony's thick mane. She knew exactly what to do now. While holding on tight, she kicked the pony on his sides as hard as she could, which drove the pony down the path, through the crowds, and towards the woods. In the mean-while, her uncle had taken his own weapons out. He always carried a good bow and arrows, and it was these that he used now. Turning his body at the waist, he aimed at the oncoming warrior and let fly an arrow, which did not hit its mark. Otter did not look back at what her uncle was doing. Her job was to guide the horse, a maneuver they had practiced many times; this allowed her uncle to pull out another arrow, his movements as smooth as spring water. The warrior was almost on them when her uncle released the arrow: this time it met its target, and the warrior fell from his horse.

Before another attacker could intercept them, Otter and her uncle headed out into the woods outside of the settlement. Breath-lessly they rode for several miles until it appeared that they were not being followed, then Uncle finally slowed his horse to give it some time to rest. Little Otter had been so frightened before her Uncle came, she had unknowingly wet herself. Even though she was all dry now, she still felt ashamed.

"Uncle, I am sorry. I was foolish to run up into the corn crib. It was just the first place I saw when I knew we were being attacked," she said, looking up into her Uncle's stoic face with her round sorrowful eyes. "I am also sorry that I have disgraced our family."

Her Uncle looked down with surprise. "Little one, how could you have done anything to disgrace our family?" he asked. "We are here and alive are we not? You helped to guide the pony very well while I fought. Is that not true as well?"

"Yes, Uncle," Little Otter replied, dreading what she had to tell her Uncle next, but honor demanded she make a clean confession. "When the warriors came, Uncle, I was so frightened, I ran blindly, but it was not until you rescued me that I realized that I had wet myself like a baby and a coward. I am ashamed," she said, bowing her head in sorrow.

"Ah, little one," her uncle chucked in an undertone," many a time I have been that frightened. When I was a boy about your age back in the homeland, I was taken on a hunt into the forest. We were hunting the big cat that was killing our stock, you know, the cat that when it yowls it sounds like a woman screaming. I wandered off from the other hunters, I got distracted, and did not pay attention to where I was going. Soon I looked up and two bow shots in front of me was that big cat, looking straight at me like I was dinner. I froze, let me tell you. I could not move, not even to raise my bow. It was just a good thing that my father had followed me and when that cat leaped at me for the kill, he shot his arrow into its heart. It fell at my feet. Then I did something I will never forget as long as I live."

Little Otter was staring up at him in amazement. She had never thought her Uncle had ever been afraid in his life. "What did you do Uncle?"

"I threw up right on top of that big cat. My father had to wash it off the cat's fur before he skinned it, so that vomit would not ruin the pelt. But, you know what? He never said a word about it to anyone, not even to remind me of it. Now I will do the same for you. It never happened, you are not disgraced. What you are is a brave girl, and I am very proud of you," said her Uncle.

Her uncle was a trusted man of the tribe. He was named Cinq Koi which means Five Puma, so named because he always sought the Creator's advice before making a big decision, even though he was not the village holy man. He was known as an honorable man, and reverent.

Soon, they began to sense others in the forest. Little Otter always thought it funny that they called these splotchy batches of treed land 'forests', which were nothing like what they knew as forests back in their Mississippi lands. There, some forests were dense, dark, moist and fruitful, and stretched for miles upon miles, while others were full of swamp water, dangerous snakes and swimming reptiles that could bite you in half. Those woods were so large that some would get lost if they went too far into them, and were never heard of again. What they called a forest in Indian Territory, however, was not nearly as dense, nor as green. The ground was dry and rocky, and what grew there tended not to get as tall as the trees from her home.

Now she could see a gathering of her village people in a small clearing. Five Puma slid off the Pony, then handed Little Otter down. She had just begun looking all around, hoping to see her mother and father, when they came out of the darkened forest and headed purposefully toward Five Puma. Their faces were tense and serious, which made Otter feel frightened again. She stayed close to her Uncle, just in case.

"Have we located all the village people yet? How many dead?" asked Uncle.

"Some, but we have not heard from anyone else from the village. This is a night for wickedness, my friend. Thank you for getting Little Otter," answered Nita Tashka, or Day Warrior, Little Otter's father.

"Day Warrior, let us sit down over here where I see a small fire. I have something to say and it is a puzzle. We must find out what it means," replied Five Puma.

The two men, both dressed in cotton shirts and dungarees with breech clouts hanging over front and back, settled by the fire, and as they did so others who had taken refuge in this part of the woods came near and sat also. Everyone's face was solemn as death, yet there was no weeping, no crying out in anguish. That too worried Five Puma, because if they were not weeping, then they were vengeful and liable to strike without thinking. Little Otter came up behind the men and sat quietly to listen. She could tell that they were concerned because something was not right about tonight's raid.

"Day Warrior, I need to ask you, did you notice something odd about the warriors on the raid?" asked Five Puma.

Day Warrior just stared ahead and nodded his head slowly. Five Puma waited for him to gather his thoughts. Choctaws did not answer quickly, but made sure of their words before they let them loose on the world. Finally, Day Warrior turned his head to Five Puma.

"Yes, brother, there was something very strange tonight. All the warriors were dressed like our Creek neighbors, but we are many miles from our border between us and them, and we have not recently had any reason to quarrel. For a war party to come all this way for an attack, there would have to be a very good reason and would have to be about something very big. Something that we would all know about," Day Warrior answered at last.

"I, too, saw these things, and a few more. Their warriors were different in some way," said Five Puma.

From the crowd around the small fire a voice of authority rang out.

"I, too, saw something very strange. These warriors did not come from the north as the Creeks would have. They came from the south. I was coming back from a day of fishing on the Red River, and they came from the other side of the river. I saw them coming and I ducked behind a big bush. They did not see me, but I saw them well: their horses were wet, soaking wet from the river, but they had foam coming from their nostrils as if they had run very far. Why would the Creeks cross over to the south side of the Red in order to cross over again and attack us from the south? It makes no sense," said Lvkna S_iti, or Yellow Snake, the War Chief.

"I disagree," cut in a voice from the circle. "They sure looked like Creeks to me and I say that we hit them hard right back, or they will think us weak, then they will come to take our land."

Several of the men and women grumbled around the fire. They were ready to form a war party and fight back. This was a huge insult to the Choctaw people.

A much older man, known to be a wise man, sat on the fringe of the circle, listening, wondering if he knew the answers to these questions, but he said nothing to the gathering.

Yellow Snake stood and waited for quiet so they would all hear his answer.

"No! We are not in our old homeland now. Our lands are guaranteed us by our treaty with the United States. The Creeks would know this, just as we know that we cannot take their lands. The United States government would send their soldiers to punish us or them. Besides, it would be pointless to run off and maybe attack someone blindly without knowing the facts. We also don't want to leave our village defenseless.

The grumbling continued, Yellow Snake raised his hand again, so that all would notice that he was about to speak again, and also to calm the assemblage.

"You know me, I am Yellow Snake, War Chief for our small village. Since we have moved into this new land, we have not had to fight for our land, even if we might have to fight for our food. Everyone knows about the many who die every day because of the bad food the agents send to us. But, I am here to tell you that it is the same all over the Indian Territory. We have no more and no less than our neighbors. Therefore, I say this, we will go back and put our little village back together, and also we will send a runner to Doaksville, where the Chief Over All is staying."

Before he could finish his words, a rider rode fast into the clearing. A young Choctaw warrior jumped from his horse and hurried to Yellow Snake.

"Yellow Snake, I bear a message for you from our village. I am to tell you that the enemy has left as quickly as they had come, leaving us with some injured, two cabins burning and five people dead. But I am also to tell you to come quickly because something is not right. We managed to kill a few of their number, and although they are dressed in traditional Creek clothing, the men underneath the clothing are not of the Creek people. We dare not move the bodies until you have seen them," said the young warrior.

Yellow Snake turned to the gathering and announced, "It seems we can go back now and we have a puzzle to figure out. Come, I don't know how much time we have before this happens again. And we have our dead to mourn as well.

It was then that the old wise man, whose name was Yanati Nashoba, or Running Wolf, felt a sting of fear that the saying passed down through his family was coming true. He would speak to no one about it yet, however. This thing had been a part of his family since time immemorial. Most people in the village knew him to be Choctaw, and that he was, but his family also told of a man who became part of his family centuries ago, who had come from across the eastern sea, but he was alone and in need of help. After giving this man help and marrying him into the family, they discovered too late that they might pay a horrible price. Possibly an ancient retribution would befall someone near his family or in it, and he was the last of them left alive after the terrible march into Indian Territory.

Then he realized that the one who might be in the most danger was a young Cherokee girl who had helped his village with some legal papers the year before. It was she who may be in dire straits, but there was nothing he could do to stop the chain of events. May Chihowa, the Creator, give her his protection.

Chapter 6
A Grand Plan

General Federico Guillermo De Almeida, paced in his suite of rooms, unconsciously stamping his feet as he went. As he restlessly walked back and forth, his secretary Juan Baltasar Aldrete, paced along with him, only walking backwards. The general did not like to see the back of someone he was talking to.

"Juan, why have we not heard about what our agents are accomplishing in Indian Territory? We should have heard something by now," complained the general, aggravated and tense. "You would think since 1836, when we began putting my plan into action, those men, who gave me grand accounts of themselves, would have some good news for me to act upon. You would think, Juan, those – those – those perros, ah you know, dogs, would realize that I can break them with one word, Juan, just one," he repeated, holding one finger in the air. "But, what does General Federico Guillermo De Almeida get for his brilliant plan to take back Texas for Mexico? Ahhhhh, you see Juan? Nothing, nothing at all. Well, when they report, you make sure to send them to me first; I want to talk to them personally. You understand me, Juan? Or do you have a better answer for me?"

Juan was nonplussed. He did not have an answer, and giving the wrong answer was not an option. He did not want to end up in prison for the rest of his life. That was what had happened to the general's last secretary. Juan began paging through some correspondence while trying to maintain the pace, but he was helpless to find anything good to say to the general. He found nothing in the letters that pertained to the problem at hand, except one letter penned in a gentle hand and addressed to, not General and not Mr., just Federico De Almeida. Juan was familiar with such a letter, and he immediately placed it in the palm of the general's hand.

"Ahhhhhhh, a letter from my dearest daughter, Angelina. I have not heard from her in at least two months. Let me see what she has to say," said the general, as he stopped his constant pacing to quickly read Angelina's words.

My Dearest Papa:

I have been waiting patiently for your return Papa, but have not even had a letter from you. I do hope that you are safe and well, but I worry, with you walking around among the gringos. I cannot think of a reason for you to visit such a place when everyone you love is here with me. All right, I will not scold throughout my letter, but I miss you terribly.

And I have news, Papa. That is why I need you here with me. Papa, I have been asked for my hand in marriage,"

At that, the general stamped his foot and said, "What is this? Juan, can you believe that some young man has had the audacity to go straight to Angelina to ask for her hand? It is unthinkable. What is becoming of our children these days, when they forget proper manners? He should have waited for me, to ask me, the Papa, first,"

Juan looked uneasy as he replied: "My General, we have been gone for a very long time. Young people do not like to wait."

"He is probably just some caballero who works on one of the ranches outside of Mexico City. Well, never mind. I will deal with that when I return to my Angelina," decided the general, as he again began to read the rest of his daughter's words.

He is a fine young man, Papa. He is from a prominent family, and he says that he has the dowry saved already. He also has an inheritance. His grandfather gave him all his property, a large ranch, horses, fields and all his slaves. He is such a lovely young man, and I do hope you will at least consider his proposal, please Papa.

I await your return, my dearest. Please write to me, and I do not mean for you to ask Juan to write the letter. I want one from you, in your own hand. Please Papa.
YourLoving Daughter
Angelina De Almeida

The general was lost in thought, worrying about the loss of his only daughter. Too soon, too soon. There is some consolation, and that is the young man's inheritance. She would automatically be a propertied woman of the city and do justice to her Papa's name.

Ah, but I have a mission to accomplish and I will see it through until the end. Then I will come home in triumph, hailed as a wise leader and possibly a wise father as well.

Juan stood in front of him with paper and pen, ready to write to Angelina for the general.

"Oh, get out of my face, out of my room. In fact," Juan held his breath, "go down to the hotel desk and see if any other messages have come in since luncheon," finished the general.

"*Si*, yes, yes. I will go now," Juan said as he quickly put all the papers on the writing desk in the room and hurried to the door of the suite.

He grabbed the crystal door knob, but it would not turn because of the slick, wet, sweat dripping from his hands. He stopped quickly to wipe them on his red waistcoat leaving visible wet streaks down the sides, then he finally got the knob to turn and he scurried out.

The general sat in the chair by the desk and rubbed his aching head. If this did not go right, his position in the government of Mexico would be forfeit. It was an impossible situation. How could he direct his spies in Indian Territory if he had no idea where they were and what they were doing? But when he thought of the glories he would receive for the successful delivery of that land they had so recently lost to the rebels, the land they now called, The Republic of Texas, he felt excitement run through his veins. He imagined the Royal Ball they would hold in his honor. If his plan worked out, he would be the most celebrated general of all time, and he would be able to live the rest of his life upon his laurels.

Ah, but it is such a touchy, painstakingly sly plan, *he thought. I hope I have selected the right individuals for the job. It requires gall and hubris to be able to pull this off. The general rose from the chair and began to pace again with his hands clasping each other behind his back as if they too would like to be far, far away from the general's tantrum.* I have taken a huge risk, though, that could reverse on me and devastate me and my plans. But, how could I attract the right kind of spies if I had not offered such a king's ransom? Be that as it may, I might need to find out a suitable replacement if and when any of my men should not be able to pull off their task without destroying themselves in the bargain.

He remembered the weeks it took to recruit the right men for the special assignment, paying them from his own stockpile of hidden wealth and priceless objects. That way, if they were caught it could not be traced to him, because everyone knew he was not a wealthy man. Year after year he had plundered villages, farms, and even churches, to amass his great worth. Even if they told, they would not be believed. Except that, he was wealthy. Probably richer than the President of Mexico. *If those men fail me now, I have only one recourse, and I don't want to deal with that man*, he thought. The man he was thinking of was ruthless, sly and had never failed in anything he was sent to do. The only problem was, he did not recognize authority. He was not frightened by the general or his threats of punishment or worse, and that unnerved him. How can you control a man if he does not fear you?

So, he had to think of something that would be worth more than mere money. He thought, I need something that this man craves, of course, if only I knew of such a thing. Wealth, I have, but I have no priceless object or papers that would entice this man to take on the project. It needs to be something a man would die to obtain. But, what if I lie? What if I tell the man about a fabled priceless object that... say... I have hidden away, and offer it to him as a reward for success? Nothing for failure. He would also take a risk. Yes, that sounds good. But, what could I offer him that would give him the impetus to go for all or nothing in Indian Territory, eh? *And so he sat at his desk to think on the problem. He had no doubt now that he would have to call in this man and, what is more, this man was in Boston now. He could have him up to his suite, private and secret, not even Juan in attendance.*

Then he remembered an old fable about a priceless Aztec object made of gold, both green and yellow, so heavy you could not wear it. Enough gold so the owner could live the rest of his life like a king. The old tale said a Spaniard had stolen the object away from the Aztecs and brought it up north. The fable also said it was with one of the tribes along the Mississippi above the Golfo de México. But he could not be worried about where the priceless object was now, only that he needed to use the lore as a lure to hire and control the worst sort of man to do his bidding.

The thought flowed through his mind, envisioning how the plan would work and how he would realize his goal. He still had time to go to the local jewelers in Boston and have something special made just for this purpose. It was going to be so convincing.

Then, for the first time that day, the general was able to sit down, relax and even have a small glass of wine along with his cigarro. His new plan was almost as good as gold.

Kitty Sutton

Coyote

65

Chapter 7
Unconvinced and Unconcerned

Coyote had spent the day dressing out the deer he had killed that morning. His friend Five Owls had invited him a few years ago, to visit him at his Osage village in Indian Territory. They first met in 1839, and it had been a rough introduction, since Coyote had been mistaken for a warrior seeking scalps, but after the scuffle that ensued, Coyote and Five Owls found they had a lot in common. That had been the year he left his Lakota village, high up above the Big River the whites call the Missouri, to search for what

Wakan Tanka, the Creator, wished for him to do with his life. His heart ached for his Lakota people, but he was unsure if his people felt the same about him. His mother had been captive to the Northern Blackfoot after a raid on their summer camp and was forced to marry her Blackfoot captor. When she returned to her people she was with child. In time she bore a half Blackfoot, half Lakota son, and Coyote was that son. Unfortunately, his divided lineage had been the blessing and the curse of his entire life.

The Northern Blackfoot, sometimes called the Blackfeet, and the Lakota had been bitter enemies for as long as anyone could recall, even though one of the Lakota tribes was also called Blackfoot. But then the Lakota considered most other plains tribes the enemy. The name "Sioux" was not a Lakota word; it was what the white men named them, and it meant, 'Little Demons'. And even though it had been no fault of her own, his mother suffered the pain of distrust by her Lakota village as she raised her half Lakota son among her people. In fact his name, Coyote, was given to him by the chief, because coyote was known as the trickster. Coyote could do good for you or play a trick on you and do bad against you. When Coyote became old enough, he left his village and traveled south in a quest to find his purpose. There had to be something he was meant to do. He did not know what he would find on his quest, and as it turned out, his eyes had been opened to a danger that would overcome his own people if they were not warned in time. His people needed to know these things in order to prepare.

After spending several months in Indian Territory, Coyote endeavored to return to his people to convince them of this great danger, namely the white men plotting ways to steal the land, the settlers who continued to cry of impending doom to the government, blaming Indians for the crimes that other white men committed, the U.S. Army which did little to help the tribes. Some of the soldiers, assigned to accompany and help the Cherokee, committed murder while marching a defenseless people from their homelands. Then the whiskey started being poured into Indian Territory, not just by lawless whiskey runners, but also by the enlisted men stationed at Fort Smith and Fort Gibson, along with the white settlers who traveled freely into Indian Territory to sell whiskey for an entirely different reason, that of gaining the land in Indian Territory. To all that had to be added the terrible diseases the whites carried with them wherever they went. Somehow the whites could survive these sicknesses, but the red man could not. He saw how these things combined to decimate the tribes, halting their economic recovery and destabilizing their governments in the new land. Everything from intentional starvation costing thousands more lives after the end of the Trail of Tears, and the incursions of outlaws like Bell Starr and her gang killing any who opposed them, to bitter disputes within the Cherokee various factions and the debilitating use of whiskey for all Indians.

These problems were on their way to the plains tribes and would work just as well against them as they did in Indian Territory, but the Lakota refused to believe they could be vanquished. Coyote would never forget the day he met in council with the head men of the Lakota. It had only been a few weeks ago, but he felt the sting of failure just as sharp now as he had that day.

Coyote had made little headway speaking to the individual chiefs and sub-chiefs in their own villages. At last summer's Sun Dance, when all the various Lakota tribal groups came together in a previously agreed upon place on the Great Plains, Coyote was given permission to speak to the newly assembled large gathering. He stood respectfully and waited for all to quiet down before speaking. Then Little Thunder solemnly bowed his head slightly, giving Coyote the floor. Coyote held the talking stick, made especially for this meeting by Coyote himself.

A talking stick was used by many tribes to keep order during a council. Whoever held the stick, had the floor and it could not be taken away from him unless he passed the stick to another speaker. The way the Lakota decorated each stick had special meaning. Red was for life, yellow for knowledge. Usually blue was for prayer and wisdom, and white for matters of the spirit. Other colors were used too, such as purple for healing, orange for feeling kinship with all things alive, and lastly, black for clarity and focus.

Coyote's stick was all yellow with dots of blue around the top and bottom. There were feathers attached which also had special meaning. Coyote had attached eagle feathers because the feathers of the eagle stood for truth and represented high ideals. Added to that Coyote had wrapped a white rabbit's fur around the middle of the stick, because rabbit brings the ability to listen with big ears. These things were obvious to everyone.

"My people and my chiefs, I give you honor and this day I hope to give to you a look into the future of all the Indian nations in the land of the tall grass," Coyote began, then he paused for effect, but already some in the council were fidgeting with impatience of what they believed they had already heard too many times.

Little Thunder, (Waki-nyan Chika), a Brule' Lakota warrior, who was reportedly the most influential young warrior of the Southern Brules, sat stoically, not looking one way or the other. He had been a friend of Coyote's boyhood mentor, a medicine man named Forgets Things, who always showed respect for Coyote.

There were many tribes represented at that Sun Dance council that day. Coyote looked and silently took note of the powerful men that had come to sit and listen, even if it was just for a few moments. The pressure was daunting when he saw all the tribes were represented this year. He looked to the west of the main arbor, where they would hold many ceremonies, and saw the camps of the Oohenonpa Lakota Oyate, Oyate means tribe in the Lakota tongue, and Oohenonpa means two Boilings and he remembered telling his Cherokee friend, Sasa, that this tribe was more commonly known as the Two Kettles Lakota Oyate, and she had laughed at the change.

Then, looking towards the south there were the camps of the Sicangu or the Burnt Thighs Lakota Oyate, and the Hunkpapa Lakota Oyate, or those that camp at the entrance. Then to the north of the main arbor were the Oglala Lakota Oyate, or those that scatter their own, and the Minniconjou Lakota Oyate, or the plants by the waters. Since they never allowed any camps to occupy the eastern area, the later arriving camps would have to squeeze in between the others who had gotten there first. This year, the late ones were the Sans Arc Lakota Oyate, or those that hunt without bows, and the Sihasapa, or the Blackfeet (not to be confused with the Northern Blackfoot, the sworn enemies of the Lakota). Also in attendance and having to squeeze in where they could find a spot were the Dakota tribes, the Santee – Siseton, the Eastern Dakotas, which had the farthest distance to travel to be in attendance, and the Yankton - Yanktonai known collectively as the Teton, Western Dakotas who, once seated for Coyote's talk, sat proudly, but obviously were feeling impatient. Together they formed the Seven Council Fires and their chief's word was law for the entire Sioux nation.

Coyote was nervous, trying to speak to such a dignified assemblage. Warriors and chiefs he barely knew, or had never met at all, sat and stared back at him with blank expressions and cold eyes. In the places of honor were old Chief Sleepy Eyes, Chief Big Foot and Chief War Eagle, to only name a few.

They also nervously watched an area just past the perimeter of the gathering where a quiet, stoic, as well as real coyote sat, waiting for his traveling companion. Coyote had explained the animal was his helper and friend, whom he called Yellow Eyes, and said they had met in Indian Territory. Having a wild coyote at the Sun Dance was a little unnerving to say the least. Some in camp said it was a bad omen, while others held Coyote in awe for having such a helper. It was obvious that the animal was wild and not tame. It did not allow anyone to approach it and it watched Coyote without ever taking his yellow eyes from him the entire time. The warriors were sure that if anyone made a violent move toward the man, the animal would strike and it would be brutal and quick. A coyote is smaller than a wolf, with agile legs and a keen intelligence, besides its strong canine teeth and snapping jaw. It was well known among the tribes that the coyote was a trickster, not to be trusted. Yet somehow this man, Coyote, had developed a connection with the wild animal that felt unnatural to some. They all would not mind if Coyote left as quickly as possible.

Earlier that day, Coyote had been introduced to a few notable young men around his own age, men who had distinguished them-selves in war and prowess, possibly headed for leadership of a village or the tribe. Young Man Afraid of His Horses seemed to be a good young man and treated Coyote with equality. Spotted Tail was about that same age, along with Red Cloud, who was a stern and quiet young man. These men also sat listening with vague interest. But Coyote would not be discouraged: he knew it would be a hard battle to convince the most feared Indian nation of the plains that they could and would fall prey to these seemingly easy to overcome weapons coming against them.

So he continued, "Many of you know that I left my village many moons ago to seek the will of Wakan Tanka, without knowing what I would find, a new purpose from the Creator, or slavery and death at the hands of an enemy. One night I happened to spot a small camp. I left my horse and went sneaking up to try and see who these warriors were. While I crouched down and listened to a language I did not know, their leader came up behind me and knocked me out. I slept for some time and when I woke, I found I had been spying on the warriors of the great Osage Nation."

Many in the gathering murmured in awe at meeting a people known to be almost as fierce as the Lakota, and living to tell about it.

Coyote went on, "Since I had left my weapons with my horse, when they found me they knew that I had not meant to kill them, so they asked me using hand sign, why I was watching them. But, that is not important. What is important is that the Osage have been tamed by the United States government, and they have had their huge lands taken from them. They have been put on lands that do not have enough game to feed their people and they are expected to dig up the earth mother and plant seeds, to stay in one place all the time, and to no longer steal horses and make war on their enemies."

Now the men were aghast with disbelief that such a thing could happen to the Osage. Their prowess in war was legendary, and they were said to be tall, well-built men and women who were feared by all their enemies. It was like saying that the moon had fallen, never to return.

Coyote had to raise his hand to encourage silence so he could continue. "I know that these things sound unbelievable. I thought so too, until I continued to travel further south into a place they now call Indian Territory. The white men have taken a large area of land, south of the Great Plains. They have made lines on their white paper, showing where the people must stay and where they cannot go. Many nations are now put in their own area of this territory, with lines that separate them from their neighbor. The white men, in their wisdom, have placed one tribe next to their own bitter enemy, and they are supposed to stay peaceable" Coyote went on, but Old Chief Sleepy Eyes had a question. Coyote nodded and handed over the talking stick.

"Did not the Osage go to war with the white soldiers? How could this thing happen if the Osage had their good bows and war clubs at their waists? This is too wild to conceive," said Chief Sleepy Eyes, then he had handed back the talking stick to Coyote.

"It may sound like this could never happen to a mighty people, but it has. The reason why I met them is because they were outside of their allotted land, so they could hunt and bring back food for their starving families. The Osage have been reduced to begging the White Father for food supplies which they were promised in a treaty. Although the White Father's chief's signed that treaty which is a promise that they will do what the writing says, they have not been keeping those promises. There have been many deaths from starvation, and the Osage are in a much reduced state," replied Coyote.

The turmoil in the assembly had gotten to a fevered pitch, but again Coyote raised his hand for quiet.

"I have much more to tell you, my people. I am sure you have heard of a great nation called the Cherokee Nation?" Many heads nodded. "For many years, they have tried to be more like the whites in every way possible. Even their women dress like the white women and the men go to white schools and send their children to learn white ways. But, this nation, so great, was forced to march for many cycles of the moon to a new land. They had to leave everything behind. Some did not even have moccasins or blankets, and many died on the way. Some were murdered by the soldiers assigned to help them, many gave up in despair and walked until they fell over in death. Women carried their dead babies many days because the soldiers would not wait so that they might send their spirits on the long walk. This once great nation lost one of three portions of their people and arrived in Indian Territory with no little ones and very few old ones to help them with their wisdom in the new land.

"I have been among these people, and their suffering has been great. Of course, the white government gave them land in exchange for their homelands, but it was not done voluntarily. In fact, it was done against some of their highest white chiefs in the white government. The Cherokee people had been a friend of the white man for many, many generations. Those people helped the whites to win against their enemies. But, the white people chose not to remember their friendship, because they can only see the land and the goods they want to take from them.

"Now that they have lost so many of their people, they are trying to rebuild in this new land. Once again, the white man has decided that this land, that no one wanted before, was something they again needed to take away from the Cherokee and other tribes in Indian Territory.

Because of the treaties that the government signed, they cannot easily take this land away, but the white settlers are determined to take this land. That is one reason why the people have been given bad food and many have died. Now, there is another weapon the white settlers are using to subdue the tribes of Indian Territory. You yourselves are familiar with the drink that makes men crazy. We ourselves have experienced the white men who come and give everyone a free drink, asking for nothing in return. The next drink must be traded for with a fine pelt or buffalo robe and by the end of the night, there are no more buffalo robes left in camp to cover our naked bodies while we are bent over spewing our stomachs out on the ground. Some of our number have even died from this drink.

"But, here on the plains, we have only seen these whiskey men very seldom, so far. In Indian Territory, the drink that makes men crazy is made by the white settlers just across the boundary of Indian Territory. They sneak wagon loads of this drink to sell to a people who have almost nothing left to them. What is more, many have been murdered because of this drink and it has been said that there is a plan to convince the white government that all of the tribes of Indian Territory are worthless and should be taken from this new land to let the white settlers come in. This I have seen and heard with my own eyes and ears.

"I also know that the Army is trying to get the plains tribes to settle on a small piece of land, just like they did to the mighty Osage and the Cherokee. I am telling you that these things are coming here and that this drink will make you not care if they take your land from you. When you drink it, you no longer want to defend your camps or gather to fight against them. I am here to warn you that the whites are like a great cloud of locusts, and they will sweep over the tribes of the Great Plains and devour you, if you do not make yourselves ready and forbid the drink they call whiskey into your camps. Forbid the taking of their gift of a free drink," said Coyote.

As he looked around the assembly, he could not tell what they thought of his words. Then a hand was raised, asking for the talking stick. Coyote was surprised to see Red Cloud stand to accept the talking stick. Coyote sat, waiting for Red Cloud's speech.

"My people, I hear these words that have been brought to us, and I wonder if something has changed among the Lakota. Are we not victorious in battle, feared by every nation that brings their horses and men up against us? How long has it been since we lost a battle? We have not seen that many white men coming here. How do you know that they will be coming up against us? Are you a future teller or spirit man now? I know of no way that the things you are afraid of, like a whining woman, will ever come to the Great Plains. And if they do, we the Lakota, will again be victorious. We will show these white men that we cannot be told where to go and where to camp, where to hunt and where to bury our dead. I am afraid, Coyote, that you are seeing things in your own head," said Red Cloud, as he laughed and offered the stick to someone else.

Chief War Eagle, looked daggers at the young man Red Cloud. He motioned for the talking stick, then all in the arbor became quiet. Chief War Eagle had been one who knew the most about the whites. He had fought with the Americans against the British in the War of 1812. After that, he had become a guide for the massive steamboats plying the waters of the Missouri. All in the council knew that War Eagle had gone to Washington City to meet with the white men. He had always been a friend to the white men and was a voice of reason within the Yanktonai, despite the fact that he was actually born to the Santee. He was born in the land that is now Minnesota, and all his ancestors were buried in that land. However, the Lakota had been pushed out of the east by white settlements, and ruled with a strong arm on the Great Plains.

"I am known to all of you, and you know that I am also victorious in battle. But I will say this. If the Americans decide to come against the Lakota, we cannot win. There are more whites than the stars at night. You are aware that I went to Washington City, the city that the white people govern from that rests on the eastern big water. It was there that I learned that the white government was, indeed, moving all Indian peoples, pushing them west of the Mother of Waters, the one they call the Mississippi River. I was very sad to hear this, because now I cannot be buried near my ancestors and I cannot go to talk to them. What Coyote is telling you is the truth, because it is what I heard would be happening, from the white man's own mouth. However, I will confess that I see no problem with taking a little of the whiskey you are so afraid of. I do not see that drinking it will cause the Lakota to not fight fiercely to push the white men back from our hunting grounds. What is there here for them? We do not have large waterways as in the east. There are no towns out here and the deep snow of the winter would surely keep them away. I advise caution, but for the time being, we have little to fear," said War Eagle as he sat down.

One after another chiefs or sub-chiefs stood to speak, most talked long about the Lakota warrior's prowess against anything the whites could bring. The problem just seemed too far away for them to worry about, and the notion that a drink could defeat the entire nation was absurd. So Coyote's mission to save his people was for nothing, since his warnings fell on deaf ears. The next day he packed his horse with food for travel and left the Sun Dance.

He decided to go and visit his friend Five Owls of the Osage. If he continued to learn all he could, maybe someday, Wakan Tanka would show him what to do with his knowledge. He only knew that he did not want to be with the Lakota people when they were defeated. As he traveled south of the high plains, on his paint pony, he thought about another friend he had made in Indian Territory. A girl. A very special girl who taught him what he needed to know to warn his own people. He had told her that he might come back. Well, maybe if things worked out, he might be able to venture further into Indian Territory from the Osages land and into the Cherokee's part of the territory. Maybe, if Wakan Tanka made it possible.

He shook off the gloom of the months he had spent trying to convince his people to prepare, make a plan, band together and make alliances with other plains tribes, all to no purpose. But, at least he had tried. They would not be able to fault him because they did not listen. Much like a story that Sasa, his friend of the Cherokee, had told him one day. He remembered as if it were yesterday. Sasa sat with him on the front porch of her new home with Jackson Halley. She was an intelligent young woman, one that hungered for knowledge and was trying to help her people. That particular day she wore her deerskin dress with the fringes at the bottom, and her moccasins which came to her knees.

"Would you like to hear a story I just learned, Coyote? I have been reading the white man's Bible. It is a book with writing on the pages and the writing came from God. People have made many copies of this book so that everyone could learn God's message. Anyway, in the Bible there is a story about something that happened many generations ago. It was a time, some years after first woman and first man had been created," said Sasa.

"I thought you said this was the white man's religion? First woman and first man are part of the Lakota legends," asked Coyote, puzzled.

"Oh, that is true, Coyote, and they are also part of the Cherokee legend as well. So there must be something to it. But the whites have it written down on paper, in a book. Anyway, the Creator saw all the badness on the earth and decided to clean the earth from all the badness of man. He would clean the earth by letting it rain until the whole earth was nothing but water. But, he did not want to destroy all of the people. So, he found a man who was a good man who had a wife and three sons, and later all three would have wives as well.

"The man's name was Noah, and God gave him a job to do, in fact he gave him several to do. Noah was told to build a very large canoe, only it was many, many times bigger. The name of this type of canoe was called an Arc. Big enough to put many animals on so they might be saved. While Noah was building this big canoe, he was supposed to go out to the people and give them a warning that their world was going to be destroyed. None of Noah's people would listen to him either. He kept telling them, over and over, for many years and in the meantime, Noah spent every other moment to build that big canoe.

"Finally, the canoe was ready, and all the different animals were put in rooms Noah had made in the Ark. Then he collected and loaded the animals, each having a mate, into the Ark. Then God made it to rain over all the earth until there were no more hills or mountains, just the

Ark floating on a world made only of water. As it rained, though, all the people that did not listen ended up dying in the water. Once the earth was clean again, God made the water go away and finally the Ark settled on top of a tall mountain, and Noah was glad that he had listened to the Creator and done his job," Sasa finished.

Coyote thought about that story from time to time. He realized that this man Noah carried a message that no one would believe or act on. That is how he felt about the message he had tried to give his people. He wanted to save them from what the tribes in Indian Territory were suffering from now, from the taking of their homelands, forcing them to live next to their enemies, and suffering starvation, to the influence of whiskey and money. Noah had done his job and so had Coyote, but it did not stop him from feeling very sorry for them because they would not listen.

Poison Woman

Chapter 8
The Stars are My Friends

Poison Woman sat on a bench outside of her sparse cab-in, shelling peas with Martha Flying-hawk, her neighbor. On pleasant days like this one, they enjoyed working to-gether, chatting and keeping each other company. Martha was less than half Poison Woman's age, but that did not matter, she enjoyed her company anyway. "I can't remem-ber a time when the people were more agitated, other than during the removal from our homelands," said Poi-son Woman, referring to the long trek to Indian Territory they now called the Trail of Tears. The Territory was abuzz with fury, sadness, vows of revenge and strife. Being one of the few elder women left to the Cherokee after the forced march, she and her brother, Medicine Man, had not been prepared for this new emergency among the tribes of Indian Territory.

When they first arrived in the new lands, she and Medicine Man put up a wigwam made of sticks and deadwood. It was not meant to last but a short time, but they had ended up living in that precarious dwelling for two years until the local young men who had helped build one of the first churches in the area, came to build this small cabin for them. They used what they could find, cutting down young trees and not letting them dry before placing them in their places for the walls of the dwelling. There just was not time to do it the right way.

"I can hear the cracking and splitting day and night as the wood dries in place. I am forever patching up holes with that local red clay I mix with cow manure and straw, then I have to cover that with that awful pine pitch to seal it, and my hands stay raw from the effort. It is an endless task, Martha." Martha only nodded, since she was having to do the same at her own cabin.

"I have got to get out of this place before I go deaf from the noise. With all this cracking and groaning you would think this cabin was a living thing," Poison Woman went on.

She had never married, but had always taken care of her brother. Her work as a healer had been satisfying enough. She ended up treating every child in the tribe sooner or later anyway.

"How were you and your brother named? My family over in South Carolina started using white names a long time ago. That I know of, there isn't anyone in my family with a Cherokee name. I never thought to ask my mother why that is so, and now it is too late. I lost her during the Nunahi-Du-na-Dlo-Hilu-I (The Trail Where They Cried) and I was not able to find her sister, my aunt, afterward," said Martha.

"My brother, Di Damv Wi S Gi or Medicine Man, had acquired his name from his predecessor when the old man died, and before my brother dies, he will try to pass the name on to the next young spirit healer, if there are any. He does not allow his real name to be spoken. He says that the person who carried it is dead, so we honor his request. Did you ever want to have a Cherokee name?" asked Poison Woman.

"Maybe," admitted Martha, looking a little embarrassed that someone might know her secret wish.

Poison Woman thought for a bit, then smiled at Martha. "My name was given to me by my brother when we were young and I was just learning to be a medicine healer," she said. "I had given him some medicine to get rid of worms in the gut. The runny stools that resulted caused him to accuse me of poisoning him, even though he had been through that same thing every spring since boyhood. It was a common remedy that our mother used on us without fail, every spring. From then on he called me A da hi hi A ge yv , or Poison Woman. That name caused the People to pause when seeking a cure from me. Just think of it, a healer named 'Poison Woman'. I learned to enjoy the expressions that crossed their faces as they absorbed the possibilities, but then, after a while, the newness wore off and then people did not think about the name any more. So, I am Poison Woman, healer to the Cherokee People. There are younger and more energetic healers now, and I don't have to work so hard when a big sickness comes. Now, after so many years, I have come to like the name. Let me see what I can do for you," she went on. "As an elder in the Woman's Council, I can give you a name. What is the thing you love, or what do you love to do?"

Martha's quick blushing was evident even through the deep tan of her normally light tan complexion, which had darkened from long days of work in the Indian Territory sun. She had to be further encouraged, but she finally found her voice.

"I love to lay on my back outside, at night, when the sky is clear and there are no campfires around, and count the star people. I...I can't ever seem to count them all, and when I come again to count, none of the stars are in the same places anymore. It is like the sky shifted, but I begin all over again. It is so relaxing. I find peace while I gaze up at their cold light. They are always there for me, and even when I find they are in a different place, they are always there. I wonder if the Creator can count them all?" she asked.

Poison Woman thought for a short while, as she went on shelling her peas and listening to them ping when they hit the side of the pottery bowl. The light wind tousled her sparse hair, and it's caress was like a baby's kiss. Then a satisfied smile washed over her face, her eyes began to twinkle, and she announced, "I have your name. Once I say it, you must keep it forever, unless your village chief decides to change it. You are now to be known as A ge yu tsa Ga go Di se s di A ni no qui si or Girl Who Counts the Stars. If you use this name, everyone will automatically know who it is they are talking about, because there are very few girls who bother to look up at the night sky."

Martha sat stunned for a while. It was so simple. Why had she not thought of that? And she could be Martha Flying-hawk to the government and on their papers, but to her people she would be Girl Who Counts the Stars. She looked at Poison Woman with tears in her eyes and said, "It is perfect. Wado for this gift. I will tell all the people in my settlement that among the Cherokee, I am 'Girl Who Counts the Stars'."

"Ah, I am sorry Medicine Man was not at home, or even nearby. He went with the other men of the local settlement, and is meeting in council. Something is happening in Indian Territory. Something dangerous that, I think, threatens all the tribes of this new land. He traveled to Tahlequah, our new Cherokee Nation's capital, to meet at the designated council grounds there. He looked grim when I saw him leave," said Poison Woman

"But, has there not been much hope in the air these days? I mean, with the forced removal behind us, the People dug right in and it seemed like overnight, they transformed this prairie land into productive crops and organized communities. It is not as bad as it was the first few months after the Trail of Tears, when we were trying to rely on the U.S. Government to send us food to subsist on, a promise never fulfilled. It was so hard for us then. It was bad enough that we lost over four thousand of our people on that wicked walk. Then we had to live with the fact that another thousand died of starvation after getting here. Useless deaths, I say. Leave it to the white man to figure out a way to take the food right out of our mouths," replied Martha. She took a deep breath of the mild fresh air, then she glanced sideways at Poison Woman, judging if she should bring up a touchy subject.

"It was rumored in our town that you helped catch some of the ones who were stealing the food allotment money. They told me that a group of men in the east had planned it all out with our Indian Agent for the temporary camp. You would think that the U.S. Army would do something about that. But, they have done nothing, and so it still goes on today in other parts of Indian Territory for some of the other tribes. It makes me shiver just to think of that time," she went on.

Poison Woman continued to shell peas, one by one, thinking on it a while. Her quiet demeanor belied the turmoil and worry she felt within. Her old wrinkled skin looked translucent in the afternoon light, and the silver blue film that covered her once dark brown eyes, reflected the light, making them seem to glow with an inner light. Poison Woman stopped her busy hands and said, "Our Cherokee leaders have vowed they will never allow the Cherokee Nation to be at the mercy of any white man who has no love for the red. That is when they began to help each other plant their crops, build their cabins and make the land productive. True, it would be a long time before it produces like the land back in New Echota and the other towns of our homeland. Just as soon as we left, they made our land a part of their states.

"But, Girl Who Counts the Stars, do not hate all the white men. Our leaders decided long ago, before you were born, that they would try to be more like the whites, and in truth we are. Just look at the way the different Cherokee factions are squabbling among themselves. First thing right off, a group of our men were so upset at our removal, they decided to murder all of the men who signed that paper to give up our land and then they all left with their families to get here first and get the best of the land. They didn't even have to walk here like we did. They took a boat ride. They call them 'The Treaty Party'. Their assassins almost succeeded, but thankfully a few got away. It is not good for our nations to be so divided. Killing each other won't help us.

"But they are no better than the Old Settlers, the ones who came here some years ago voluntarily. Once we arrived with the Chief Overall, John Ross, they said they didn't want a chief. Now they are called the 'Old Settlers'. Then, there is the Ross Party. They are so busy with fighting the U.S. Government, fighting the Old Settlers and fighting the Treaty Party, that they have had little time to figure things out for us and our families," she concluded, shaking her head solemnly.

The Cherokee Nation was finding this new land different, in many ways, from the eastern homelands. Once they figured out how to deal with the differences in the soil, the available water and finding out what types of crops grew well in this hotter climate, they began to see an increase, even a profit on their hard labors.

The young women had avoided pregnancy for the first three years, making sure they had dependable food sources before subjecting young ones to what could be a very short life. Some of them discretely went to Poison Woman for the necessary herbs to make sure a child did not even start. Most families had lost loved ones, even whole families gone, all but one. The majority of deaths were among the very old, the sick and the young. So many children died that the nation looked as if they had left their children back east. Now, with crops doing well, cabins finished and families putting down roots, the young women had begun producing offspring. It was a happy sight to see.

All was not rosy in Indian Territory, though. All along its borders, there were skirmishes and raids. Some of them were from the wild Indians of the plains, unhappy that the U.S. Government had given the civilized tribes their customary hunting grounds. On the northern border were the Osage, who did not understand what they had done when they signed over their lands for the settlement of the Cherokee. One Osage chief remarked that, yes, they had sold that land to the White Father, but they did not sell the animals that lived on that land so the animals were still theirs to hunt, not belonging to the Cherokee. So, that was the cause of many disagreements.

On the western border were what the civilized tribes called the "Wild Indians". They meant the Indians that clung to a nomadic lifestyle and who did not plant crops, but existed on roots, berries, and the meat they could hunt and kill. Their entire way of life was based on the buffalo and its many uses. Those tribes, like the Pawnee, Kickapoo, Lakota, Delaware, Shoshone and Cheyenne, just to name only a few of the many tribes of the central plains, had been used to hunting for buffalo within what was now Indian Territory. The notion of physical boundaries was completely foreign to them, and when they had to be ejected from these lands, they came back with vengeance in their hearts to raid and steal horses, livestock and captives.

Poison Woman had heard that even worse trouble was brewing at the southern border, which separated Indian Territory from the Republic of Texas. Only a few years ago, that had been Mexico's land. Several tribes moved there, invited by Mexico who gave them the land. After Mexico won her freedom from Spain, they set about installing the new Mexican government. The white settlers in the land also came by invitation from the Mexicans, but once the new government of Mexico took over from Spain, many grievances arose against Mexico. The white settlers did not like the new Mexican government, so they began to resist until it was a full scale war. By 1836 Texas had won, which Mexico was still not happy about.

There were several Indian villages—not in Indian Territory, but settled now in Texas—that were also coming under attack from the Texans. In turn, they decided to raid the Choctaw and the Chickasaw and others along the border. It seemed an endless cycle of revenge. It made Poison Woman happy she was further north, and at the same time it made her feel weary with the thought that it would never end. Poison Woman and Medicine Man lived very near where their temporary camp had been. They had access to Fort Smith, in Arkansas, or they could travel in another direction and go to the Cherokee capitol, Tahlequah. They did not want to move into a town, but were happy just being in the country.

The eastern border was with Arkansas and the white settlers. Why did white people always want whatever the Indians had? The fact that it had been granted to the Indians by treaty made no difference to the white families pushing their way west, looking for a place to settle. The government had pushed the tribes into Indian Territory because it was a place most settlers did not want to settle. Life was not easy here, to say the least. But, once the tribes were moved here, the whites all around decided that it was a land filled with milk and honey, desirable in every way, and then set about finding ways to undermine the civilized tribes in order to obtain it.

Poison Woman looked at Girl Who Counts The Stars, noticing the youth that gave her body energy. Nothing like being an old, dried up woman to make you long for the days of your youth. It will be the responsibility of young people like her to take over for the elders, and she hoped that they would not make the same mistakes all over again.

Chapter 9
Blind Ambition

The man walked out of the Cornhill Coffee House eatery, which was not one of the finest in Boston, but was adequate to his needs. Still, they charged $0.75, which was higher than some fine eateries in New York. Everything had been fresh, though, especially the seafood, just as he liked it. It was his habit to indulge in a big meal before taking on an important meeting.

Manuel Munos Mendoza was a wily, thin, short man. His black hair was combed so that the sides came forward to caress his cheeks, which drew attention to them. That was unfortunate, since Manuel was not a particularly handsome man; to make a finer point of it, he was plain. No matter how he dressed, nor how much he spent on his clothes, he always seemed to look like a well-dressed Mexican peasant, as well he might, since his parents were peasants. His linage–or lack of it–disappeared once he opened his wallet to pay, accidentally showing off the bills he carried. One might worry that it was a dangerous time to be flashing about the money on your person, but Manuel was as swift as a striking snake. He knew more ways to disable a man, or a woman, for that matter, than could be counted; and was always ready for the unexpected.

Well, the unexpected was what he craved, so he begged for it to come to him. And no matter how it was tried, Manuel always came out on top. He doubted he could ever be bested. At least, he had not lost yet, though many had tried and ended up broken men. He did not try to break women in the same way… women were easily controlled, shallow of mind and not a match for someone like himself. There was one thing that Manuel believed fervently, and that was that women were only a little higher than dogs. Sure, it was pleasant to spend some quality time with some floozy, but in the end, she would always turn out to be just as stupid as the rest. No wonder men ruled the world.

Today he was on his way to see a general. He was taking his time, though, since it did not do to let people like generals feel they were in control when no one controlled Manuel Munoz Mendoza. Ever. Manuel was only partially sure of the content of today's meeting, but it did not matter. He would not take any new assignment unless it benefited him mightily. He walked down the street to the corner and turned on Tremont. The hotel was only a few blocks away. At least it was The Tremont House Hotel, and not some log cabin in the woods. He had had enough of those for a while.

The United States had just come through the worst six year downturn in their economy. They called it the Panic of 1837, and it caused many to lose their businesses and homes. But, Manuel did not care one whit about that. It was his own pocket that mattered, and six years of depression was cramping his plans to retire a wealthy man. Not just wealthy, but richer than Midas. If there was a way, he would find it.

He walked steadily, but not hurriedly. He carried a crystal topped walking stick with his gray wool suit, and his waistcoat had a brocade front of gray and cream with a satiny gleam. His gold pocket watch sat securely in its own pocket while its gold chain swung with the movement of his stride. The watch fob was attached to a special button on the front of his waistcoat. Over his suit, he wore a black with gray stripe frock coat. Today he wore his gray beaver skin top hat. He knew he looked the epitome of wealth and refinement. He thought it comical the way people could be influenced, and he knew how to do that better than any man alive.

The desk manager personally escorted Manuel up to the general's rooms. He was supremely confident, at ease, and sure of himself. He also felt he knew what this meeting might be about.

"Do come in, Señor," Juan invited Manuel into the front sitting room.

"Good afternoon, Señor Mendoza. You are expected. Please help yourself to some refreshment and the general will be with you shortly. I must depart. The general is sending me on an errand," Juan went on, as he donned his hat.

Manuel had not said a word yet. It was obvious that the general wanted a private meeting, to which not even his assistant was allowed to be present. He chuckled to himself. This may be the most lucrative assignment yet, and I may even have uses for whatever information I glean here to use as a little, shall we say, incentive for the general to continue to send money and opportunities my way. Yes, I am interested already, even though I do not know yet what he intends. *The door to the general's private room opened.*

The general was wearing a black and red silk satin smoking jacket over his day clothes, minus his coat. He held a cigar in one hand and his other was placed in the silky pocket. The general's smile seemed genuine as he strode forward to shake Mendoza's hand with a short bow included.

"Ah, Mr. Mendoza. So kind of you to drop by for our little visit. I trust your stay in Boston is proving advantageous? Yes, well, I am happy that I could count on your presence so quickly," the general greeted him.

"The pleasure is all mine General De Almeida, I assure you. Let me be of service to you and I will be happy," replied Mendoza, with a slight smile, or what passed for a genuine smile.

"Fine, fine. Help yourself to some refreshment if you desire it. After our meeting, if concluded satisfactorily, I will open a very good wine I have with me. Now, there is a little job that I need you to take care of. It is a delicate thing and should be done in the utmost secrecy. I know that I can trust you to maintain this just between us, yes?" asked the general.

"I would not want it any other way, my General," said Mr. Mendoza

"Fine, fine, and may I assume that you are not averse to accumulating an untold amount of wealth, my good friend," added the general, chuckling a bit.

Mendoza smiled momentarily. "Of course, that is my wish, as I know it is also yours, General. Before we discuss what you wish me to do for you, since it is likely I will take the assignment—with the right incentives, of course—let us discuss this wealth you speak of first," he said with a gleam in his eyes, for wealth was what he sought. Money bought power, the kind of power to rule things behind the scenes and the power to make things happen to benefit him, as opposed to anything charitable a person could waste money on.

"This is a very important mission for Mexico. There is no greater honor that serving your county, Mr. Mendoza, which in itself can be a great reward, do you not think? However, this assignment can also give you the opportunity to own untold wealth, more than you can imagine," promised the general.

Mendoza frowned a little: something was off about this offer.

"If you don't mind me asking, General, but if you truly have such wealth to give, why do you not keep it for yourself? I had always thought you to be a modest man of modest means, a public servant. How is it you can offer me something so valuable, when you could just as likely have it for yourself?" he objected.

"Ah, but there are things you don't know yet. First of all, I have means that have already amounted to more than can fill a huge building, even if no one knows that I have such wealth. However, I have an item in my possession that I recognize as priceless. It is made of the purest of gold. Just its weight in gold is a king's ransom, but the item itself is worth much more than its gold content, no... no, I have misspoken, it is a national treasure that has been lost for hundreds of years. It came from the Aztec, Moctezuma himself. It is a golden snake on top of a grotesque head, said to have come off of his palace wall. He, no doubt, wore this when performing acts of sacrifice as we have heard of in the tales of our country. This priceless object has been hidden away for centuries, and just recently came into my hands, quite by accident," explained the general.

"I wish to see such a thing, General. I imagine it would be very beautiful, eh?" said Mendoza.

"Oh, dear, I am so sorry, but I cannot travel with such a thing, no. I have left it in a secret hiding place. I can only go there once in a great while, or my secret will be known. However, my friend, I do have a drawing of it. I first did a sketch myself, then I called in one of our finest artists to make it look as real as it is. I told him it was for a government project. He did not know the difference," said the general.

He then went to the desk by the window and pulled out of a leather satchel an artistic painting of a magnificent Aztec wall decoration. The object was so very unusual, with a serpent coiled, ready to strike, on its head. Its empty eye sockets bespoke of outrageous bloody ceremonies. The coiling serpent's eyes carried Mexican Opal of deepest depths and gleam.

The size shown seemed to be what an adult man could wear. It was magnificent. But Mendoza remembered something which made him a little suspicious.

"But, General, this looks just like the head and serpent we hear of in our folk tales. I did not think it to be real. What a magnificent thing. Just how did you come by this artifact, may I ask?" he said.

"One of the things that I do for Mexico is to collect the taxes and to help return stolen property once it is found. You know, taxes are collected from the poor, but also from the rich as well. It is up to me to decide if something a man possesses is stolen property. I came upon some very fine things that a widow had received in her husband's will.

Well, my good man. I took one look and determined that her husband must have been a terrible thief, for she possessed many things that her husband had collected, which he was not wealthy enough to own. The artifact was among these things. The widow had no idea of its worth, but I am sure it is the same one we have heard tell of so many times in our lives," glibly answered the general.

"And naturally you took charge of the item. What would Mexico do if they found that I have it? Hm?"

"They do not even know of its existence. To them, it is still just a myth, and you would be hailed as a great hero for possessing such a prize. Like I said before, this item is priceless. You would not even have to sell it. Just owning it would open many doors for you. You know how that works. Once you are known to have money, then people are eager to give more to you. It happens to me all the time," said the general.

Mendoza was not an innocent. He knew that there was something the general was not telling him, but regardless of that, he had many ways to deal with him when the time came. The general only thought he could outsmart Mendoza. As for the head with the Golden Serpent, he would know best what could be done with such a prize. Not only that, but the general had just confided to him his many overstepping of the laws of Mexico. Having control over such a high standing person in the Mexican Government was also worth its weight in gold. So he made his decision.

"How do I know you actually have this thing? A picture can be drawn without it being real. What proof do I have that this is indeed my prize?" he asked.

"Ah, I see your point, my good friend. Yes, I do have some assurance for you," replied the general, as he opened the desk drawer to pull out a small box, handing it to his visitor. "Go ahead, Mendoza, open it. In fact, you may keep it if you take the mission."

Mendoza lifted the top lid of the box to reveal a pad of cotton. He set the lid aside and slipped the cotton away to expose a golden tail of a rattlesnake, broken off at one end as if it had come off from something much bigger. It had weight, and it gleamed even in the low light of the room. For a moment he was speechless. The general saw the question on his face and answered before he could ask.

"Yes, yes. This is the end of the serpent's tail, which broke off from the object as I was, uh, removing it from the widow's house. You see, it is completely real," he finished.

Stunned, Mendoza stared at the object the general had placed in the palm of his hand. His mind quickly ran through several scenarios of life with the wealth that was promised.

"Then, I am willing to consider such a payment. However, first I must know what you need me to do for such a fine thing. I believe, General, we are going to be close friends, indeed," he promised.

"Good, good," approved the general, rubbing his hands together. "The task I have in mind is not an easy one, but given your expertise I feel that you are the only man for the job. That is why the payment is so high, because this job I have for you may help Mexico regain the land we lost to the Texans, the very land they now call, The Republic of Texas. Bah! The name itself is like rot in my mouth. I have come up with a foolproof plan, and if you can successfully get this thing started, it will probably accomplish itself, then once the first phase is successful, Mexico will know what to do next.

"Now, my friend, come over to the desk and let me draw you a diagram of the people and places that are an essential part of this plan. Now, you see here, this is the Mexico border as it is now after our war against the Texans, and here is the Republic of Texas, and here is the southern border of Indian Territory which belongs to the United States. What I want you to do is...."

Chapter 10
Ruined Dreams and Broken Hearts

After coming home from Poison Woman's cabin, Martha Flying-hawk worked diligently to get what little they had onto the supper table before her husband, David, walked through the door. She did not want him to have an excuse to take his unhappiness out on her, which happened more often now than before they left their Tennessee Cherokee homeland.

Martha had been a young girl of fifteen when she married David. He was from the a ni a wi or Deer Clan, which was known as the hunters of the tribe. Hunting was his specialty, since he had been brought up from a long line of excellent hunters and that was how all the men in his family were raised, to provide meat for the family and to take care of the animals. He knew all about preparing the hides for all kinds of purposes, and his family was well respected. After coming to Indian Territory, Martha noticed that he seemed to have lost himself.

Martha's family was of the a Ni GI lo, hi, or the Long Hair clan. It was known as the peaceful clan and many Peace Chiefs emerged from it. Within that clan there were three sub-clans, the Twister, Wind and Strangers. Her family had long belonged to the Strangers Sub-Clan. It had carried much more significance many years ago, when tribes warred against each other and invariably the tribe would end up with captured people from other tribes, many of them children. It was the Strangers Clan that helped these new ones. Many of the families of this clan adopted the "strangers" into their own families and treated them equally, as their own.

It had been a very good marriage, until they came to Indian Territory. Now she needed her skills as a peacemaker on a daily basis, just to deal with her own husband. They were extremely poor, mostly because David refused to work his land. He just did not seem to be able to change his way of life. They were all having to make adjustments, some were adjusting better than others, but David was slowly becoming someone else, someone she did not recognize because his heart had changed, and hers had not.

She thought, the most exciting and wonderful thing that has happened to me, and I can't tell David. Any mention of our life before the move throws him into a rage, so mentioning about my new Cherokee name "Girl Who

Counts the Stars" is completely out of the question. I don't know how long I can keep this up. I am so worried. I haven't confided in anyone, not even Poison Woman.

One good thing is, David hasn't hit me yet, but he has come very close to it. I imagine that he will, eventually. Then what should I do? If my parents were alive, I could just set David's things outside the door, divorce him, and then go to live with my family, but, the tribal elders say that women cannot do that anymore. We have to do it by some laws or something. It is all too confusing. When I think that I might tell someone and get me some help, David seems to know that I have reached my breaking point, and he will become all apologetic and try to do better, only to fall back on his old ways again. Ways like drinking whiskey, running around with that outlaw crowd, and spending the night with one of those bought women. He thinks I don't know about that. How could I not know it when he comes home with perfume on him? I don't even own any perfume, so I am pretty sure of what he is doing.

I know about the disease that is passed on from those women, and I don't want it. That seems like a pretty good reason why I have stopped having relations with David. But, he doesn't seem to care or want me anyway... at least he has not acted like he even noticed. He is not the man I married. May the Creator protect me from the evil that has taken over some of our people, my own husband in particular.

Martha ran to the window of the wooden shack they lived in. There was yet no glass in the open frame. Smoothing down the wrinkles in her calico skirt, she tried not to worry about the large greasy stains she could not seem to get out, no matter how much she washed it. Even the bright blue color of the calico was now gone, covered over by dirt and stains. Martha stood there barefoot on the dirt floor, dreading the evening and what it might bring.

She was supposed to have a log cabin and a working farm by now. She would happily help David take care of it. Unfortunately, he took no interest in learning even the basics of farming, so she had had to do odd jobs for her neighbors for food while she tried to keep a small garden close to the shack. She didn't know where he went every day, but he would be gone for a few hours and invariably come home in a foul mood. She could not think what she might do to help her David, the young, strong Cherokee she had married, if that man still existed.

Standing at the window, nothing was moving. Nothing and no one was coming down the road to the shack. That was both good news and bad. She hated waiting for the bad to fall on her head, usually as a surprise. She wanted to get it over with for the night, then he would go off drinking and she could get some rest until the next day, when she would have to figure out how to put food on the table again. She did not know what else to do, so she did nothing at all, except sit by the window and watch for her husband to come home and begin the cycle over again.

Deep in a copse of trees, David sat a pony he had not owned until just a few short minutes before. He waited quietly while the men pursuing him passed him by. He had always marveled at the stupidity of some people. The men from the nearby farm, just outside of Tahlequah, had assumed that a thief would gallop hell bent for leather after stealing a horse. But, David was smart, much smarter than anyone knew. He had taken the pony and after galloping away, he found a shallow stream to walk the pony up the middle on the rocky bed, water splashing some, but not enough so as anyone could hear as yet. He had continued for several miles before leaving the stream bed when he found a dry, rocky slope, which would not show his passing once the water dripping from the pony's hooves quickly dried in the Indian Territory heat. Then he had stealthily walked his mount into this dark clump of trees, vines and bushes. After dismounting and tying the pony to a branch, he quickly backtracked to make sure no path existed to give his location away.

The searchers had gone barreling past, thinking he was headed for the Arkansas border. They would lather their mounts up good before they finally realized they were following their own noses. He had been extra careful to choose a pony with few markings, common color and not much to distinguish it from any other farm pony in these parts. Even if the men doubled back, they still would not catch him, and once they actually found the pony, he will have already sold the thing to a stranger and headed out for parts unknown.

This was not hard work. Not like farming, which he despised. He was extremely bitter about the Cherokees' removal from their homes in the east, where he had been a fine hunter. Many families had looked up to him and needed him to help supply their meat, because it was what he was truly good at. Never had he ever imagined he would be expected to put plow to dirt, and for what? Just as soon as they get used to this place, he knew the government would find a way to take this away as well. So, what's the use to work that hard when the white man can take whatever he darn well pleases, just because it belongs to an Indian?

David had made the long trek from Georgia. He witnessed the wholesale death, his people dropping like flies and those soldiers sitting up on their stout mules just watching, not trying to help. He had even seen the murder of an old Cherokee elder who was not walking as fast as a soldier wanted him to. That old man ended his days with a bayonet in the back. The injustice of it all was more than he could take.

He had his wife back at the cabin, but he hated to go there of a night and see the mournful look on her face, it just made him want to slap it off, and sometimes he almost did. *Doesn't she understand that I was just not cut out to be a farmer? Oh well, this is the best way to get some money,* he thought. But, usually before he finally headed on home, the money would be long gone. Drank up in whiskey and ale, with nothing to give to Martha.

What he really needed was something that made him more money than stealing just a pony or two. He had tried to think of different schemes to work, but this was all new to him. He had never tried to be a thief before.

He rode a little further south before he cut east. He was headed for a small secluded place where men like him did business. He sat the brown and tan pony, with his dirty, worn deer skins hanging on him, some of them in shreds. His hair hung down his back in greasy hanks, since he did not even bother to tie it back anymore. He was barely recognizable from the man he used to pride himself to be, but that life was gone now, and no use to pine for it, like trying to bring back the dead. There was no going back, ever.

Chapter 11
The Guardian

Wheezer lay on the bed, next to Sasa who was sleeping fitfully. She tossed and turned, making him unable to get a good night's sleep as well. Sitting up, he looked at Sasa's young face with the moonlight streaming through the window of her bedroom at their hotel in Boston. He sensed no danger and could see no reason for Sasa's unease. Wheezer scooted over the comforter to lick Sasa's cheek. Still asleep, she whisked her hand as if to ward off flies. Wheezer sighed, and decided to take a walk around the suite to check on his other humans, asleep in their room.

Anna usually kept their bedroom door closed and tonight was no different. Jackson and Anna did not like company in their bed. Wheezer never could figure out why that was, but he let them have their way and did not whine about it. He padded to every corner of the suite, checking, listening, and sensing if there might be any danger to his sleeping family. On his way back to Sasa's room, he almost passed the suite's door when he heard a slight creak. He turned to investigate the sound. It seemed to be coming from the door itself, in fact the door was not quite closed.

First, he placed his delicate, glossy black nose in the crack in the door and took a good sniff. He did not expect to smell much of anything at this late hour, when everyone was asleep, so he was surprised when the wafting aroma of pipe tobacco came drifting by. This peaked his curiosity. Since the big fire at Jackson's ranch in Van Buren, Arkansas, which scared Wheezer so much he ran until he was lost in the forest, the smell of smoke made him worry. That was the summer Wheezer had met Sasa when she saved his life from a snake bite. That made the smell of smoke, any kind of smoke, especially troubling to him, and he needed to find where it was coming from.

Nosing the door open a little further, Wheezer slipped out of the suite. The smoke seemed to be coming from the lobby area, so he quietly slipped down the marble staircase, which had been dimly lit for the night hours. When he reached the lobby, the smell was much stronger, so much so that he began to be alarmed. Standing in the shadows, he watched the night manager go about his business, noticing that the man was not particularly worried about the smell of smoke. He kept alert while the fur skin on his back began to ripple with tension and the hairs that ran down the middle of his back began to stand up straight and stiff.

Wheezer moved forward, trotting past the front desk and following the scent to a doorway into what looked like a small dining room. All along one wall was a dark, high table or counter, as long as the length of the room, with mirrors behind it. Glasses and bottles glittered in the dim light from flickering candles on the tables. There seemed to be no one there, but then Wheezer noticed a bit of movement all the way to the back of the room, in the far corner. Slowly, he slipped and weaved through the empty chair legs, brushing the white linen tablecloths that hung from each table, getting closer and closer to the source of the scented smoke until a voice stopped him in his tracks.

Wheezer crouched under a table, so that the white table-cloth hanging down the sides concealed his presence, and he held extremely still while he tried to discern if this smoke was any danger to his sleeping humans. While he crouched there, he became privy to a conversation between two men. One of them spoke with a heavy accent Wheezer had already heard before. It was like the accent of the Mexican man who came to work sometimes on Jackson's ranch, and it made it difficult to understand the English. Just the same, Wheezer got the impression that at least one these men was dangerous. One of them had the smell of fear sweat on him, even though they did not appear to be in distress. Of course, in his experience with humans, he knew that the mood could change in an instant. He would have to get closer to tell which man it was.

"I am not sure what you want me to say, Señor. You want to know about the young lady in the hotel who is brown like me, but is not Mexican? You say she is really a no good Indian, but Señor, the young lady you speak of is just that, a lady. Señor, there is no way for a red Indian to change its spots, even if they tried for their whole lives to do it. I think you are dreaming," said Pedro, the hotel grounds-keeper.

"I say, Suh, that it is her. She fits the bill all right. My poor dead father would cry out from the grave if I let this opportunity pass me by without wreaking vengeance upon her head for the awful death of my poor papa. I don't know how she made so many changes, but I been asking around town, but everyone has been fooled by this act she is puttin' on. I have be sure, though. You say that she is with a man and his wife? I had not heard that she even knew any white families, the little I know about her. Do you know the name of the man who rented the hotel suite?" asked the young man.

"Sì, Señor, I do know it, but I do not want to lose my job here at the hotel if you make problems for me. Jobs are very hard to find for someone like me, a refugee from the Mexican war. I just want to be left alone to take care of my family," said Pedro, with a worried look.

The young man looked extremely frustrated, but after a moment he calmed down.

"Don't be daft man. I would never do anything here. Everyone knows that I am a gentleman of high standing in the Boston community, just as my father was until that vixen interfered. And you will be well paid for the information, Suh. I assure you, the great city of Boston will not be alarmed in any way, should this be the right girl. What is the man's name, Suh? I am growing very impatient with you," the young man slurred.

Pedro looked all around the room, except for down, and nodded his head slightly before crossing himself and murmuring a quick prayer.

"The name of the man that the lady is with is a Mr. Jackson Halley, Señor. That is all I know. Now, may I get back to my family? They will be waking up soon, and I have not had one hour of sleep yet," asked Pedro.

The young man looked stunned, almost paralyzed. Then he slowly drew some money out of his coat pocket, giving the entire bundle to Pedro. Pedro's eyes grew large and he hesitated to take it, but the young man shooed him away with a flick of his hand without even looking at him. Pedro hated to leave this man he did not really know, a man who had been drinking heavily since they had sat down, and that was at least a couple of hours ago. Pedro's conscience was eating at him already, and he had not yet stood up from the table.

"Señor, don't you think it is time for you to also go to your room? I know you have much to grieve over, but it will all look better in the morning, Señor," he pleaded.

The young man was still brooding, and Pedro was not even sure the man knew he was still there. Then he began to speak, so Pedro politely stayed to listen. However, his concern for the young Indian girl who was now obviously a lady, was growing by the second and it was making him angry that he even told the man whom the room was registered to.

"I have asked others, and they say that she is the one that helped to catch the Indian Agent that was stealing from the Indian's food allotment back in '39. That has to be her. I swore that I would get even with that girl if it was the last thing I did, Suh. And that I plan to do. Do you know how my father died, Suh? He was eaten by wolves," slurred the young man, as he downed another whiskey. "And it was her fault."

"I am sorry, Señor, but I just don't believe that little slip of a thing could have had anything to do with wolves. It is too unbelievable. Besides, I heard that your "beloved Papa" killed some people when he went to Indian Territory. If I were you, I would slow down some, before you end up like him," said Pedro, who was now thoroughly ready to leave.

Upon hearing the slur concerning his father, the young man jumped up to strike at Pedro, but missed, being too drunk to see straight. Since Pedro was still sitting, the man's swing carried his body around and down closer to the floor, and his fist came around right in front of Wheezer's nose. Wheezer was startled and quickly jumped up to defend himself. But the man had overbalanced and found himself on his hands and knees, face to face with the formidable Wheezer.

The young man was not sure he was not hallucinating this apparition, but quickly decided it was real enough when Wheezer pulled his lips up and to the sides to expose every gleaming white sharp canine tooth at his disposal, snarling and spitting in the young man's face.

"Oh God, it's a wolf. Ach! Help! He will rip my throat out," he began screaming at the top of his lungs.

Pedro's back was to Wheezer, so he was not able to turn around and see what the man was screaming about, and just then the man grabbed at both of Pedro's arms, trying to leverage himself to get up and run away.

Wheezer could hear the footsteps coming from the lobby and figured that these people would take care of the bad man among them, so he quickly wove his body through the chair legs again where no one could see his progress. He reached the front lobby where there was no longer anyone to see his passage and sprinted up the marble staircase like a streak of light. It was not that he tried not to be seen, there was just no one there to see that he had been there.

Once upstairs, he slipped into the still slightly ajar door to his suite, turned and rose up on his back legs to put his front paws on the door to close it, then he ran into Sasa's room to lay on the bed and protect her if that man decided to follow him. It was a good night's work and he rested, alert but comfortable, the rest of the night.

Chapter 12
Life is But a Picnic

"Anna, won't you be coming with us?" asked Sasa, as she readied herself for the first picnic of the season.

"Uh, no, dear. This picnic is really for you young people, so that you can get to know them and make some more intimate friendships than can be done at a tea party. This time, the young men are invited, and it is you young ladies who will be responsible for keeping the conversation and entertainment on a light and airy note. It is supposed to be a gay and happy outing in the sunshine," said Anna, with a slight upward curve to her lips.

"I don't have the faintest idea of how to be, uh, entertaining. What am I supposed to do, get up and show them how Indians dance around a fire?" blurted Sasa.

"That would be utterly ridiculous, Sasa. In fact, it is the last thing you should do. You already know how to act like a lady, so go out and try to have some fun for a change," countered Anna.

Fun. Sasa could name it many things, but fun was not one of them. She was beginning to be impatient with the utter uselessness of the activities these young people thought to be an important part of their days. All the while, Sasa never lost sight of the people who must tag along in order to answer to their master's every wish and whim. It was the height of laziness, as far as she was concerned, to summon a maid–forcing her to stop whatever she was doing in another part of the house–and then to have her walk the ten feet across the room to pick up a shawl that the wearer had dropped on the floor in the first place. What a waste of time.

Sasa could almost rant if the Halleys would let her, but Anna had said it was all part of the white high society, and that she had to learn how to blend in to accomplish her purpose in the future. But, it was darn hard. She already wished to be back home on the frontier. She knew changes were happening daily in Indian Territory. The pull on her heart to be with her people was almost overwhelming. Instead, she heaved a huge sigh, donned her prettiest spring bonnet and started for the door, then stopped a moment.

"Since this is outside, is there any harm in taking Wheezer this time? He is so lonely when I go away, and it would make me feel much better if he were along," she asked.

Jackson had heard the request from his room and peeked around the door opening.

"I don't see why not. When I used to go on these little outings, I distinctly remember a young lady named… Uh, Othelia, I think it was… taking her little puffball of a dog with her. At least, I think it was a dog, I never checked under all that fur to make sure. Everyone thought it jolly of her to have brought her 'darling' pet along. Wheezer is so much better than that useless ball of fur, your friends might be very entertained by him, indeed," he answered.

"Do you really think so, Jackson? I mean, you know how Wheezer can get sometimes," cautioned Anna.

"Don't worry Anna, I will have a talk with him. He truly knows what I am saying, I know he does. He will be good, won't you boy?" asked Sasa.

But, Wheezer was already at the door with his lead in his mouth, waiting patiently.

Anna said, "Well, I guess that answers that."

They had agreed to all meet at the Standish home first for elevenses, what Sasa learned was what the English called the early tea before luncheon, and from there they would regroup to consolidate the carriages needed for the transporting of the group. While en route, Sasa had that conversation with Wheezer she had promised Anna and Jackson. Wheezer sat beside her in the carriage, so it was not hard to garner his attention.

"Now Wheezer, you heard what Anna said. You are to be on your best behavior. Please try not to disrupt the picnic. No eating off of anyone's plate. No walking across the food area, and no jumping into ladies' laps. They may like you very much, but they will not want their dresses ruined," said Sasa, as Wheezer gazed intently at her, taking in every word.

Sasa was promptly on time, but there were still a few who had not arrived as yet. She stepped from the carriage with the help of the driver, something she would never get used to, alighting by the front entrance of the Standish mansion. She straightened her peach cotton dress which also had a sheer batiste floral printed layer over the plain cotton peach fabric underneath. Her bonnet was the simple kind that tied under the chin, but also had a sheer veil attached which could be lowered if needed. As usual, her gloves were white, but instead of kid, she had chosen to wear cotton today, in case she got food on them during the picnic. She carried with her a small purse that featured silk tassels hanging from the bottom. She did not have much to carry in it, but it was part of the overall outfit, so she put a small change purse in and a drawstring bag of treats for Wheezer.

It was apparent that elevenses were being held under the Cherry trees in the private garden on the south side of the house. Sasa was escorted to the location by the Standish's footman, who then handed her off to Caroline Standish. Wheezer was wide eyed and enjoying the new experience exceedingly.

"Oh, Sasa, I am so glad you could make it. I realize that our picnic was planned so close to the Spring Ball next week, but if I had postponed it, we would have never been able to work it in between all the other things going on in the weeks to come," said Caroline.

"I am still not used to going to all of the parties and dances, teas and exhibits. My head is in a whirl. I am so happy to have you to help me cope. Oh, by the way, Caroline, I brought Wheezer. I truly hope you don't mind. He loves the outdoors and most of your friends have not gotten to meet him. He is really very smart and fun to be with. Do you mind terribly?" asked Sasa, biting at her lower lip.

Caroline looked down at Wheezer, seeing him for the first time. Wheezer seemed to know that this moment was crucial to his staying on the outing, because he then sat back using his tail to keep him from falling backward, held his paws up very politely and worked his mouth into one of his best grins, showing his pretty front teeth which looked almost like human teeth.

Caroline began to giggle, then erupted into hearty laughter. Sasa and Wheezer looked at each other, waiting for Caroline to control her mirth.

"Yes, yes, of course. He will be the life of the party, dear one," giggled Caroline, as she patted Wheezer on the head.

Sasa could tell that Caroline had made a friend that day. Wheezer looked smitten by the lovely fair lady who patted him, for now he was up and wagging his tail–what there was of it–furiously. Knowing that Wheezer liked at least one of these society people helped her to relax a bit.

Slowly, but steadily, other invitees began to arrive, some of which Sasa had met already at other teas and dinner parties she had been to. There were also a few she had not met yet, but who seemed eager to make her acquaintance. Gazing around the beautiful garden, Sasa could see the kitchen servants coming and going to load the carriages with the food for their picnic. Most of the picnics that she had been to back in Van Buren, Arkansas, included traditional food from her tribe. She was curious about what types of food white people would bring, with nothing to do but spend their money on something as simple as an outside meal in a park.

"Caroline, I see your cook and her helpers have the food ready. I am interested in learning what Bostonians bring to a picnic. I am sure it is very different from what we would bring to one, living on the frontier," she said, trying to introduce the subject without being too obvious.

"Well, here in the East we love to share recipes, so I don't mind in the slightest. In fact, I am quite proud of our cook. She has been with my family for years and years, and after I married Mr. Standish, my family asked her to come live with us. She does not share every recipe with me, because some she keeps secret, but I can tell you what it is and what it is made from," answered Caroline, as they moved closer to the door the kitchen helpers were emerging from.

Callie, the cook, came out of the kitchen door, just in time for Caroline to ask for the list of foods they were packing for the short trip. Callie, a short round, redheaded, but strongly muscled Irish-woman, reached in her pocket and pulled out a well-worn and grease stained list, handing it over to her mistress, then she continued on.

"Let's see here," said Caroline, as she examined the list. "I see we have rusk and mulberry jam and whipped cream to spread on it."

Sasa looked dumbfounded, and Caroline noticed her distress.

"Oh dear. I do apologize. You may not be used to some of our everyday foods, so if you don't mind, I will explain what it is too," she offered, while Sasa breathed a sigh of relief that she did not have to say she had never heard of rusk.

"Rusk, I believe, is a type of dry, crunchy bread, like toast. The cook bakes it twice. Once in a long roll, then after it cools, she cuts it in slices and bakes it until both sides are nicely browned. Generally, she will do up enough to last the family a good month or two and wraps them up in a linen towel. Most of the time we eat them dry and cool, but if we want them warmed, she just holds them over the kitchen fire. Next on the list is, oh how wonderful, she has made a Sea Pie. I have no idea why they call it that, because it has nothing to do with the sea. I know you have had pie, but this is a meat pie. With the pie crust and all, except instead of fruit, they put in all kinds of meat. This one probably has split pigeons, turkey pieces, slices of veal and some mutton. They put in some kind of a gravy and bake it. You will just love it, Sasa," said Caroline.

"I truthfully have to say that I have never had it before," confessed Sasa.

"Don't worry a bit, dear Sasa. Let's see here, she has another pie here. My, her handwriting is atrocious. Looks like a beef foot pie."

"But Caroline, beef don't have feet."

"Oh, it is just what they call it. It is really the lower part of the leg, minus the hoof. They take the 'feet' and put them in cold water for a week at least. They change the water daily, then they boil them until the meat falls off the bones and the knee joint comes apart. Some of the oil that comes off of that boiling we call, 'Neetsfoot Oil' and it is good for rubbing into your saddle or anything leather," said Caroline.

"How is it that you know about how to do it?" asked Sasa.

"Well, my Papa wanted all his children to learn how to take care of themselves. We learned how to ride, to hitch and unhitch a horse from a trap or cart, and we had to take care of all the leather things that go with riding a horse. If you don't rub Neetsfoot oil in your saddle, it will soon crack and dry out.

"Anyway, this Foot Pie also has apples, suet, wine, raisins, cinnamon, mace and sugar. I know it sounds odd, but I promise you will like it. You can eat it hot or cold, so that makes it good for a picnic. Now, next on the list. It looks like we have Syllabubs to drink."

"Syllabubs? What a crazy name. What on earth can that be, Caroline. You're not fooling me, are you?" asked Sasa.

"Now this is something I know you're going to like. It is made from our wonderful apple cider, and they add sugar and grate nutmeg into it. Then they add milk to some kind of liquor, I think brandy. You add it all together just before you drink it and it is wonderful," said Caroline.

Sasa had a sour look on her face, because she could not imagine putting milk into apple cider. However, she would give it a try. How bad could it be, anyway? She looked down at Wheezer, who waited patiently on his lead, and wondered if he would find this food tasty. She decided that he would eat almost anything.

"That's fine, really. If you don't like Syllabubs, you are sure to like the Spruce Beer we are bringing. Cook makes it every summer. It is like other beers or ales, but we also add molasses and Essence of Spruce before it is corked. It is very refreshing on a hot summer day. Then of course we have the regular cucumber sandwiches, fresh fruit, and cake too. We will all come back stuffed," finished Caroline.

Somehow, Sasa thought she might not be as stuffed as the others after the picnic. The list of foods Caroline's cook had prepared sounded like somebody's bad dream, but she would make sure she tried everything. These were things she needed to learn about. Caroline watched her for a moment.

"Sasa, do you think you could share some of your native foods with me?" she asked then. "Papa told me that some of the foods we eat all the time now, originally were taught to us by the Indians who lived in this area. In fact, he says that our first colony would have died, had it not been for the wise Indians. After he told me that, I have always had a deep, abiding respect for them, and I would dearly love to have some of their recipes. Sometimes, Callie lets me in the kitchen to cook something myself, although, a society lady is not supposed to lift a finger. I love to cook, but don't tell anyone. I don't need the others looking down their noses at me," she added.

After everyone had had their cup of tea and a cookie or two, they piled in their carriages and headed out to the country. Actually, it was a large palatial park that belonged to a wealthy landowner who had given his permission for the outing. Most of the land was under cultivation, but several acres were grass with a few trees for shade here and there. There was room for various games as well. The area was beside virgin forest land that had never been cleared.

The group settled at the top of a large mound, so they would have the best view. They had brought along a couple of ladies' maids and some help from the kitchen to prepare the spread while the young people sat in groups of four or five chatting and laughing together. Sasa was having a wonderful time.

The food proved to be not a bad as Sasa had thought it would be; it was definitely different, but some of it was very good. After they ate, Albert made his way over to her group and sat down beside her to talk. He looked so natural in the bright sunshine, but Sasa had to remind herself that he was a pampered, wealthy young man and that her roots were vastly different. She did not want to encourage him.

Soon they were sitting amiably, chatting, when another young man approached and asked to join their small group. Evidently, Albert knew the young man, because a strange look came over his face when he introduced himself.

"Most kind of you to have invited me for this very fine outing, Mrs. Standish. I did not see Steven in the group. Could he not come?" said the young man.

"No, I am afraid he had business in town and could not be with us today, but Albert was gracious enough to agree to accompany me. Papa caught me at the last moment and mentioned that Mr. Alderhide, our banker, asked if we might include you. I am glad you were able to accept our late invitation," replied Caroline.

Sasa, felt the mood had changed somehow, but she could not put her finger on what had changed. She saw Albert throw a surreptitious and meaningful glance at Caroline, who returned the curious gaze.

"Yes, I am pleased to be here. Mr. Alderhide was my father's banker as well, and I suppose he has been passed down to me after my father's death. He thinks I should get out more often than I do, now that I am alone. I hope it was not an imposition to have me along on such short notice," said the young man.

Albert realized that Sasa had not said anything, and finally remembered that this young man and Sasa had not been properly introduced. He hated to have to be the one to do it, but good manners must be shown.

"I am afraid that we have been remiss in our duty to our guests, sir. You and our lady friend have not been introduced. May I introduce you to Sasa Halley, lately of Van Buren, Arkansas, and Sasa, may I introduce Mr. Allan Jeffries of Boston," he said.

"It is so nice to meet you, Miss Halley. I had heard of your visit, but had not thought I would have the pleasure of your acquaintance," said Mr. Jeffries, with a smile that did not reach his eyes.

Something was whirling around in Sasa's mind, something elusive but important, and while she sat through the pleasantries, it finally came to her, and hit her like an arrow to the chest. He said his name was Jeffries, but there could be any number of Jeffries in a city like Boston. She turned to look at Caroline, who slightly nodded her head at her and all at once she had no doubt. Anna had told Caroline Sasa's history, and she must be aware of her difficult first year in Indian Territory. With Caroline's small nod, Sasa knew, without a single qualm, that this man, Allan Jeffries, was the son of the man who had tried to kill Mr. Andrew Halley, Jackson's father, and also the man who had tried to kill her. But, what was worse was that this was the son of the man who was responsible for the premeditated poisoning of her little brother, Usti Yansa, Little Buffalo in the English language, and the starvation of over 1,000 of her people after they came to Indian Territory. True, Allan Jeffries' father had died a fitting death. A pack of wolves had attacked him from behind, dragging him into the night. Since the killer had already disarmed them all, there had been no weapon available and there was no saving him. Sasa's heart broke a little. She had not thought about the man's family, or even to inquire to find out anything about him. At the time, she was just relieved that it was over. She looked at Allan, and suddenly, she did not know what to say to this tragic figure before her.

There seemed to be no words, nothing to say to begin a conversation. The silence grew quickly while Mr. Jeffries kept his eyes on Sasa's face. As the seconds ticked by, Sasa began to see a small change in his expression, going from intense probing to mild curiosity. A scream broke the silence like a shot and everyone looked in that direction. Several feet away, Miss Abigail Cole was standing looking down at the ground and screaming.

"Snake, oh heaven help me, I think I will faint," Miss Cole yelled, and no less than five young men came to her aid.

Even so, no one seemed to know what to do. Sasa waited, however. She felt she should not check it out since Anna had told her that women were not supposed to know what to do in a situation like this. She was supposed to lean on the strong arms of a male companion. However, Abigail continued to caterwaul, while the men around her seemed helpless in the extreme. Wheezer was tugging at his lead, and the last thing she wanted Wheezer to do was to go and attack a snake in front of all of the guests.

Finally, Sasa had had enough.

"Caroline, would you please hold tight to Wheezer's lead for me?" she asked.

"Sasa, you can't think of going over there. I forbid it. You will be bitten," protested Caroline, then a thought came to her mouth before she was able to stop its exit. "Beside, even if Abigail gets bitten, the snake will probably die first." Immediately, Caroline looked around to find out who may have heard her heartfelt sentiment.

But Sasa was already striding over to the scene, not in small, dainty womanish strides, but long capable strides. She had lost patience, and more than that, she felt disdain for women who seemed to love being the damsel in distress she had read about in the book of fairy tales Anna had given her one Christmas. She walked up to Abigail, who took no notice and continued her tirade. Sasa looked down, then heaved a tremendous sigh.

"Miss Cole," she yelled to get Abigail's attention. "Oh dear. Miss Cole, you are not in danger. Please stop this diatribe. You are upsetting the other guests."

But Abigail was enjoying her moment of drama too much. So Sasa had no choice. She could see it was up to her to stop this ridiculous outburst. She bent and picked up the small adolescent Garter snake directly behind the head. She held it in front of Abigail's face to show her it had been a non-venomous snake, but she promptly fainted dead away as the young fops around her cushioned her fall. Watching Abigail faint had been surreal to Sasa: it had never occurred to her that anyone could be frightened of the common garden snake.

Then anger came up into her throat as bitter as bile. She turned to look at each young man who had been there to cushion Abigail's fall. She wanted to shout at them for being weak and cowardly. Even children had more sense, in her opinion. Each young man looked back at her out of wide, bewildered eyes. Quickly her anger cooled. She realized that catching snakes was as foreign to these educated young men, as riding in carriages and going to teas was to her.

Sasa turned around and walked the few yards to the edge of the forest. Of course, no one accompanied her.

"Osiyo (Hello) little one. You are at the wrong place at the wrong time. They did not know you were only eating the ants that came to feast on our picnic food. Do not forget your life was precious to me. Maybe we will meet again someday and you can return the favor. Wado," she said. Presently, she bent down and gently placed the snake on the ground. It paused for a moment, testing the air with its tongue, then slithered away into the forest. Sasa looked back at the group. They were all looking at her as if she had grown horns. *Oh, well. Whatever comes, comes,* she thought. As she walked back to the group, Allan Jeffries strode out to meet her. She was surprised by the mixture of admiration and vexation on his face. She walked back to the picnic with him by her side. Now her thoughts were no longer on picking up snakes in the grass, but averting the attention of a possible snake in the flesh.

All in all, the picnic had been enjoyable, but different. Later that evening, as she laid out her riding outfit for tomorrow's game they called Polo, she realized that she had felt like she had been holding her breath all day long.

It was as if something was about to happen, but nothing of any great import did, at least that day.

After checking on all the items she would need the next day, she stopped in the middle of the room. She could see herself in the mirror above the vanity where Sarah dressed her hair every day. Scrutinizing herself from head to toe, she still could not put her finger on what had changed about her. Sasa had never really thought of herself as a woman, like the women in her tribe or even the white women. But the person staring back at her was definitely a woman and for some unknown reason, she felt afraid.

She gave her body a little shake to drive away the morose thoughts. It was time to get ready for a good night's sleep, and maybe she would read a bit with the abundant candles the hotel supplied to them. She read for a while, but felt it too hard to concentrate, so she doused the candles and with Wheezer by her side, went to sleep.

The next day, at the Polo match, she strolled the grounds with the other young ladies, watching the game they called Polo. It was an odd game, she thought. It seemed to consist of hitting a tiny ball while galloping on horseback, using a long stick with a small, sort of, club at the end. They had set up goals at either end, which she understood immediately, because the game all Indian tribes played, called Stick Ball, used the same type of goal line. However, Polo was not nearly as exciting as her traditional Stick Ball games where frequently there were broken limbs and players knocked unconscious. Another difference was that the Polo game was only for men, when in many tribes, women played Stick Ball and were as aggressive as the men. The only interest the Polo held for her was the fancy horse maneuvering the riders used on their steeds.

As she strolled along with the other young ladies, they stopped to watch the game for a little while at this new vantage point. Sasa stayed at the back of the group which put her closer to the groups of seated men and women, sipping tea and coffee during the game. Her mind wandered from the game, and soon tuned in on a conversation a group of men seated behind her men were having.

"I was told that she has had the same education as any of the law students would receive, but I don't understand why. She can't try a case or even represent a client. Even if she were not a woman, there will never be an Indian lawyer. What good would learning law do for a woman? The next thing you know, they will all want to own property and vote," said the first man.

"Don't say that Samuel, or you may have to eat your words. I heard just last week of a woman who writes a popular column in a paper called The *National Anti-Slavery Standard.* She has been giving something she calls, Women's Rights, particular attention. Her column is called, *Letters From New York*, where she answers women's questions. Her answers give vent to her ideas of what women should be allowed to do, including vote, own property and oppose their husband's views, even publicly. Right now it seems to be localized, but this is the kind of thing that could catch fire and spread," said his friend.

"That's right. I've heard of that. It has the men in my club rather put out. I think her name is Lydia Child, or some such. As I told my friends at the club, pay no attention to it. It is a phase, surely, and will pass quickly. Just like all those abolitionists, crying foul. And as for the Indian girl, maybe she does have some aptitude, but like my father always says, you cannot make a silk purse out of a sow's ear, eh," another.

Sasa was furious, and not being one to hold her tongue when she felt strongly about a matter, she turned around and said; "Sirs, I think you have been showing some rather rude behavior, especially for gentlemen of society. You see I am standing right in front of you, and yet you discuss my education as if I were not here listening to every word. Are you so threatened by my receiving an education, usually only afforded to white males, that you think nothing of sitting around like a bunch of laundry women, gossiping your heads off? Why not just ask me? I am right here. Or are you the sort who view women as invisible, except when they can be seen hanging on your arm as some sort of embellishment?

"So to save you the effort it would take to be the gentlemen you purport to be, I will give you the answer you seek. I sought to learn the laws of the United States in order to be of service to my own people in an advisory capacity only. I was groomed in the social graces so that I might better understand your views and possibly help the white lawmakers to better understand the Cherokee and any other Native tribe. I wish to be an instrument in the advance-ment of peace and understanding to both peoples. Is not promoting peace of Christian value? Is your view of your world so narrow that you cannot see the benefit of such a course?

"And lastly, gentlemen, I do not pretend to be a "silk purse" nor am I a "sow's ear". I am a woman, born to a people who lived on this continent for several thousand years before you "discovered" it. I am as proud of my race as any of you may be, only my roots are here, not in some country over the great oceans from where your people fled to immigrate here, so they might be free. Free to do as you pleased, take whatever you wanted and free to enslave other races. Is it so hard to imagine that the people you enslave or entrap onto reservations want the same thing? The same freedoms that your people traveled from far and wide, at great risk to their lives, to attain? Maybe, gentlemen, you are the ones who are in need of a better education. If you need any pointers on the subject, I would be happy to advise you. Good day," she concluded.

Before she could walk away a clapping of a single individual began in the crowd that had gathered around the confrontation. Then another and another, until the majority of the women, and some men were applauding her comments. Caroline came to her side, placed her arm through Sasa's and they strolled on, leaving the men she spoke to, white faced and in shock.

That evening, as she readied for bed, she thought about her day. Would she ever understand these people? As she walked by the chifferobe, she felt drawn to open the door and pull out the gown she would wear to the Ball, on Saturday. It was an important event, for it would be her first where she would be presented to white society. Was she only fooling herself? It is true she received much encouragement today, however, she was still dismayed by the unfair attitudes some held to.

She pulled the dress from the hook it was on and held it up in the flickering candlelight. It was the palest of ice blue, almost white. Low off the shoulders and with a tremendous amount of fabric devoted to the gathered full skirt. There were no less than six starched petticoats to hold the skirt out. The corset would push her breasts up and crimp her waist in so much she would have a hard time breathing. There were a pair of matching long kid gloves that went to the elbow and a lace shawl she would drape over her arms. The shoes were heeled pumps with a satin covering in the same color of the dress, and there was a sweet ruffle of fabric and a glass jewel in the middle at the top of each shoe. Anna said she was having some flowers made to go in Sasa's hair after Sarah finished arranging it.

As she gazed dreamily at the dress, she was suddenly reminded of a gift she had received before she left Indian Territory. The gift was from a Choctaw elder who had visited Tahlequah while she was also there. He seemed to know her from somewhere, but she had no idea where that might have been. On her last day in town, he said he had a present for her. She had it with her in her jewelry box and it would be just the thing to wear on her wrist over the kid glove.

The thought of the Ball was exciting, but also frightening. It was a challenge which she would meet head on, as she did all of her challenges. No matter what might happen, she had a responsibility now to help her people, and learning to be as much a lady as any white woman was an important part of it. *So, let Saturday come,* she thought. *I will be ready.*

Chapter 13
The World On His Shoulders

Indian Territory was abuzz with anxiety and stress. Reports of raids were coming in from all corners of Indian Territory, and in all cases, the source of the raid could not be determined. John Ross, Principal Chief of the Cherokee Nation, was certain there was something they were missing, some small piece of the puzzle that would explain it all.

The tribe was just now beginning to prosper, despite the deepening division between the various parties within his nation. His people had been making steady progress and now they were producing plenty of corn and wheat, beef, pork and mutton, squash, beans and pumpkins to feed the entire lot of Cherokee people in Indian Territory. If they continued to prosper as they had, they would produce enough goods to sell to the settlers or to ship out to the other states, thus making a nice profit. The portion given to the Cherokee government would be used to build schools, saw mills, a brick works, as well as needed government buildings, the first of which would be a courthouse in Tahlequah. If they were to function as a true government, they must have a courthouse.

On a more personal level, Chief Ross had to decide where he would build his home. At the moment, his accommodations were filling his needs, but he wanted to build a fine home that the People could feel proud of. There was so much to do, and he must not be seen as weak, or his adversaries would be there to rip him and his administration apart.

He had considered the news of the mysterious raids, mostly happening near the Texas border, to be an embarrassment aimed at him. On the other hand, the reports did not seem to have any connection to him or the Cherokee People. He could feel that something was not right about it though. He felt down in his gut that whatever was going on, first of all, was not raids between Indian Territory tribes. All of the accused tribes had denied such raids. Anyway, why would they take time to raid when there was so much work to do for each of the Indian nations in the territory? All the chiefs knew that infighting would be counterproductive to the health and welfare of all the tribes.

The newspapers had named the Cherokee's removal from their homeland and property as the Trail of Tears. That it was, however the Cherokee were not the only ones to suffer from that same scenario of being ripped from home and hearth, and forced to walk to a new land. Other tribes had suffered just as much as the Cherokee, so it did not make sense for any of the tribes to be raiding their own neighbors.

The Cherokee could not stand another blow at this time, not when the People were just gaining momentum. Chief Ross felt he was being pulled in too many directions. His frequent trips to Washington City caused him much stress and sleepless nights, just to come away with one failure after another. Occasionally, he would win the People some consideration, but the thing that really mattered, the thing that his people were desperate for, was the payment of their claims against the U.S. Government and Treasury for property and spoilage that had been promised in writing. The government had promised to repay the individual Cherokees for all the livestock, goods and homes they had to abandon to white settlers. The continued withholding of those funds was unconscionable, since it had already been agreed upon.

After hours of meditating on the perplexing problems of the raids near the border tribes, Chief Ross came to the conclusion that it was a particular problem that must be solved as quickly as possible. He finally came to a decision. He sat down at his desk, removed a sheet of paper from the right hand drawer, opened his inkwell, prepared his pen nub to receive the black, slick ink, and wrote a note to his assistant, Mr. Joseph Vann.

Assistant Chief Joseph Vann
March 9, 1843

Sir: I believe the particular problem we discussed a fortnight ago concerning the anonymous raids occurring regularly in all tribal nations within Indian Territory, mer-

its a closer investigation. Please attend me at your earliest convenience. I wish to discuss the steps I believe we need to take in order to benefit all Indian Territory, and especially the Cherokee. It is my intention to mount a vigorous investigation.

Chief John Ross

Chief Ross folded the missive in from each corner over-lapping in the middle, then melted a generous glob of sealing wax on it and embedded his seal in the cooling wax. He handed it to a waiting attendant with the instructions to find Assistant Chief Vann wherever he might be found and deliver the message, then sat back in his creaking desk chair to work out possible solutions to this conundrum.

Chapter 14
No Rest for the Wicked

Mendoza would need to take the fastest way to Indian Territory, which was steam ship from the Boston harbor, down the east coast, around Florida Territory, then up into the much calmer waters of the Gulf of Mexico and into the mouth of the Mississippi River to a port in a city called New Orleans. Then he would board a river steamer going up the Mississippi until they reached the Arkansas River, head west on the Arkansas, and finally branch off to the west on the Canadian River. There he would find certain bands of Kickapoo and Kiowa who, for their own reasons, were working as his allies in his latest endeavor.

He presumed it had not taken much to hire several raiding parties from those tribes, since they were already mad as hornets at the Texans. Of course, they would not understand his reasons for wanting them to speed up their disruption of life in the territory, but they would have the satisfaction of seeing the Texan settlers afraid half out of their minds with visions of slaughter in their beds.

Even with these so-called allies, things were going very slowly. The process needed to be advanced. The general had put this task in his capable hands. If he could just get Indian Territory to the flash point, an Indian Civil War would erupt so quickly they would never know how it happened. To implement his plans, though, he needed more information. Someone from the Cherokees had already been found to help with that, and since they were the largest of the tribes, and were already fighting among themselves, this person would probably not be noticed. And if Mendoza had to, he could easily complicate things there since there were many different factions. One of his agents had already zeroed in on a Cherokee man who was needy and at the same time unhappy with his own nation. This man had already provided much information, but Mendoza was also planning to visit some of the southern tribes in Indian Territory. He was curious if they knew anything about the Golden Serpent.

Mendoza had tried his best to research the artifact among Mexico's historians, asking about the 'Golden Serpent' of legend that the general had promised him. He never found anything definitive about its whereabouts, or even if it had ever existed. The legend said that it had been given to one family of Indians, but nothing further was known about it; he remembered, however, his own mother telling him the story of the great Aztec leader, and of the fate of that once great nation. She never failed to include the tale about the Golden Serpent, and how it was still out there, somewhere, waiting to be rescued from anonymity. There was no better person than himself, one who had an appreciation for fine living and beautiful things. That is why, deep down, he knew the general probably did not actually have it. The idea had sparked such a desire in him that even the slightest hope of finding it burned in his soul, and each day he increasingly felt it was his destiny to own it. Now he would not let anything stop him from his goal, for he would own the Golden Serpent. The general did not know it yet, but he would pay Mendoza much money for his deception.

General Federico Guillermo De Almeida carefully prepared for his night at Boston's Spring Ball. He knew he was only invited for propriety's sake. He was a foreign dignitary in the United States.

It would have been a tremendous insult to Mexico had they not invited me. Even though the United States is constantly involved in skirmishes along our border, they are not, as yet, declaring an all-out war against Mexico, *he thought.*

The general was not worried about his acceptance. He was only there to represent the dignity of the new Government of Mexico, and after this night, he would head south to the Mexican border's bastions to regroup his covert forces. He laughed out loud when he remembered that the U.S. Army was still not aware of the systematic nature of Mexico's consistent attacks. And, he knew, they had no clue or hint of what was really going on with the raids in Indian Territory or their purpose. He wanted it to stay that way for some time in the future, to give his plan time to come to fruition. On the one hand, the general had no doubt of Mendoza's ability to pull this ruse off, but on the other hand he was much more worried about the man himself. He would have to be very careful once the deed was accomplished, for then was when Mendoza would want what had been promised to him. He would have to make sure that Mendoza was denied access to his presence at his home at that point, and at his offices as well.

It would not matter, because once the goal was accomplished, El Presidente would be showering praises on General De Almeida, and he was sure that President Nicolas Bravo would not care what it took or what promises he had had to make to make it real for Mexico. Since Bravo had been appointed in 1842 as Interim President of the Republic of Mexico by Santa Anna himself, he would want to hang on to the presidency if he could. What better way than to regain some of their lost territory under his presidency?

In the meantime, he needed to be as likable and approachable to the Americans as possible. Looking harmless, when he wanted to, was a specialty of his. He had no qualms to turn the tables around and be as hard as he needed to be when the time came. Hard choices had to be made. Empires did not build themselves.

And then, would not my daughter, Angelina, think the world of her papa; enough to allow me to choose the right husband for her, as it should be, and not some smiling snake, coming around to steal my little one away from her loving family? *he thought. Yes, the success of this venture meant everything. And it was too brilliant not to succeed.*

Too bad that the Golden Serpent was not real. Even hearing himself tell the story, made his own blood quicken. What a prize it would have been, had he believed it was real. It was a children's bedtime story, and where it originated was anyone's guess.

Tonight, he would enjoy himself. He had no reason to worry. It would all go as planned and General Federico Guillermo De Almeida began attaching all the medals and ribbons to his newly pressed uniform showing the honors and praise he had received from his government, before calling for Juan to begin to dress him for the ball.

Juan tapped on the bedroom door.

"Yes, yes, Juan. Come in, you offish lump. It is time for you to assist me in dressing. I want to look my very best this night," said the general, but Juan just stood in the doorway with a hesitant look on his face.

"Oh, what is it now? I haven't time to solve all your little problems," griped the general.

"Oh, sì, Your Excellency, I have your clean dress coat and also your top hat, which has been brushed and steamed to perfection, Your Excellency, and I already have the carriage waiting in the street. The driver has his instructions. I took the liberty, Excellency, to polish your shoes for the ball. I hope they are satisfactory, Excellency," said Juan, with obvious anxiety.

"Juan, why do you always have to bother me with small, insignificant details? I have no time to pat you on the head now. Just tell me if the errand I sent you on earlier was accomplished while you help me dress," demanded the general.

"Sì, Your Excellency, it was accepted just as you said it would be. Only..." Juan faltered and dropped a cufflink on the floor.

"Only what? Don't tell me they cannot comply with my instructions, Juan. I have no time to argue with these Americans," barked the general.

"Uh, no, everything went fine," said Juan, getting up from the floor after finding the cufflink. "They accepted the article, only they questioned the reason why I could not reveal my source for the information. They were hesitant to publish the news article when they personally did not hear of the problems," he explained, cringing back, making himself ready for a blow.

"Ah. Just as I had hoped. That is good, Juan. Since they don't know whom the information came from, they will be intrigued all the more. At the very worst, they will just print the article. It would be best if they sent a newspaperman into Indian Territory to verify the article. By then, Indian Territory should be erupting into chaos. Those news people have a great tendency to exaggerate their facts. I am counting on that, Juan," gloated the general, in a much better mood.

Juan bowed himself out of the room. He was not sure why the general had written an article about civil war within Indian Territory. He knew for a fact that the general had not been within a few hundred miles of that area of the U.S. Plus, Juan was privy to almost everything that came in for the general and however many visitors he had had here in Boston, which was very few, to be sure, there had been none that would have had any such information about Indian Territory. And, most curious of all, why would the general care about Indian Territory in the first place? General De Almeida was supposed to be here to represent Mexico, and as far as Juan knew, Mexico had no interest in the tribes of that area.

Juan did not like not knowing what was going on with the general, because it was his job to assist His Excellency in anything he needed to accomplish his duties. It would mean the loss of his position with the government of Mexico, if he were to be found uninformed and unprepared. He had to be a little more observant, and he would start tonight after the general left for the Ball. He was a loyal Mexican who wanted the best for his relatively new country, and if sometimes he could help the general without him even knowing, he was sure the general would eventually appreciate all his hard conscientious work. Once he knew what the general was working on, he would be able to find a way to help, even if the general was not aware of it.

Chapter 15
Going To The Ball

The stars were just about to pop out of the spring heavens as Sasa gazed up from her window. It was hard to see as much of the heavens here as she could in Van Buren, Arkansas. There, the celestial display seemed so close a person could almost touch it. Here in Boston, there were too many lights, both in the streets and from buildings and tall structures, to see the sky clearly, but it felt good just to know it was there and always would be, the same sky she had traveled under when walking the Trail of Tears with her parents and little brother, the ones she could not say their names out loud anymore. The same sky that hovered over Indian Territory was also Boston's to gaze at. It calmed her, as she continued to ready herself for the grand evening.

Sarah had already done her hair in the latest style. It was put up on the back of her head with fat long rolls of curls on either side of her face. She would not wear a hat for the short carriage ride. Instead, she wore jewels placed in various places on her head. The effect was stunning, like having the stars come and sit on your head. The jewels seemed to pick up any light, even if it was only a candle flame in the room: the light danced through them and back out again, fractured into mini beams of colored rays.

She was almost ready, she only needed a few finishing touches. She opened the dresser drawer, and drew out the small wooden box the Choctaw elder had handed her. Out of it she drew a bracelet of gold. Attached to it was one single charm, an ancient Indian head with a bright golden snake coiling at the top, its mouth opened to strike. The charm was very small, only about half an inch tall and wide, secured onto the gold bracelet.

The elder had given her a name, but not where it came from. He called it the Golden Serpent, and said she was to protect it always. It was a puzzle, and Sasa could not figure out why the elder went to such lengths to give her this gift. Maybe someday she would know.

The bracelet sparkled warmly on her ice blue opera gloves. Now she was fully ready. She would be riding over with Anna and Jackson, but unfortunately, Wheezer could not attend. He watched her dress from atop the bed, trying to figure out why she would be dressing so differently. So before she left, she bent down to look into Wheezer's warm brown eyes.

"Wheezer, my black white whiskers, I will not be gone for very long. I will be back very soon, but you cannot come with me. So, I ask you to guard the room for us. Wado my friend.

Wheezer listened attentively, but licked his lips throughout Sasa's instructions. Sasa knew that it generally meant he did not like what was being said or done.

"It is all right, Wheezer. Do not worry for me. I will be back tonight," she promised, and with that she went out to the sitting room to await Anna and Jackson since they would be going together.

As Sasa closed the suite door behind her, Anna and Jackson, Wheezer began to pace. Something worried him. One moment he would try to lay down on Sasa's bed and the next he would be on one of the overstuffed chairs in the main sitting room, trying to see out of the window. He could not get comfortable in any position. He paced continually for hours, but would not relent his vigil until he saw Sasa walk through the suite door again.

As the carriage pulled up in front of Caroline and Steven Standish's large and ornate mansion in the very best part of Boston, Sasa gazed out in excitement and curiosity. She had been to this house at least two times before, but it was in the daytime. The house looked so different at night, with all the candelabra's bright with candlelight. Even seen from the outside, it looked alive.

Jackson handed Anna down from the carriage, then turned for Sasa's hand as well. She was having to get used to being helped in this way by white men. They liked to believe that women were too fragile to do anything strenuous or difficult. She did not object, though, because she had decided to try and not be argumentative.

The group prepared to enter through the front double doors when they were stopped by the footman. Jackson seemed to know what was wanted and Sasa saw him hand the attendant their invitations. Their small group was then led through the foyer where they stopped to allow the maid and butler to take any hats or cloaks they wished to take off before proceeding to the entrance to the ball-room. Even though Sasa had been in this house before, she had not seen all the rooms and certainly not this huge ballroom. An orchestra was playing beautiful music while a man announced the group. When Sasa's name was mentioned, she saw several people turn to stare, but the look on their faces was not angry or cool, showed only smiles and appreciation. She held herself with proper posture, just as Anna had taught her.

Nothing in her short life had prepared her for the beauty and elegance of the ballroom she had been ushered into. The windows seemed to go from floor to ceiling with great, green velvet drapes swagged on either side. The oak wood floor glistened and the music made her want to move with it. The couples on the floor were dancing one of the newest dances, called the Waltz. Anna had made sure Sasa had received dance instruction as part of her curriculum, but she never could have imagined the beauty of so many couples all going in the same direction to the three beat measure. Color swirled before her whenever she had the chance to watch. Otherwise, she always had a partner and was twirling to the intoxicating sound of the music itself. It was, by far, the most exhilarating experience in her young life, almost like the book Anna had given her to read, Alice in Wonderland. Only this felt like, Sasa in Wonderland. Now she knew beyond the shadow of a doubt that her People and other tribes were in a different world entirely. This made her wonder about how she would bridge the gap, or even if she should.

For now, she was content to enjoy the moments, as each young man dressed in black cutaway dress coats, black tie, starched white collars danced past her. Their vests varied somewhat. Some had plain white, stiff vests which seemed to hold them in like a lady's corset, while others wore satin brocades or expensive wools with metallic threads. Only the boldest of men would venture to wear anything with a different color, other than the accepted black and white for dress. The same went for their coats and pants. They were always black, but could vary a little in cut, quality of fabric and length of use.

Sasa thought, so that is why the men pay so much attention to the women. We are the only ones wearing any sort of color and showing any part of actual skin. I have no idea how I will be able to explain this evening to my Cherokee elders, like Medicine Man and Poison Woman, who specifically told me they wanted to know these things when I came back.

Just at that moment, Sasa began gazing around the room in search of something.

"Sasa. What on earth are you gazing at?" asked Anna, as she approached her.

"Anna, have you ever had the feeling that you were being watched?" she asked.

"I would say that you have a whole room of people gazing at you. So far, you are the Belle of the Ball," replied Anna, with a wide grin.

"What? What do you mean, Anna?" asked Sasa, alarmed that maybe she might be an object of mocking.

"Nothing to worry yourself over. Most women here dream of being the Belle of the Ball someday. You don't seem to even notice that you have danced every dance, each with a different man. I dare say, you will probably have to have a new dance card if you keep that up" said Anna.

As it was, Sasa's dance card dangling from her wrist by a satin ribbon, had every dance claimed by men she had never met. The last dance was spoken for, and that one belonged to Jackson Halley. She had to pencil it in herself because Jackson could not get close enough to do it himself. There were so many men wanting a dance with her that she thought it would be easier if she just took the dance card off of her wrist and passed it around the room.

"No, I mean, what does that mean, 'Belle of the Ball'? I have never heard that phrase," she said, not understanding the term.

"Oh, I am sorry dear. It means that you are the prettiest, the most sought after for a dance, and the most desired girl at the ball. It is exciting. I know from personal experience. Most exhilarating. However, there is a downside to it that can't be helped. Unfortunately, you will discover some of the other young women in the room are not so pleased about it. It is their eyes that may be gazing at you with true malevolent feelings. Every ball has a Belle, and tonight it is you," Anna told her, with joy sparkling out of her blue eyes.

Sasa looked at Anna, who was as beautiful a woman as any here. She had her hair done very prettily with flowers pinned in it at the back. Her figure was still that of a young woman and Sasa told her just that.

"Oh, but Sasa, I am married. In other words, I am not available for courtship. The young men want to dance with you to see if you might be as sweet as you look, and the married men want to dance with you to remember their youth and how they chose their own wives, with whom they may or may not still be in love with. And you are a mystery. Exotic, but refined. This would be a very dull crowd, indeed, if they could not appreciate your virtues.

But don't succumb to their smooth talk, Sasa. Most men are not trustworthy, when it comes to women, even if they have wealth, fine clothes, or are highly placed in society. In fact, those are the ones to look out for and protect yourself from," Anna whispered in her ear. "Just be polite and enjoy the ball. I have to find Jackson now, and see who might be making eyes at him.

Laughing, Anna glided away, a vision of pale gold and emerald green satin accents around the full skirt, along the low neckline and around the off shoulder caplets. The flowers in her hair were made of silk with golden threads and green leaves.

After Anna had disappeared into the crowd of bystanders around the dance floor, Sasa again experienced the feeling of being watched. The hair at the back of her exposed neck stood up and a cold chill ran down her spine. She knew that these eyes were not just watching, but spying on her, and it gave her a sudden feeling of alarm which she was forced to push out of her mind. After all, what harm could come to her here, with so many people at the ball? And so she continued to dance.

Jackson was enjoying the ball immensely. Not for the dancing in itself, however, but for the various interesting people who happened to be there. Many of the attendees were old acquaintances from the many years his father, Andrew Halley, kept an office in Boston. Halley's Financial was a well-known lending house to which a great deal of business in town owed their successful enterprises.

He stood in the back, close to the refreshment table, watching Sasa whirl around the floor with yet another partner. A grin creased his handsome, suntanned face, just thinking about Sasa and all of the fun it had been to show his and Anna's world to her. Jackson already had an intimate knowledge of Cherokee life and customs. He had spent most of his youth running and playing through the hills and woods in and around the Cherokee homelands, back in Georgia, with his Cherokee best friend, and business partner, Archibald Flint. He had been just a small boy in 1825, when the Cherokee national legislature designated an area central to the Cherokee Nation in Georgia and named it New Echota. It was the site of the first Indian language newspaper office, and was built near the headwaters of the Oostanaula River. Jackson's father conducted much business there because he helped provide start-up money to various enterprises the Cherokees undertook.

It had been a lucrative arrangement for both parties, until the forced removal of the Cherokee Nation in 1838-39. The Cherokees out produced the white settlers around them and had produced other goods to sell to white buyers. Most Cherokee families lived in the same fashion as any of the other settlers and farmers, and some were quite wealthy. These facts were what attracted the attention and fueled the desire for the Cherokee's land, and their removal almost toppled Halley's Financial, since the U.S. Government chose not to recognize any liens on Cherokee property that protected the various loans. Andrew had felt the sting of the removal just as much as the Cherokee, but not the deathly consequences the Cherokee suffered, considering the four thousand that died along that walk the Cherokees called *'nu na hi du na tlo hi lu I'*, or The Trail Where They Cried. The English newspapers shortened it to The Trail of Tears.

All of his experience with the Cherokee had helped Jackson, as he took on the task of preparing Sasa for the white world. Actually, she had surprised him with her great intellect and ability to learn quickly. She was a marvel to him and, as he had no children yet with Anna, he felt very fatherly toward Sasa. Making her his ward was the only option when he was still an unmarried male. But, when he married Anna in 1841, he began the process of legally adopting Sasa, so that she would have all the rights of any white woman in the United States. So far, her introduction into society was a success and he was extremely proud of her as he watched her from the sidelines.

"Why you ole dog, you!" said a booming voice from his left side, and at first Jackson had no idea the title was being aimed at him. Then the apparition approached, and he almost choked on his punch when he finally recognized Isaiah Barnes, frontiersman extraordinaire.

Isaiah was a hard man to miss, taller than an oak tree and so wide of shoulders he could block the light of the front door, with hands that were bigger than two of most men's hands put together. The most astonishing thing of all, however, was the clothes he wore. Jackson had never seen the man in anything other than skins tanned by one of the tribes out west, but today Isaiah was in dress kit. He wore the finest cutaway black suit, gold brocaded satin vest, and fine black pants to match. He looked every bit the well brought up man about town. Even his long, brown hair was pulled back into a queue, clean and well combed. His long full beard had been trimmed and now was only about two inches long, in perfect keeping with the style there in the east.

"Isaiah? Is that really you? I hardly know you without your skins and fur hat on. Fancy, you showing up at the spring ball in Boston, of all places," said an astonished Jackson.

It was natural that Jackson felt that way, since Isaiah had always been the rugged type, liking the open spaces and traveling camp life common to buffalo hunters and fur trade mountaineers. Isaiah had a way with everyone, though, from the lowest of the low to the high born elite. The thing was, he never bothered to acknowledge that he was any different and so was just as good. It was not in the things he said, but in what he did with his life and for his friends. Most people, no matter their station in life, were proud if they could call Isaiah Barnes their friend. And so was Jackson.

"Well, you see, pard'ner, I am actually just apassin' through. I have some friends in this here ole town an' they asked me ta come, an' so here I am. Only goin' ta be here just a few days, then I'm aheading on down ta Indian Territory ta hire on at Fort Gibson. Ole Nathan Boone is afixin' on takin' an expedition up a ways ta give some protection ta them pilgrims drivin' their wagon trains on the Santa Fe Trail. He wrote me all 'bout it, an' he also says Ole General Zachary Taylor has asked him ta search for a place them Osages call the Salt Plains. Seems Ole Zack's been ahearin' stories 'bout some big salt flats up there and is mighty eager ta find out if'n its true. Seems like a dandy time ta me, so I'm aheadin' on ta Fort Gibson. Gotta be there by June, so I aim ta be there early like.

"Hey now, Jackson, don't you live close ta there? I heard tell you is in the mule breeding business. That so?" asked Isaiah.

"Yes, you heard right, Isaiah. I have a spread across the river from Fort Smith, at a fairly new town named after President Van Buren," replied Jackson, with a satisfied smile.

"How about your pap? I ain't seen hide nor hair a him since... wall... come ta think of it, since '38, just afor them bigwhigs up in Washington City booted them Cherokee off'n their land. That was some poor bull, that was.

Thought your pap's business was goin' under, then I heard he bounced back right smart like.

"So you went and got you a ranch ta raise mules for the army post and all them blue shirts, have ya? Well, I guess a man's gotta make a livin' if''n he can. I just can't figger asittin' in one spot for so long. Don't seem like any fun ta me, no sir. Naw, I think I woulda stayed up in them ole mountains and collect plews, if'n the fur trade hadn't agone belly up. What is a mountain man s'posed ta do? I never did take me a mountain wife, although them pretty squaws in some of them tribes I wintered with a time or two woulda been happy as jumpin' rabbits if'n I decided ta settle down a bit. Naw, not for me, son, not for me. Is that ranch akeepin' you busy, son?" asked Isaiah, as he stopped to take a deep breath. Then he reached for a pocket where there was none in the dress clothes he had on. Jackson grinned knowingly. One of the things he had almost never seen Isaiah without was his chaw of tobacco bulging out the side of one or the other of his cheeks, but there was no room in his present attire for his usual twist of wilderness tobacco they called a plug.

"It's doing just fine. When you get back from your exploration, why don't you come on over and stay a spell with us? You know I have a missus now? Her name is Anna. She is the one over there in the light gold and green with the face of an angel," said Jackson, proudly.

Isaiah turned and squinted as if he needed glasses.

"Well I'll be hornswoggled, you gone and got a real keeper and I never even got the chance ta compete for her. I guess I'll just stay a bachelor, then, but that's all right by me anyways," he commented, while sporting the biggest grin he could manage on his weathered face.

"Later, I will introduce you to my ward. Her name is Sasa," added Jackson.

"Sasa? Isn't that an Indian name? Sounds, let's see, Choctaw? No, Cherokee! That's it, Cherokee. I used ta know a few your pap introduced me ta, way back when he was just startin' ta loan money ta the tribe," said Isaiah.

"I can't fool you, Isaiah. Yes, she is Cherokee. And I will be most happy to tell you the whole story, but maybe we'd better do that over drinks before you leave. I see my wife giving me the 'come here and dance with me' look. Let's go over, so that I can introduce you in person," said Jackson.

The dancers whirled, the women chatted, the young girls giggled and Anna smiled from across the room. It was turning out to be a good evening's entertainment, but he couldn't help thinking about his beloved ranch, so far away. He had fallen in love with the frontier and being back in Boston, even for this short time, made him realize the fine life he lived without all the finery and society. How grateful he was that Anna was happy to live there with him, and happy to help him prepare Sasa as well. He was a fortunate man.

Sasa was led off of the dance floor by a blushing, very young man who could barely squeak out a conversation during their dance. The general could not help thinking what a fine looking woman she was, even from afar. At the moment, she was trying to make the young man feel relaxed in her presence, but it was obvious she had no notion what was making him so nervous. She had thanked the young man, and the general made sure that upon turning Sasa would come face to face with him. He noticed right away that they were of a height so that he could look directly into her eyes.

Sasa, for her part, was startled by his presence. She saw he was not formidable in height, for he was almost her own height of five feet, five inches, but he had the bearing of a chief and an arrogance about him that repulsed her immediately. Unfortunately, when she looked at her dance card, it said, "His Excellency, General Federico Guillermo De Almeida, Republic of Mexico".

"*Buenas tardes, señorita*. Ah, I see you have consulted your dance card and found your next dance is with this poor representative ...uh, how you say, ambassador... of a small nation. I hope you will not deny me the privilege of dancing with the most beautiful *señorita* at the ball, eh?" said the general.

Now that he was closer to this lady who he had thought was just another member of these stupid American's elite circles, he was astonished to see in Sasa's deep brown eyes and golden tan skin, what he knew to be an Indian. He did not yet know what tribe, but he was even more puzzled at her presence among these people. He had known Americans to be extremely prejudicial and destroyers of the native tribes. This young lady's presence here was such an anomaly, he had to find out more about her, and he would begin immediately, while he had her in his arms.

They began the dance easily enough, and it was a slow waltz, so it afforded him the chance to hold a conversation she could not run from.

"If you will excuse the impertinence, young lady, but I had someone fill out the dance cards for me, so I do not actually know your name. I am..." he began, but Sasa cut him off.

"I know your name," she said, abruptly. "I read it. You are a Mexican general. General DeAlmeida, are you not? I am Sasa Halley." And she said no more.

"Uh, why yes. So, your name is Sasa. Such an unusual name. What does it mean?" he asked.

"It means Swan in my native tongue. I am Cherokee, sir, and the ward of Mr. Jackson Halley," she said, rather curtly.

The general's thoughts where reorganizing themselves from a jumble of wrong assumptions. Yes, he could see it now. She was a native Indian. He had had his way with a few of them of various tribes. Most tribes did not mind selling or trading the charms of their squaws, and he had thought them all to be the same, frisky females with loose morals. He gazed at Sasa as they danced and wondered if she was as loose as the ones he had bedded. His mind drifted back to relive some of the passion and abandon he had indulged in, and without thinking through his next move, and without caring where he was or in what company, for after all, he was allowed anything he pleased in Mexico, including any man's wife if he so chose, he quickly drew close to Sasa, allowing his hand to slip from her waist to where her bottom would be.

"I have a room at the Tremont Hotel, young lady. Why don't we slip out of here and spend the night under my sheets, eh?" the general whispered in her ear.

As quick as lightning, Sasa drew herself back, her arm flying through the air in a blur striking him with one hand across his face, and began to swing her other hand to match the force of the first when the general caught her wrist.

"Oh, I do so like a fiery woman, you should be much fun," he said, but as he spoke, he noticed the light glinting off of the charm hanging from the fine chain on her wrist. The image froze him on the spot, for he recognized the icon of the Golden Serpent, or what he had always been told it looked like. His face hardened like stone, while everything and everyone, disappeared from his conscious mind. All that existed was the charm, Sasa, and himself, alone.

"Where did you get that charm?" he asked through his teeth, as he gripped Sasa's wrist.

Sasa, knew that she could defeat this terrible man had she not been constrained by protocol and good manners here in this grand ballroom. He held her wrist in an iron grip, but did not seem to notice that the music had ceased while all in attendance had turned to stare at the pair standing nearly in the middle of the dance floor. She struggled to get loose. His dark eyes bored into hers with intense purpose, but she had no clue of what he wanted from her that could explain his ungentlemanly actions.

"Ah, my pet," he growled through gritted teeth. "You cannot go until you tell me where did you receive such a fine gift?"

"Naw, I think not, pilgrim. What I think is that you had better unhand the young lady or I will be forced ta mess up all those pretty doodads you got there all over your chest. And then we would have ta send you back to Mexico in more than the one piece ya come here with. Then we'd have ta tell Mexico what a fine feller they done sent over to see us," cut in a voice as stern as iron and quiet as death.

The voice came from behind him, and the general began to smile, but as he turned his head, he found he was staring down the long throat of a Paterson Colt .36, a kind of weapon he was painfully familiar with, since it was the same gun used by the lethal and triumphant Texas Rangers. It suddenly dawned on him where he was, and silently damned himself for giving free rein to his desires. He had wanted to keep a low profile. Now he would not be able to move among these people as he had before.

"I am most sorry," he said, as he slowly let go of Sasa's wrist, but she did not retreat.

"I hadn't had the pleasure ta be introduced ta you yet, Sasa, but I am a good friend of Jackson and his pap. So, what exactly did this varmint do ta get you riled up enough ta slap him, not once, but two times?" asked Isaiah.

Jackson arrived just then, and the scene was paralyzing. Isaiah was still holding his Colt, nose high at the general, Sasa was still fuming, ready to explode, and the general seemed to be astonished that everyone was making such a fuss.

"He wanted what no man can have without my consent, he put his hand much lower than my waist and he wanted to know where I got my bracelet from. I slapped him because he suggested that I go with him and get in his bed," said Sasa.

Almost everyone in the room gasped, as much for the bad deed as for the plain speech that came from Sasa. Women were not supposed to even hint that they knew of such things, but Sasa had been asked, so she answered.

"Now Mister General whatever ya are, I have ta confess that I don't take kindly ta no Mexican generals being among us, but I didn't do the invitin'. But, I am doin' the uninvitin' here and now. So I suggest ya get, and get fast, because if'n I see you in town after tonight, I am goin' ta make sure ya don't get home. Is that clear enough for ya, General?" asked Isaiah.

"It is, sir. I am not sure what is going on here, or why you white people are being so nice to an Indian squaw. What I offered her was no better than she deserved to...." said the general.

Fortunately for everyone else, he could not finish the sentence. Without a moment's hesitation, Jackson swung his dress cane, cracking the general over the head, leaving a bloody dent there with its heavy metal finial top. The man slumped to the floor. A trickle of blood running down his forehead and onto his clean military coat with all its medals. While several other men took charge of throwing the general into his carriage with instructions to leave town this very night, Sasa found herself surrounded by all the young ladies she had made friends with this season. Their eyes were wide, their cheeks blushed, and it was plain that this was the most exciting thing they had experienced in their young lives.

It was still early in the evening, so instead of breaking up the ball, the incident was quickly set aside and the strings sprang to life again. Sasa would have to write this in her journal, and then try to figure out what it all meant. A short time later, she again felt the concentrated stare boring through her, but when she quickly turned around, saw no one but the other dancers and attendees of the ball. It was troubling to say the least.

Chapter 16
A Profound Obsession

It was unfortunate that there had been all that commotion to disturb everyone at the dance. He wanted Sasa to be calm, relaxed and unsuspecting, with her guard down, for his plan to succeed. He had not planned on the confrontation in the middle of the ballroom, but he could not cry over mistakes now. If he were to be able to grab the girl and get away clean, he had to put that unsettling incident out of his mind.

There she was now, beginning another dance with yet another man. Had she no shame? Why would any of them willingly choose to dance with her? Surely they knew she is one of those Cherokee squaws. Really, any squaw from any tribe should be regarded as beneath contempt. Just the fact that Sasa had been wined and dined the last few weeks in Boston was a sign that Americans were letting down their guard. Don't these people realize she is a murderess? She should be put to death, if not tortured. That oversight would be rectified. He would see to it that justice was accomplished, and then these fine people would know the brave thing he had done for them, and he would no longer be barred from their intimate acquaintances.

As Sasa danced, though, he began to appreciate her grace and beauty. Without realizing it, he briefly smiled when he saw an extremely young man stumble while trying to impress her. He knew what that felt like too. He had been young at one time, young and inexperienced. But, that was before.

He ached with anxiety as he watched her dance around the floor. He dared not approach her, but the thoughts that swirled in his mind made him feel feverish and shaky. The night before had been spent in gross indecision and uncertainty. He knew he should just leave her well enough alone, but every time he saw her, his blood boiled with indignation and disgust.

And there she was, the center of attention, admired by all, even those who hated Indians felt she had accomplished the complete transformation, from Indian savage to a well-bred, well-educated and socially acceptable young lady. But, it was not enough for him. No amount of grooming was going to assuage the violent anger he felt for this girl, for she was responsible for a heinous crime. How the government let this squaw get away with the murder of his father, he would never know.

Making her pay for it was what had consumed his every waking thought, but she continued to perplex him.

When he met her at the picnic, she realized who he was, but she showed no shame, no regret as far as he could see. That alone inflamed his hatred. Now she was here, enjoying all that society could offer her, while that same society had begun to turn their backs on him. He never had found out why. Why was it that whenever any of the old family friends looked at him, their eyes immediately drew down, not wanting to meet his gaze, as if he had done something shameful? It was maddening, especially since he was the one who had lost his own father, the last of his family on this mortal earth.

Finding the right opportunity to strike had become his obsession, and so he stood there, staring holes through her back, willing her to feel the hate he was throwing at her and waiting for the right time. It would come, and soon.

The Choctaw elder, Running Wolf, had made sure he had not been followed when he left on his two week journey from the small village they called Sakti Chaha, which meant "a steep place" or "cliffy", a few hours ride from Fort Towson and not far from the new Choctaw capitol town called Doaksville.

He was equally as cautious when he returned. His task was a grave one, and he felt in his bones that he had a sacred duty to carry out all that had been required of him by his father, and his father before him. When he was given this task, he knew it would be far into the future, but he never thought that he would be alone by then, and without a single person left of his family. That fact made his duty a heavy weight. He had sworn to tell no one, and he had mostly stood by his promise, except on two occasions. The first time he had broken his promise was when a young man who walked beside him on the terrible trip from their homeland, stumbled and fell against him. He had been carrying the object in his arms, wrapped in elk hide.

The force of the man's fall pushed it out of his grasp and onto the ground. The man quickly got back up and proceeded to help Running Wolf pick his burden up from the ground. Upon doing so, a portion of the hide fell away, revealing the gleaming gold scales peeking through. Running Wolf quickly covered it back up and endeavored to separate himself from his fellow traveler, but it was too late. Running Wolf had seen the questions in the man's eyes, and he knew that he had created a liability for himself.

Until recently, he had not been approached about the object, and no one had come looking for him in the village. Regardless, someone would come. It was too great a discovery for the young man to refrain from speaking about it to someone. It was inevitable that someone would seek him out in order to possess it. He had to think quickly to devise a plan. Running Wolf had thought long and hard after arriving in Indian Territory. Realizing that there was no one left to pass down his duty to within his own family, he had to find someone with a clean heart, someone who did not know greed or harbor hurtful schemes against others. He had found such a one, and her name was Sasa Halley. She was a young woman of the Cherokee.

He had not yet given the girl any information about the object, but made her promise she would come back to the village after her long trip to Boston. As a reminder, he had given her a fine gold chain bracelet with one small charm dangling from it. The charm was as close as he could come to a representation of the object itself, using his skill as a metal worker in silver and gold jewelry. The gift would bind her to him, and she would keep her promise to come back. But now he wondered if giving her that charm had been a terrible mistake. On the one hand, he may have endangered her, without allowing her to truly understand why she needed to be cautious, and on the other hand, if someone saw the charm, it might lead that someone straight back to him.

That was the reason why he decided to give the object a new home, one that no human needed to protect. He still debated on telling Sasa of its very general location, and this he would need to consider carefully. Even so, he would not be able to direct anyone to the object, for the simple reason that he himself could not retrace his footsteps to find it again. He had taken great risk to find a place to put it. This he did in the dark of the moon along some nameless river. Once he had spotted the river in the twilight, he waited until deep darkness had robbed all color and shape from his eyes. Then he stumbled along its bank for several miles unaware of the danger. At any moment he might have stepped into a pit or fallen and broken his leg, but he wanted to be sure that he hid the object even from his own eyes. He groped with his hands until he found just the right place and there it rested. His task complete, he left before the moon rose and gave its light, and he was far away by morning. Now the object was safe, but also lost to him and that was as it should be.

For his entire life, the life of his father and his father's father, and on and on back into the mist of time when each generation of his family had guarded the artifact, it had caused great pain and sorrow. That thing brought nothing but danger, but the promise must be kept. There had even been one or two of the men in his line who were slaughtered in order to find out its whereabouts. Each generation had guarded it and remained faithful to the promise given to a dying Spanish soldier. Since the day the object came into his people's village, so many generations ago, until now, it had been a burden almost too horrible for the men of his family to withstand. Hopefully now, he would be free of it and the greedy men who would seek it. Little did they know that every person who had sought to possess it lost their lives because of their greed, while the one who had possessed it did not want it, but was forced to protect it. All because of a promise made by his ancestors. Honor demanded that he kept the promise, just as if he had uttered it himself.

As he walked back to his new, and possibly temporary, village, he felt confident that it was truly gone forever, and that no man would be tainted by the blood that had been spilled for it. Finally, he came to his small home on the outskirts of the fairly new community. It had begun as a camp and it slowly blossomed into a small town in only six years. On the other hand, at the current rate of death from starvation, and with the raids terrorizing them, it might only be a temporary settlement.

There was no one there to welcome him home, no one had even noticed he had been gone. Now he would have to wait and be observant to any strangers suddenly appearing in town. He sensed his ordeal might not be over yet, but there was nothing else he could think of doing and no way to help protect the young Cherokee girl, the only person who carried the symbol of his ancestors' long burden. For now, he would have to pray to the One above and wait. May the Creator see his good heart, and help him and the girl, Sasa.

The watcher had tried to keep an eye on the old Indian. He had been surprised at how fast the old man could move if he needed to. The watcher had been assigned to keep an eye on this village in the Choctaw lands of Indian Territory, but it was very hard. It took him weeks to finally make a list of likely suspects. Then his employer had come and narrowed it down to this one individual. For several more weeks, he had watched his every move. Being darker skinned was a plus in this village of dark skinned Indians, even if no one would take him for an Indian, except maybe in the dark.

Thinking of the dark, he felt like punishing himself for not seeing where the old man had disappeared to a few weeks ago. The old man had vanished on one of the darkest nights of the month. He surmised that about the same time the old Indian was sneaking out of town, unseen, he had not been watching, because he was spending some time with one of the Indian girls in the village. Money was scarce here and he found that it did not take much to entice a young squaw to share his bed, but, it had cost him dearly. If his employer found out, it could mean his life.

Too late now to worry about it. What was more disconcerting was the fact that the old man had been gone for several days. The watcher had tried backtracking to see where he had been, but it had rained on the tracks and they were so faint, he lost the trail. It irked him that he had no clue why he had to keep an eye on the old man in the first place. He had never tracked anyone in the red clay that passed for soil all around the area.

The Indian was back now and the watcher held off on his own comforts to keep a better eye on his movements. He had been told to watch for a package of indiscriminate size. If he spotted the old man carrying a package, the watcher was to follow and see where he took it. Then once the old man was gone, he was to retrieve it, not open it under any circumstances, not tell anyone he had it, place it in the underground box they had buried a few miles south of town, and then send for him.

Nothing like that had happened yet. One last instruction chilled him to the core. His life would be forfeit if he opened it, and the same would happen if he told anyone of his purpose there. That was easy. He could not look at it, since he had not found it, and he could not tell of his purpose either, since he would have had to know it to begin with. He smiled to himself for a second, then continued his vigil.

Chapter 17
Undeserved Riches

The payment, this time, was more money than David Flying-hawk had ever seen in one place before, but—sadly—the men just told him that it would be the last of the information they needed from him. Well, this should last him a good long while. Maybe he should leave the territory, move away from his tribe and live off of this money until something better came along. Of course, David wasn't thinking of Martha, his wife, in the slightest. He had quit thinking of her when he stopped going home to check in.

She could just find another dirt grubber to plant her farm. It would not be him. That has always been and always would be woman's work.

He could not stand seeing her in the same dress day after day. It was the dress she had worn when the soldiers came to get them and herd them to Indian Territory, and it had been mended so many times you could not see the design on the fabric anymore. Martha herself was looking so old and haggard, always pawing all over him with her worried little voice. He did not need that kind of thing, especially the way she begged for him to go dig in the dirt. He should have walked away long ago.

Now, he was a bigger man. The other men of his tribe would sit up and listen now that he possessed so much money, but, first he wanted to go have a drink at one of the bars in Fort Smith. It did not matter to them if he was an Indian, they always had a drink for any Indian whenever they scraped up enough money.

It was still early spring and he could see the fog his breath made in the frosty air. He decided he would stop over at O'Tooles, one of the newer grog shops in the middle of town. Carefully he made his way there, making sure not to give offense to any of the white soldiers, then slipped down the street and into the dimly lit drinking establishment.

"I want drink whiskey, I pay," he said, as he thrust out the money he had been paid. Eyes popped around the room and whispers began, obviously wondering about his fine turn of fortune. Two clean cut Cherokee who were sitting in a dark corner, not drinking, but apparently waiting for something, approached David from behind and he flinched when he saw them.

"What are you afraid of, David? Have we not been your neighbors these many long years back in Georgia?

Are you not glad to see us?" said the taller of the two men. "Hey, we noticed you have a lot of money there. You better be careful tonight as you go home, David. Someone is likely going to steal that wad off of you, if you keep showing it to everyone."

So David wisely put the money in his pocket, but it was too late, everyone in the room had seen the money, and some of the eyes looking his way glowed with intense desire.

"I... uh... I did some work for a man and got paid today. That's all," he hastily explained.

The two Cherokees looked at him with disbelief stamped on their faces. David was unable to think what else he might say to John Hummingbird and Alexander Sutton. John, the taller of the two, had sat on the Cherokee council for the Wolf Clan for many years, and was a respected elder and supporter of Chief John Ross's party. Alexander Sutton was a wealthy rancher and farmer. He had come over early to Indian Territory, when it was clear that the tribe would be made to leave their homes. Wisely, he had sold all his stock and household to make the trip for him and his small family, a wife and two teenage sons, by steamboat, the year before the long march, which had claimed so many of the People. Because of coming early, he had been able to claim the best of the available land for his ranch.

Of course, there was a group of Cherokees who had arrived and claimed the finest parts of the Cherokee land years before Alexander Sutton. They were the Old Settlers, the two hundred or so Cherokees who pulled up stakes as much as seventeen years before the forced removal, and who first settled in Arkansas at the behest of the U.S. Government. Then the government decided that they wanted all the Cherokee to reside in Indian Territory, so they moved again. They were the first Cherokees to come to Indian Territory and they possessed the choicest of land, were well established and a bit unhappy to have Chief John Ross declare himself to be the Chief Over All.

Alexander silently and calmly gazed at David, then he spoke, quietly, so their conversation would not be overheard by the white men drinking not far from them.

"David, we have noticed that you are not coming home to take care of your wife, Martha. We find that very strange. I remember a time when nothing could separate the two of you. What has changed?" asked Alexander.

David was shocked at the question. He had never supposed anyone paid the least bit of attention to any of his wanderings. He turned to look at John, only to find the same knowing look in his eyes, but he could not fathom how they would know anything. Quickly, he decided the best thing to do would be to leave and ride toward Indian Territory as if he were going home. He would then double back and get the drink he now needed badly.

"Uh, I think I will get on back home. I am really not all that thirsty," he announced, then he turned and walked out of the small grog shop. David would have to use the Army ferry to get back to the other side. After guiding his horse onto the landing on the other side of the Arkansas, he headed in the direction of his little shack and the wife who waited for him, but with no intention of arriving there.

While David left the grog shop, Alexander noticed two of the white men gazing at the open doorway and whispering to one another. He looked at John, who nodded his head seriously. Immediately, but not hurrying, the two Cherokees walked out, then quickly mounted their horses and made it to the Army ferry just in time to make the next crossing after the one David took.

Alexander looked back at the small town and noticed the two white men coming out of the shop together to find their horses. Once outside, the men hoisted themselves up into their saddles and headed for the Army ferry. John and Alexander would not have much time, but they knew just what to do.

David kept his horse at a steady pace, but not so fast that he would be forced to give the horse a rest. He did not want to stop anywhere along the way and intended to double back after a few miles. When he made the decision to turn and go back along another route, he found the two Cherokees close upon him. There was no escape, because if he ran, they would surely know he had something to hide. Fear sweat broke out under his dungarees, staining the underarms and neck of the calico ribbon shirt he had recently bought after receiving his great payment. Somehow, David knew that his tribal brothers were more than curious about his recent gain. As they approached, he smiled wanly.

"Ho there, David. Hold up, we would like to talk with you. Maybe smoke the pipe. Let's find a shady spot with some privacy and have a council," suggested Alexander.

David could only nod and go with them. Soon they found a quiet spot, not easily seen from the trail, and they picketed their horses much further away, around a rock formation and behind some brush. David was not sure why they had walked so far to picket the horses. They made their way back and sat down on one of the horse blankets, then John pulled out from his parfleche both his pipe and a special tobacco which included his own secret blend of herbs, seeds and leaves. David knew immediately they would all three begin the time honored pipe ceremony, but he dreaded it, because it would be unthinkable for him to lie or dishonor himself during or after the pipe ceremony. In all tribes, this was known to all. Someone who could not keep an agreement made after smoking the pipe was less than human and lost much status among the People.

During the calm silence before lighting the tobacco, Alexander signaled to John and David, putting his first finger to his lips to signal "keep silent". David was unsure what was happening. Why were they having to be quiet? They were in their own Cherokee Territory now, weren't they? Still, he obeyed and sat in silence. His eyes widened when he first heard horses coming down the very same trail he had just been on, then he recognized the two men from the grog shop, who held carbines across their laps, ready to use them at a moment's notice.

David resorted to the common signs that used fingers, hands and arms in a variety of positions. It was a common sign language that almost every tribe learned from childhood. Without it, none of the tribes would have been able to trade goods, food or make peace in council. David signed, "They are only two, let us attack now and surprise them."

Alexander shook his head to decline the idea, and shot him a stern look, in case he felt he could do it anyway. The three Cherokee watched as the two white men tried to pick up their trail. Fortunately, they had stopped in a particularly rocky area, and in any case most white men were lousy trackers. Since they did not bother to dismount from their horses, they missed the small telltale signs that the three Cherokees had stopped there. The men spurred their horses onward, then all was quiet again.

As they then began the quiet passing of the pipe, offering it to the four directions, the earth and then the sky, David racked his brain for some excuse to explain why he might have that much money, but he knew they would not swallow any story he might concoct. He was caught like a mouse in a bobcat's mouth, not yet crushed and eaten, but knowing he soon would be… and if not by his tribal brothers, by the two white men who would probably come back to find where they had lost the trail.

The ceremony finished and the pipe replaced, the part of this meeting he knew would come was finally upon him. The other two men sat and looked at him with open, inquisitive eyes. He knew what they wanted to know without even asking them. This was not something he had planned on. He had no escape. Smoking the pipe was binding, so he resigned himself to speak the truth.

"Why did we have to walk all that way to picket the horses? Now we will have to walk back and get them, and I am already tired," he asked, irritably.

John smirked a little, then said, "What kind of a hunter are you? Did you not realize that the horses of those men would smell our horses and then they would speak to each other? That would have been death for us."

David turned red under the tan skin around his ears and neck. He knew he had been lazy about such things for some time. He thought Indian Territory was a safe place.

"My brothers, I have been struggling to live. I am not made to be a farmer and my special skill of hunting and making meat is useless here in Indian Territory. The game has long since been hunted out. What is a man to do?" he pleaded.

John and Alexander looked solemnly at him.

"Tell us. Do not leave anything out. Later, we will build a sweat lodge and we will chase out this badness that seems to have you in its grip. But speak low and do not make a sound if those men come back. We do not want the Army here trying to catch Indians who would attack any upstanding white men," said Alexander Sutton, with a small chuckle.

David bowed his head, thought for a moment and allowed his dream to leave Indian Territory behind vanish into mist. He prepared himself, getting comfortable on the horse blanket.

"It began not long after we arrived in Indian Territory in 1839. There was a traveler who approached me while I was trying to dig up that hard ground we call a farm. This man looked to be Spanish or like the Mexico Indians. He agreed with me that planting and farming was women's work and then said that I could make much more money by helping some of his friends learn about the tribes in Indian Territory. So, every few weeks, he came back and asked me specific questions. On the next visit he expected me to have the answers and then I would be paid," said David, looking about nervously.

"What sort of information did this man want from you?" asked John.

"First he said that the white government needed to pay for what they had done to the Cherokee and, of course, I agreed. He said there was a way to make them suffer and I was all for that. He did not tell me the whole plan until recently, but if it works, it should get back good at all those rich whites," answered David.

John and Alexander gazed with alarm at each other. Could this Cherokee brother believe that there would not be consequences if anyone meddled in the United States plan for Indian Territory? That same white government that had gladly sacrificed thousands of Indian lives from many tribes, just to herd them all here. David was playing with fire, and he did not even know.

"He recently told me he was from the Mexican government, and that the best way to get back at the United States would be to keep them from getting Texas, and that he would make sure the United States could not keep Texas and make it one of their states. Some of the ideas he had were very farfetched, but the money he offered was too good to pass up. He said he needed as much information about all the tribes in Indian Territory, things like who was whose enemies and how many people does each tribe have, where they like to camp and where are the towns in Indian Territory. He said I would not have to do anything but give him this information and I would be rich. And see here? Here is the money he brought me this morning," said David.

"Something does not add up here," said John. "I think we need to take him to Chief Ross. Maybe he will understand what he is talking about," he added.

"Hey, wait a minute. I never said I would go and talk to the Chief. You never said anything about that. No, I am not going," objected David, emphatically.

"You either go with us now, or we will make sure those two white men find you. They will take all your money, and they will kill you. Remember, it is not against the law in any of this land to kill an Indian. They won't even have to answer for being in Indian Territory without a permit. You would be dead and dust before anyone figured it out," countered Alexander.

David bowed his head again. There was no way out of this, because he knew what they said about the white men trailing them was true. So they mounted their horses and carefully picked their way over the small gravel rocks in the area, heading for Tahlequah, where Chief John Ross kept an office at the new Cherokee Nation.

175

Cherokee Chief John Ross

Chapter 18
A Terrible Burden

Nothing could be harder, Chief Ross was thinking, than try-ing to get all the various factions of the Cherokee together to talk and agree on something extremely important, let alone something that must be kept secret. In spite of his misgivings, he called a meeting of all of the chiefs and sub-chiefs of his nation, regardless of the party or faction. Even his most bitter enemy was invited. Now, whether they came or not was a totally different question. Chances were that some would find any number of reasons not to attend, thinking that Chief Ross was in some sort of personal crisis of his own making and having no intention of helping him. This meeting, however, would be for the welfare of the entire nation, indeed the entirety of the whole of Indian Territory. How he would present the grave situation to the invitees was something he was anxiously debating with himself.

He sat by his office window, gazing out at the newly budding trees off in the distance, but only seeing the questions swimming in his mind. It all seemed to happen so fast, but he knew that it only felt that way because he had not known what was happening under his own nose for many months. It wasn't as if he had not had his hands full with government business, trying to get justice from the U.S. Government, which was a long and tedious job with enemies around every corner. Not only did he have part of his own nation against him, he also had certain white entities working tirelessly against the entire Cherokee Nation.

It was a dangerous game those white men of power were playing. They pretended to side with Ross against his enemies, but if there was anything he had learned in all his years as Chief of the Cherokee, it was that if a white man in power was patting you on the back, you had to watch out for the knife in his other hand. He wanted to say that to the Treaty and the Old Settlers Parties, but he knew it would fall on deaf ears. His enemies were so eager to cause Ross to fail that they would take any friendship from the white U.S. Govern-ment they could get, but Ross knew that these government men had reasons of their own to want Ross out of office, and they had nothing to do with championing the views of the Treaty or Old Settlers Parties.

What Ross actually believed was that these government men, who consisted of Indian agents, generals, senators and congressmen, had a separate agenda, and that these men would cozy up to those other Cherokee factions in order to drive between them a wedge so big it could never be brought right. Once the Cherokee government dissolved into separate factions, these men of power would, with a mighty swipe, sweep the Cherokee away, dissolving them as a nation and finding justification to take back the territory given them by treaty. He could not allow that to happen, so he continued to plug along, trying to find goals in common to bring them all together again.

However, the emergency meeting this night was far more important than just one nation in Indian Territory: this concerned the welfare of Indian Territory in its totality. The meeting was not a governmental procedure, but more like an emergency meeting of those in authority.

Just before the meeting began, he sat close to the window in the large log building the Cherokee government used for all manner of official business. It could hold, at the most, fifty men, if some stood... and some would have to stand for there were not enough chairs for this meeting. He could remember back when he was a child, when meetings of this sort were held in a much different manner. It had been the last era of the power of the women's council. Whites could not stand the fact that the women owned the land and that they held enormous power within the Cherokee nation, so they pushed and bullied their views onto the nation, making women something less than they should be. The Cherokees ultimate mistake was to give up their long held ways in order to be more like the whites. In the end it did them no good, and here they sat, in a land foreign to them, with hard problems to solve.

The men filtered in quietly, choosing sides of the room along with their party lines. They probably assumed this would be a political meeting, regardless of what he had announced to the contrary. There was George Guess, otherwise known as Sequoyah. John felt he could depend on George. Then, his good friend and past editor of the Cherokee Phoenix, Elija Hicks. George Lowrey, Tsa-Tsi-Agi-Li, who was Assistant Chief, had come early to greet the men as they entered the meeting. Even his arch enemy, Stand Watie, skulked in, obviously suspicious of Ross's intentions. It looked as if many of the headmen, sub-chiefs and Cherokee government office holders had come. That was a great relief to him.

Many of them dressed in a portion of the traditional Cherokee attire, with their turban-like hats and colorful coats in bright colors of vibrant red, cobalt blue and sun yellow, with handmade moccasins on their feet. Some dressed in plain dungarees, like any white settler would wear, chambray shirts and heavy leather, square toed boots. A few, though, were dressed like white men, much like the chief also dressed. Sober black or gray cutaway coats, stiff white collars and cuffs, sedate shirtwaists or vests and leather dress shoes. He often wondered if a Cherokee's mode of dress could be correlated with his political views. He would have to think on that one later.

He allowed himself to occupy his mind with the recent questioning of David Flying-hawk. If there was a Cherokee with less honor than this man, he did not know of one. Even his old enemy Stand Watie had a measure of honor. But this man, David, lacked any feelings of duty to his heritage, his nation, and even his wife. He had betrayed them all. John Ross had questioned the man himself just the day before yesterday, when he had learned the terrible truth.

John Hummingbird and Alexander Sutton had brought the sullen man to him and the story that unfolded was a chilling one indeed. The wretch had no idea he had betrayed, not just his own family, but his nation and every other nation in Indian Territory. John Ross determined to keep David's name out of it, or he would be a man marked for death. Chief Ross did not believe a man should pay with his life for being stupid, lazy and ignorant, although he did not deserve much else. He was thankful that John and Alexander had known enough to question how David had come into so much money. Both young men were of the same clan as Martha Flying-hawk, the wolf clan, and so they felt it to be their right to investigate the reason why David was not providing for her. Just this morning, he heard that Martha, after learning of her husband's disloyalty, had set his things out in the yard of their farm, which meant they were now divorced. David was free now, to go where he would, but ironically, he pleaded for Martha to take him back. John hoped she did not, and that David would leave Indian Territory.

The Chief looked up to see that the room was almost filled to capacity. He nodded to his secretary, who then called the meeting to order. Once the room quieted, Chief Ross rose from his chair to address the gathering.

"Osiyo, Brothers, I have called you all here this evening to discuss..." he began, but was rudely interrupted immediately.

"We don't want any of your patronizing, Ross. Just state why you wanted us all here and let us go. I have work to do," said one of the attendees.

"Tom Maker, I will get on with it, if you allow me to finish a sentence. Believe me, this is something you are going to want to hear," replied Chief Ross.

Others in the room looked astonished at Tom Maker for such a rude interruption. When the room settled again, Chief Ross continued.

"First, even though it will take a bit of time, I want your solemn oath that you will tell no one of tonight's meeting. I must prevail upon each of you to solemnly swear that what you learn in this room tonight will go no further. Not your wives, not the Indian Agent, not other tribesmen, not any whites outside of our own nation, and especially not the U.S. Government in all its many forms, is to be allowed to know what we know until at which time it is safe. If you agree, we will smoke the pipe, if you will not be bound by this oath, then you may be excused," he said, in a voice that brooked no argument.

Great turmoil erupted in the room. Each man looking at his neighbor and wondering if any secret revealed this way could be kept from white ears. When the room quieted, the chief continued.

"Assistant Chief George Lowrey has prepared the pipe. If it burns out along the way, we will put more of the sacred tobacco in and re-ignite it. Before we begin, is there anyone who cannot keep this oath?" he asked.

Then he silently waited for anyone that wanted to leave the room to do so, but no one did. Even Stand Watie sat in open curiosity. John was sure they were all wondering, what would cause the Chief of the Cherokees to call a meeting such as this and require an oath, then smoking the pipe to seal it among so many men.

Almost an hour later, the passing of the pipe had finished. They had only had to fill the pipe four times. Each smoker honored the four directions and the sun and earth. Since they were all burning to know what this unusual meeting was all about, they did not tarry with the pipe.

"Now, my brothers, I have a request I must ask of you. I ask that whatever political beliefs you have, whatever party you identify with, and whatever grievances you may have with me, you put them aside for now. Let all sides remain inert, suspended for a short time while we hammer out a plan to counter a great threat to our nation.

"Some intelligence has come into my possession which is very troubling. It is now known that Mexico has had for some time spies among us. Not just the Cherokee alone, but every Indian Territory tribe.

"The purpose was to gather information about us and our enemies in order to use it to our detriment. A plot has been uncovered, revealing the intentions of Mexico to try to start a civil war within Indian Territory.

"You, I am sure, know of the many raids happening along the Texas and Indian Territory border. Some of them are genuine skirmishes between known entities. At the same time, there has been an alarming increase of these raids. We have had reports of raiding between neighboring tribes, where the accused raiding tribe swears it had not been them. If this had happened only one time, it would not have been noted. However, this scenario has played out many times in southern Indian Territory," said the chief.

"But that is down there by the Choctaw, the Creek and Chickasaw. What does that have to do with the Cherokee Nation?" asked one of the headmen.

"You are right in questioning it. I did not know the answer until just recently and once I considered what I now know to be true, I can see very clearly how these raids are meant to affect the entire Indian Territory.

"I think you are all aware that if Civil War in Indian Territory were to happen, there would be no telling what the United States would do to all of the tribes of Indian Territory. They have proven they are not above going against their own treaty provisions. If this happened, the United States could rationalize taking our new land away from us and then dissolve the tribes. Remember that many of the displaced whites who were farm steading here before the government made them move back into Arkansas, would love to have this land taken from us," said Ross. The closed room erupted in a commotion that threatened to burst into argument.

"Gentlemen, gentlemen, brothers, please be seated and listen. All will be revealed to you, but you must refrain from all this turmoil until I give you all the facts," said Chief Ross, as he motioned with his hands for them to sit down and calm themselves.

One of the headmen from the Old Settlers stood up to address the chief. "This all sounds so far-fetched. You are asking us to believe that now, after the bulk of the Cherokee finally arrived here, a plot springs up to take this land away from all of us? Your story is just that, a story."

"I have irrefutable proof that Mexico has been sending agents into our midst to learn about each Indian Territory nation. Questions such as where our villages are, who are our enemies within the territory, are only some of what they have learned about us. Then they have paid the Texas tribes of the Kiowa and Kickapoo to dress as the enemy of a tribe within Indian Territory and then go and raid them, in the hopes that they will believe they had been brutally raided by their enemy and probably a neighbor. It is hard enough that the United States forced us to live next to our traditional enemies. Now, Mexico is hoping to spark the flame of war that would destroy every nation in Indian Territory," explained Ross.

"How can you possibly know all of that, Chief, and why in heaven, would Mexico come all that way up here to meddle in our business anyway?" hollered one of the attendees.

"I cannot divulge how I know, but suffice it to say, they have successfully infiltrated our own nation, not to mention the other nations of the territory. We believe we know the reason, but until I check it out, I do not want to comment on their complete plan. I can say that it is not our nations that they want to harm, and they don't want our land. We are just a means to an end for something they want...something far greater indeed." answered Ross.

"So what can we do about it? It all seems so bizarre, if you ask me. If that is what they are really doing, I don't see how we could stop them, short of a war," cut in another attendee.

"I have been giving considerable thought to that, and I think I have a plan to puncture their balloon without ever having a war. In fact, it will be just the opposite. I called this meeting so that all the headmen, sub-chiefs and leaders of our people would be aware of this threat, so that they can keep an eye on their own people. The spy, or spies, are still here among us. They might even look like Indians. There is no call to go accosting strangers. I want you all to say nothing, just be aware. Once I have a plan worked out, I will ask each of you to provide assistance in foiling their plot. Remember that we must stop the cause for civil war among all the tribes of Indian Territory and that it is not just about the Cherokee. In our next meeting, a fortnight hence, I will tell you the reason for the raids," finished John Ross.

The group looked stunned, unsure of the next step. Reassuringly, he began to see nodding heads, even Stand Watie seemed to have put away his grievances, at least for the moment. Actually, John Ross was somewhat surprised to see Stand there. Almost a year back, in Benton County, Arkansas, Stand Watie got into a bitter fight with another Cherokee, James Foreman and Stand ended up killing Foreman before riding off on his horse. Stand gave himself up to authorities, but was allowed to go home until the trial. That trial had not commenced as yet, but witnesses said that Foreman had set out several days before the fight to find and kill Watie. They just happened to meet at a small grocery in Benton County. Foreman was a vicious, violent, fighting man and was dangerous anytime he had his back up. John was sure Watie would be acquitted, eventually.

The men were allowed to leave, but as John stood there, Stand turned and walked up to him instead.

"Don't think it is over between us, Ross. I know you had something to do with the murders of the men who signed that treaty, and I won't stand still for you to do it to me either," said Watie.

"I have said it before, Stand, and I will say it again. I had absolutely nothing to do with those murders. I may have been unhappy, even furious, with those men for selling our homeland, but I would never condone murder under any circumstances. I have no desire to kill you, Stand. I want to find some way to negotiate peace between us, but that discussion will have to wait until this present crisis has been abated. Know this, however: I will not lay down and play dead either, no matter how much I want peace, if it means giving up anything for the People. They have already given enough, in gallons of blood, spread over seven hundred miles or more. On the other hand, I am extremely glad of your assistance in this present matter," countered Chief Ross, standing firm in front of Stand.

"Well, once my trial is over, we are going to have to come to terms with some issues, and I guess we shall see what we shall see, eh?" replied Stand, with bitterness boiling in his eyes when he left.

Only Assistant Chief, George Lowrey now remained in the room with John, and it felt oddly silent and cold.

"Do you think they all will keep it to themselves, Chief?" asked George

"Time will tell, George. I was certainly surprised to have Stand's cooperation, though. He may not participate in our plans, but at least he is not going to work against us either. We can thank the Creator for that. Ah, George, I am tired, but there is so much more to do this night. Can you stay while I work out some ideas? I need to sound them out and see if they make any sense at all. Nothing we do will be foolproof, George, but I am willing to try. What I am thinking of doing has never been done by any tribe that I know of, in the Americas and I . . ." continued John… "I may even write a short letter to President Sam Houston, even if I doubt there is anything he would be able to tell us. This has been going on under our very noses. Plus, I hear he has his hands full as it is, holding Mexico off at the Texas border. No, I don't think I will worry him with this. So," he concluded, rubbing his hands together to warm them, "let's get started."

They would work late into the night and for some days to come. Hopefully, they would get it right.

Chapter 19
A Change of Plans

Manuel Munos Mendoza had a firm rule that was about to be broken, and he could do absolutely nothing about it. He had been waiting at the shipyard office, which stayed open as late as ten o'clock at night, especially when the Boston Bay was crowded with ships and boats hurrying to fill their holds, or unload them, so that they could get to the next port. Each ship's Captain needed to have his manifest signed by the harbor master. In his case, he wanted to buy his steamship ticket for his return trip down the coast and around the two Floridas (as Mexico had named them before the Americans took the land). First, he would go around the large "foot" of land, the original Florida. Then the ship would dock at New Orleans near the mouth of the Mississippi river, that flowed through the area Mexico had named Florida West. Now, New Orleans was part of the state of Louisiana. His strict rule, so far unbroken, allowed no contact between his employer, whomever that may be at the time, and himself in public. Not even with the employee of the person who had hired him. He liked to leave a very cold trail behind him.

Fumbling along a few yards down the dock from him, in the darkness lighted by the many ship lamps about, was Juan, the general's assistant. Cold rage was building inside him; he wanted no encumbrances to complicate his plans, but there was nowhere to run, since the office clerk had stepped out for his dinner and the office was temporarily closed. Obviously, Juan was looking for him. Mendoza found a dark corner, and as Juan stumbled by, he reached out and abruptly yanked him into the shadows with him.

Juan let out a high pitched squeal that Mendoza promptly silenced, putting his hand over his mouth and warning him in agitated whispers to make no more noise.

"What, pray tell, are you doing out here?" Mendoza hissed through gritted teeth.

"My master, the General, has sent me to find you. There has been an unfortunate, altercation and he needs your help," answered a shaken Juan.

"An altercation? Does he not realize how dangerous it is for us to be seen together? It would be dangerous for both of us, to say the least. What could be so important that he calls me to help him at this late date? I am ready to take tomorrow's steamship, and I will not be delayed," countered Mendoza.

"Señor, a most terrible thing happened to the general. He had been invited to the Spring Ball and the information is a little vague. It seems that the gentlemen attending bodily threw him out, instructing him to leave town immediately. He says there is something very important he must do, however, and that he needs your help," replied Juan.

"So what is that to me? I don't see what I can do about it. I have nothing to do with the elite society of this city. I was here for a specific purpose, that purpose was accomplished, and now I must go back without delay," insisted Mendoza.

"Ah, sì, Señor, the general thought you might say something like that, so he told me to tell you, that it is about the Golden Serpent and a beautiful young girl. The general said he has proof that she knows something about the artifact, and we must keep her from divulging what she knows to anyone. It could hurt the ongoing project he has you working on. Please come, Señor. The general, he is in such a rage after those gringos tossed him into his carriage. If I don't come back with you, the general said he would have my hide," babbled Juan.

Mendoza squinted his eyes, thinking it through. Did this general think he was stupid? No, he probably was panicking and imagining things. Who could know anything about the ancient artifact? Least of all a woman, at that.

"Ah well, I suppose I can spare him a little of my time" he conceded. "But! I will not miss this steamboat. It is essential that I get back to... uh... to my project immediately."

"Sì, sì, Señor Mendoza. Gracias. Follow me, it is not far. The general says he will explain it all when you come.

Wheezer's pacing became more frantic. He resorted to jumping at the door knob, but it would not open as before. He jogged from room to room, to jump on the furniture closest to the window, but even when he could see down to the sidewalk, he still did not see Sasa, or any of his other family either. He felt extremely worried, and agitated to the point of frenzy. Something bad was about to happen, and he needed to get to Sasa.

As the evening wore on, he became tired. Panting, he loped over to the water bowl to slurp up some cool water, then he tried his best to calm himself enough to gain his energy back. However, the respite did not last long, for he was soon pacing again.

After the tense moments while the general was being escorted out of the ballroom, Sasa went to the ladies parlor, set up especially for this night, so the ladies could freshen themselves, straighten any article of clothing gone astray and, if needed, take ones shoes off for a rest. Most of the ladies at the ball carried with them a small compact of powder. If any of them used anything more daring, it was kept at home and used in secret.

When Sasa returned to the ballroom, several dance partners were eager to claim another dance with her. For the moment, she declined them all so that she might sit beside Anna on one of the red silk brocade settees that lined the walls around the room. The episode with the general had been upsetting.

She was amazed to think that after all those years of training and hard work, no matter what she looked like, or how good her manners, some people would always only see the Indian in her. What was the use to even try, if she was going to meet up with the likes of the general? A disgusting man she hoped she would never meet again. Nonetheless, she knew deep in her heart why she was making this gargantuan effort. It was for her people... not just herself, but for all of the tribes of Indian Territory.

Anna had told her that there were people she would meet and subjects she could discuss that an Indian man would never be able to. Just as the reverse was also true. Given the chance that she would find a hearing ear among the white man's government, she could use her schooling in the best possible way. It was a chance she needed to take. She vowed to set some of her inborn pride aside. The very same pride that kept all Indian tribes from getting along with one another.

Anna sat close to her on the same settee. She looked lovingly at Sasa and held her hand while they watched the other dancers.

"Are you going to be all right, my dear?" she asked her.

"It was unsettling, but I suppose that I will have to know how to handle such things in the future. If I had been in my deer skins, he would not have a hand to grab with right about now," answered Sasa, as they both laughed at the thought.

Sasa turned her head to look around the room.

"Is something else bothering you? I have seen you look around the room several times tonight. You look concerned," observed Anna.

"Anna, I can't put my finger on it, but I feel that someone is staring at me, and not the other dancers. I keep checking every time I feel it at the back of my neck, but when I look, I can see no one looking at me. All the same, I know someone is staring at me, and it is not a good feeling," said a worried Sasa.

"Well, you have fulfilled the obligations for dances on your dance card. So, any time you wish to go home, we will be happy to depart. Balls are not Jackson's idea of fun anymore, so I know he won't mind a bit. I'll tell you what. Why don't you go collect your wrap and tell the footman or butler that we will want ours? By that time, I should be able to pry Jackson away from Isaiah's side. They are just talking about hunting, guns and horses anyway," proposed Anna.

Sasa's answering smile was enough of an response. Anna nodded her head and they stood and walked in separate directions.

It looked like his chance was coming. She had left Mrs. Halley's side and was coming down the halls to find the butler. It was a good thing that he had already taken care of him. He would wake up later with a large bump on his head and no idea who had hit him.

He needed something to subdue her and to muffle her screams, so he grabbed some other lady's thick cape with a fur lining off of the cloak rack behind him and concealed himself behind the heavy velvet curtain, waiting for her to brush by, but to his astonish-ment, she came right into the cloak room with him. It was now or never, and it had to be now, for how would he live with himself if he did not take his chance?

She stopped just inside the doorway, probably looking for the attendant. Then, as she turned to look back the way she had come, he sprang out, throwing the cloak over her head and gripping her hard around her midsection, pinning her arms down.

Wheezer's alarm became so great that he threw himself against the door, then began barking wildly. He raked his sharp claws down the door, making a terrible noise. The barking and pounding on the door could be heard almost throughout the hotel. Finally, the desk manager strode up the steps, two at a time, wondering what was going on. He had met Wheezer and the Halleys had been in this suite of room for several weeks, and never had he heard one peep from that dog. So he could only think that something must be wrong.

The manager dashed to the door, inserted his key and quickly opened it, fully expecting to find a burglar or something of that sort. Instead, when he opened the door, a whirlwind of Jack Russell, swept past him and down the stairs, only touching every few steps, just enough to propel his taut body forward and outward.

The manager stood stunned, not knowing what just happened. But one thing was for sure. The Halleys were going to be unhappy with him. One reason would be for letting their dog out of the room, and the other would be for the bill he would charge the Halleys for the damages the dog had made to the door. This most certainly was going to be a difficult evening.

Wheezer stopped every few moments to sniff the ground. The scent was very faint, but at least he had one. He hurried on and finally came to a large building blazing with lights. Wheezer had no time to think about where he was going. There was no one at the open door of this place where he could hear music, so he bounded right through the doorway, running full tilt into the middle of the ballroom where he stopped. The music stopped as well while all stared at this new intruder.

From out of this crowd of strangers, Wheezer heard a familiar voice. Jackson stepped through the crowed.

"Wheezer, boy? What are you doing here? Wheezer, what's wrong boy?" asked Jackson.

Wheezer ran at Jackson, but did not wag his tail and greet him as usual. Jackson, knew his dog and knew the signs: something was gravely wrong. Before the family could follow Wheezer back to the hotel, he would have to round up Anna, who had just appeared at his elbow, and Sasa.

"Anna, where is Sasa? Wheezer would not be here if some-thing were not wrong. I don't see her on the dance floor," said Jackson quickly.

"Jackson, I sent her to get her wrap and to tell the attendant we would be leaving, but that was several minutes ago and she has not returned," replied a suddenly worried Anna.

Jackson looked down at Wheezer's earnest face and shaking legs and knew what he needed to do.

"Wheezer, find Sasa, boy. Find Sasa," he ordered.

Wheezer had already picked up her scent and with his master's command, he circled several places around the ballroom, before finally taking off down the hallway at a full run. Jackson was right behind him, sliding on the slick marble floors as they weaved through rooms until they finally came to a scullery room with an outside door, standing open.

Wheezer stopped, looking up at Jackson for instructions. Jackson, looked outside to see that the door led to the mews where the horses were kept and where the stable boy lived. He looked down at Wheezer and noticed that just outside, on the ground, was a glove. An ice blue formal glove, the very same that Sasa had worn that night. Jackson stepped outside and scooped up the glove, just as Anna appeared at the door, with the men of the house close behind. Jackson held out his find.

"That is Sasa's. I am sure of it," said Anna.

Isaiah pushed through the doorway.

"Jackson, I know that I am just an old Mountain Man, but with your dog's help, maybe I can track whoever took Sasa. And if'in I find that it was that varmint, the general, I am going to tear him limb from limb. I saw your dog come in, an if'in he could track your girl all the way through Boston ta find y'all here, wall I guess he's a good enough huntin' dog for me," he said.

Jackson was too dumbfounded to answer. He had never thought that Sasa could come to any harm in a city he knew so well.

Wheezer, on the other hand, was ready to go and was beg-ging for the signal to seek out Sasa.

"Jackson, I know this is a surprise, but we need to track this man now, while the tracks are fresh and Wheezer is here. Between the two of us, I am sure we can wrestle up this here pilgrim," begged Isaiah.

Jackson nodded, not saying a word. Isaiah, walked a few steps, then turned, thought etched deep in his face.

"Oh, an I forgot to say, they found the butler in the hall closet. He'd been hit over the head, but I think he's goin to be just fine after the headache wears off. Okay, Wheezer, let's get to it," said Isaiah, as they started off into the gloom of the night.

Chapter 20
Men and Their Plots

General De Almeida paced beside his carriage, as he waited for Mendoza to arrive. He knew he only had a short span of time in which to accomplish what he wished to do. Hopefully, he would be on a boat headed out to sea and then to Mexico before the Americans figured it out. He doubted very seriously that anyone would be willing to spend good money to search for the Indian girl Sasa.

He knew she was still dancing at the ball. After being thrown out of that gathering for something as silly as groping an Indian girl, he had come up with the idea to take her far away from her white friends, but he had little time in which to do this, plus he did not want to be seen. He fully believed the mountain man's promise to kill him if he tarried in Boston. Fortunately, there was a ship leaving for South America whose captain he knew could be persuaded, with the right remuneration, to stop first at the Mexico port city of Tampico. From there, he would have access to his operatives in Texas and Indian Territory.

His change in plans only meant that he had to work fast. He was seething by the time Juan finally came around the corner. Right behind him was Mendoza. He did not look too happy, but that would change when he explained everything.

"Ah, Juan, you surely took enough time. The music inside has stopped, but could just be because of some special announcement, or a change in the dance they will do. I know it can't be over yet. These Americans, they love their dances. No, I think you are here on time," whispered General De Almeida, while looking over his shoulder.

The general then threw a conspiratorial glance at Mendoza, but he had just opened his mouth for his next word when a loud clatter of hooves, the frenzied sound of a whip and a black coach and four rounded the corner, coming so close to them that Juan had to reach out to grab the general by the arm and pull him out of harm's way. As the coach whirled onto the main thoroughfare, the general shouted epithets of a decidedly obscene nature.

"General, please keep your voice down. You have been thrown out of this place, this very night, and I do not wish to be found here with you," growled Mendoza.

The general seemed to start, as if he had forgotten where he was and why he was there. Taking a deep breath, he began to explain the reason for his summons to Mendoza,

"I forget myself. You are right, Señor Mendoza. Now, for the explanations. Tonight, at this very dance, I met a young woman " he began.

"You call me over here to talk about one of your women? General De Almeida, have you taken leave of your senses? We are engaged in a most secret endeavor and should not be seen together under any circumstances. I shall now go back to the shipyard," Mendoza interrupted him, rather huffily.

"No, no, no, Señor Mendoza. That is not what I called you for. Please, just stand still for a moment while I explain. It turned out that this young lady is really a Cherokee Indian who also is Jackson Halley's ward. He and his wife have educated her as a proper lady, and why they would want to do that is totally beyond me. Anyway, while I danced with her, I happened to notice a bracelet she wore around her satin glove. On that bracelet is the spitting image of the artifact I told you about days ago. I am sure that it was handmade, most likely by some Indian or other, but the point is that someone, somewhere, seems to know an awful lot of details about the artifact. No one has ever really seen it, but the image was exactly as it had been described to me," said the general.

"Wait a minute. You told me that you had the artifact in your possession. Why would you care about how it had been described? You supposedly have the real thing. Is that not so, General?" objected Mendoza, as his eyes turned to black agates.

The general realized he had made a grave error in implying he had not actually seen it.

"Uh, no, Senor Mendoza, I do have it. I am talking about the way it had been described to me before I found it. It has occurred to me that this Indian squaw knows something about it. She may even know that I have it, or there could even be two such gems. At any rate, we can't afford to flaunt the knowledge of this great thing. Would we not want to keep prying eyes away from our agreement, eh?" he countered, making it up as he went.

"That had better be the case, Your Excellency, for if I find out you have lied to me, our partnership may come to an untimely end," warned Mendoza, with a menacing glare.

"Yes, yes, yes, what I have told you is the truth, Mendoza. Now I need your help. The young girl is inside, dancing, and I wish to grab her and cart her off with me to Mexico, and while we are on our trip, I can thoroughly question all she knows about the Golden Serpent artifact. She has not met Juan, so I can send him inside to ask for her to come to the back. He can say that some other Indian wishes to speak with her. When she comes out of the door, we can grab her, gag her mouth and throw her into my own carriage, which is waiting in the first stall of the mews," said the general.

Mendoza was thoughtful for a moment, but he soon nodded his head. While they were giving instructions for Juan to carry out the first part of the plan, however, another clamorous sound came from the back of the building: this time it was loud voices that split the night. Mendoza took a peek around the corner to see what it all was about; after a few minutes, he drew back into the safety of the dark side of the building, an odd smile on his face.

"What is it, Mendoza? What is happening? Why are you smiling?" snarled the general, fully agitated by now.

"It is too late, my dear General. Your bird has flown. Someone else has beaten you to her. That black carriage that flew by and almost cost you your life, was driven by the kidnapper of the young lady you yourself wished to kidnap. It is amusing, do you not think?" explained Mendoza.

He peeked around the corner again, signaling for quiet while he listened to the discussion going on at the back of the building, then he quickly withdrew.

"General, I believe, if you do not want to be discovered here, we must leave this place, right away. A man named Isaiah and an oddly familiar dog are coming this way, presumably trying to track the young lady and her abductor," he quickly reported.

The three hurried out to the street, crossing it in time to turn and watch Isaiah turn right instead of crossing. The general breathed a sigh of relief.

"Thank you, Señor Mendoza. That is the man who swore to kill me if he saw me in this city after tonight. Now we shall never know anything about this girl, even if I feel it is important. I guess we will have to leave this town and hope this does not blow up in our faces," he grumbled in a despondent tone.

Juan stood silently by and listened carefully. He often did that. It helped him to learn things that could be useful to him later, maybe even help him keep his well-paying job.

Mendoza pondered for a few moments, then nodded his head in agreement.

"Your Excellency, might I make a suggestion that would serve us both? This Isaiah and the young lady's adoptive family have never met me. So, I will stay a couple more days here in Boston to see what transpires. If they rescue the girl, I possibly could find out what you want to know. You, on the other hand, should get on your boat and head for Mexico, as you planned. I will be your eyes and ears, sì?" he suggested.

The general had more than a few misgivings about this solution. On the one hand, he did not think Mendoza would find out that he did not have the artifact, which was the only thing against his staying here. On the other hand, the plus side was that he might really find out something important, and if the girl was rescued, he could still question her eventually anyway.

He finally nodded his agreement and they parted after the general told Mendoza all he knew about the girl and the people she was with. Mendoza was glad he had not bought his steamship ticket yet, since he had some suspicion that he was not being told everything by the general. He harbored no illusions about De Almeida's truthful-ness, for he knew him to be a self-serving scoundrel, but as long as he kept that in mind, he could outsmart him and still wind up with the prize in the end. Now all he needed to do was to keep an eye on the girl's hotel where the Halleys were staying. The matter of the kidnapping was either going to end with Sasa's death by the hand of the kidnapper, or with her being rescued, in which case he would need to embark on the new additional assignment of watching Sasa's every move, even to the point of following her to Indian Territory.

Mendoza watched as the general and Juan headed for the carriage hidden in the mews. He noticed Juan turn to stare back at him. Juan was an odd duck as far as Mendoza was concerned. Largely to be ignored, but not completely. With that, he headed back to the hotel to see if they still had his room

Chapter 21
Friends Are Where You Find Them

It was dark, so dark, where the man had left her. Dark and cold, the room smelled like mold and felt moist. The air did not move, at least she could not feel it move on her face, and it was too dark to see anything. She was tied to a chair, with her arms attached to each side rung. Each foot was tied to each front chair leg, but she did not know when it had happened. Her head ached, so she assumed that she had been hit there to keep her quiet. The last thing she remembered was having something thrown over her head, a brief struggle and then darkness. When she awoke, it was still like being asleep, because darkness closed in around her and there was absolutely nothing that gave off any sort of faint light. Even a lighting bug would have been welcome.

Even though she did not remember much of the savage hands that had grabbed her, she was not as frightened as she thought she should be. Sitting there in the dark, she had time to examine her own mind, her deepest feelings and thoughts. There was naught else to do, other than sleep. Somehow she knew her life was about to change.

It was one of those turning moments her dear mother used to speak of. She could almost hear her mother say, "My daughter, there will come a time, maybe one or maybe many, that your life will change direction. One moment you are sure you know what is going to happen next, and the next moment something happens that you cannot control, that changes even your own thoughts about life." At the time, Sasa had no idea what her mother had meant; she had only been nine summers old. It was a bit funny how this was coming back to her mind now. Why was she thinking in these positive terms when her life could be just about to end? Why did she not feel the urgency and desperation any captive would feel at this moment? It made her head hurt to think in circles.

The paradox was, if she was totally calm and unafraid, why were there streaks of water leaking from her eyes and running down her face? Sasa thought about that. Wasn't it possible that her body had a different reaction to things than her mind? That had to be the case. Regardless of her situation now, she willed her eyes to dry. She shook her head and whipped her face on the coat she had been abducted in, that still hung on her shoulders. It looked expensive. It was really too bad that some woman at the Ball had lost her coat. Then, as she pondered how ludicrous it was to worry about the woman's lost coat while she sat there, not knowing if she would live or die that day, she suddenly laughed. Her thoughts then strayed to the old Choctaw man who had given her the bracelet. Now, that was a true puzzle. The first question she asked herself was: Why did the old man say he had made it especially for her? She did not know him, and had never met him before going down into Choctaw country to help with someone's legal papers. Then again, why did that Mexican general want to know so much about the bracelet? Maybe it was he who had abducted her from the ball. He was such a bold man, she supposed he was arrogant enough to do it. The odd thing was, even when she danced with the general, she still had had that feeling that someone was staring at her from behind. Was it the general, or someone else who so roughly had grabbed her and consigned her to the chair she now struggled to untie herself from?

Another thought burst into her head. She thought of Wheezer. With this thought, she felt urgency, but not hers. She realized she was feeling *his* urgency. They were so in tune with one another, she could almost feel his tortured worry.

Soon, her body forced her to remember that she had needs that had to be answered. She needed to relieve herself, but had no idea if her abductor would provide this basic necessity, nor how long she had been in that damp dark room. Her fingers could feel her dress draped over the chair seat, which told her she still wore her ball gown. The right glove was still on, and it felt like so was the bracelet on her wrist over the glove, but her left glove was gone. Now she remembered pulling it off quickly, and dropping it as she was being dragged out of the building. In that fleeting moment, she had wanted to give Jackson–and possibly Wheezer–something that told them she had not left of her own free will. She did not know how far her abductor had driven, so the glove may not be of much help at all.

She had been musing on these things when she began to hear faint noises. She finally recognized the sound of footsteps. Suddenly, a door was thrown open and a bright, blinding light kept her from seeing much at all. She was able to see that the light was coming from the top of a stairwell, whose steps were old and wooden, and she finally realized she was in a basement. She had never been in an actual basement before, only a root cellar her family kept at home in Georgia. The realization did not alarm her. In fact, she felt curious about how it had been made.

A man began coming down the wooden steps. He did not walk with a cane, so he must not be old. She could only see his silhouette because of the bright light behind him. When he stepped off of the last step, she looked at the floor and saw he wore a good pair of leather, dress shoes.

The man cleared his throat. "Miss Halley, today is a day of retribution. You are going to pay with your own life for the life you took from me," he said.

Sasa was astonished. This was impossible.

"I have taken no life, sir. What on earth are you talking about? I have never taken the life of anything other than an animal for food," she replied.

"Ah, you would say that, wouldn't you? But I have the proof. I have the testimony of others that tells me of your guilt. You are guilty of killing my father, and I will have justice. Soon. Very soon, Miss Jezebel," countered the man.

Sasa thought she detected a familiar tone in his voice. He had a definite southern drawl. Did she know this person?

"Sir, I still have no idea what you are talking about. What man, who was he? If I am guilty of murder, sir, then why have I not been arrested for a crime?" she asked, becoming agitated.

"I asked the same question myself. I refuse to talk about that now. I have already passed judgment. You are guilty, and you will pay," he said.

"All right, I see you have made yourself, judge and jury. If you think me such a criminal, why do you not take me to the local constable? Surely, they will want a trial to hear what the evidence may be," argued Sasa.

"NO!" the man yelled. "They are all Yankee liars. They have already told me a bunch of lies, which I refuse to believe. You are the one who is guilty. You killed my father."

Sasa was incredulous now.

"I most certainly have never killed a man, ever. Who was your father and why do you refuse to discuss this like a civilized person?" she exclaimed.

"Ha, ha, that is a laugh. Civilized. You have no right to even say the word. You are just a dirty Indian, and you have no idea what civilized means," he said.

Sasa stopped for a moment. This conversation was degrading quickly, and she needed something to keep him talking. First, though, she needed to take care of her bodily needs, then she could better face this new threat.

"Sir, before you go to the trouble of killing me, would you please allow me to relieve myself? Regardless of your opinion, I am an educated lady and I at least expect a modicum of allowance," she said calmly.

She could see that had startled him a bit. It had interrupted his tirade, and he now searched for a way to get it back. But it was no use. She had asked him a civilized question, asking for something no gentleman could refuse, but he decided he would not give her the luxury of the inside bathroom.

"I will untie you, but don't think you can escape. There is no way out of here except those stairs, and I certainly won't let you pass. There is a bucket over there, in the corner, with a pitcher of water close by. I will be back soon, so get it done quickly," he said. Then, "You will rue the day you slaughtered a wonderful man like Colonel Jeffries, my father," then he left her with a small lantern with only a bit of candle. That would not last long at all. At least now she knew who he was. Even so, she could not fathom why this man thought she had been responsible for his father's death.

Isaiah and Wheezer had stopped at the street in front of the great house where the ball had been held. The dancing was continuing and that was as it should be. It wouldn't help to have a group of hysterical people running around Boston to try and find the kidnapper. For this, Wheezer and Isaiah needed quiet and time to sniff the ground, smell the air and think clear thoughts. Time was of the essence. Wheezer was sniffing furiously, but Isaiah had no clues that he could count on. It was dark and difficult to see the ground clearly enough to track. And what was he looking for anyway? This was not like tracking in the mountains. He would have to rely on Wheezer.

Isaiah heard footsteps running up behind him. With a cat's quick reaction, he pulled a revolver from his belt, just under his dress coat, and whirled around to meet the danger, but it turned out to be Jackson.

"Did you forget somethin', Jackson, my boy?" said Isaiah, as he put his revolver discretely away.

"Anna and I decided that it would be better for me to help in the search. I know Wheezer pretty well, I know his signals. It can only help you, so Anna is calling her carriage, and is going to wait at the Hotel. There are questions to be asked there as well, like how Wheezer got out. She wanted to come also, but she can't very well trudge through Boston streets in her ball gown, can she?" explained an out of breath Jackson.

"Well, Jackson, I'm thinkin' this person had to be someone who knows Boston, maybe lives here, an' knew a quick way to get shut of any followers. Our little ole' ace in the hole is Wheezer here. I think he has found some scent now. Not sure what to expect of this here dog, never have seen one like him afore, but I believe he is a mighty smart un, that's a darn sight better than nothin' atall," said Isaiah.

Jackson watched Wheezer, nose to the grimy street, searching for a clue. Then looked in the opposite direction and noticed some-thing sparkling in the lamplight of the streetlamps lining the street. He trotted over to pick it up and knew immediately that it belonged to Sasa. Isaiah and Wheezer rushed to Jackson. Wheezer took a whiff and automatically his stubby tail went up along with his perky ears.

"Isaiah, this is Sasa's shoe clip. They were a gift from Anna last year. This was her first opportunity to wear them. She must have kicked her feet and one fell off," explained Jackson.

Wheezer sniffed, again, and wagged his tail, then began to find scent further up, and when he began trotting in that direction the men took off after Wheezer. At least they had a start.

Thank goodness one of the men had allowed Jackson to borrow his small pistol. At least he had something, if it was needed.

"Hope you can keep up my boy, I don't want to have to carry you, no how," teased Isaiah.

Jackson only smiled and kept up just fine, as the three of them ran into the night.

Sasa could not hear any voices above her, nor could she smell anything significant. After she took care of her ablutions, she sat back in her chair, avoiding the dirty floor, and began to think back to the terrible night when Colonel Jeffries surprised her and her new found friends, Anna and Jackson, at the temporary camp in Indian Territory. That was the camp where both her mother and father had died, losses followed by the mysterious death of her five year old little brother, Usti Yansa, or Little Buffalo. It was a painful memory.

That was a night to remember, and she had believed she would never have to think about it again. But here she was, being forced to dredge up all the old hurts, the terrible rage against the white men who had orchestrated her little brother's cruel death. Allan Jeffries had it all wrong, however. She had not killed his father, but she had no idea how she would convince him of it. He was not really a bad sort, just misinformed and hurt. Sasa had no idea who had told him lies, because there had been no one else there to witness his father's demise besides herself, Jackson, Anna, David and Archibald Flint, Jackson good friends, and Wheezer. But, how could she go about proving it to a man who wanted to believe her a villain?

The basement door swung open again with a loud bang against the wall, knocking plaster off where the knob had hit it and Allan stormed down the steps. Obviously, he had worked himself up to doing something he was not used to doing.

Finally he was at the last step. Allan Jeffries held a revolver out away from his body. It occurred to Sasa that this man was unused to using a gun. No one who used a gun on a regular basis would hold it that way, because the kickback from the black powder load in the barrel would be fierce. It could whip back and he could end up braining himself, if he were not careful. Just then, that knowledge and observation gave Sasa an idea.

"Well, have you had time to talk to whatever god you pray to? What is it? The Sun god? The Moon? What?" said Allan, already agitated.

"Actually Allan, the Cherokee have been mostly Christians for many decades. We are not the wild Indians of the plains. But no, I did not pray. I was more interested in trying to figure out who told you all those lies and why," said Sasa.

"Stop! Don't say my name. You have not the right, murderer," yelled Allan.

He took a few steps closer. Sasa stood slowly, stretching her legs and yawning, before bending down to seemingly straighten her skirt. She demurely turned away from Allan, as a Lady would do to keep from showing her ankle. Then, like a flash of light, she whipped her body upward, her arm also streaking upward, knocking the gun from Allan's hand. Her own hand was not empty. In it she had her trusty Green Mountain knife which had served her so well in the past, sharpened and ready for any needed task. Stunned and confused, Allan was not quick enough to stop Sasa from grabbing his shirt collar from behind and placing the sharp knife edge just under his chin. He was paralyzed by fear, for it was obvious he had not been trained in any type of self-defense.

Sasa, whispered in his ear, deadly serious.

"Sit yourself down, Allan. You aren't going to like this much," she said menacingly.

"What...what are you goin' to do," he sobbed. "See, I said from the start you were a murderer. Now you are going to finish the job you started with my poor father." Looking as if she was not listening, Sasa tied his hands in the exact way he had tied hers. Then his feet. Next she searched the basement's dark recesses for another wooden chair. Finally, she found one that was barely serviceable, but it was all there was available. It would have to do.

"What do you need that for? Why don't you just stab me and get it over with," he blubbered.

Sasa's scalp began to tingle, her face grew hot with intense emotion. How could this man spout these filthy lies? She had lost so much, and yet she was still trying to understand. Playing on his fear, Sasa only looked into his eyes with serious intent. It unnerved him so much he almost swooned, until she threw some cold water in his face.

"Why do you hesitate? Strike quickly; kill me as you did my father!" he screamed.

Instead, she positioned the chair just in front of him and quietly sat. Without worrying about showing her ankle, she replaced her knife back in its sheath tied to the outside of her leg. She never went anywhere without it, even a grand ball.

"Now, Allan, we are going to go over the events of that spring of 1839. I was there, you know that, but whoever told you those things, lied to you. I know everyone who witnessed your father's death, and they are all part of my family, or close friends. Just what did this person tell you? How did this person say your father died?" asked Sasa.

"He...uh, said you walked up to him, stabbed him, then cut his body up and threw it away. He said that is why there was nothing to bury. What did my father ever do to you?" he said, defeated.

"All right, I will take your last question first. What did he do to me? Let's start with why he was in Indian Territory. Allan, what business was your father in, where did he get the money to buy this grand house in Boston?" asked Sasa.

"Well, his business was always out of town. He said he was a sort of buyer and seller—a merchant—but I never knew of what, and I never have seen anybody who worked with him, so I am not really sure. After he died, the money stopped coming to the bank. Now the house will have to be sold to pay for our debts and there will be nothing left for me. I will be as poor as the Irish immigrants pouring into our harbor. All I know is the money dried up," a resentful Allan murmured.

"Allan, I know what business your father was in and where he got the money for this grand house. Your father was part of a conspiracy to skim the money the government paid the Indian Agents in Indian Territory for the purpose of purchasing food for the Indians they forced into leaving their homes, all they owned, their tools, land, livestock, keepsakes, you name it, behind them. When we arrived in Indian Territory, we had nothing but the clothes on our backs. Every family had someone die on the Trail Where They Cried. I lost both my father and mother. Our nation alone lost over four thousand people on that trip, some without shoes, walking on snow and ice. No blankets, no medicine, and most of the time we were not given even the time to bury our dead.

"Our nation signed a treaty with the United States govern-ment that they would provide food allotments in Indian Territory, until we were established with a place to live, fields plowed, churches and schools set up. Can you imagine it, Allan? Then try to imagine being there with nothing and getting your package of food, and it is full of worms, the meat spoiled and diseased. None of it edible, none of it nourishing," Sasa explained.

"Day after day, week after week we would ask our agent, and he would give us no answers as to why we were not getting the right food. Did you know that the Indian Agent of our temporary camp was Anna's father? Mr. Edwards was in 'business' with your father, secretly. I am sure they are not the only ones, because it is still happening. That first year the Cherokee lost another one thousand people to starvation. Not sickness, not warfare. We starved so that your father could buy you this big grand house, because his business was stealing the money from the food allotments that were supposed to keep the Indian tribes in Indian Territory alive," said Sasa.

Allan looked ashen, and for a moment he was unable to speak.

"No, that can't be. That is too monstrous to be the works of my father. He was not like that," he finally replied.

"Yes, he was that man. Let me tell you what else your father did, and then how he really died. Do you remember meeting Jackson Halley, my guardian? At the time, I had not met him yet. His father had been appointed by the U. S. War Department to hold the money for those food shipments in escrow until the time it would be paid to the various suppliers of food. Some suppliers are honest, but some were part of the conspiracy as well. They were paid for good food, but delivered bad rations and split the money with your father and Agent Edwards. Mr. Andrew Halley, Jackson's father, found a discrepancy, however, and went to check up on one of the suppliers at a warehouse in St. Louis, where your father gunned him down and left him for dead, but not before Mr. Halley shot your father in the foot with a small pistol. Mr. Halley almost died," said Sasa.

Allan, sat stunned. Could this have been his father? Was that where the money had been coming from? Was that why he couldn't find any record of what his father's business really was? Allan could not speak, and he could barely breathe while staring in disbelief at Sasa, who took it as a gesture for her to continue.

"Mr. Halley was taken to a St. Louis doctor who worked on him for days, but when he awoke, he remembered something your father had said before leaving the warehouse. He had said he was headed for Indian Territory to kill Jackson Halley, his son.

"It was found out that he had acquired the help of a country doctor and some clothes and boots as he traveled. He stuck his bloody foot into a boot, then ignored it while riding west through Missouri, then south through Kansas. That whole time, he never thought to check his foot, change the bandage, or give it a bath. As he traveled, he got sick from the blood poisoning in his foot and by the time he arrived in our camp, the night he died, he was out of his head and he stunk to high heaven because his foot and leg were full of gangrene. He was so intent on killing Jackson Halley that he had never thought to protect himself against anyone or anything that might have followed him.

"He caught us all that night, when Mr. Edwards had us at gunpoint to murder us all. Do you want to know how we found out that Mr. Edwards and someone else were stealing from us?" Sasa asked, then she went on without waiting for an answer.

"It all started when my little brother died a strange death. With Wheezer's and Jackson's help, we found out that your father and Mr. Edwards had murdered my little brother, because he had seen them collecting their cut of the money. He was only five, and he did not speak English. I am sure he had no idea what he was seeing, but their own guilt and greed led them to kill an innocent Indian boy. Of course, all of the Indians could die as far as they were concerned. That may have been the plan all along, and still may be." Now her voice was emotionally charged, too.

"But, my father could not stand there and murder a child in cold blood," argued Allan.

"No, you are right. He killed him by proxy. Mr. Edwards and your father, together soaked a wooden toy with rat poison and gave it to him, then had someone tell him that it had magical powers and if he licked it often, his wish would come true. The more he licked it, the closer to death he came. In fact, we have an eye witness to the deed. Our house manager, and his former housekeeper, saw him do it. They had no idea she had been watching, and listening to their plan," she said.

"But, how did my father die? I don't understand," Allan whined, while squirming in his seat, not to free himself, but with feelings of horror and disbelief.

"He had always planned on killing Mr. Edwards. He shot him first, while we just stood there, then he held the gun on us all; it was at that moment that Wheezer, my dog, began to bark at something in the darkness. The next thing we knew, a pack of wolves crept up behind your father, lured by the smell of his rotting flesh, dragged him into the darkness and then tore him to pieces. That is the real reason why there was nothing to bury. And the man who told you he had been there, was not. However, I would bet you anything that he was an associate of your father's 'business', and saw no reason to tell you the truth," finished Sasa.

Allan sat with his head down, thinking. His situation grew hellish in his mind as he saw for the first time what and who his father had been. He mindlessly dug his fingers into his palms, bringing blood that quickly dripped to the cold floor. Tears and sweat commingled as they ran down his face. As the pictures Sasa had painted for him with her words formed in his mind, he could find no way to reject them. He had refused for so long the rumors that ran rampant around town and that had made him a reluctant guest at parties and picnics. The worst, though, was the fact that he had deluded himself. All the while, real people suffered, suffered unto death, while he sat in his father's fine house in Boston. Then another terrible thought choked him.

"If this is true, I am not only poor, but socially ruined. How can I hold my head up in this town after finding out what my own father did?" he wept.

Sasa gazed at the sorrowful young man and felt deep pity for his disillusionment.

"Give me a little bit. I'll think on it. I daresay, some in this town, in this country, would applaud him and rail at his opposers for stopping him before he completed his task. Meanwhile, if I untie you, are you going to try and kill me again? If so, let me get my knife out and we can see what happens," she replied.

Allan bowed his head, ashamed of himself. Tears ran afresh down his handsome face, his blue eyes so full of them the color could barely be seen. Slowly he nodded his head, but just the same, Sasa remained on her guard.

Wheezer surged ahead, finally scenting something stronger than just the smell of the carriage wheels. Soon, they turned down a tree lined lane, that was made all the darker for the abundance of tall oaks on either side. The entrance to a great house was difficult to make out, totally dark except for some faint light coming from some inner room, but Wheezer seemed to know just where to go.

As they ran past the front door and circled around the side to the back, Jackson was wondering if they had made a terrible mistake, but Isaiah had no such doubts and continued on where Wheezer led. By and by, they arrived at the scullery door and discovered it standing open. They could plainly see where the light was coming from and indeed the room was practically ablaze with it.

With each step closer, Wheezer's fur rose a little further on his back until a ridge of fur was standing straight up when they came to the back door. Without stopping, Wheezer rushed into the house, finding the door to the basement open and a well of darkness beyond the steps. Isaiah noticed the glint of Wheezer's white canines, now more exposed. Wheezer had pulled his upper lip up and away from his teeth. This trait of the Jack Russell Terrier, he would learn later, gave them the ability to open their mouths much wider than most breeds of dog.

Sasa's scent was too strong for Wheezer to stop, so he bounded down the steps, not bothering to look for places to plant his paw. Whatever his paw touched, he used it to propel himself forward and straight into Sasa's arms. She had just finished untying Allan's feet.

The reunion of Wheezer and Sasa was intense. Allan had not moved while Sasa calmed her dog, whispering into his ear and allowing him to clean her face. Then, when he began to rise from the chair, a huge human paw of a hand planted on his chest and pushed him back into his seat.

Sasa, placed her hand on Isaiah's sleeve, gazing seriously into his eyes. She had only known Isaiah for a short time that very night, but her eyes spoke volumes to him. He released the pressure he held on Allan's chest and unclenched the other hand's fist, which had been prepared for a thundering blow to Allan's jaw.

"I am so happy to see you all, but Isaiah, this has just been a big misunderstanding. Now that I understand it, I think it is time for us to go back to the hotel and talk this over. Allan, I wish you to accompany us so that you can add any information that I lack. I may have a solution to this dilemma, but first I think that Anna will be worried out of her mind," she said.

Jackson and Isaiah both looked dubious, but acquiesced anyway. This story ought to be good. Sasa finally took the time to talk to Wheezer.

"Hello, my Black White Whiskers. You always come in the nick of time, don't you? As always, I owe you my life, dear Black White Whiskers. I love you. Wado," whispered Sasa into Wheezer's ear, for that name was a secret special name between them.

Wheezer, gazed into her eyes. The love that flowed between them was palpable, yet there were no more words uttered. Wheezer clamored up on Sasa's lap, licking her face thoroughly, then he turned and barked several times at Allan, as if to bawl him out.

"Yes, I know, Wheezer. I am sorry. I will not do it again. Please forgive me?" Allan told him directly.

Sasa watched this exchange with mild surprise and pleasure. Wheezer, for his part, was not sure if Allan could be trusted yet. He would be watched first before Wheezer would give his approval.

As they exited the house, Jackson noticed that Allan had left the door open.

"Don't you want to close and lock your door, Allan?" he asked.

"Why? This house was bought with blood money. I want nothing to do with it anymore. It can burn down, for all I care," Allan replied sincerely.

The four walked to the end of the lane, hailed a carriage and proceeded to the hotel for a full night of explanations. It was surely going to be interesting.

George Lowrey

Chapter 22
Genius or Madness?

The Assistant Chief of the Cherokees, George Lowrey, sat in his chair, still as a mouse. Had he heard what he thought he heard Chief John Ross say? How could this be? Had John lost his own mind after struggling to keep their nation together against all odds? No, he did not believe John to be delusional, but maybe he was being foolhardy or was suffering from impossible optimism. The plan that Chief Ross had just laid out to him was fantasy, pure, unadulterated fantasy.

"John, I don't know what to say to that. It is unbelievable, really. How were you able to come up with such a plan when it has never been done before, ever?" he asked, incredulous.

"It was simple, really. You have to admit, everything else we discussed had little to no chance of working. The problem is, we can't attack the Mexican spies and provocateurs, because we don't know who they are, or what they are planning next. We are blind to their movements and only know where they have been after a raid happens. By then, they are long gone," explained an excited Chief Ross.

"What about rounding up the Kickapoo and Kiowa, or lodging a complaint with the Indian Agent? We could even go so far as to ask the Army to do something?" suggested George.

Chief Ross bowed his head, then shook it slowly.

"No, that wouldn't work. We dare not interfere with the Kiowa or the Kickapoo. They are angry at Texans, and they think this is a way to get back at them. It is too difficult to explain what is really happening to them, and even if we could, they are not likely to care what happens to the tribes here in Indian Territory. It is enough that we will invite them to attend.

"As for your other suggestion, think George, think. We certainly don't want to invite the Army to do anything more than what they are doing now. You know how Washington City can use any foothold they can get to pry concessions from us. I want the Army as far away from us as possible. It is enough that they have a fort at Fort Gibson. As for the Indian Agents, there is only one that I will invite to attend my planned 'Gathering of Nations'. I still don't trust anyone who works for the government of Washington City. Their allegiance is to them at all times, not to us.

"Remember that there are several agents still involved in skimming off the money from the food allotments. I heard that the Osage are in a bad way. They have had many deaths from starvation. They have not taken to farming very well, so they have not been able to rely on their own crops as we did after that first year here when we lost over a thousand of our people. However, I understand that some of them have become good ranchers and are now raising cattle. And the Choctaw are steadily losing their people to starvation, year after year. I don't know if their agent is involved, but they are clearly not getting good food. That is a different problem, though. We will have to set aside these other things until after we have our gathering," said Chief Ross.

"Yes, I suppose we can't do too many things at one time. So tell me, why you think that inviting all the different tribes within a few days travel to come to this big gathering would work, when no one has ever done it before?" asked George.

"The very fact that it is new and unique, never been done before, will aid in its success. Don't you see? If we send runners out in all directions with our invitations to come to a big gathering of nations, where peace will reign while we treatise for a month or more, and if we send the white wampum beads as proof of our good intentions, the tribes will clamor to select their own delegates to accept the invitation, out of sheer curiosity, if for no other reason," replied Chief Ross.

"Well, when you say it like that, it sounds doable, but I still worry that your own tribe will reject your idea. What is to keep the likes of Stand Watie from trying to sabotage your plans?" objected George.

"I am confident that Stand will not be that stupid. He stands to be able to speak at this gathering, appear to be the big man. He won't pass up this opportunity to show his political strength when he finds out that Agent Pierce Butler will be coming. Stand has always wanted that agent on his side. No, I think we don't have to worry about him," reasoned Chief Ross.

"Aren't you worried about the Army showing up to this?" asked George.

"Yes, at first I was, George. But, once I thought about it, they will be confused and lost if they do come. Think about it. Each tribe that speaks a different language will have to be translated into several other languages. The Army Officers as well as Agent Butler will not be able to keep up with all that is said. As soon as we have enough translators in as many of the languages as possible, we will be able to get our message across to those whom we want to hear it. It probably won't be easy, but it is our best shot," said Chief Ross.

"But, what about the plains tribes you mentioned. Why on earth are you going to involve non-Indian Territory tribes in this venture, eh?" insisted George.

"George, it only helps us to have them here. We are trying to stop the Mexican government from hiring other Indians to raid within Indian Territory. If we use the white wampum beads and each tribe pledges upon those beads, there will be no way for Mexico to get their foot in again. As far as I can think, this is our only option to stop the spies and Mexican agents from using Indian Territory to achieve their own plans for Texas. Remember, Texas is what the Mexicans want, not our land. However, they don't care about any of our tribes. If we don't stop them, then we will be killing ourselves," explained the chief.

George paced back and forth, looking pensive still. Thoughts were racing through his head so fast, he could hardly put words to them. Finally, he stopped in the middle of the chief's office.

"Chief Ross, what about the great cultural differences between the tribes from the east, who have become mostly civilized with white ways, and the plains tribes who are still debating how many white men there are? What I mean to say is, the plains tribes do not have the experience with what we face east of us. Some in the north, like the Sioux, have steadfastly refused to believe any reports on the cities and populations of the white man. I know a Sergeant in the Army Dragoons who told me that some of those tribes are in such a remote area that they think white men don't have white women or children since they have never seen any yet. There are bound to be problems along those lines. How do you propose to counter them?" he queried, and allowed himself a sigh of relief, feeling he had stated it well.

The chief thought the question an extremely intelligent one, and wondered why he had not thought of it. Sitting at his worn desk, he steepled his hands together while he pondered on it.

"You know, George, I think we must be very diplomatic in that direction. We need to keep this council of chiefs discussing the problems at hand. If we venture beyond that, we stand to get into an argument we can't win, because they will not believe how things really stand until they actually see them with their own eyes. I don't know when that will be, but I know it is not going to be here at our meeting. We must keep them on the subject at all times. They will understand what the wampum is. It is universally used for all sorts of important things, especially sealing agreements," he finally replied.

"I thank the Creator that we were able to bring the sacred wampum with us from our homeland, plus more of the beads if we need them. And it looks like we will need more. What do you propose to do, Chief?" said George

John Ross walked over to a place behind his desk, which concealed a special metal lined cubbyhole that only the chief and his assistant knew how to open. Within its dark recesses were many of the Cherokee Tribe's important legal documents, several sacred artifacts and the wampum belts, including a large sack of the white and also black wampum beads, made from certain shells from the eastern coastal regions. It was not known just how old the oldest of the belts was, but they were all precious to the Cherokees.

Wampum had a long and varied history in the Americas, from being used to seal a treaty, to currency for trade items. When the English came and ran out of coin, they would accept Wampum from the Cherokees and other tribes. What Chief Ross needed them for now was to cement some very important agreements between many tribes. A truly monumental effort.

The chief took the belts out gingerly, then the canvas bag of loose beads. George walked over to look inside. He puzzled a moment or two.

"Will this be enough, Chief?" he then asked.

"Let us hope so. This is one of the things that I have been thinking about. No nation has ever had such a meeting as we plan, so we must be ready with enough wampum belts for each chief who agrees to abide by the peace agreement. The ones we have already made will not be enough for what we have planned. In the past, we used the best beaders among our older women to make more belts. Usually we chose them from the women's societies. We knew that they would treat this duty with the proper reverence. However, after the forced march, we are left with few old ones, whether they are good beaders or not. Sadly, those societies have not had a chance to completely recover from losing so many to death on the march and then death in the camps from starvation, so we will have to choose from all the women, not respecting their age, to make more of the wampum. Who do we have near Tahlequah that might remember the traditional way to make it? I don't want to send the wampum too far from us for safety's sake," Ross answered.

"I can only think of one who is fairly close, but she is very old indeed. I'd bet she could supervise the younger ones, and that would give the young ones a chance to have the tradition passed down to them, so the chain won't be broken. The woman I am thinking of is Poison Woman… you know, the one who is the medicine maker and teaches our girls about herbs. Or she used to. She and her brother Medicine Man, have been keeping quiet since that terrible incident at Fort Smith, in '40. In fact, I remember that year she helped a Lakota man to learn our language and all about what had happened to the tribes east of the Mississippi. I heard he went home to see if he could warn his people about what was coming. I sure hope they listened.

"Anyway, she has always been a good beader, and she can teach the younger ones, I am sure, if we ask her in the right way. She has a young friend also who does some beading. Not sure where she is at the moment, but maybe Poison Woman would like to have her help with the other women we send to her. Her name is Sasa Halley. She became the ward of our friend Jackson Halley, so that he could help to give her a good education," said George.

On hearing Sasa's name, Chief Ross's face brightened. He smiled at George and heaved a big sigh.

"That was her name. Do you know I have been wracking my brain to remember that girl's name for days now? Yes, I know all about that excellent education. Did you know that she was taught right there on Jackson Halley's ranch? Ole Andrew Halley, Jackson's father who helped our nation back in Georgia so many times, arranged for a law professor to spend several years on the ranch, giving that girl an education that has never been had by any woman, anywhere. Not even a white woman has had an education like that. Last time I talked with Nathan Boone, he said that she would have the qualifications to be a lawyer, if such a thing were permitted. Andrew told the professor that at the end he had to give her the same kind of test he would give his male law students, to pass the bar examination. Nathan said that the professor, who was none too happy to be pulled away from his comfy university, had to stay until that girl knew enough to pass the bar with honors.

"Nathan said that she surprised them all. She finished in half the time, and finished with marks as good as his best students back east. She must be some woman, George. I barely remember her as a little skinny kid running around her father's farm in Georgia. Boy, does that make me feel old.

"I was trying to remember her name so that I could send her an invitation to come and help with the peace council," concluded the chief.

George raised his eyebrows high and began to shake his head from side to side.

"You know, Chief, some who have converted to more white ways than Cherokee, will not be happy to see a woman in such an important position at a peace council," said George.

"I thought of that too, and I think I can keep her in an advisory capacity. I know that she learned some of the Lakota language from that young Lakota that year. She may even know some other languages, but mainly, I am going to want her to help me keep the U.S. Government in the dark as to what this meeting is all about. If they get involved other than being invited as a guest, they will try to use it as their own springboard to harangue the plains tribes, and I won't have it. We are in just as much danger from the white government as we are from the Mexican one.

"And there is another thing she can do that a man cannot. Some of the tribes we will invite have never given their women important places in their councils as we have, so a woman standing around the grounds will be practically invisible. The men will feel free to talk amongst themselves without knowing that a very smart young lady is soaking it all in. It would be our best tool to keep any bad incidents from happening to ruin this council. At all costs, George, we must succeed.

"Yes, have Poison Woman choose several girls to do the wampum beading and see if she can tell you where Sasa is at the moment. What I last heard is that they all took a trip to Boston, at least that was the rumor. I am not sure they are back. If they are not back yet, tell Poison Woman to let Sasa know Chief Ross would like to have a meeting with her at her earliest convenience.

"Now, we need to sit down here with the list of the invitees. Figure out who the runners will be to take the invitations and set a date for the meeting. There are lots of things to figure out, like how long it will last, how many should be brought in their delegations, and we will also have to think about feeding that many, maybe hundreds. We will need to figure out how many tribes to invite first, so we know how many wampum belts the women must make.

"My servants at the house will bring us dinner, so if you have a mind to, pull off that coat and let's get started. Now the first tribe to invite, I think would be..."

They worked for many hours that night and for a few more nights to come. Every detail had to be hammered out, every possible misstep must have a contingency plan. Plus, they had to decide on the protocol for the council. The rules for everyone's conduct, no matter who they were, would need to be made plain to the attendees. So much could go wrong with something this big. Sometimes, Chief Ross wondered if he could pull it off, but, there was no other avenue to fix this problem. This was it, and he was the man to implement it, and he prayed the Creator would bless his efforts.

Chapter 23
Age With Wisdom

The spring days were getting warmer, the daylight stretching longer. It was the busy time of planting and readying the ground for each of the hearty crops they would harvest later in the fall. Poison Woman was not thinking of any of those things, however. She was long past having the energy to help in the fields, and besides, she had no husband, only her brother who was a respected spiritual man. It was true that Medicine Man could be difficult at times, but he had stood by her for all of the terrible years of fighting with the whites, and he now saw to it that the various farms round about provided them with adequate food to add to her contribution of roots and greens, berries and nuts she gleaned from the land. She always made herself busy now, trying to pass on her knowledge to the young ones. Many in their tribe were gone and a huge gap in the handing down of tribal knowledge had to be breached, or it would be lost.

Just the week before, the Chief of the Cherokees himself had sent her a personal request to gather as many young women that would care to learn, and teach them the art of wampum belt making. He would provide the materials, if she would teach the women, or even the young girls that would be women soon. They could not afford to be picky with so few young people available. He had also added that she should not talk to outsiders—or gossip—about her assignment, adding that the reason for that would be made clear to her in due time. Well, she had no problem doing that, since she rarely talked to very many people anyway.

Today, she had summoned Martha, or Girl Who Counts The Stars, to see if she would like to help in the project. They also asked for Sasa, but she had not yet returned from her trip to Boston. Hopefully it would be soon, she was anxious to see the girl and looked on her as something like a granddaughter. When Sasa did return, she was to tell her of Chief Ross's request to come to Tahlequah for a special assignment. What an honor it was to be asked, and she was sure that Sasa was up to the task, whatever that task might be. Poison Woman knew it must be something very specific, if the Chief had to have a woman instead of one of his headmen carry the task out.

"You are daydreaming again, grandmother," said Martha.

"Oh, my girl, I do that a lot lately. I guess it is something that old people do. Let's get back to what we were discussing. I have asked you here to see if you would like to learn to make wampum belts that will be used for a special purpose. Don't ask me about it, I can't tell you. I only have a little time to teach it, plus I will have to have more helpers than just you. If you know of some dependable and good hearted girls who would like to learn, we will need them soon," said Poison Woman.

Martha's eyes gleamed like black agate as Poison Woman talked. She had languished on her farm for too long. After she kicked her no-good husband out, she went about her days in utter silence. There was no one to speak to, laugh with or even yell at. Now, she could look forward to something special and the company of Poison Woman on a daily basis, at least for a while.

"Why, yes, grandmother. I would be honored and I do know of a few I can ask, who did not die last winter during the starvation times. I will do this thing this afternoon and let you know in the morning," she answered, flushing from the excitement of the appointment.

"Well, granddaughter, you should probably be off at it now. Hopefully you will bring any who want to learn in the morning, bright and early. I don't have much time to teach it. Be sure that you only choose those with good hearts, no one selfish, none who might be practicing witchery, and none who play around with the white men at Fort Smith. Good hearts only, you understand?" repeated Poison Woman, with her gravelly voice.

"Yes, yes, I understand grandmother. I will be back tomorrow. I know just who to ask. Are you sure you can't tell me what this is for?" asked Martha.

"No! The Chief did not tell me, and anyway it is not for us to ask such questions. It is an honor just to learn the technique. I imagine we will learn what they are for by and by, eh? Now, off with you," Poison Woman ordered crisply.

She watched as Martha trotted down the road. The girl did not own a horse since that good for nothing man left, but she was young and fit. She would get by and prosper eventually. There was a need now for more children of the Cherokee. Some Cherokee man would see Martha, see her hard working body, and join with her to farm that land and make new Cherokee babies.

Medicine Man

Just then, Medicine Man strolled out onto the porch, scratch-ing his almost bare head and yawning after his morning nap.

"Gossiping again, I see. Well, I guess you have to do something to while the hours away," he commented.

"Yes, like you do by sleeping them away. Don't you worry about what I do with my time, you old Cherokee, I am doing some-thing honorable and important. I think one of the Birdsong brothers brought you some game; I did not see what, but it looked like rabbits, to be skinned and cleaned for our supper. Go do that, or go back and take your mid-morning nap now," she countered.

He yawned again, scratched his chest and went back to his robes inside the hastily built, wooden structure that served as their home now. He probably would not won-der about it until he saw the wampum beads in her lap. That would get his attention in a big way, for he knew that he would be required to pray over them and give prop-er thanks to the Creator. Maybe by then she would know more herself.

Poison Woman informed the runner who had come with the message from the chief that Sasa was not back yet, but that she would probably be the first to know when they were back, other than the people at the Halley ranch, of course. She decided that as soon as word of Sasa's re-turn came, she would ask one of the younger Cherokees to take her into Van Buren. She could not put something like this in a message for someone else's ears. It was ob-vious that if the chief refrained from telling someone like Poison Woman, then it was information not to be bandied about carelessly. Medicine Man may already know some-thing about this, since she remembered that he had at-tended a special meeting in Tahlequah a few weeks before.

He refused to tell her what that had been about, so she surmised this special assignment she was given must be connected to it in some way.

What puzzled her was the large amount of wampum bead belts she was required to make. She could not remember a time when so many were needed. Her own mother, who taught her the wampum belt making technique, had never mentioned the old chiefs needing more than four or five. Six belts would have raised the eyebrows of the women making them. In this case, Chief Ross asked for thirty. That was an unbelievable number of wampum belts to be needed at any one time. Even when they made peace with an enemy, they never required more than four to exchange between chiefs.

It did no good to sit and wonder, and it was not getting the work done. The messenger from the chief had brought a large sack of handmade wampum beads, from both white and black shells, sinew and needles, along with everything else required for her assignment. There were also red wampum beads, but they were not kept with the white so that the peace of the beads would not be tainted with war or disagreement. The first thing she would do, would be to check every bead for its fitness to be in an important symbol of peace. Medicine Man had been given a long plank table the year before, on which they ate their meals. She would have to use that for her work surface. To prevent the beads from falling through any gaps in the planks of the table, she would lay a piece of canvas or duck on top. That way they would not lose any of the precious beads. Each bead had been lovingly shaped.

The technique she used had been passed down to her from her own mother. She did not know if any of the other women had different ways, because she had never seen anyone else make wampum except her mother. She put her wide brimmed hat on as protection from the morning sun, grabbed a canvas bag she had kept coffee in and headed for the nearby creek. Once there she looked closely for a small inlet where sand, pulverized into tiny, shiny pieces, lay flat to the banks. She was careful not to pick up any small stones, only the fine sand. Once back at her table, she poured out a small portion of the sand in front of her and smoothed it level, about the size of a pie plate, then she laid the good wampum beads on the sand. There would be no way they would roll off of the table as long as they were safely in the sand, plus the sand helped to give the beads a bit of polished gleam.

Next she went to a small shelf in the corner of the small room. There she removed what looked like a four foot piece of rope. This was sinew, taken from a winter kill and allowed to dry. Now she took it out to the front yard where a large tree stump sat up and grabbing a hand sized stone she began to pound on the sinew until it began to separate into several lengths of strong fiber. This is what she would use to hold the wampum beads together.

Poison woman set to work, barely looking up while the sun took its trip across the sky. In the afternoon, Martha returned with no less than three Cherokee young women who seemed excited to be included.

"I thought I should come back today and make sure my selection was good. Do you approve of these young women, Poison Woman?" asked Martha, smiling.

Poison Woman nodded her head. She stopped worrying about why she was asked to help, and began to enjoy the company of the young women. The only thing lacking in this gathering was the smaller children and other elderly Cherokees, like herself, who were few in the Cherokee Nation these days. Most of the missing died during the forced march out of their homeland in 1838, but there were many who had escaped along the way, so their numbers were greatly reduced by the time they had arrived. Not to mention the ones the nation had lost after getting to Indian Territory.

It was odd, she thought, that even if her friends Sasa and Jackson Halley had discovered the ones who were keeping the Cherokee from getting their promised government food allotments that had not put a stop to it. She expected the government to sweep in and make amends for the tragedy, but the practice was still going on in every Indian nation in Indian Territory and beyond. There were still hundreds of dead every year. She often wondered if the government wanted them all to die off. It would not really surprise her. She once heard a soldier say that the only good Indian was a dead Indian, then laugh as if he had made a great joke.

Those stupid soldiers thought that most of the Cherokee did not speak English, so they felt safe in saying anything they wanted. Little did they know that the Cherokee heard and they understood. Most of the Indians in Indian Territory wanted nothing to do with the Army and their soldiers, most of whom were nothing but dirty dogs, anyway.

The days to come, filled with busy beading, would fill her with joy and mounting anticipation, thinking about what the Chief was working on. And if it turned out that this was her and her brother's last summer alive, she knew she would be content because she had been part of something momentous, whatever it was.

Chapter 24
An Unusual Invitation

Coyote had spent many moons with his friends, the Osage, in Indian Territory, and during that time he had learned many things about the white men who were coming to settle the vast lands presently occupied by the many tribes of the plains. The Osage had had a great deal of contact and negotiations with the U.S. Army and were well informed about their abilities. Many Osage owned guns, besides the bows and arrows they normally carried, but the Army was forcing them to remain peaceful, surrounded as they were by their traditional enemies. There were still small battles being fought.

The Cherokees had a few sub-chiefs who were stubborn and wanted to continue their raiding against the Osage, and it took stiff discipline to keep the Osage young men from setting off from their villages to retaliate. There had been many murders among the Cherokee, within their own nation, which kept Chief Ross' hands full. However, it took stiff discipline to keep the Osage young men from setting off from their villages to retaliate, and even so it was hard to keep warriors from taking up the red road.

Coyote missed his mother back in Lakota country, to the north and west of where he was now, sitting in front of a good fire, its flames lapping against a good buffalo hump, which was some of the best meat one could have, as far as his people were concerned. While at the Osage village, Coyote and Yellow Eyes had been treated to the meat from cattle, which he found to be mushy and tasteless compared to the enriching meat of the buffalo. The Osage, much to their dislike, were being forced to raise cattle, because the increased population of white settlers was keeping the buffalo far away. There were also other meats, including fish, but buffalo was a staple of the majority of plains tribes.

Coyote sat in front of the fire, his right hand gently stroking Yellow Eyes' back. Coyote was the only human, besides Sasa, the girl of the Cherokee south of the Osage, that Yellow Eyes would allow to touch his fur. He was not as fidgety here with the Osage as he was while Coyote visited his own Lakota village. The small coyote knew he was not welcome there, but would not part from Coyote's side. The elders thought it unnatural for him to be friends with a real wild coyote, but Coyote, now a man, told them that Coyote was his name forever more and that it was only right that his helper be a real coyote. He grew irritated with those people, because of their stiff-necked refusal to listen to talk of anything outside of their known world. If they had not seen—or experienced–it, then for them it did not exist. Finally, he had had to leave, which had been fine with Yellow Eyes.

He remembered back when he met Five Owls, the Osage leader of a small village just outside of the Indian Territory line. That area was called Kansas Territory, but you hardly knew when you crossed over into Indian Territory. It did not make sense to Coyote. There were Indians on both sides of this imaginary line, but he tried not to wonder why white men did things. Coyote had been caught by Five Owls, as he watched their hunting camp up in the long-grass country one night. He came very close to being killed by Five Owls, but they were far away from the land the Osage were supposed to stay in, so Five Owls resisted hurting Coyote. They became fast friends, though, as they traveled south, back to the land the white government said they had to stay in.

Those memories were sad and good. Sad because the Osage were still starving to death. Many hundreds had already died of starvation. Five Owls had explained that the white government had promised to feed them if they moved away from their homes into this barren place close to the tall grass area. It was the same situation he had seen in Indian Territory where the Cherokees lived.

Five Owls' Osage name was Sata Wapoke and the Osage people were known as Wazhazhe, but the called themselves Ni-U-Kon-Ska, or People of the Middle Waters. They took that name for themselves after they had been chased away from their Kentucky homeland by the Iroquois Indians and pushed west and south until they came to a place where all the big rivers emptied into one huge river. Five Owls told him the white called that river the Mississippi.

Coyote sat to watch the village activity. These Osage people were very different from those in his Lakota village. They were a very tall people, and were good to look upon. Even their women were tall. Their faces seemed to have some traces of the white race. Some had dark bronzed skin, and some had a much lighter skin, but all could be fierce if called upon to fight. He admired them and was happy to call Five Owls his friend. They had spent many hours helping Coyote to learn their language. Now he spoke it fairly fluently, and understood much of what was being said around him.

On the other hand, when Coyote was alone and he had some privacy, he began to have deep thoughts about his quest. It seemed another lifetime from when he had left his village for the first time to seek what Wakan Tanka wanted him to do with his life, one springtime evening at the hour when it is hard to see well because the light is still there, but yet it is not. That thought made him wonder if he was just fooling himself, like the dim dusk light fooled the eyes into not seeing what was plainly there. After he left the Lakota for the last time, his heart had been opened up and emptied by the realization that he could do nothing to stop the events that were about to engulf all the tribes of the plains.

The whites called this year 1843. Only ten years ago an Indian hardly ever saw a white man on the plains unless he was one of the fur trappers or mountain men. Now he was seeing with his own eyes the wagons heading west, full of white people looking for a better life. That too, made him wonder. What more did they want from their life that they already did not have? The white man was always telling the Indians that his life was so much better than an Indian's life, and that the tribes needed to all turn into white men if they wanted to enjoy what they enjoyed. They called it civilization. On his trip away from his people's northern village, up close to the upper Missouri River, he had crossed a wide expanse that hundreds of wagons had driven over. It had been beaten down so badly that he didn't think a plant would ever grow in those dusty tracks again. He had decided to make a camp in a secluded spot and wait a few days to see what might be coming down that road. It had only been three days when he saw an aberration. Huge wagons with white cloth the white men made in the east, called canvas, over tops of rounded ribs of wood, were rolling down that road. There were so many that it took two hours for them to finally pass. Each wagon was drawn by two or three spans of oxen or mules like those Jackson Halley raised in Arkansas, and carried several people, not to mention all the various ones who walked alongside them, continuously yelling foul, bad white man words at the mules as the wagons rolled down that dusty road.

Now it was real. Now it had started to happen, exactly as he had told his people it would, but the thought did not give him any satisfaction. He would rather not be right.

It was at these thoughtful times that he also thought of Sasa, down in Van Buren, next to Indian Territory. She was really not all that far away, just an easy two to three day ride, but he knew that Sasa had been spending her time learning everything she could about being a white woman. He knew why, but her knowing so much put up a wall between them. She was losing some of her Indian ways and leaving him behind. He had never told her that he liked her. The last time he saw her, she was fourteen, almost fifteen. For Indians, that was way past marriageable age, but he had known that white men, like Jackson, thought of that age as still being a child, so he had said nothing. Now he doubted he would ever see Sasa again, and that thought saddened him even more.

Sometimes he thought about his wild coyote, Yellow Eyes. The Osage people gave the wild coyote a wide berth. They never challenged him, and the children never tried to engage him in play, as they would a dog. Yellow Eyes was content to be side by side with Coyote, even sleeping next to him on his robes, but Coyote had noticed a feral look in his friend's eyes when he looked at others.

Even though Coyote fed him every day, Yellow Eyes needed to hunt from time to time. He supposed it was the wildness in him. Coyote was pleased to have him as a friend, any way that the wild coyote chose to be with him. He could not help thinking there was something special this wild animal was given to him to do. Only time would tell what that might be.

It was late afternoon, with a snapping cold breeze threaten-ing to chase the early spring away, when a runner arrived from one of the tribes that lived in Indian Territory. It set the village to buzzing. Coyote did not get to see who the runner was, but he did not have to wait long to find out. A young woman with solemn eyes approached.

"Coyote, my chief wishes that you come to his lodge as soon as you are able. Do you know which lodge it is?" asked the messenger.

"Yes. Please tell the Chief, I will be there soon," answered Coyote.

Before setting off for the meeting, he knelt down to be eye to eye with Yellow Eyes.

"Ah, Yellow Eyes, my brother. I must go to the chief's lodge You may come with me, but you must stay outside of the lodge. Since I am an outsider, this must be a really important meeting for them to call me.. If you do not want to wait outside of the lodge, then you can wait here," he told him.

With that finished, he stood and walked quickly to his destination. As he walked, he noticed that the noise of the village had stopped and everything was hushed. It made him feel nervous. Yellow Eyes stopped just outside of the lodge, while Coyote entered the darkened enclosure. The space was part of a long grass covered lodge they called a longhouse. Many families lived in just one, but this large longhouse was the private domain of only the chief and his wives, and also hosted official tribal councils.

Coyote stepped in and waited to be told where he was to sit. Already Chief Bellzer (Shin-gah-was-sa) and Black Dog of the Osage were in the places of most honor around the central fire pit; there were also other sub-chiefs sitting on benches built along the sides. Since he was not of their tribe, Coyote assumed he would be told to sit in the place of least honor. He waited patiently to be recognized, then Chief Bellzer pointed to a free space around the central fire. That gave him pause, as he did not feel he deserved any special consideration from these mighty chiefs.

As with most Native tribes, they observed the pipe ceremony before any word was spoken. No matter how long this took, no important thing was discussed until it was finished. When the pipe was wiped clean, put back in its special pouch, and entrusted to a young man whose job it was to take care of such things, the meeting began. Chief Bellzer spoke first.

"On this day, a runner from the Cherokees in the south has come with a special invitation. It is something we have never received before, and we want to ask you all to listen to this message, then tell us what is in your hearts. The message asks us to select a delegation of head men to travel to the Cherokees for a special meeting about peace. It says there will be many tribes there, possibly some of our enemies as well, and that if we do them the honor to come, we are to come as peace chiefs for the time we are with them. This message is from their Chief Over All, Chief John Ross. He also states that there is an important reason for us to come, one that may protect all the tribes who attend," he said.

He looked gravely at them all. No one spoke, for he still had the floor and was not finished. Solemnly, he raised his arm, and lying in his hand was a belt of the precious white wampum beads.

"When a request is also accompanied with the offer of the white wampum beads, it is serious indeed. There is no more sacred talisman of peace among all the tribes. If we accept the white wampum, then we must also agree to come to this council in peace. But hear my words, if any of you are selected to attend with Chief Black Dog and me, since I will accompany him too, and you agree to go in peace, but then change your mind once you see your enemy there and shame the word of the Osage Nation, your life will be ours to take or enslave as we will. The spirit of the white wampum will not be broken by the Osage," he added, then he sat down.

Questions were put to the chiefs, *What if our enemy provokes us?* And *why should we go if our enemies also attend?* One by one the chiefs impressed upon them the seriousness of their oath upon the white wampum. Then Black Dog looked at Coyote.

"Tell me, Man of the Tall Grass, what you know of the Cherokee now living where our people used to live. Will they abide by their promises? Will they also keep the peace, if we venture into their territory?" said Black Dog.

Coyote rose from his seat to address the great Osage chiefs. "I had the advantage of being among these people for almost a full cycle of the moon. They are like any other people, some good, some bad. Nevertheless, they are closer to white man's ways than any of the other tribes. Even so, I am positive they will abide by their own requirement. I would take them at their word," he answered.

"It is also said that you speak their Cherokee language; also Lakota, Delaware and English, plus now the Osage tongue. Would you be willing to accompany us to this peace council as an interpreter, to help us hear the words of the other chiefs as they speak? And would you also spend some evenings before we leave teaching us some of the Cherokees' ways?" Black Dog asked

Coyote was honored and resolute. He bowed his head in assent, and the rest of the council continued to discuss the possible reasons for the invitation.

Outside of the lodge of the chief, Yellow Eyes began to worry. He had expected Coyote to come out quicker. The Osage villagers walked past him, giving him a wide berth, but Yellow Eyes was not watching them. He crouched on his belly and scooted, inch by inch until his muzzle was just underneath the hide covering of the doorway.

Coyote was preparing to take his leave of the chiefs when both Chief Bellzer and Chief Black Dog saw the muzzle peeking through, along with a small portion of the animal's eyes. Motioning for Coyote to sit again, Chief Bellzer smiled at the comical nature of the situation, then he sobered and looked grim.

"I have been told from Five Owls the story about how you got your name. He explained how your village could not forgive you for something that was not in your control. Here with the Osage, once we take a person into our lodge and they make children for us, we then do not worry about the other blood of the other people that runs in his veins, but that does not mean that we do not have concerns about having Coyote and Yellow Eyes in our midst. It is for that reason that I will now tell you the story of how Coyote is responsible for the forever death that you cannot come back from. This story has been passed down since time began, so take it to heart, my son, and know why your friend Yellow Eyes makes the People wary," said Chief Bellzer.

All the men who had been preparing to leave gave a faint smile and sat down again in their places in the lodge to wait for the chief to tell about death. And so he began.

"In the beginning, there was no death. All the People never died, and it got very crowded until there was no more room for any new people. The wise chiefs called a council, so they might decide what to do. There was much argument because some said that people should die and then come back into the world after some time. But, Coyote jumped up and said that people should die for forever. He said there would not be enough to eat if everyone kept coming back, and besides that, there was not enough room for everyone. Then some of the other chiefs worried that there would no longer be happiness because of all the ones dying for forever.

By the time the council ended, Coyote was the only one that believed the People should die and go away for forever.

When the council was over, all the medicine men of the People gathered together and built a very big grass lodge, facing the east, of course. Then they called all of the men of the tribe so that they might tell them what they had decided. They said that the medicine house was a special house, and that after the people died, they would come to this house and would be made to come back to life. The most important chief medicine man explained that he would put a large white and black eagle feather on top of the grass house. He said that this feather would, all of a sudden, become heavy with blood and would then fall over. When the People saw this happen, then they would know that someone had died. Then all of the medicine men would come to the special grass house to sing the songs to call the spirit of the dead to the special grass house. It would be then that a spirit would enter it and would become alive again. All of the People rejoiced about the fine wisdom their medicine men had made for them, because death had been the most feared thing of all.

One day they finally saw the eagle feather turn bloody and fall, just as the medicine men had said it would. So they knew that someone had died. The medicine men gathered in the special grass house to sing for the spirit of the dead to come to them. It was on the tenth day that a whirlwind blew out of the west. Ominously, it circled the special grass house, then it finally entered through the entrance in the east. The People were amazed to see that from that whirlwind a handsome young man appeared, who had been murdered by another tribe. There was much rejoicing in the camp. Everyone danced and sang, all except Coyote. He was very displeased. He thought his rules were better than all the other medicine men's rules. Then it came that another feather became bloody and fell over again. Coyote saw it, then picked up the feather and quickly went to the special grass house. He took the seat near the door. When the medicine men came, he sat and sang with them for many days. Finally, he heard the whirlwind approaching, so he closed the door before the whirlwind could come into the house. The spirit that was in the whirl-

wind passed on by without stopping. So it was that Coyote introduced the idea of permanent death, and so the People from that time bitterly grieved about the dead and could not be consoled. So now, it became known that whenever anyone meets a whirlwind or hears the wind whistle, he will say: "There is someone wandering about." Unhappily, since the day that Coyote closed the door, the spirits of the dead have wandered over the earth, trying to find some place to go, until at last they find the road to the spirit land.

After that day, Coyote was always running and running. He never came back to the People, for he was ashamed for what he had done. And we know that Coyote is always skinny because he is starving. No one will give him food, or a kind word, for evermore."

Chief Bellzer ended the Osage death story, and looked search-ingly at Coyote.

"You have proved to be a good man, Coyote. Our people are happy to see you day to day. They enjoy hearing your people's stories by their fires, at night, and having you play a good game of stickball with our men. What they are not so sure about is Yellow Eyes. They remember this story that they have heard since childhood, and from generation to generation, and they are afraid. What may I tell my people, Coyote, to ease their fears?" he asked.

Coyote thought for a moment, then he seemed to come to a decision. He opened his eyes wide and stood tall, with his arms by his sides. Wearing only a breech cloth, leggings and his medicine pouch hanging from his neck, he glistened from the reflections of the firelight off of the bear grease that covered his exposed skin. His stance was powerful and his grace and goodness were almost visible all around him.

"Whether it is wise or good in your eyes, my chief, I do not know, but I would like to tell you what I believe. In your story I feel you are missing a minor detail. Coyote in your story is a medicine creature who meets with the other medicine men from the time beyond beginning. He is a spirit creature, and has already done all the damage he can do to all of the People. Yellow Eyes, however, is not a medicine creature in that way. He does not make decisions for the People. He is my spirit helper. He has never interfered in any decisions in my life, or in the lives of others, except for one occasion when he saved many lives, one night in Van Buren, Arkansas. Coyote is not his name. That is my name, but I was forced to take it. It was not of my own choosing. The creature staring at us from under the door covering is Yellow Eyes, and he is here only because I am here. He only wants to help me as I go on my quest, seeking what Wakan Tanka wishes me to do with my life. It may very well be that Wakan Tanka has something for him to do as well, and has asked him to be by my side. I am made to think that Yellow Eyes is a blessing for all the People of all the tribes. I cannot say why I am made to think that, but it is in my heart and my head. Yellow Eyes is not Coyote, the medicine creature you speak of. I am certain on that," he replied.

"Ah, that is a very good answer, my son. These things I did know. I wanted to see if you also knew them as well. It was important to me because of my sending you back down into Indian Territory to help the Osage understand why Chief Ross has called a meeting of friends and enemies alike. This has never been done before. I wanted to see if you thought of Yellow Eyes in any other way than your spirit helper who is alive and in flesh and fur. Even now he guards you and protects you. I am made to think that he does have this purpose that you speak of. So now, I will send you along with Yellow Eyes to attend us. Now, you must let one of the women give you some food and after you have eaten, return here so that we may discuss this meeting we will attend," finished Chief Bellzer.

Black Dog had talked only briefly during the entire council. Now he made known that he would like to speak.

"You all know me, I am Black Dog of the Osage, and I am one of the most feared of warriors among the Osage. Now, I must think about my people in peace and not war, not raiding. I too would have you go for those purposes, and more. I am made to think that this meeting we go to will prove to be one of the most important of our generation. I have seen the light that shines in your helper's eyes. If we are confused about why he accompanies you, he is not. There is determination in his gait. When he looks at the Osage, he does not growl, does not show his teeth in fear, does not glare upon the People, nor look upon them as meat. That is why I am made to think that the Osage also have a purpose that is connected to Yellow Eyes. He will be honored among us, and the People will be told that Yellow Eyes is not Coyote from the beginning times. The Osage, Coyote and Yellow Eyes, together we will all be tested. That is all I have to say," he declared and then he sat.

Coyote was astonished and honored. Yellow Eyes seemed to have understood Black Dog's talk and ventured further into the lodge. Now half of his body was inside and half was outside, but there was a glint in his eyes that had not been there before. Coyote nodded his head in agreement. The council was ended and he met Yellow Eyes on the outside of the lodge entrance. There was no wagging of his tail and no eye contact, only the determined step to his gait Black Dog had commented on and that determination bled through to Coyote. Finally, he realized, this may be the work that Wakan Tanka wanted him for. Time would tell, of course. Only time would tell.

Chapter 25
A-sailing We Will Go

The ship was listing easily in the wind as the pilot guided it past the many islands that were strung out from the tip of what the Spanish had called Florida East. The sun was a thing to behold, but the wind was mildly chilly on Sasa's face. Isaiah had told her that Florida got extremely hot during the long summer days, and the women all carried umbrellas and fans, but still wore their long dresses with long sleeves and high collars when they walked in the parks. However, the native women were known to wear not nearly as much, and when the first explorers had come here and met them for the first time, the women all wore nothing at all on top and a type of short skirt below. It was natural for them, he had said. Just like it was natural for her people to dress like the Cherokee.

She liked Isaiah very much, even though he was a white man. He had known many tribes in his lifetime and she felt he understood them better than some of the politicians who said they wanted to "help" the native peoples. He never looked anything but kindly at Sasa, and she never felt him undressing her with his eyes. For that she was extremely thankful. She could not wait to get home to the ranch and be near to her people in Indian Territory again. After this trip to Boston, she thought she never ever wanted to go back.

Wheezer had walked smartly beside Sasa as many trips around the deck as she would allow him. Occasionally, they would meet other passengers taking the air as well. Wheezer sat obediently while Sasa chatted briefly. However, one such occurrence made the hair on his back stand up.

As they walked by a solitary man, Wheezer noticed the man turning around to stare at Sasa. Then on the next round, the man stopped to introduce himself.

"Ah, hello, dear lady, I see you walk for the air as I do, sì? And what a lovely dog you have. Allow me to introduce myself, I am Manuel Munos Mendoza, of the Mexican government. I am going to see the frontier. I have seen the cities in the east, and now I go to the middle, yes?" he lied.

"Hello...uh...well my name is Miss Halley. Pleased to make your acquaintance," Sasa answered, a little uncomfortable for not having been properly introduced. Men did not come up to young ladies and tell them their names.

Already, Wheezer was growling fiercely at Mendoza'sfeet. Sasa felt she must hurry on before Wheezer did something they would both regret. Besides, she trusted Wheezer's opinion about people she did not know, and she was glad to break away. Further down the deck, Sasa stopped to lean on the side and gaze at the sea and its beauty, having already forgotten her discomfort in meeting that strange man. Wheezer, on the other hand, had not forgotten. He knew what he smelled, and it was not good at all.

Wheezer was at her feet, sitting patiently, waiting for Sasa to walk again around the deck. While on the ship, she kept a leash on him during their frequent walks in case he might accidentally fall overboard. The sun was bright, even though it was beginning its descent to the west, and the salt breeze was like velvet on her skin. She remembered how her mother would tell her stories of when the Cherokees lived closer to the coast and traded with other tribes the precious shells to make beads and decorations for the women much further inland. She thought she could get to like being by the sea, but Arkansas and Indian Territory were basically in the middle of the continent. Truly, her people had been pushed a long way from their original home.

Wheezer never left her side these days. Especially after that terrible kidnapping. Her mouth quirked in a one-sided smile when she thought of that night when they left Allan Jeffries mansion to go to their hotel.

Allan Jeffries proved to be a much better man than his father, just as Anna was so much better than her father had been. Both, once facts were discussed, understood the horrible feelings that churned inside them, once they both had found out what their fathers really were. "Monsters," Allan had said, and Anna had not disagreed. It was plain that she had stronger words for what she thought of her father, but did not say them, just calling him, "inhuman". Time was spent that night explaining exactly what the two men had done to the Cherokee people. As Allan listened, his face became contorted with remorse and revulsion. It was a hard thing to watch. They talked the night through and morning was only an hour away when Allan asked if he could accompany the family to Van Buren, Arkansas.

"I want to see what the frontier is all about, I want to work like a man should work and learn to make my own way, Suh. Would you be willing to hire me, Mr. Halley? I know how to ride well, but I don't know much else about what happens on a ranch. Pay me what you will, I want to earn my way up. I implore you to give me that chance, Suh," he said.

"Well, I don't mind hiring on another worker, Mr. Jeffries, how-ever, you must know that you will be working, not just with some other Cherokee workers, but also for my partner who is a full blooded Cherokee. There will be no room for racial bias on our ranch, sir. Can you do that?" replied Jackson Halley.

Allan said yes, most exuberantly, and the deal was struck. Not very many minutes later, Sasa broke in on the discussion.

"Jackson, I know you are enjoying your friends and past acquaintances, but I feel it is time to go home," she announced.

Everyone stopped talking and stared in her direction. Even Isaiah was stunned.

"Let me be plain, sir. I have had as much society as I want at this time, and I have a feeling that I am needed at home. It is only a feeling, but I have learned not to ignore them when they come to me. I have enjoyed much of what this trip has offered, and I have learned a tremendous amount, but it will not feel right if we stay," she finished.

It was Jackson who broke the impasse.

"I would like nothing more, Sasa, if it is all right with Anna," he agreed.

They all looked toward Anna, who was giving the biggest smile she could manage. She wanted to go home, too.

"I already have booked passage on a sailing ship bound for New Orleans. We could all go together if it pleases you," suggested Isaiah. As it turned out, a ship had just left that morning and they would have to wait about four long days for the next one, which was the one Isaiah was booked for anyway. Now they were more than three quarters of the way to the New Orleans port where they would then get passage on a steamer to take them the rest of the way, or at least to where the Arkansas River met the Mississippi, and then a very short ride on a flatboat up the Arkansas to Fort Smith. How she longed to be there at that moment. Hopefully, she would be home by the middle of May.

After their long walk on the deck of the ship, Sasa and Wheezer went down to their cramped cabin. There was no room for Wheezer to play, but he seemed to not mind it so much as long as he was able to see and touch Sasa. She sat on her bunk in the room she shared with Wheezer. Anna and Jackson occupied another room, and Isaiah offered the other bunk in his room to Allan Jeffries. That was fine with Sasa, for she loved to read and think.

She lay back against the wall at the back of her bunk, pulled Wheezer up onto her lap and wrapped her tan arms around his furred body. Wheezer had developed some funny attitudes in Boston, which he now displayed. He held his head perfectly still and erect, as if a painter was painting his portrait. Eyes straight ahead with a fixed stare at nothing but the other wall, he was waiting for the multitude of compliments he had received by her society friends. He found that if he struck a pose they would begin to compliment him on his ears, his perfect nose, his beautiful brown eyes. Every manner of compliment he soaked up like a sponge. Now he expected Sasa to do the same.

And why not? thought Sasa. *He is a beautiful boy, and he deserves any compliment I can muster.* So she began, "Just look at you. How handsome you are. Your nose is so black and smooth, your fur is soft and shiny. And your ears, I can't say enough about your ears. Especially the way they perk up and flip over at the tips. You are indeed a special friend. And just look at how intelligent you are. One can see it in your beautiful brown eyes. I really don't know how we could do without such a beautiful friend as our Wheezer," she said.

Wheezer held his head perfectly straight, and moved only his eyes to look sideways at Sasa. He wrinkled his brow a little bit, and Sasa had to giggle.

"Oh, Wheezer...ha ha ha ha, you are so taken with yourself. The compliments are over for now. Thank you for letting me gaze at your magnificence," she said with a wide smile.

Wheezer took his cue and relaxed from his posing, leaned his body back and placed his slender head against Sasa's breast. He remained content to stay there until the bell for dinner rang. She promised Wheezer to bring him back his dinner, then locked him in the room and was off in a flash.

He lay down on Sasa's bed, not liking to be without her, but he was hungry and he knew she would bring him something to eat. He had been in the darkening cabin for a few more minutes when he heard a scratching at the door lock. Immediately he hopped down from the bed and ran to sniff at the bottom of the door to catch the scent of the person coming in. It hit him like a lightning bolt; a scent he knew to be danger. He began to bare his teeth and growl. The longer the person fiddled with the lock, the louder Wheezer became until he began to bark frantically. Wheezer heard some epithets from the other side of the door and then the person was gone. But he was still frantic by the time Sasa returned.

"Oh, Wheezer. I told you I would be back. You did not have to make such a fuss. It is not like you to disturb everyone. I can't imagine what has gotten into you. Well, I am here now, so let us just settle down and have the food I brought for the both of us. The cook let me bring my plate back to my room tonight if I promised to bring it and utensils back," Sasa told him.

But Wheezer was not listening. He was running back and forth the short distance from her little table and chair and the door, continuing to sniff at the underneath edge. Sasa knew her dog well, and it did not go unnoticed.

"Wheezer boy, come and sit here. Come, now, Wheezer," she commanded.

Wheezer abandoned the door and came with bright eyes and a tilted head.

"Wheezer, did someone come here while I was gone?" she asked.

Wheezer turned and looked at the door and growled, intensely serious.

"Ah, I see. Was this someone I know?" she asked him.

Wheezer barked two times. Sasa contemplated for a moment, then moved to the door with Wheezer on her heals. She opened the door to examine if there had been a note left for her, maybe pinned to it, but as she scanned down the old creaky door, she noticed something odd about the lock, which had been original when the ship was built and was old and corroded. What had drawn her attention was the shiny scrapings around the area where the key went in. She looked closely, and saw the tiny shavings from some sharp instrument someone had used to try and open her door.

"All right. Now, Wheezer, did this person try to open my door?" she asked.

She barely got the question out before Wheezer was answering with a frenzied bark. She calmed him the best she could, then after giving him his food, she sat at the little desk to write a note to Jackson, who's bunk was next door; once done, she quickly folded it and slid it under their door. If someone was trying to get into her room, she did not want them to know that she knew it by pinning a note to Jackson's door. This way, he or Anna would see the note paper on the bare floorboards when they came in from dinner. They would have to have a meeting. And soon.

Chapter 26
Them Injuns Is Gettin' Restless

The spring rains had been falling for a good three days, but that did not stop Harvey Castor and his fellow Arkansan Militia troop from slogging their way across the prairie in route to Fort Gibson. The eight men walked and rode warily, carrying their old flintlocks ready for any attacking, marauding red Indians who hungered for white meat, who might try to surprise them. They had taken a vote and these eight had been chosen to risk their lives, riding into treacherous Indian Territory, so that they might summon the help of the Army at Fort Gibson in repelling the expected slaughter of white settlers along the Arkansas border.

"All right now, boys, I think I can see the outbuildings of the fort up yonder, but don't you relax your vigil none. These wily redskins would just as soon kilt you as look at you, so keep your powder good and dry and a sharp eye out for any approaching trouble," said Harvey over his shoulder, as he continued to slosh through the muddy, rain soaked, road to the fort, walking next to his lame horse. He rubbed his scruffy beard with scummy hands, his clothes not being much better off.

Harvey had been elected as the leader of the group only because his uncle Clem had been in the Army and had once attacked a village of Seminole Indians down south. His friends and neighbors considered him the resident expert on any type of redskin, no matter what the tribe. Almost none in the community could read nor write, so all news was carried to them verbally, being embellished, twisted and made-up as it circulated.

Harvey Cooke had seen some of the so-called friendly Indians come into town, back at Fort Smith, but he had never actually spoken to one. He was feeling more than nervous, now that he was in actual Indian Territory. It was easy to talk big when he was surrounded by all his buddies, while they listened to his made up stories with rapt attention. It gained him free drinks, dinner at his neighbors table, and a status as yet undetermined. He had been forced to accept the appointment for this committee, representing all the Arkansas militias for this particular errand, or he would have lost face. He could not afford anyone to realize how afraid he was of just setting foot over the border.

"Harvey, I don't rightly know if'n we can shoot anyone on this side of the border. Did you ask the commander back at Fort Smith what we can do if'n we're attacked?" asked Ned Struthers, who had abandoned his farm to make this trip with the militiamen. Plus, he considered it an honor to accompany Harvey. Ned's wife of seven years was back home on the farmstead, birthing another baby in as many years. This trip gave him a little break.

The militiamen were nervous, since there were many Indians camped out all around the fort. They seemed to be waiting on some-thing. The men saw no hostility among the Indians, but they kept their guns at the ready. Harvey stopped to look up at Ned atop his big Missouri mule, and grimaced.

"Yes, Ned, I did. Long story short, we don't have any right to shoot so much as a rabbit in Indian Territory. But, I'm tellin you now, boys, I don't intend on lettin myself be kilt by no Indian, and that's a fact. So's you might as well be ready if trouble comes, cause I ain't awaitin for the U.S. Army to arrive to stop it. Now, as we agreed, when we get to the fort, I will do most of the talkin. You boys are here to show that our country folk are serious. If'n they ask you a question, then you can pipe in. Got it?" reminded Harvey.

The resulting grumble became the men's assumed assent to the plan. Each man continued on, some walking like Harvey, leading their horses, and some riding. Each man kept a piece of oilcloth draped over the flintlock of their guns to keep the rain water out. Slowly, they came across more camps of various types of structures. Some looked like grass huts, while others were real log cabins. While passing one such cabin in progress, the men all noticed the clothing worn by the men doing the construction. If some had not had a long black braid hanging down their backs, it would have passed for a white settlement, with exception of one other detail. The majority of camps they had passed revealed a cleaner people by far. The militia members stared in awe, as their assumptions about how Indians lived began to conflict with all the stories they had so gullibly gulped down.

But Harvey only sneered at them. "Look at them buggers," he said. "They is tryin to copy us whites. Afore you know it, they will cut their hair short and start eatin with a knife and fork. But, they don't fool me none. Once a Indian, always a Indian. Just keep on a-goin, boys."

After about another hour of travel, slogging ankle deep in red mud while the rain continued to pour down on them, they came to the post's front gate and were welcomed by the sergeant on duty. Wanting to appear professional, Harvey strode up to the sergeant and gave him a smart salute. The sergeant had more to do than he could shake a stick at, so he barely raised his arm in a return greeting and pointed the men to the main office. He did not stand around long enough to find out what they wanted.

Harvey figured it differently and decided the sergeant had assumed Harvey's right to belong there; emboldened, he strode up towards the office. The fort grounds were much bigger than the men from Arkansas had thought it would be. Everywhere there was activity. Men were being drilled on the parade ground, workers were working on more buildings to accommodate guests and the sutler, whose store was to the side of the Army offices, was already doing a good bit of business.

Ned got off of his mule and hurried up to Harvey. Something was itching at him.

"Hey, Harvey. Look on over yonder. Do you see what I see? They is lettin the redskins come into the fort. Heck, they is even selling stuff to them. And looky at that, Harvey. A few of them Indians is totin guns. I thought they had them taken away. Now, I don't feel none too safe. That's not what you told us, Harvey," said Ned, as he scratched his lice ridden scalp.

Harvey only growled a warning to drop the subject. Even so, Ned continued to keep an eye on it all. This was not what Harvey had counted on. He had expected the men to be dutifully awed by what they saw, proving that their friend and commander was indeed a brave and courageous man. With every step, he was beginning to look like the blow hard he was.

A duty officer stepped up to the group, saluted smartly, taking in all that they were.

"Welcome to Fort Gibson, sirs. I am Sergeant William Cutright. May I be of service?" he said.

"Well, now. Finally, some welcome to a group of true Americans. Ah...hem. Yes, I am Harvey Cooke, and I am temporary commander of this special unit of Arkansas Militia. We come to discuss some grave concerns our countrymen would like you to be aware of. We been instructed to speak with the commander or the highest rank available at the fort. If'n you are it, then I guess we got to settle on you," explained Harvey.

"Uh...Yes, sir. Our commander is here at this time; however, I will have to see if he has time to accept your visit," replied the sergeant

"Now, son, you make sure he knows exactly who we is, 'cause our militia is responsible for a mighty big area, and y'all just might need us pretty soon. What we got to say is derned important and we come all this way to tell him," insisted Harvey at the sergeants retreat-ing backside.

The group stood stock still for a good twenty minutes before the sergeant stepped out to beckon them inside. As the men passed Sergeant Cutright, he was forced to pull out a handkerchief from his breast pocket to place it over his nose. Even on the frontier, he had not smelled anything as bad as this, except for a rotting corpse. He quickly announced them into his commander's office and practically ran for the relative fresh air of the stable yard.

Harvey stood, giving his imitation of a salute to the man standing behind the dark cherry desk.

"Good afternoon, gentlemen. I am Colonel William Daven-port. May I be of service to you? I understand you are from the Arkansas Militia, are you not?" said the colonel.

"Uh, yes sir. We is. Harvey Cooke is the name, and these are my men. We been sent to ask for help and protection along our Arkansas border with Indian Territory from the coming Indian wars about to descend on the good white folk of Arkansas," said Harvey matter-of-factly.

The colonel's bushy brown eyebrow raised a good quarter inch, and at the same time the stench of the men finally reached his nostrils. First thing before answering them, he strode over to the one window of his office and raised the sash, but did not return to his desk. This made no impact on Harvey.

"Now, what is this you say about an Indian uprising? I have not heard of anything. Where and when has this attack happened? How many are dead? What tribe attacked you? Come on man, give me the details so that I can muster a detail," said the agitated Colonel.

"Well, now, Colonel Davenport, sir, there ain't yet been any attack. You see, we been seeing more and more of these redskins a-comin into town. They is even building shelters and such up close to the border and all. Ain't there some law agin them coming so close to us whites a-livin in Arkansas? We got women and chillins to think on and we never seen so many all in one space afore. We even heard tell of some big doins comin to that Cherokee big town. Let's see, Talley Squaw, I think they calls it. Ain't there no law about them comin together, nor nothing?" pleaded Harvey.

The colonel was hard pressed to hold his temper. He had no time for scatterbrained yahoos taking up his day.

"Mr. Cooke, as far as I am aware, there has been no uprising against any white settlement. Any trouble we have heard of so far are skirmishes between Indian tribes. And no, the Army cannot send details out just to wait in case there might be an attack. I am sorry for your long trip, but there is nothing I can do for you, save give you some advice," he replied.

"What might that be, Colonel? The Arkansas militia is ready and willing to obey any command you might make of us. We each have a gun of our own and we are ready," said Harvey.

Before he spoke, the colonel had a thought come into his head.

"Mr. Cooke, are you representing all of the Arkansas militia, or some part of it? Now, before you answer, let me remind you that I am acquainted with the main ranking officers of the Arkansas militia, and I find it very odd that they have not sent me a correspondence informing me of the exact needs and reasons for this visit," he warned, with a pointedly stern expression.

Harvey was hard pressed now, since he had blown himself up to his men as being a respected militia man with the Army. He also was not sure what the colonel had just said.

"Well, sir, I don't know what this correy-spon-dance is. We don't got no letter 'cause none of us can read one anyways. I guess I can say that our militia is from the three settlements south of Fort Smith. We ain't part of no other group. But, that don't mean we ain't got a problem with them thievin redskins. We can feel it in our bones. Can't you do nothin to help protect us settlers?" replied Harvey, he thought eloquently.

Now the colonel's rage was mounting, but long practice helped him hold back.

"Men, here is my advice. Go home. Farm. Live. Work. But, until there is a real uprising, there is nothing I can do, and I have no more time to devote to your request. Oh, and one more thing. I advise you to get in contact with the Arkansas Militia headquarters. In fact, I have received a copy of an order issued by them. Let me read this to you gentlemen," said the colonel, then he stepped to his desk, found the copy he had spoken of and with an evil glint in his eyes, read it.

"Militia Order

All persons liable to Military duty in the first Battalion, 13th Regiment, Arkansas Militia, are hereby ordered to attend a Battalion Muster, at the State House, in the City of Little Rock, on Saturday, the first day of April next, at 10 o'clock, A.M., Armed and equipped as the law directs.

Commandants of companies are also notified to hold company musters, at their respective muster grounds, on Saturday, the 25th of March inst.
E. Walters, Lt. Col.
Commanding 1st Battalion
13th Regiment, Arkansas Militia
Little Rock, March 14, 1843

"It is my understanding, gentlemen, that they are getting ready for a war with Mexico. So if it is fighting you want to do, go on to Little Rock and report to Lt. Col. Walters as quickly as you can, since this order is not that old. We will check in to your concerns about a possible Indian uprising. Unless, of course, some of you brave men would like to join the Army and be assigned to this post."

Harvey now began to squirm. He had no desire to go off to fight a war, he only wanted to be seen as a heroic Indian fighter. He fumbled with his slouch hat, quickly saluted, and forced his way past his own men in retreat. The next thing the Colonel knew, the men had mounted their mules and nags, heading out of the fort gate.

Colonel Davenport watched them go for a time, then shouted for the orderly. "Have the Officer of the Day get some men and find something to fan the air, sheets or cloth, anything to fan the stench out of this building," he ordered. Then, "Heaven help the unit that admits that lot into their ranks."

"Sergeant Cutright, please attend," he went on. "Sergeant, has there been any rumor of any gathering of large numbers of Indians recently?"

"No, sir, I have not heard anything, but I can check with people we know in the area, traders and such, that might know and report, sir," answered the sergeant.

"Yes, but be quick about it. I think it is a bunch of silliness, but if there is something going on, I need to know," concluded Colonel Davenport.

"Yes, sir,"

Colonel Davenport then went back to his reports concerning activities along the Indian Territory's border with Texas and possible insurgents from Mexico. Now that was something to worry about.

As Harvey and his men slogged their way back towards the border, they were forced to pass the very same Indians they had passed going the other way. Groups of four or five makeshift dwellings made of sticks and hide, and some canvas tipis were grouped together here and there. Harvey was feeling embarrassed, angry and combative. He paid little attention, barely looking up as they rode past the dwellings. He had been sure the Army would jump to have an opportunity to kill them some Indians, but when they failed to react, he lost face with his men.

Soon they were passing a lone dwelling. It was the kind of rounded mound covered with old hides the Indian called wigwams. Harvey could see a squaw cooking over a fire with a youngster helping to bring her firewood. Before they approached Harvey's tempter got the best of him.

"Them knuckleheads is just too dang lazy, that's what. Somebody better teach them how to keep these injuns in their place," he mumbled. His men could not figure out what he was talking about. Weren't these injuns in the place the government wanted them in right now? But, before they could ask him, Harvey jumped from his horse to approach the squaw and what he could see was probably her son of about twelve. Easy pickins, he thought.

"All right now, you. Squaw woman. We here good white men been travelin for a peace now and we is hungry and tired. I think you been whipping up some victuals there and you just might as well figger on feedin us too, especially as seein as how you got to do what us white men say. Just like the United States Army, we is Arkansas Militia Men," he abruptly said to her and then turned to his men to say, "Boys, this here red injun squaw is goin to dish us up some of them victuals she is stirring in her pot. So come on and get down here, tie your mounts to a bush and let's get to some eatin."

The men looked stunned. Where did Harvey get his nerve? When Harvey looked back at his men, they had not dismounted, but were staring past him at something that put instant fear in their eyes. Harvey swung around to see what the problem was and came face to chest with the biggest, red headed Scotch-Irish, U.S. Army soldier he had ever seen, and some sort of officer to boot. He was speechless and could not seem to move his spindly legs. The man was wearing his uniform pants with his suspenders hanging down on either side of him. He had no shirt on, and this gave the men a good view of the man's musculature, which was mighty indeed. His hands were twice the size of any normal man. His flaming red hair carried from the top of his head to a grand mustache and down to the man's huge chest.

"Now gents. Did I hear you correctly, me man. Ye want me wife to feed the lot of ye, do ya? Well now, I heard ye telling me sweet woman ye wanted her to give ye what was in her pot. Let's see now. Why don't ye just have a seat there and sample it for your men before we feed the lot of ye? Mrs. Guild, would you please ladle up a bowl of what ye got in that pot. We will make sure it is to our friend's liking first. Then, if the men want to join him, we can surely dish them up some as well," said the burly officer.

Mrs. Guild, obviously the soldier's wife, looked uncertain, then after seeing the twinkle in her husband's eye, she nodded, fetched a wooden bowl, ladled up a rather thin soup, handed it to Harvey with a spoon and waited.

"Now, let's see how ye like me wife's cooking. Come on, down the hatch," ordered Sergeant Guild.

Harvey looked down at the soup in his bowl, but could not tell what kind of broth it was. It had to be good because the woman had been stirring it over the fire for some time. Harvey raised the bowl and as it touched his lips, he felt the soldier's huge mitt brace it up against his lips.

"Now, me friend, drink it all up. Ye said ye wanted what was in her pot, so now drink it down and let's be done with it," said Sergeant Guild.

When the liquid hit Harvey's tongue, he realized it had not been soup at all. In fact, Harvey was very familiar with the taste, since his own mam used to wash his mouth out with it whenever he had said a bad word. The "soup" in the squaw's pot was her laundry and he was drinking the wash water with lye soap in it. He coughed, sputtered and struggled against the strong officer until the liquid was gone from the bowl. When he was released, he felt sure he was going to vomit. Stumbling to his horse, he could hear the sergeant clearly as he said, "I better not ever see ye on this side of the border again, me friend. I don't let no man, woman or child, talk to me sweet woman like that.

"And, by the way, if ye do happen to vomit it back up, ye men ought to catch it in your hats, take it to the creek and take a bath. Ye are the stinkinest bunch of ya-hoos I have ever smelled in me short life. Now be off with ye, and don't ye be coming back," added Sergeant Guild as he put his huge arm around his Cherokee wife who had been doing her husband's laundry that day. They watched as the men hurried their horses to greater speeds as if the devil was running behind them.

Chapter 27
Trouble At Sea

Allan Jeffries was worried. So much had happened to him in the last few weeks that it was continuing to change his life almost daily. That was not all bad, really, because even though he had lost his misplaced affection and respect for his father, he had gained new acquaintances, friends, and possibly a new direction for his life. Those things were not what worried him now. It was the safety of these same acquaintances and friends who were even now on board the same ship heading for New Orleans, where they would transfer to a steamboat for the last leg of their voyage. His worries focused on the odd things that had been occurring, almost daily to his new friend Sasa.

Someone had been trying to break into her room, and even though they had not yet been successful, there was no way to anticipate any further attempts. So, he had taken to following Sasa, at a distance of a few yards, wherever she roamed the ship. And Jackson was keeping an eye on her room. It was almost laughable, when he thought of the danger he had put her in, not so long ago, something for which he was sorry in the extreme. All the more reason why he could not let anything happen to her, if only to assuage his own guilt.

The only question mark in his mind was about a certain passenger who had spoken to her on several occasions, but had done nothing more than that. What he did regard as a significant clue to the man's intentions was that Wheezer always growled fiercely whenever this man approached Sasa. Wheezer always stood his ground and never allowed the stranger to step within striking distance. The only problem with that was Allan had no inkling what that meant. He had never seen a dog with the intelligence of Wheezer before. All he could do was to continue to watch and wait.

Wheezer's reaction to the odd man that spoke to her every day, while she strolled the deck of the ship, had not been lost on Sasa. She kept her suspicions to herself, though, because she felt safe with Wheezer at her side, and moreover she was not without resources herself. Something that young Allan Jeffries had learned the hard way. She smiled to herself.

Her exceptional mind did take note of certain apparent facts. He was Mexican, as was the man who accosted her at the ball. Both men had asked her about her bracelet, which baffled her. The bracelet was not worth a terrible amount of money, there were no stones on it and the chain was fairly thin, yet each man seemed to be curious about the design of the charm, and she had very little information about the significance of it. Both men had asked who had made it for her, but she had evaded answering that question, not knowing exactly why. She just knew down deep that neither man had any right to even speak to her, much less draw information from her about her acquaintances.

She was so happy that this leg of the trip was almost done and she would soon be settled in a much nicer room on a fairly new steamboat, heading north on the Mississippi River toward home. The beginning of her trip to Boston was a blur. She barely remembered the ship voyage even though she had never before seen the ocean or even imagined the size of the ships they used to ply the waves, so on the way back she took more time to take in the view. Some days, there would be dolphins racing along beside the ship. The captain explained what they were, since she had never heard of an animal that looked like a fish, swam in the ocean, but breathed air and was not a fish at all. During her intense studies in law, math, English and some science, the professor had not dwelt much on what he considered common knowledge, but it was knowledge Sasa hungered for, and each day of life gave her new opportunities to learn.

She had missed the ranch and she was anxious to get reacquainted with Penny and her puppies. Penny had been such a wonderful gift since she was also a Jack Russell Terrier, bred by the originator of the breed, Rev. John Russell in England, who had specifically sent her to the Halleys so she would be mated to Wheezer and thus begin the breed in America. And Penny's first litter had already been spoken for even before it was successfully bred. Of course, Wheezer and his exploits had something to do with their reason for wanting one of the pups. Since they were headed back earlier than they had planned, she would arrive back at the ranch about the same time Arch Flint, Jackson's business partner, a Cherokee, would be weaning them from their mother.

As Sasa stood gazing out to sea, musing about the puppies, she saw movement out of the corner of her eye. It was that man, Mr. Mendoza. His back was turned from her, which gave her enough time to scurry to the hatch which led to her room, followed by Wheezer who, upon noticing the man beginning to turn around, emitted a low growl as he trotted down the steps after Sasa. Allan also saw the evasive action, but chose to stay on deck, out of the way, to see how the man reacted to Sasa's disappearance, and he was soon rewarded with seeing the man begin to look in the various places where she usually strolled, in such a way as to give him the feeling that the man had known Sasa had been there only a moment before, but had escaped his notice. Now, Allan had a face and a name to consider and discuss with Jackson.

He would be relieved when they transferred to the steamboat. Hopefully, the man's journey would end at New Orleans.

Mendoza was frustrated when he considered all the days he had been on the same ship with the Indian girl, without getting to know anything more than he did to begin with. Since the general had ruined his trip to Boston because of wanting–no needing–to know more about the bracelet, now he also felt the need to know. Something was not quite straight about the story the general had told him about the artifact. If he indeed had it, then why did he care if some Indian squaw had a worthless charm on a flimsy chain with a face on it that the general imagined could be the same artifact? It made no sense, unless the general did not actually have it. Maybe he did not even believe it existed, but once he saw the charm decided he had found a clue to its location. Mendoza seriously doubted the general had such a priceless item.

Then it finally occurred to him that the general had thought to get his services for nothing. Be that as it may, he was a hard man to take advantage of and much cleverer than anyone gave him credit for. Yes, he would do his token service to continue the raids into Indian Territory for the general, but now his new mission was to investigate if the charm on the squaw's wrist was a real clue to locating one of the most priceless objects known to the Mexican people. Were he to find it, he would never have to work another day in his life and he would receive requests from people like the general for a piece of his time for an audience. It was worth the effort. The more he thought of the Golden Serpent, the more he lusted for the wealth it could provide, and because he allowed this lust to grow, he lost a little of his cold, calm, calculating mind.

Chapter 28
The Watcher

It was dusk in the temporary settlement of the small com-munity of Choctaw Indians, where Little Otter and her family still lived, down south of the Canadian River. The constant raids, poverty and the lack of government allot-ment food created starving times for her people. Ever since that first attack, when Little Otter had experienced her first scary raid, she maintained a constant look out for strang-ers who did not belong. She often woke up in the middle of the night, screaming because she had dreamed that she was again trapped in the tall corn crib on a black night when a marauding band of an unknown tribe attacked her friends and family, newly arrived in Indian Territory.

It had been many months since that terrible night when her uncle, Five Puma, had rescued her from certain death, during the first of many raids. She had not forgotten the lesson that, although they were in a place that was called Choctaw country, a part of Indian Territory given to the Choctaw by treaty, it did not necessarily mean they were safe. She had already lost many of her family to starvation, and between the raids and the lack of food, some of the Choctaw were having a difficult time establishing permanent towns. Her uncle told her she must remain vigilant, keeping her eyes open to new dangers, especially strangers who may wander into the settlement. It did not matter if the stranger was white, Indian or Mexican, she was to take notice at all times, and then tell her uncle.

For an almost eight summers old girl, she had good eyes and she could fade into shadows easily. She had the advantage of being a child, which meant she got overlooked by most people, especially if they were hiding from other adults. On this early evening, Little Otter saw a man crouching in the grass, not far from Running Wolf's lodge. She hid and waited to see what he was doing, but he continued to watch the lodge. Whenever Running Wolf emerged, the man looked sharply and kept his eyes on him, making sure Running Wolf never left his sight even if he just went to the midden to relieve himself.

When the sun was down and the moon had not yet risen, she slipped out of her dark hiding place and ran to Five Puma's house. Her uncle smiled wide and was happy to see her.

"Ah, little one, how has your day been, eh? I bet you

are tired after a fine spring day like today," he said, as she dashed into his arms.

"Uncle, there is a stranger. A watcher, behind Running Wolf's lodge. He has been there for a long time and he is keeping his eyes on our elder. I stayed to watch, to make sure of what he was doing. I made sure he did not see me, but he is still there. It is night now, and I am worried for our elder," she blurted out, excitedly.

Five Puma, grabbed the girl by her shoulders to steady her, "Where, by the elder's lodge, did you see this man, Little Otter?"

"He is hiding deep in the patch of last year's tall grass about two arrow shots from the back of the elder's lodge," she explained.

At that, Five Puma quickly ran out of his lodge to find more warriors, before he would approach this hidden watcher.

Little Otter slipped back to her hidden watching place and waited. She looked back toward her uncle's house and noticed at least five warriors, plus Five Puma, circling around so they might approach the watcher from behind. She could no longer see the watcher and she hoped that he had not disappeared. She soon knew he had not left when she heard the sounds of a fight, out in the field of tall grass. She heard someone scream, then silence. After a time, she saw her uncle come out of the field without the other warriors and she stepped out of her special spot to greet him.

"Uncle, I heard a fight. Did anyone get hurt? Are you all right?" she asked worriedly.

"All is fine now. You did a very good job, as good as any young warrior could do. I am proud of you," he replied, as he bent down to look at her, eye to eye. "With your watching out for us, the strangers don't stand a chance, eh."

She did not understand what these strangers wanted with her people, but that did not matter. Keeping her friends and family safe was the important thing. She went home and slipped into bed, hoping that another watcher did not come in the night to replace the last one.

The next morning, Five Puma headed for the lodge of Running Wolf, one of the oldest of the Choctaw elders living in the Choctaw portion of Indian Territory. His steps were determined and ponderous. Five Puma had so much on his mind, what with all the raids going on. If the Choctaw were not being raided—and then accusing a neighboring tribe of the crime—then they were being blamed for some other raid in the territory they did not do. He did not need any more worries, much less outsiders coming into their territory to cause fear and panic with rumors and innuendo. His family had not yet settled in a permanent place because his people were being terrorized.

This new problem had the marks of a threat to one of the respected elders of their community, but there was little anyone could do to protect the old man. He really could do nothing more that warn him of some impending danger and try to protect him. None of the Choctaw chiefs wanted to ask for help from the army because the tribe had lost all faith in their so-called white brothers. He had a second reason for calling on the old elder, and it was that he might be of help in an unexpected way.

Five Puma stepped up to the hide covering the wooden door frame, dusty and swinging in the spring breeze. Running Wolf sat inside the shack, making marks and pictures on a special hide he kept to count the seasons and their highlights. Five Puma scratched on the piece of hide and waited.

"No need to stand there, Five Puma, just come in and seat yourself. I am almost finished with this. I assume you are here for a serious reason, or you would not be at my door," said Running Wolf, as he finished with a mark on the hide and deftly laid it over a small meat drying rack set beside him.

"Say, I would like to have a talk, grandfather, but it would be better if we walk out away from the settlement. Do you feel like taking a short stroll, grandfather?" asked Five Puma, sincerely hoping the old man was up to the task.

"They did not name me Running Wolf for no reason, my son. I think I would like a walk. We can take the prairie road that leads north, then head over to a shady spot by a creek that runs off of the Canadian River. Does that suit you?" suggested Running Wolf.

Five Puma nodded his assent and they headed off together. The younger man was in his prime, with broad shoulders and limber body. He was a skilled horseman and accurate with bow and arrow or gun. He provided well for his family and, on occasion, for the community. He wore only a breechcloth and leggings of deerskin. On his feet were moccasins, and he had an intricately beaded belt around his waist.

The elder walking beside him was slight of build, shorter and somewhat stooped in the shoulders, with his gray white hair pulled back into a single braid. He always wore the same plain clothes, a white cotton twill shirt and trousers made out of a tough woven material and dyed indigo blue. He owned ceremonial skins, but wore them only on special occasions now, since game was getting very scarce and he was finding it hard to come up with the necessary buckskin to make more. Also, he no longer had a woman at his lodge who could scrape and tan the hides, then sew them for him. It was easier to take what the missionaries gave him to wear, which was more like any white settler would wear. Sometime later, they found an old log washed up from the recent spring flood and took a seat by a creek. They had not said a word to each other up to that moment. Five Puma, who was trying to organize his thoughts before he presented them to the elder, was in no hurry, and Running Wolf was happy to allow the younger man however much time he needed, because he sensed that this meeting was somewhat serious, requiring the secretive nature to the site chosen for it.

They sat amiably, watching the muddy water flow past them, but not really seeing it. Then Five Puma began to explain the reason for the unusual meeting.

"Grandfather, you know that since all this raiding began some months ago, we have been very careful to watch when strangers come through our territory. There has not been just one, but five curious men, traveling around our country, asking questions about the Choctaws. Now they are asking questions about you. What is especially odd is that all of these men, who came through at different times, sometimes weeks apart, have all been Mexicans.

"Some of our sub-chiefs became suspicious and began to keep track of what these men were trying to find out. At first, it was not about you in particular. They were asking about an elder whose family ties go back to the peoples and tribes living close to the Aztecs. Unfortunately, one of our number who is trapped by the whiskey drink, spouted off about you and your family.

"That is when we noticed that the strangers began to ask about you specifically. We have been very careful to watch for the arrival of any strangers, and we have done our best to make sure they left with no information, but last night we found one of these men hiding out in the brush, watching your lodge. I am worried that you may come to some harm, because we do not know what they want, or why they are bothering with our Choctaw grandfather," he concluded.

"Where is this man now, my son?"

"Well, we made sure he would remember to not come back here again. I am afraid that during the struggle, his arm was broken. He would not tell us why he was watching your lodge. We told him we would break the other arm if we saw him again. I am sure, though, that he will not be the last. I don't know what these men want, and I am not sure I want to know. What I want is to make sure you are safe and no harm comes to you."

"It may not be something you can stop from happening. Do you and the headmen have any suggestions for this old man?" asked Running Wolf, now looking all around the area and finally seeing at least one of their warriors not far away.

"As a matter of fact, we do. Recently, we received a runner from the Cherokee Chief John Ross, inviting us to a special peace council in Tahlequah. It must be a very important meeting, because they sent us a white wampum belt. We are sending a delegation to this meeting and we thought that you might like to be one of the ones we send. Even though you are not a chief or sub-chief, you are a most respected elder, and it would give you some protection for the next few months as you travel and attend the council. If we put our group together soon and get us all on the road, you would have plenty of time to get there, even if we walked instead of riding. I have been chosen to be one of the group. Since we know of the danger, we would be there for your protection as well," said Five Puma, hoping the elder would not take offense at the suggestion.

Running Wolf seemed to be thinking hard on the matter. Occasionally, he muttered things that Five Puma did not understand at first, until he talked to himself a little louder, saying, "And it will all be over by the end of the peace council. Then, after I am gone, no one will know." Then the elder became more aware of his surroundings, as if waking up.

"Five Puma, I would be honored to attend this meeting. In fact, I think I am supposed to be there. I will be ready on the day you say we are to leave, but I will have to borrow a horse. As you know, we have had so many starving among the Choctaw that I gave my horse as meat for the families with children. He was old anyway," he replied.

"I believe we can provide you with a horse, one that has not been eaten as yet," agreed the headman with a wry grin and a twinkle in his deep brown eyes.

The two men talked and joked on the way back to the settlement, but Running Wolf knew how close to danger he was. He knew what those strangers were looking for, but he had already hidden the thing where even he could not find it, so there was no longer any danger to it. As for himself, he did not fear death, he only feared failure in his responsibility to guard it and to keep it away from the greedy hands of men who would kill to possess it. To some men, it was only a myth, like a bedtime story, but, he knew it was real and that so much blood had already been spilled because of the greed of men who valued gold over human life.

He also knew that this would be his last summer, and he was content that he had fulfilled the promise made by his family and passed down to him, to keep the object safe and away from those who killed for gold.

He was pleased to be invited to the peace council, more pleased than anyone could possibly imagine, because he knew that the girl would be there, even if he could not explain how he knew this. She would be there, and his duty would be fulfilled.

Chapter 29
Wheezer's Very Bad Day

Wheezer had never seen so many people in all his short life. There were even more than in Boston, the big city they had been to. This place seemed to be all people, everywhere. Besides the crushing crowds, the aromas that wafted past his regal nose enticed him and gave him a desire to go and find the source of those scents. However, he could not leave Sasa's side: no matter what scents passed his nose, he had to stay at her side. It was good that they were not hurrying along, but were standing in a line waiting to board the big steamship.

He was used to seeing muted colors, in fact, color was not something he usually focused on, but this city was so colorful that he was having a hard time figuring out body lines. Some people think that dogs don't see color, but Wheezer could tell them that was not true. He only saw fewer colors than humans, and not much variance in shade. It was enough to make a jumbled, confusing mess of the scene passing in front of him now. He was not afraid, however, because Sasa had his lead firmly in her hand, and that meant there was no danger of him getting lost. Until a particular scent passed by... a scent that signaled danger to every hair of Wheezer's back. He could not see the man, and he did know it was a man, but, all the same, he did not budge from Sasa's side.

Finally, it was time to board the great steamboat. Sasa and her family had waited in line for some time, and a great multitude were lined up behind them. Once the gang plank was set out and the gate opened to accept the passengers, Sasa began to feel the crowd pressing down on her from behind. Some squeezed in front of her and she lost sight of Jackson and the rest of her group. As they inched forward, she felt she was being pushed along by those behind them who wanted to get to the best spaces on the deck because they had not booked rooms as the Halley's had. These travelers would be sleeping on deck, come rain or shine, and many of them knew that there were better places than others that would provide better protection from the hot sun and inclement weather, and they knew it was first come first served.

Then, a blur suddenly whooshed by and before Wheezer knew what was happening, he was being dragged away on his lead, which had been cut. Sasa was not aware of the change and Wheezer barked furiously for her, but she was unable to hear him and was none the wiser since she still held the looped end of his lead tightly in her hand and the din of the crowd had increased to deafening proportions.

As Wheezer struggled, hands tried to reach down to grab him around his body to pick him up, but he quickly showed them what weapons resided inside his mouth as he squirmed this way and that, almost wiggling out of his collar. Before he could free himself, however, he felt a sharp blow to the side of his head and the world went black.

Sasa finally stepped onto the deck, but was immediately stopped by the purser.

"Yes, miss, may I see your ticket?" he said.

"Certainly," she said as those behind her continued to push at her back.

"You there, stop your pushing and shoving, or you will not come aboard," the man ordered, with an apologetic look back to Sasa. "Your ticket is in order…"

Sasa was admitted past the purser, whose duty was to check passenger documents, tickets and to ask if any valuables needed stowing in the captain's safe.

She finally made it to her designated stateroom and stepped inside. She held the door open for Wheezer and looked down to find Wheezer gone and the limp end of his lead hanging from her hand. Cold fear swept through her body. Immediately, she dropped all her carry-on luggage and parcels, running wildly back to the deck, port side, to yell for him. She realized that Wheezer had not left her side willingly and so she ran to Jackson's stateroom, next to hers.

Sasa banged on his stateroom door which was opened quickly.

"Sasa, what is the matter? Is there a problem in

your room?" Jackson asked, but judging by the look in her eyes, he quickly realized it had to be something terrible.

"Jackson, Anna, someone has taken Wheezer. They cut his lead and he is just vanished. I don't see him on the docks. I have called him several times. I don't know what to do. I got to my room and found his lead cut, but no Wheezer. Jackson, someone knew what they were doing. The captain is going to get underway quickly. I won't leave without him, Jackson. If I have to jump into the water, I will not leave without Wheezer," Sasa said, at the point of tears.

Jackson too was upset by the theft of his friend. Without losing time trying to figure out why he had been stolen, he grabbed Sasa's hand and they made their way to the captain, who was already in the pilot house above. Before they could reach him, the paddle wheels began to turn.

"You go on to tell the captain, I will go back to the rail to look for him," shouted Sasa.

"Right," said Jackson.

The boat began to move from the dock. The last of the lines had been drawn in and the anchor lifted. The loud chugging of the steam engines drowned out most sounds. Sasa looked back at the pilot house and could see Jackson yelling at the captain with his arms waving around frantically.

In a small alleyway close to the dock, Wheezer began to come to. He opened his eyes, but was a bit confused. His first thought was about Sasa. Where was she? His head hurt and blood began to drip down over one eye. He was alone in the alley and there was no one to restrict his movements. Like a shot he catapulted out of the alley toward the retreating steamship. He reached the edge of the dock and began barking furiously. "Sasa, Sasa, don't leave me. I am here. Sasa, see me," he barked, over and over.

On the deck, Sasa finally saw him. The boat was already several yards from the dock and the paddle wheels were continuing to churn the water. She yelled back to Wheezer. She began to remove her light jacket and her shoes to jump over the rail, but before she could finish, Wheezer jumped off of the dock and was swimming vigorously after the boat.

Sasa looked down at the running paddle wheels and gasped. She turned and yelled to Jackson in the pilot house and kept pointing at the wheels.

"Jackson, tell them to stop the wheels, Wheezer is in the water. Wheezer is swimming to the boat. Jackson, tell them to stop," she yelled.

She could see Jackson becoming even more frantic. He banged his fist on the control board in front of him. The captain thought for a second, then nodded to the pilot to shut the wheels down.

"I will have you know, sir, that this will cost not just time, but money as well," said Captain Magellen.

"Never mind that, I will pay for the money lost. Our dog was stolen from us on the dock while we waited. He has run from his captors and is now in the water swimming to reach us," explained Jackson, now that the captain could finally hear what he was saying.

"A dog, you say? Stolen from you on the dock? Why, I have never heard of such a thing. Why would anyone want to steal a dog? There are lots of them running around here with no owners they can have," he countered.

"None are like this dog, Captain. This dog was the first of his kind to come to America. He has saved people's lives and helped to solve crimes. Captain, if we don't find a way to get him on board, my ward will jump over the rail. She will not leave her faithful companion behind," said Jackson with emphasis.

"Oh, very well," Magellen capitulated, then he turned and went on, "First Officer Sands, get however many men you need and get that dog aboard so that we can be on our way. In all my years, I have never seen anything of the like, sir. I hope the compensation to the ship's funds will be worth it to you."

The captain left the pilot house with Jackson, making their way to Sasa who stood anxiously shouting encouragement to Wheezer.

Wheezer was a bit dizzy. He kept on paddling toward the boat. The water had calmed a bit, now that they stopped the paddle wheels, but he felt things were becoming hazy. He had to keep going, had to keep trying to reach Sasa.

Jackson, the captain and Sasa were now at the rail, when from the far side of the dock, gunshots rang out.

"What the? What in tar-nation is that man shooting at?" the captain yelled to his men who were just then lowering themselves down into a rowboat.

Jackson concentrated his focus on the man and realized with a start, "He is shooting at Wheezer, my dog. Is there anyone on deck that can return fire, sir? That crazy man could injure not just the dog, but your men as well."

As Jackson and Sasa looked on with horror, each shot came closer and closer still to hitting Wheezer, who was now not making much progress in the water. To Jackson's surprise, the captain himself pulled out from under his jacket one of the new repeater guns and returned the man's fire. When his shots came very close to hitting his target, the man turned and fled into the shadows between the shipping buildings off the docks.

Jackson had been watching intently during the shooting, and when the man's hat flew off from one of the captain's shots he could clearly see the man was either

Mexican or a southern Indian. Allan and Anna were now beside him at the railing.

Sasa's tear streamed eyes were only for Wheezer. She realized that he was barely holding his own. The men in the rowboat only needed a minute more to reach him in the water, but if he stopped paddling, he would sink. Realizing he needed help staying awake, she yelled to him, "Wheezer, Wheezer boy. Keep going Wheezer, keep swimming. That's right. Let the men help you into the boat Wheezer. They are going to bring you to me. That's a good boy Wheezer, keep going," she encouraged him until the men finally reached him. One of them grabbed Wheezer by the scruff of his neck and pulled him into the boat. Wheezer allowed them to help and once he knew he was in safe hands, he fainted dead away.

Wheezer was placed in Sasa's arms and she immediately took him to her room. Sitting down on her bed, she held him as one holds a baby, while she quickly dried him off with a towel hanging beside the wash basin and pitcher full of clean river water. Anna was beside her, trying to help. Sasa was distraught, with tears flowing down her cheeks so copiously she could barely see to examine him, so Anna took over that duty.

"Sasa, he is not dead, only unconscious. He's lost a lot of blood from his head and it looks like one of the bullets grazed his thigh," she finally said, as she ripped apart some of her cotton petticoat to make temporary bandages to staunch the bleeding. "He needs rest and when he wakes, he'll need you. It is important that he gets liquids. Then when he can take them, some soft foods to eat. If you will stay with him, I will make sure your meals are brought to your room and I will order what Wheezer needs... maybe, even some broth would help him. I will go speak to the ship's cook, if they will show me where the galley is. Don't worry, Sasa, he will recover. From the look of the marks around his neck, he struggled violently to get out of his lead. And see here, there's a bit of skin hanging on his fang where he must have bitten his assailant," Anna went on. "I hope he got a good chunk."

"But why? I don't understand it. Why take him, just to hurt him and walk away? What possible benefit would that accomplish?" asked Sasa.

From the door to her room a voice answered, "It is obvious, Sasa. They wanted to separate you from your protector. They did not want the dog, they wanted to be able to get at you, and Wheezer was in their way. I have thought about this for a while, and it is the only thing that makes any sense," answered Allan, with Jackson nodding his agreement right behind him.

"You said 'they'. How do you know it was not just the man on the docks?" asked Sasa.

"It makes sense that there must be at least two. One to separate you from your dog, and one to get at you on the ship. That means that it is you who are in danger, Sasa. So we must be vigilant to figure out why. Maybe today's attempt has something to do with some of the other strange things that happened during this trip, besides my own atrocious mistakes," said Allan.

Isaiah knocked on the entrance where Allan and Jackson blocked the view inside.

"What's agoin' on? I heard tell, some no-good yahoo tried to kill our dog," said Isaiah.

They all turned to him in unison, then allowed him access to the room. Isaiah approached the bed where Sasa sat with Wheezer now laying in her arms as she rocked him gently back and forth, and he looked the dog over. "Sasa, I

been around some," he then said, quietly, "an I knows animals. I think he ain't been mortally wounded. Just give 'em
some time, gal, an it'll be all right. Now, Isaiah his-self is
agonna keep watch over you an your'n. They ain't agonna
even get close to this here cabin door, Miss Sasa. Don't you
worry none, see?"

Sasa looked deep in the big mountain man's eyes
and just nodded, for she could not trust herself to utter a
word. They all filed out of the small cabin. Anna was the
last and said she would go to the galley right away.

Wheezer and Sasa were alone as Sasa continued
to rock, back and forth, back and forth, her tears dropping
down onto Wheezer's muzzle. Occasionally, she wiped the
wet drops from his face. After a while, she felt so tired she
could not hold her eyes open any longer, so she laid down,
putting Wheezer in the crux of her arm, and pulled the cover
from the bed over her and her friend. Together they slept.

Chapter 30
Best Laid Plans

Mendoza was angrier than he had ever been in his entire life. What was supposed to be a perfect plan to remove the protection—in the form of a scrappy dog—from the squaw he had been following since Boston, had been ruined by sheer chance when the dog recovered enough to make it on to the steamboat. It was enough to make him scream, but he could not take the chance and was forced to control his rage.

It seemed every way he turned to learn more about the charm which had dangled on the girls bracelet had been blocked, his purpose thwarted. He had been standing in a shadowed area of the boat's deck as he watched the drama play out. He could not understand what kept the girl and the dog so inseparable. He had hoped to befriend her in order to get the needed information, but the dog turned out to be too savvy, and he seemed to know his scent. Every time Mendoza got near the girl, the dog gave a warning growl. Too bad his hired help on the dock did not go ahead and bash the little mongrel's brains out.

He had come to the conclusion that the general's purpose in this entire venture was to locate the very artifact he claimed to already possess. All this business of starting a civil war in Indian Territory so that Mexico could take Texas back, now seemed a ridiculous scheme, destined to failure. After careful consideration, he finally decided that he would completely forget about carrying out the general's instructions to further this stupid plan, and concentrate his considerable talents on finding the artifact. He became convinced that it was something he was destined to have, and would not allow anyone to get in his way, not even a mangy dog or a foul squaw in a white girl's clothing. Yes! This artifact must be his, and no one else's.

He retired to the saloon where food could be found; during the day it was open to the ladies as well as to the men, but at night it was only for men, so he could have a respite there and think out a plan to achieve his goal. This time, he would not rely on anyone but himself. Even if he had to follow her into Indian Territory, he would not hesitate. Eventually, she must lead him to what he sought. He reasoned that for her to have the charm, she must have had it made, maybe by a jeweler, to remind her of the artifact in her keeping, so she had to know where it was, and maybe she had other valuable things tucked away. It was obvious. How could an Indian squaw, a Cherokee no less, have the kind of money it took to garner the education, the clothes and the entrance into Boston society she obviously possessed? He did not believe for a moment that a white man would willingly pay for it. In fact, he imagined that the man must have made her his ward because she was wealthy in her own right, and since women could not manage their own property by U.S. law, he had made himself her legal guardian. Very clever of him. Almost as clever as Mendoza himself. Clever, indeed.

Colonel Davenport leaned far back in his polished walnut swivel desk chair, tapping the tips of his fingers on the top edge of the letter he had just received from his commanding officer in Washington City. Fort Gibson was considered to be at the edge of the frontier, and in a very strategic location to watch the activities of the various tribes. On the other hand, Fort Gibson had also become the place where all complaints stopped, since there was no one down the line to pass them off to. Whenever the colonel received correspondence from Washington City, he knew without looking, it meant either work or trouble, or both, in no particular order. Evidently, Indian Affairs officials had been receiving letters, many letters, about the movement of hundreds of Indians in small groups in and around Indian Territory. Judging from previous exaggerations told by panicked settlers in the past, hundreds could mean ten or twenty.

The reports seemed to indicate that all the groups were traveling in a direction that would bring them to the same location. No one was sure what their destination would be, exactly, and even if there had been no violence to speak of, the movement of so many different tribes of Indians was making the nearby border states very nervous.

It also puzzled Colonel Davenport. If they were all traveling to the same destination, how would his troops be able to keep the peace? It was bad enough when only two different tribes met, so whatever was prompting this activity could potentially be a surprise box of trouble for Indian Territory.

It aggravated him as well. Headquarters wanted him to somehow put a stop to them gathering, if that was their intention, but the fact was that they had every right to convene. He had sent a few patrols out, even if there was nothing for them to do but come back to Fort Gibson. There was no disturbance of the peace, that is except the continued tribal raiding close to the border of Texas.

As far as all the raiding went, in every case his officers had investigated, no guilty party could be found. Not that the raids did not happen, they most certainly had happened, but there was some confusion as to exactly what group of Indians were responsible for them. Arrows found at the raid locations indicated certain nearby tribes, but none had had the individual markings each warrior would have made on them. Without those individual markings, a warrior could not count the kill or the coup, and in the Colonel's experience that went against all known practices of any of the tribes within the territory. Each arrow should have had not just the tribal way of making it, but it should have had the maker's decorations or marks. It was the way each warrior identified his own. It also had something to do with the spiritual power they breathed into their weapons. Guns were different, they were anonymous. No one ever marked a bullet. They tended to stay inside the target they smacked into.

He had to be very careful of how he approached any of the tribal governments in Indian Territory. They had certain rights by treaty, and even though he distrusted and even hated most Indians, he refused to break the law he had sworn to uphold. He had at least expected to hear from the various Indian Agents if there was something to be concerned about. He was curious about how all this movement could go on and the agents know nothing of the matter.

The evening before, at dinner with his wife, he had explained the problem. Mrs. Davenport had a very practical head, so much so that if she had been a man, she would have made a good statesman. He generally at least considered her suggestions, if only to keep the peace at home. Last night, she offered a suggestion that, after he heard it, he felt he should have thought of it himself.

"My dear, don't you think that a visit with Chief John Ross would be in order? It stands to reason, he would be the easiest chief to deal with, and you have the added benefit that he is an educated man. I actually admire the Cherokees," Mrs. Davenport said.

"Admire them? Balderdash! Why in the world would you admire any Indian tribe?" replied the colonel.

"Oh, but dear, the Cherokee are the closest to white ways of any of the tribes in the territory. They almost all read and write their own language, and you have to admit they had built up quite a profitable industry back east before their removal. They are almost all Christians. So, if you are careful and respectful of how you approach him, Chief Ross may oblige you in answering your questions. No matter your personal feelings about their race, dear, to his people, he is like the president. If you go in there stomping and blowing like a bull buffalo, don't expect much cooperation. But, yes, I truly believe he is the one to ask," Mrs. Davenport said.

It was true that the Cherokee were the tribe most converted to white ways, and had been an educated people for many decades, so it stood to reason that they would take a leading role in the politics of the region. The infighting within the Cherokee Nation was not good, but their relations with the other tribes were fairly stable. Mrs. Davenport's suggestion had merit.

His decision made, he called for the Officer of the Day and ordered for runners to be sent to both Pierce and Chief Ross with a suggested date and time for a meeting in Tahlequah. Hopefully, they would have their answer in a day or two. He was determined to get to the bottom of this, but just as his wife had said, diplomatically. All there was left to do on that front was wait.

The Golden Serpent sat, propped up in the place where Running Wolf had left it. It was a fitting place for any kind of serpent, especially one made of gold. Alone, its sightless eyes stared from deep shadow. Occasionally, the sun would be at just the right spot to shoot a ray or two that would pierce the shadows far enough to reach its gleaming gold surfaces, which reflected a bright shine, but there was no one to see it. And because of its location, if anyone was unlucky enough to see it, their life would last only seconds before being snuffed out. And so time waited in the silent gloom of the Golden Serpent's forever home. Time and unforeseen circumstances would tell if its gleaming surface would ever be exposed to human eyes again.

Chapter 31
An Unwelcome Visitor

The spring was looking glorious. As it got warmer, every-thing began to take on that irresistible palette of green shades which words cannot do justice to. At least, that is what Chief John Ross thought as he rode his buggy into the surrounding country of Tahlequah, Indian Territory. This trip had been devoted to checking on how the planting was progressing on some of the major farms close in to Tahlequah. He marveled at his own people and their in-genuity. When he considered all of the tragedy they had

had to bear during the last four years, it bolstered him up so much that he wanted to work harder for them, if such a thing was even possible. When he was not working for his people in and around Tahlequah, he was in Washington City trying to represent the Cherokee and their legal rights. Many of those rights were agreed by treaty with the U.S. Government, but were being ignored as if the treaty never existed. Today, however, he did not have to wonder about that. A momentous day was approaching and, so far, he had been successful in keeping the Army, the U.S. Government and his own Cherokee Indian Agent, in the dark as to the purpose of the upcoming peace conference.

After his tour of the nearby farms, he turned around and headed for Park Hill. His dusty black one-horse buggy came to a stop in front of the new Ramada being constructed in honor of the peace council soon to begin. It was the largest structure of its kind his people had built in his memory. Park Hill, near Tahlequah, was the site that had been chosen for the actual conference. There was plenty of room for the various tribes to set up their camps, water flowed nearby, and it was altogether a pleasant place to hold the conference.

Chief Ross sat his buggy and watched the workers as they put the finishing touches on the roof, which consisted of two peaked, four sided, pyramids atop large hewed log poles extending at least twenty feet high. This would allow the speakers to be heard because the peaked roof would catch the sound and reflect it back on the listening audience. Tiered benches were being constructed as well as a speaker's platform. The platform was rather large so that it could accommodate several government observers, plus the Cherokee Indian Agent. Each speaker would stand at the podium to deliver his oration. To either side of the podium they had planned more than one area for interpreters to stand while translating for the various tribes in attendance.

It was all coming together fairly quickly. Even though many of the headmen in the tribe had been far from excited about the prospects of the peace council being a success, when the first runners came in with news of the various tribal commitments to attend, the People started putting their hearts into the preparation. It was not hard to realize that the Cherokee's honor would be at stake if they lacked enthusiasm for the momentous occasion. Only the headmen who had attended the secret planning councils knew the real reason for their attempt to bring all the regional tribes together. Chief Ross hoped that it would stay that way as long as possible.

He looked up at the grand wooden structure and smiled with pride for his people and their ability to work together. It was not always so. Especially when it involved tribal politics, reimbursement monies due the tribe, or the murders relating to the illegal signing of the treaty selling all of the Cherokee lands out from under the Cherokee people's feet. Chief Ross knew that some in the tribe thought he had sanctioned the murders of three of the treaty signers. It was like talking to air whenever he denied any part in it, but he had spoken the truth. He hoped that something like this peace council might help to pull his people together, instead of destroying them from within.

Only time would tell, he thought, as he turned his horse and trotted for Tahlequah, satisfied with the work. So much was at stake, and the biggest stake of all was whether or not the tribes would be able to hold on to the land they had been given. If the plot to start a civil war within Indian Territory among the tribes succeeded, he could not imagine what might happen to all the Indian peoples inhabiting it as a punishment. It must be prevented from happening. At all cost.

As he pulled up to the temporary log building he was using as his office, he noticed that several Army horses, each bearing the Army's brand clearly on its rump, had been left waiting, hitched up to the hitching post in front of the building. *Now what*, he thought. He hoped that whatever this was about, it would only take a short amount of time. He had many things to attend to.

Chief Ross handed the reins of his horse and buggy over to the stable hand who was waiting patiently for them, then he bounded up to the office door, taking the steps two at a time, took a deep breath, and went in. As he entered, his eyes took a little bit to adjust to the dim light inside his office, but he did not need them because even before he entered the room he had been able to hear a man's boots pacing back and forth in there. The pacing man stopped his steps and looked relieved to see him. On his part, Chef Ross was relieved as well that it had not been any other pesky Army officer, but Colonel Davenport from Fort Gibson and his aide; at least, he knew where he stood with this man. Colonel Davenport did not have a good opinion of Indians of any sort, and he did not approve of them trading at Fort Gibson, but he had been overruled by is commanding officer in Washington City, so he now made the best of an unpleasant situation and conducted business with any of the several Indian Territory tribes.

On the other hand, there was no love lost as far as Chief Ross was concerned. He had no use for the Army, especially after the "legal" murders that took place on the Trail of Tears by soldiers who were never brought to justice for their crimes. He had no inducement to be civil, except that he was a gentleman through and through. It was still very trying whenever the two men had to communicate.

"Good afternoon Chief Ross. I was beginning to think you were not going to show up at your own office today," accused the colonel.

"Please forgive the oversight, Colonel Davenport. I will henceforth stay in my office on the off chance you might drop by one day without notice," bantered back Chief Ross.

Now that the verbal shots had been fired by each opponent, a silence ensued for a minute, then Colonel Davenport proceeded with his business without acknowledging the potshots.

"I did send an invitation for us to meet, but I received no return letter. I had also asked Cherokee Agent Pierce M. Butler to attend as well, and when I did not hear from either of you, I made plans to come for a visit myself. Agent Butler was not available today."

"So, what brings the colonel all the way to Tahlequah and Park Hill that is so urgent?"

"Ah, Chief Ross, we have been getting some alarming complaints at Fort Gibson lately. Reports have been coming in that certain Indians from various tribes have been gathering in and around Tahlequah in the past few days. What do you have to say about this?" asked Colonel Davenport.

"Oh, well, I guess it does seem unusual for Indians to be congregating in Indian Territory, where the populace is mostly...let's see...uh...Indian. In these complaints, has something been charged against any individuals or tribes?" countered Ross.

"No. No offenses have been actually reported, but the settlers in Arkansas are getting mighty nervous, especially when they see what seems to be a large gathering of Indians. They want to know if there is going to be a war dance, or are you trying to bring the rains? What is the purpose of the gathering?" asked Colonel Davenport.

"Excuse me, Colonel, but I seem to remember that there are no laws governing our tribe other than the laws we make for ourselves, or have you forgotten that we are a sovereign tribe?" Ross reminded him.

"No, I have not forgotten that fact, even though I strongly disagreed with it when the treaty was drawn up," said Davenport.

"Oh, you mean the fraudulent treaty by which our ancestral lands in Georgia were stolen from us? I don't think it matters what you objected to; and as far as the settlers in Arkansas are concerned, tell them that they can start to worry when we send *them* an invitation.

"And Colonel, if you knew anything about the Cherokee, you would know that we have not danced the war dance for some time. Besides that, there would be no reason to call the rains because it has been raining off and on for days. So why don't you get down to the actual questions you want answered, and stop hiding behind the skirts of those ignorant Arkansas squatters? I have business to attend to, and it does not involve holding the Army's hand," replied Chief Ross.

Colonel Davenport bristled, opening his mouth to bellow out a rebuke when he realized where he was. It chafed him that he could not cow Chief Ross, and for that he had to give him a grudging respect.

"Chief, the Army would like to know more about what type of gathering you are preparing. I have seen the building going on over at Park Hill. It is not every day that such a thing is built. My commander wants to know what it will be used for. Could you please enlighten us?" he asked through his teeth.

Chief Ross thought for a moment or two. It had been agreed among the headmen and elders that they would not fully reveal what they were doing or why, but he had to say something that would mollify the whites' shaky nervous systems.

"My dearest Colonel Davenport, we have invited the tribes of Indian Territory and some tribes close in to the territory, to come to a peace council. Our aim is to reaffirm our traditional ways and to proclaim that peace should exist between us, since we are forced to live so close together. There is nothing sinister about this meeting, and it will not have anything whatsoever to do with war. This is strictly a "come be my brother" council," he finally replied.

"I just can't get my mind around it, Chief Ross. As far as I am aware, there has never been a meeting quite like this one ever before. Can you explain why?" insisted the colonel.

"Very simply put, Colonel, we have never been forced off our lands and made to live in such a small area, side by side with those who used to be our enemies before. What would you have us do, sir?"

"Well, uh...you could let the government do this for you. We have always had success with our dealings with the tribes. It seems a logical choice."

"No, I am afraid it will not do in this case, sir. You deem it a success only because you have forced the rules and we must obey. Keep in mind, Colonel, that there is nothing in the treaty preventing us from making friends with our neighbors, and we don't need the white man for that," said Chief Ross emphatically.

Colonel Davenport paced the floor, apparently not happy with the way the conversation was going. He had thought that the tribes would jump at the chance to have the Army take care of this for them... but what did Indians know, anyway? At the very least, he had to be at this meeting and report the discussions to Washington City.

"Well, Chief Ross, it sounds like a mighty fine meeting. Would I be too rude to ask if I and a few government observers could come to watch? It is a novel approach, and we might be able to learn from your example," he said, while thinking *"unlikely in the extreme"*.

Now Chief Ross was painted in a small corner. He had not wanted any participation by the government, so how was he going to make this work?

"Colonel Davenport, we will be happy to have you come, but only as observers, you understand. I also want you to limit it to only a few people, including our illustrious Cherokee Agent Pierce M. Butler. However, at no time would you have any duties to perform on this occasion. If there is any need for discipline during this conference, we already have our own peacekeeping force on hand. And at no time any of the white settlers from outside of Indian Territory will be allowed to attend. We do have some whites who have married into our tribes and we are leaving it up to each tribe to decide who they send as delegates. If you come, you can be accommodated on the platform behind the lectern. However, sir, if you try to insert yourself into our conference, we will require you to leave our council. Is this understood, sir?" he said with stiff resolve.

"Quite, sir. How many days should we plan on, two... three?"

Chief Ross's eyes began to glitter in amusement.

"We will be meeting for at least one month, sir, or longer," he informed him.

The colonel was taken aback by the length of a meeting such as this. He could foresee no way that the tribes could meet without starting a ruckus, but if he—or any of his government represent-atives—was to be allowed there, he would have to agree to a non-interference agree-ment. *Well, no matter*, he thought. *They will be begging for my help probably within three days of the beginning of the talks.* He did not know of any redskins that could keep their heads, once riled, and he thought he would enjoy that, when the time came.

The chief watched as the colonel mounted his horse and departed in a cloud of dust. He could cross this task off the list of this day's agenda. All seemed to be going well, and Davenport smiled as he thought, *I give that council two days before bedlam erupts and they all end up drunk and disorderly.*

Chapter 32
A Close Call

Sasa woke abruptly in the middle of the night. She could still hear the engines as they pushed and pulled, and with her mind's eye she could see the paddle wheels swirling through the murky Mississippi water. She wondered what had woken her out of her sound sleep. Finally, she felt a wetness flow under her nightdress as she lay beside Wheezer on the cot in her cabin.

Quickly, she reached for her oil lamp and deftly brought light into the small cramped room. Immediately, she noticed that Wheezer was on his side, moving his legs strangely. His back was arched and his tongue was hanging out. He had urinated in the bed – the wetness that had woken her up – and she now noticed that he had defecated as well. He seemed to not be breathing much, if at all. She jumped out of her cot and pounded on the wall to alert Jackson and Anna, in the next cabin, that she was in need of their help, but when the door opened after just a second, she was surprised to see Isaiah. He must have been sleeping at her doorway, protecting her as he had promised he would.

"Isaiah, there is something wrong with Wheezer. He has urinated in the bed and he is moving funny," she pleaded.

"Hush now, little lady. Just let ole Isaiah take a look here. Consarnit, I wish there was more light," replied Isaiah.

Just then the door was opened again by Jackson, with Anna rushing in carrying a second lamp. Isaiah gave a quick nod of acknowledgment, but did not take his attention away from Wheezer.

Anna noticed the state Sasa's night dress was in.

"Sasa, come into my room and let's get you changed into something dry. Isaiah will do everything he can for Wheezer, and you won't be gone but a moment," she urged her.

Sasa looked at Isaiah, and when he nodded his assurances she reluctantly rushed out of the room with Anna. Upon her return, Wheezer seemed more relaxed, no longer thrashing, but still not conscious. She looked up at Isaiah, hoping to hear a good prognosis, but the mountain man did not have the heart to raise her hopes.

Kneeling down next to the cot, so he might be able to look at Sasa, face to face, he hesitated just a moment. Before he could say anything, Sasa broke down in violent tears. As she rocked Wheezer, back and forth, stroking his shiny furry head, she sobbed harder than she had at any time in her life.

Finally, Isaiah was able to speak. "Sasa, me gal, it could go either way... you know he had a bad crack on that hard head a his today. But, I'm a-thinkin he's a real fighter. He could even be able to hear you a-sobbin on him like a river been let loose in the forest. Why, you might even be a-makin him think he's dead already. If'n you don't want him a-thinkin he should just go on ahead an die, I expects you oughta be a-sayin prettier things in them pointy ears a his.

Sasa looked down at Wheezer as she took in the suggestion Isaiah had made. Finally, she looked up long enough to meet Isaiah's eyes and gave a nod. Isaiah knew that meant she would try her very best, but it would be hard.

"Now little lady, I'm a-gonna be right outside this here door. If'n you need me, just call my name," he added, as he left the cabin.

Jackson, knelt down, placing his hand on Sasa's, then Anna placed hers on top of theirs.

"Sasa, Anna and I are right next door, as you know, but we want you to remember that we are also here with you in our hearts. If you need to talk, day or night, just let us know. Meanwhile, we are going to be praying for the safe return to health of your friend and ours. He started out in life on the other side of the ocean. He came to me as a gift, but—be that as it may—he has never been my dog. I was only keeping him until he could meet you. I know Wheezer loves all of us, but you are the most important person in his life, so for his sake, try to let him know you are here, waiting for his return. Just knowing that will help him get better," said Jackson, before he and Anna left for their cabin.

Sasa was exhausted, but that did not matter in the least. Her best friend needed her and she would not let him down. She dried her eyes first, then she began talking to him in a more natural tone. She talked about all the things they would do together. She spoke about Penny back home in Van Buren, Arkansas, who waited for his return with her brood of puppies running around the ranch.

"Oh, now Wheezer, you don't want to miss the chance to run those little puppies ragged, now do you? You will have to try real hard to get better. If you don't, then Masey won't have you to chase out of her kitchen. She sounds mad, but let me tell you, she secretly loves it. She looks forward to your visits to her kitchen. And I think I saw her slip you a cookie one day.

"Then, of course, there are all my friends in Indian Territory. They are depending on you, Wheezer. Especially Poison Woman. She even told me that she intends on making a special beaded collar for you to wear on formal occasions. Won't that be nice?" And on and on it went. All through that night and day, into the afternoon, when a knock sounded at the door.

Isaiah had excused himself to answer a call of nature, so Sasa just beckoned them to come in. To her surprise, it was Captain Magellen. He came into the small space, briefly looking at the dog and sniffed as if he smelled something bad.

"Uh, young lady. I have been informed by another passenger that you have a dying animal in this cabin. I can't stress this any harder than to say you must dispose of said animal as quickly as possible. We can't have the other animals, or even people, becoming ill because of one sickly dog, now can we? Oh, I don't know why I am trying to talk to an ignorant Indian. Where are your masters? I guess that it is to them I should have spoken in the first place," said the captain.

Sasa was so stunned she could only stare at the man with her mouth open. Then she recalled herself.

"Captain, sir. Whomever said these things has misinformed you. The dog in question is the same dog Mr. Jackson Halley paid you a large sum of money the day before yesterday to save from the water. This dog is not just an animal, his name is Wheezer and he is better trained than many humans, I dare say," she replied.

"Now see here, young lady. I don't know who has taught you to say those few intelligent words, but they don't fool me one little bit. Now, you just get yourself up and find your masters before I take a strap to your behind this minute," yelled Captain Magellen.

"Or you will do what, again?" growled a voice from the doorway.

She needn't have to worry, for just as the captain had finished with his diatribe, Isaiah came up behind him to utter those frightening words, and in an instant Jackson and Anna were there as well. The captain was not a large man, and Isaiah not only towered over him but was double his width and muscle as well. As Isaiah looked down on the captain, he uttered a nervous hiccup. Then Jackson pushed past Isaiah, in part from fear of what he might do to the captain, and in part to do it to the captain himself.

"What is the meaning of this, Captain? I could hear you from my cabin. Why are you speaking to my ward as if she were a bond girl or slave? And I demand to know who is telling you that this dog has some kind of illness that could harm the other passengers or animals on this boat!" His face had turned a bright red and his fists were ready for a good brawl.

"Now, Mr. Jackson, I had no way of knowing this was your, shall we say, concubine?"

"What…" screamed Jackson. "I said "ward", as in "adopted", you idiot. Your mind must be so far in the gutter you can't get it out of it. This girl has been given a university education, she has taken all the tests and has passed them. However, something has just occurred to me, sir. Do you own this boat?" asked Jackson.

"Well, uh…no, I do not. I am hired to operate it as captain by Wells and Sons, a shipping concern out of New York. This was their first venture into steamship transport. I assure you, sir, that they are of the utmost upright and honorable of men. They support my decisions and have faith in my abilities. Why do you ask?"

"Ah, Wells and Sons. I happen to know Herald Wells. In fact, he is still paying us, Halley's Financial, for the loan on this tub. So in essence, you are riding in our boat and you better go mind your own business, or you won't have a job or a reference," countered Jackson.

The captain was dumbstruck. He practically ran from the cabin and showed no signs of slowing even when he passed Isaiah.

"I am so sorry, Sasa. That was so uncalled for," Jackson said then, but Sasa was not listening. She was too busy smiling down at Wheezer, who was gazing back at her with loving brown eyes. Satisfied his beloved Sasa was with him, he closed his eyes for a more natural sleep.

For the next few days, Sasa and Wheezer kept to their own cabin with Isaiah to guard them while Wheezer recuperated, much to the displeasure of the shadowy individual on the boat who still wanted to dispose of Wheezer any way he could. Finally, the day came when the steamboat stopped at a small outpost where the Arkansas River meets the Mississippi. They would take on new loads of logs for the burners to make the steam and let off passengers who would either walk or take a ferry boat to their destination. In Sasa and her family's case, they would have to take a small flatboat that would take them across the Mississippi to the Arkansas and up it until they reached Fort Smith, where they would be let off on the Van Buren side of the river and then pay to have a runner to send a wagon from the ranch for all their luggage. It was the best feeling in all the world to Sasa. Home to what she knew the best. Home to her families in Indian Territory and in Arkansas, Indian and white alike. That was where her heart was now.

Chapter 33
Travelers

By various modes of travel, General Federico Guillermo De Almeida had made his way from Boston to his covert operations camp on the Red River, a bit east of the border of Indian Territory. From this position, he was able to direct the strikes and raids perpetrated on the various tribes just across the Texas border. He had expected to meet Mendoza there, since that man had orders to follow that vixen of a squaw and find out who her contact was concerning the Golden Serpent artifact, then to meet him here at his covert camp to help accomplish the inciting of the Indian Territory civil war, but there had been no word from him.

Worse news followed. The raids on the various towns and tribes of Indian Territory were no longer causing the horror and fright they once were. It was reported that now the raided camp or town was only asking their people questions, picking up the spent arrows and holding hidden councils. De Almeida could not imagine what had gotten into those dumb Indians, but they were acting exceedingly strange. Maybe, they were too ignorant to figure out a neighboring tribe had attacked them. At this rate, no civil war would start and his fine plan to help his nation win back the land now called Texas was fading fast. He had thought this venture would be a simple thing. He had sold the idea to El Presidente himself. If this did not work out, it would be his own neck in a hangman's noose. For the first time ever, he thought about ways to avoid his leader's wrath. The possibility of considering desertion loomed large in his mind, and he gave a visible shudder at the thought.

A few miles north of Tahlequah, the delegation of Osage was making their way south for the Peace Council. By now the warriors and their Chiefs were trail worn and dusty. They had hunted along the way and there had been no unpleasant surprises, but the weather was hot and the ground dry. Their ponies pranced along the rocky ground, their desire to take off at a hard gallop so great that they constantly had to rein them in. On each Indian saddle was a small barrel of Indian whiskey, made of pure corn liquor, cut with chilies and tobacco, watered down, but no less dangerous and firmly strapped down. The chiefs had ordered that no drinks would be taken until their arrival. The warriors were hard pressed and thirsty for the strong drink.

However, Coyote had no desire for the intoxicating influence of the Indian whiskey they carried. He had already seen too much of the results of drinking that foul smelling stuff, and he believed the tribes were under attack in a silent war of attrition, with whiskey being used as the sole weapon against them. Yellow Eyes walked along beside his pony as an honored member of the delegation.

As Coyote rode along, he let his mind wander where it would, and he soon found himself thinking of Sasa. He wondered what had become of her, and if she had married. There had been little time to get to know each other better, those few years back when he had gone on his quest. Now would be different. He hoped she would still be there, but there was every possibility she would not, and that thought made him a bit sad, indeed.

He traveled light, wearing just the breech clout and his leggings and moccasins. He would have removed his leggings, but the weeds and brushes along the route were bad enough to tear the skin and inflame wounds that were already there.

As they rode or walked along the faint trail down into Cherokee Territory, they chatted. Excitement was building for the conference to come.

"Sata Wapoke (Five Owls), I believe we will soon be passing the place where I stayed with the Cherokee. I doubt that Poison Woman and Medicine Man will be there, since it had been a temporary camp site, but there are sure to be many Cherokee farms along the way, and we may see other groups coming for the same reason. Are you looking forward to this meeting?" asked Coyote.

"Ah, Coyote, I do not know what to expect, but… yes, I am excited and curious to see the other peace council delegations, many of whose we have fought in battle. I am hoping they will honor the white wampum and not cause any trouble there. My Chiefs say that if there is trouble, they are prepared to give as good as they get and better, but on my part I am hoping that there will be no trouble, for I wish to hear all of the various Chiefs give their peace speeches, and I am also curious to know why they called this council. It has never happened before, and if it turns out badly, it may never happen again. What do you think?" replied Five Owls.

Coyote thought for a moment before he answered.

"I am also interested in the speeches, but I am hoping to see a Cherokee friend of mine, the maiden I told you about, Sasa. I am sure she will be much changed. I hope she remembers me," said Coyote.

"Ah, are you in love, my friend?"

"Love? We have never spoken of such a thing. She is a friend."

"But friends can become lovers, yes?

"Yes, in my tribe as well, friends can become lovers, but I am not sure she is thinking along those terms. She may not even have thought of me like I have thought of her."

"My friend, I assure you, she has thought of you. If not, then she is no woman I would want to know. Ha haha-hahahaha," laughed Five Owls.

And on they walked, ever closer to the place called Park Hill, near Tahlequah. Some they met along the way pointed them in the correct direction, giving them kindly advice on roads to take. Every face had a smile on it, and many of these same people would also be at the confer-ence, just to watch.

In the meantime, Running Wolf and his party of Choctaw headmen and chiefs were making their way from the opposite direction. Little did they know that the Watcher was trailing along behind, far behind, waiting for the opportunity to carry out his orders.

Mendoza also stepped off of the steamboat, but made sure he did not get near the Halley party of travelers. He especially kept his distance from Wheezer. When the flatboat was brought, he told the owner that he wanted to be taken separately. The boat owner agreed for extra money. So Mendoza watched the Halleys embark and go across the Mississippi while he waited. He did not want them to realize they were being followed, and he was sure he had succeeded in keeping their curiosity away from him.

The loggers had worked fast and furious to get the logs they had cut down that morning for the steam boat safely loaded into the boat's boiler room hold. There were six men plus the logging boss, all big and burly. The Halleys had long since loaded themselves onto the flatboat and had gone. Mendoza watched the steam boat paddle its way towards other ports along the Mississippi, as he settled himself down on a low rock. The loggers took a break in their long day, for a bite to eat.

"Hello, my fine friends. Do any of you know the Halleys from Van Buren, Arkansas? They were the folks that just left on the flatboat," asked Mendoza.

The men looked at him with slitted, hateful eyes, then their leader answered in clipped sharp tones.

"Well, now, I don't see as how you needs to know any such a thing. On the whole, I don't remember as you have ever been in these parts affore, and I don't rightly believe any of us are your fine friend. You look far more like one of them there Mexicans to me, so let me give you some free advice. Get your business done quick-like and get on outta here. We don't cotton to any foreigners round these parts," he warned.

"Sirs, I assure you that..." Mendoza managed to reply before he was interrupted.

"Don't matter, no how. We don't care a fiddle faddle about your assurancing. You just better get yourself on outta these parts soon, or you won't have a head to talk outta."

"But, Sirs, I mean no disrespect. I just want to..."

"No, you don't and no, you won't," the logging boss's final words rang out. There was no room to argue.

Mendoza only smiled benignly.

As dusk arrived, the longboat had not yet come back and Mendoza was extremely unhappy. He had wanted to get at least across the Mississippi, if not to Fort Smith or Van Buren. *If these men knew who they were talking to,* he thought, *they might know it is very dangerous to treat me, Mendoza, in that fashion, especially since they are illiterate swine.*

A thought came to him unbidden, but it made perfect sense to him. He watched the men start a campfire, so it seemed they would stay the night on the boat landing. The longboat captain arrived and informed Mendoza that he would have to wait until morning for his ride. He had nothing to argue about it, though, because the delay would serve a purpose not thought of before.

It was a night with little light from the moon, as it was covered by high flying clouds. The campfire had burned low and all the loggers were asleep, positioned around it, feet first. The loggers had paid no attention to Mendoza, nor did they invite him to their fire or share their food with him, but he had no problem going without food for as long as necessary. His mind was on other things.

In the dark, he carefully walked to the tree line where the loggers had been harvesting trees for the steamboats that stopped for fuel, and there he waited patiently. Through the night, each man rose to relieve himself. When he did, Mendoza would make a noise that was definitely not a noise from nature, and each time the logger would follow to see what the disturbance was. Of course, each one investigated brandishing some kind of weapon they had at hand, but since the glowing coals of the campfire gave them momentary blindness, Mendoza had the advantage and each time there was one less logger to greet the morning sun. Stealthily, he unsheathed a dagger that was very sharp on both sides of the blade, and it took so little effort with each man, as he slipped the sharp blade between their shoulders and it was over.

By morning when the flatboat was ready to take him across, there were no loggers in sight, only Mendoza, who mentioned the loggers had started early and were in the woods. It would be some time before anyone figured it out, and by then he would have accomplished his mission and been on his way, out of the United States.

"Well, I don't reckon why I slept so deep that I did not hear those men this morning. I musta been tired, though. Why in heck didn't they wake me for breakfast?" complained the flatboat operator, then he noticed the camp fire was cold and no breakfast had been cooked that morning. "I guess they was too much in a hurry to eat. Oh well, are you ready? I reckon I will catch breakfast over ta the fort after I drop you off."

"Have a good breakfast, sir. I will wait as well, until I see my friends across the river from the fort. I am quite anxious to get on out of here, so let's get going," replied Mendoza amiably. *Too bad for the next steam boat to dock here expecting logs for their boilers,* he thought. *I guess they are going to have to send the men on the boat to do their own chopping.* And he giggled quietly.

Chapter 34
Invitation For Peace

The light was just beginning to fade from the afternoon sky when the Halleys pulled up to their ranch in Van Buren. One of the hands had been sent with a wagon to assist them in getting home.

Sasa and Wheezer jumped down off of the sideboard and almost instantly a blinding streak of fur went buzzing past them, then circled around and made another pass. This time closer. After several more rounds at high speed, Penny came to a panting standstill, a smile from ear to ear on her funny Jack Russell face. Her ears, which naturally bent in the middle and were placed either side of the top of her head, were now standing straight up as she started jumping up and down, up and down, until finally Sasa rushed over to give her a big hug. Wheezer reached Penny first, however, and proceeded to give her little bites on the sides of her head, his form of kisses between dogs.

"Penny, oh Penny, I am so happy to see you. Good girl, now sit so we can see you better, sit!" ordered Sasa.

Before Sasa could get a good look at Penny, out of the barn rushed five whirling dervishes in various markings on white fur. Two had a round patch of black fur circling the right eye. One had a round dark tan spot at the base of its tail. One had one black ear and one dark tan ear, and the last pup, the runt it seemed, was all white except a black spot on the tip end of his cropped tail.

Sasa was so overwhelmed that she sat down in the grass and let the dogs crawl all over her, licking her lips, nipping at her clothes and tugging at the leather of her shoe as she laughed uproariously. It was obvious she did not want to be rescued, so the rest of the Halley party traipsed through the main entrance to Jackson's grand house.

"Wait a minute, wait a minute. Come on guys, let me up. Oh for heaven's sake, stop tugging on my clothes!" She would just get her feet under her in order to stand when a pup would jump to grab her sleeve and pull her down again, but she finally managed to get up, and after thoroughly loving and petting the brood, she grabbed her bag and parasol and headed for the house. Wheezer stayed behind to play with the pups and Penny. All in all, it was a great homecoming.

An hour later, they sat at the table, eating one of Masey's fine meals with Archibald Flint, Jackson's best friend, foreman and part owner of the ranch.

"Jackson, we must talk. There is something big happening in Tahlequah. Chief Ross sent a messenger requesting that Sasa join him at the "Grand June Peace Council." It is the first ever council of its kind. It has all been pretty secret. The Chief would like you and Sasa to come to Tahlequah. She is needed, but I can't say why. You are to be her...how do you say in English...her protector. They did not tell me why she is needed, all I know is that the white wampum beads were sent out to all of the Indian Territory tribes and as far as the Rockies, down into Texas and north to Illinois, in invitation to this conference," said Arch.

"The word you are looking for, my friend, is chaperone. It is French, and means the same thing as protector. Well now, this sounds interesting. How long are we needed?" asked Jackson.

"I am made to think three or four weeks."

"Three or four weeks? We just got back from a long trip and we have to leave again? Darn, I was hoping for some rest. What do you say, Sasa?"

"Well, since I don't know what Chief Ross has in mind, I suppose I ought to go and talk with him," said Sasa.

"There is no time, Sasa. The various chiefs and warriors have already started arriving. They have set up a huge shed with three foot wide planks for its roof, in Park Hill, where the council grounds were for the last big council of the headmen of the Cherokee," said Arch.

Sasa thought it over for a bit, but there was really nothing she could do but go. If her Chief needed her, then she must go. In fact, was that not the reason why she had got all that education, so she could help her people?

"But what about the army? Where are they in all of this?" she asked.

"Chief Ross has told them nothing. They have been allowed a certain number of observers, but that is all they are there for. They have nothing to do with this conference. Much to their surprise, Chief Ross is not telling them much. They have been making threats that they will bring in the troops and break it all up, and the white settlers across the border into Arkansas are up in arms, claiming they will all be murdered in their beds with this many Indians on the loose, but, the chief stood his ground. He pointed out that the Cherokee are a sovereign nation, and that they have every right to hold a conference and invite whomever they choose. That didn't sit well with them, so the chief agreed to let some of the brass come, including Agent Pierce Butler. I don't know who else will attend, but I can tell you they won't have any way of understanding what is going on during most of the speeches, since they will be translated into all the various tribes tongues but not into English. Hahahahahahaha." laughed Arch. "You will need to leave in the morning if you are to get there on time, Sasa. Oh, and Wheezer is also invited."

Sasa heaved a big sigh and put down her napkin.

"There is nothing to do but go, Jackson, which means I need to get some sleep. Good evening all, and Masey, this meal was the best I have eaten since I left home. Wado, Masey," she said, as she left the table for her room.

Bright and early next morning, Jackson and Sasa were repacked and on the road to Tahlequah. The farewell to Anna was tearful and Allan was feeling left out. The wagon started down the dusty road towards Tahlequah, but stopped before they had gotten very far. Turning in his seat, Jackson beckoned to Allan to get his bags packed quickly and jump in the wagon, because he was sure that Chief Ross would not mind and he and Allen could try to be of help if they needed it.

The trip would take all day and possibly part of tomorrow as well, since it took longer to cover that distance in a wagon. Sasa had made sure to pack all of her best ceremonial clothes and the few small things she had made for Wheezer to wear on special occasions.

By the time Mendoza approached the ranch, the wagon was a few hours ahead of him. By asking at the house, he received the barest of information and when no one was watching him, he slipped down the same road his quarry had taken.

Chapter 35
The Great June International
Peace Council of 1843

The meeting grounds of Park Hill near Tahlequah was swamped with delegates. Some had brought their women and children as well, so they might cook and help the men in any way they needed. The various tribal groups were separated only by a few yards. So far there were just under four thousand souls attending, the host nation, the Cherokees, included. Everyone knew the object of the conference was peace, so all of the various warriors were on their best behavior. At least that is what Sasa thought when she picked her way through the crowded campsites in search of Chief John Ross. Their wagon had slowed them down some, so they arrived after the official start of the conference.

She finally saw the huge, newly built open shack, like a pole barn without walls, and she headed for it. As she got closer, she marveled at the way the sound carried right out into the audience and even further. The effect must be in the way it was built, she thought. She could clearly hear Chief Ross speaking in Cherokee. As she got closer, she could vividly see all the bright colors of everyone's best clothes. She had also donned her best ceremonial dress and regalia, her high top moccasins and the wonderful turquoise jewelry she had received as a graduation gift from friends.

It was a few moments before she realized that observers from the U.S. Army were there, as well as a few other white men whom she did not know. Among the Army attendees she noticed Colonel Alberson, and behind him was Colonel Davenport from Fort Gibson.

She glanced back at Chief Ross and thought how grand and proud he seemed as he talked of the reason for this conference. He said:

Brothers, when we look back to the history of our race we see some green spots that are pleasing to us. We also see many things to make our hearts sad. When we look back on the days when the first council fires were kindled, around which the pipe of peace was smoked, we are grateful to our Creator for having united the hearts of the red men in peace; for it is in peace only that our women and children can enjoy happiness and increase in numbers. By peace our condition has been improved in the pursuits of civilized life. We should, therefore, extend the hand of peace from tribe to tribe, till peace is established between every nation of red men within the reach of our voice.

Brothers, when we call to mind the early associations which endeared us to the land that gave birth to our forefathers, where we were brought up in peace to taste the blessings of civilized life; when we see that our fires have there been extinguished, and our families removed to a new and distant home, we cannot but feel sorry. But the designs of Providence are mysterious: and we should not, therefore, despair of once more enjoying the blessings of peace in our new home.

Brothers, by this removal tribes hitherto distant from each other have become neighbors, and those hitherto unacquainted have become known to each other. There are, however, numerous other tribes with whom we are still strangers.

Brothers, it is for renewing in the West the ancient talk of our forefathers, and of perpetuating forever the old pipe of peace, and of extending them from nation to nation, and of adopting such international laws as may redress the wrongs done by the people of our respective tribes to each other, that you have been invited to attend the present Council. Let us, therefore, so act that the peace which existed between our forefathers may be pursued, and that we may always live as members of the same family.

As he continued to talk, Sasa gazed at the crowd of Chiefs preparing themselves to give their own talks. This was when she noticed the interpreters positioned around and in front of the various clusters of like speaking tribes. There was only one to translate to the white men and Sasa doubted that he would be able to translate any more than two or three of the speakers, if that. Likely, he could only translate from the Cherokee language.

She skirted the large crowd, walking several yards away from the forum, looking for familiar faces. She did not yet know what Chief Ross wanted her to do here. She could barely hear him giving his speech now, when she happened into an area reserved for barrels of what she assumed to be strong drink or whiskey. She was very familiar with what they looked like. Then she noticed that the barrels were being carried one by one over to a man with an ax. A barrel was being placed in a rocky crevice and was split wide open, letting the whiskey spill out.

"What is going on here? Does Chief Ross know you are ruining all this whiskey? Although, it is not a bad idea, I must say," asked Sasa.

"Osiyo. Yes, the Chief asked us to empty all of this before it ruins his conference," said the man with the ax.

"There are so many barrels. This is going to take a while," she observed.

"At last count, there were fourteen hundred barrels, brought by all the various tribes. I sure hope they do not give the war cry over our disposing of it all. The Chief says this is not a party, and that the delegates can party when they get back home. So, when the groups come in, we take the barrels away and stack them here until we can get to them. Don't know where it is all going. I sure hate to think that some farmer down the way will have whiskey in his well for some time to come," the man replied while they all laughed.

Sasa gave a short nod and continued on her way. She was familiar with this area, but it looked totally transformed by all the delegates and their families. Thankfully, there was water readily available and Chief Ross had prepared by buying up a lot of the corn crop of the previous year. Now that it was the beginning of summer, there were thousands of vegetable gardens that would yield their fruits for the visitors and the local families alike. The Cherokee people were known to be generous, even with people from far away, like Ireland, where the potato famine caused so many to starve to death; the Cherokee had opened their arms and hearts to the Irish and helped them whenever they could.

Finally, it sounded as if the council had adjourned for the lunch period. The food for the entire council was being provided by the Cherokees, so there was no lack of food for any campfire. Sasa caught sight of Chief Ross, heading toward his camp area which he would occupy for the duration of the council, and she quickly picked up her step so that she would converge on his path. Chief Ross was jolted out of his innermost thoughts by her sudden appearance.

"Osiyo, daughter. I am overjoyed that you were able to make it to the council," he said.

"I am pleased to have been invited. I was told that you had need of me during the council. What can I do for you that all of your other people could not do as well as I?" Sasa replied.

Chief Ross looked around, as if to check to see if they were being watched. "Let us not discuss this here," he then said. "Come to my camp. My lunch is waiting for me there and I am sure I will have plenty to share. We can discuss the reason why I called for you after we eat." Then he looked down at Wheezer, who had remained silent even though there were thousands of strangers around him. "Ah, Wheezer, you have come to help your friend, Sasa. I am indebted to you my friend. I will make sure you are fed, as well. Eh?" Then they moved off towards his large tent. Before they entered the tent Wheezer turned his head, seeming to search the crowd, then uttered a low unmistakable warning, but to whom, Sasa was unsure.

Deep in the crowd there was a man, taken by everybody for just another Indian, for he was dressed in fine buckskins and his skin had a brown cast to it, only a shade different from all the others. His hair was long and black, and he had a cord wrapped around his head to hold it back. He remembered the close call, and the luck that he had found a lone Indian, traveling to the Peace Conference. However, he felt it had taken him an eternity to learn where the People were traveling to. It seemed that the towns were emptying of their inhabitants. When he had stopped an elderly couple, he thankfully found the woman could speak English.

"I'll bet you can't speak English, old squaw," he said.

"Well, ugly man, I most certainly do speak English. What do you take me for, some uneducated white person from Arkansas? Who are you?" she countered, with as much disgust as he had also shown.

"Uh, Mendoza, mam'. I just want to know where everyone is going?" he said.

Interrupting the conversation, a young woman came walking up to them on the road. Little did that young woman know, her arrival prevented him from taking care of the old couple. It was no matter, since the girl Sasa was unlikely to know such a pair as that, but he hated that he had given them his name.

"Don't you know nothing? The Cherokee have invited all the Indians as far as we can run, to a big shindig down at Tahlequah. Ain't you heard about it?" she said. "Hello, Martha. You going to the conference? Come on along with us, we like the company."

"I would love to Grandmother Poison Woman," accepted Martha.

The old man standing beside Poison Woman only stood and watched.

"Say, have you seen a young Indian girl, riding with a white guy? I think they were headed this way. Her name is Sasa," said the man.

Startled, and now looking as if she suspected him of some-thing, the old woman only shook her head as they turned as a group and continued on their way.

By that time, there were more people on the road, so he held back so that he might make a plan on what to do. As the day came to a close, the sun dipped below the horizon and still, he stood in the shadows, trying to decide what to do next. Sasa was heading for the conference, that much he knew from the Halley's cook. He had barely finished talking when a little dog came barking and showing his teeth, escorting him out of the yard in no uncertain terms.

He finally settled on a course of action. Now he only needed to waylay an Indian with clothes that would fit him.

He saw his opportunity coming up the road and it was hard for anyone to see where the man hid behind some bushes. Finally, when the man walked just past his location, he jumped out, pulled his knife and dispatched him so quickly he had no time to scream. The blade slid neatly between his shoulder blades. Next, he took the man's clothes and regalia. And then lastly, he scalped the young man in a most unusual way. It would be a long time before anyone finding the body would figure out why.

Yes, Mendoza had made it just ahead of his quarry. In fact, he happened upon a delegation of some Indians, he didn't care what tribe, and walked in just behind them. If anyone spoke to him, he just pointed to his throat as if he was unable to speak.

There were thousands of people and campsites here. It might make it more difficult for him to find Sasa, but he knew he eventually would. He made his own small camp, accepted the food that was provided by his Chero-kee hosts, and waited.

Chapter 36
An Abundance of Love and Cooperation

Having finished her meal, Sasa now waited patiently for her host and Chief to finish and explain why he needed her here at the Peace Conference. He finally wiped his mouth and came to sit close to her so that their words would not be overheard.

"Daughter, wado for coming. I know you have just finished a long trip back from Boston, but you can help us with a very sticky situation here at the conference," he began.

"What could you possibly need, sir, that I could supply? Of course, I am always ready and willing to help my people, and I am honored to be invited," she said.

"Where did you leave Jackson? I assume you did not come alone." he asked.

"I believe he stopped at the Flints' campsite. Do you remember Archibald Flint? Arch and his family run our ranch, and Arch is partners with Jackson. I don't think Arch will make it down here until Jackson goes back to take over for him. He may make it for a couple of the last days. Jackson stopped at their camp to let them know, so they would not be looking for him until later," explained Sasa.

"But you have Wheezer by your side, and for that I am very glad. Sasa, this might be a bit tricky. You see, we have not told the govern-ment much about this con-ference. If they knew, they would try to take it over, and once that happened, it would be ruined. They never abide by their own treaties and they lack honor. They don't understand the Wampum and they don't care to understand the way we Indians think. Since you are a young woman now, and you have that fine education, I thought you could just get close to the United States observers, to keep track of their conversations—you know, if they want to bring in troops, that sort of thing—and then come to tell me. With your education, you will understand them better than any of our translators. We need that here, we need you, to help watch out for the Cherokee's interests and for all the tribes meeting here in good faith. If we fail at this conference, they might not participate the next time, and I am hoping the various Indian Territory tribes will take turns hosting the conference every few years, without any help from the United States. Do you think you can do this for your chief?" asked Chief Ross.

Sasa was stunned. It was a heavy responsibility to take on. But, how could she refuse? She could not.

"Yes, my chief, I will be at your service. Can you please tell me what to watch for, what phrases might spell trouble, that sort of thing?" said Sasa.

The lunch break was almost over, and the next speaker was due to take his turn on the platform. So far Sasa saw Muskogees or Creeks, Choctaws, Chickasaws, Shawnees, Pankeshaws, Seminoles, Delawares, Caddoes and Kickapoos. There were still tribes coming in. The Osage had not made it yet, nor had the Quapaws or Peorias. Chief Ross had told her that eighteen wampum runners had returned with an acceptance of their invitation. So there would be even more than these she already knew were coming.

She found herself back under the great expanse of the wooden roof, over the main part of the council. She silently walked over close to the back of the platform, where the United States representatives were sitting with the Cherokee Agent Pierce M. Butler, and she took a seat to listen. Next up to speak was the War Chief from Tucka-batchemicco, part of the Upper Creek division of the Musk-ogees, or Creeks. He was to give only a small talk this day, and a much longer one when all of the tribes had reported present.

He stood up on the podium in his grand outfit. On his head he wore a bowl-like cap with feathers coming out of the middle and more hanging down over all its sides. He wore a white shirt with a black silk cravat, his undercoat was a mild pink and his over jacket was of light gray wool with fleur de lis printed on the fabric. Its shoulder seams attached off shoulder with a small ruffle. The sleeves had a yellow stripe and the coat had yellow piping. The coat wrapped and was held together with a sash of the same gray color. He carried a shoulder bag which matched his coat. He looked magnificent.

He stood tall and said

"Brothers--I rise up this day to give a small talk. The talk I am going to deliver, will be around the Council Fire of the Muskogees, with a bright sky above. The white beads which I hold in my hand, I am going to send to our Grand Father, the Delaware. In the time of our Forefathers, he sent to us a stalk and some beads, saying: Your ears are stopped, and your eyes have dust in them-receive these emblems, they will open your ears, and wipe out the dust from your eyes. These were the words we once received from the Dela-wares, the intention of which was to open the White path of peace, that we might train up our children in it.

I am now tracing up the old customs of our Fathers, and what I am saying is understood by all of our old people present. I also speak in the presence of Gov. Butler, and Col. Logan, Agents for the Cherokees and Creeks, and Lieutenant Flint, of the United States army. This talk is given that those who are not present may hear it also. As we have lately had some difficulty with some of our red brethren, we now send these beads to our Grand Father, the Delaware, that the White path so lately stained with blood may be cleaned, and that some plan may be fallen upon for the preservation of peace, and to prevent the further shedding of the blood of any of our brethren. The persons who were killed, from what I can learn, were of the tribe called the Pawnee Mahas--a tribe that but few of us have ever seen.

Brothers--We have traveled a long way from the course of the rising sun. Before coming to the land we now inhabit, we heard a great deal about our brethren who dwelt far towards the setting sun. Since arriving and kindling here our new fires, we have had the pleasure to see some of our western brethren, and have taken great interest in explaining to them the ways of our Forefathers. In former times, our fathers knew nothing of the emblem's I hold in my hands, as in those days there was nothing but war and bloodshed among the people. But since the adoption of these emblems, and the use of them for making peace between different tribes, becoming a custom among the Red people, they have proved of great benefit, and form the ground work of training our children in the path of peace. The white beads and tobacco, which I send to the different tribes, are to cleanse the path which has lately been stained with blood; and I wish all those who hear this talk, to take it home with them, and to tell it to their children and grandchildren, and to advise them to walk in the straight path of peace. It is given around the Great Council Fire, and must not be forgotten as long as the sun rises and sets--or the waters run and the trees grow. I will send this talk to our Grand Father, the Delaware, with the request that he will send it with some beads and tobacco, to the Pawnee Mahas, and say to them that the path that leads to their country is grown up--when they receive them.The path will be opened, and purified of the stain of blood. No more blood must be spilt. I will also send word to them, that hereafter, when traveling the path, should they happen to see blood or bones, they must think that they have been caused by lightning, a fall from a horse, or through some accident. The red people, like other populous nations, have among them some bad people, who will, probably, stain the path by spilling blood. Should any do so we feel that it will be our duty to rise up with our arms, and joining our friends, put a stop to it. I send also some tobacco and beads to our Grand Father, the Delaware, with a request that he will send them and this talk to the Shawnees, Wy-andotts and Kickapoos. I am done."

Sasa was surprised the speech was so eloquent. She barely noticed the time it took to listen. The Army representatives were moving around to allow one of their number to reach the podium. She thought, *Oh no, I hope they don't cause a riot,* then giggled to herself. The man who now stood before the podium was Colonel Alberson. He seemed a puffy type of person. His uniform bulged out around the middle, which made his two rows of silver buttons sparkle and gleam. He also wore a cravat, but it was rumpled and so was his uniform, for that matter. There was dust on his black boots and his hair stuck out from all sides. All Sasa could do was listen and try to keep from either laughing or being incensed. He said:

"We are in the path of our forefathers: I have but few words to say, but will say them in the same spirit of those I have heard speak. The new Race know but little, or nothing of the habits of our fathers.

I remember to have seen a similar council in former times-this is in the original way. The path is thus kept white and clean, even to each other's doors.

The little difficulty that occurred a short time back. I now regard wiped out by this white path, and I am glad to see the white path re-newed and extended to the Northern Tribes, and I am glad to see all uniting to keep clear this path. I hope all nations will join and assist in keeping this path open and clear of obstructions.

When I reach home, I will explain to my people, what I have witnessed and heard here; and I will also use my influence with the different tribes to get them to inculcate and teach the same to their children. This is all. A short talk is often better than a long one and all sufficient. I would like to have a copy of the proceedings here, to read to my people when I get home. I am glad to see the Agents present. When I get home I will call a council and invite our Agent."

He bowed slightly and made his way back to his chair. By that time, the afternoon session was done. Now the chiefs would meet together privately to settle specific business. It was just as well. Sasa was seething after Colonel Alberson's talk, because it was ridiculous.

Jackson found her under the council roof shaking her head.

"What is the problem, young lady? Did someone say something that didn't taste all that good? Hahahaha," he laughed.

"No, Jackson. It is just that Colonel that just finished talking said some pretty dumb things. They should have never let him talk. First he insults us by saying we are a "new" race, like we just were invented. We were here long before he was born, in fact before his distant ancestors were born in Europe. Then when he talks about the "white" path, he is really talking about his white ways and teachings, not the white path of peace. Is he so totally ignorant of what the wampum colors represent?" replied Sasa, with mounting irritation.

"Whoa now, Sasa. It's no use to get upset. Remember, they are just observers. They think the tribes hang on their every word, but if you had looked around you would have seen many get up and leave during his talk. Your brothers and sisters in all these tribes have closed their ears to him, so you need to do the same. Just try to forget it. He likes to hear himself talk anyway," said Jackson.

"I suppose he does. It just boggles my mind how he could get it all so wrong," she replied.

"The same way they have gotten it wrong for several hundred years now. So let's go get something to eat. The Flints are cooking up something special for you. All your Cherokee favorites. Fry Bread too," said Jackson.

"Thank you, Jackson. I don't know what I would have done without you and Wheezer. Speaking of Wheezer, I don't see him. I will have to find him first, then I will be right there," said Sasa.

She started out making a circle around the council hut, but did not see him. As she searched, she began to worry. It was not long ago that someone had been trying to hurt him. As she walked the outer perimeter she began to feel frantic. She was almost ready to tell Jackson, when she saw him romping in an adjacent field with another dog... but wait, it was not a dog at all. Wheezer was playing with a coyote. As Sasa got closer she was relieved to discover that Wheezer was playing with a longtime friend, Yellow Eyes, the coyote that had befriended her and her family several years ago. And where ever you saw Yellow Eyes, you were almost certain to also find Coyote, the Lakota.

As Sasa turned to look around for him, she was surprised to find him just behind her. But with the corner of her eye, she also saw a strange Indian that seemed to be sneaking up on Wheezer. At the appearance of Coyote, the man faded into the brush. That was most unsettling.

"Ha, you never saw me, Sasa. You are losing your skills with all of that book learning you have been doing," joked Coyote.

"That was only because I was looking for Wheezer. But maybe you are right, seriously. Let me take a look at you. You look grand, and you may be the only Lakota to attend," she answered happily.

"In honor of the friends that brought me, I today am an Osage. I was invited in case there are those who speak a language that I can translate. Then I will do that for the Osage delegation. You know, Black Dog is here. I had the honor of being asked by him to come. I don't think anyone says no to Black Dog," said Coyote.

"Not if they value their scalp," agreed Sasa, and they laughed together.

But, still there was that feeling of being stalked that stayed in her mind. She was not sure if she even saw it now, but the thought would not go away.

She and Coyote with their friends Yellow Eyes and Wheezer, walked off into the crowd, talking and laughing.

Mendoza crept out of the bushes, but pretended to be pulling up his breechclout after urinating. He was careful to not get too friendly with any of the delegations since they all spoke their tribe's tongue. He could speak a bit of Cherokee, so he took his food at their camps. Up to this moment, he had thought he had an opportunity to grab the dog, but at the last minute the girl was there with a very stout looking brave, and his opportunity was lost. Now he would have to wait.

And wait he did. Days went by with many speeches from the council hut. Even Sequoyah, the Cherokee who invented the Cherokee alphabet, spoke. But nothing would take Mendoza's mind from his purpose.

Chapter 37
We Are A Beautiful People

The 1843 Grand International Peace Council was well underway. Sasa had been so happy in Coyote's company, she had forgotten all about stalking figures. After all, this was her people's land now. The Cherokee were one of the most respected tribes in Indian Territory because of their skill in adapting the white ways to their businesses and agriculture. The Trail of Tears had taken its toll on them, but with the vision of Chief John Ross and the hard work of the Cherokee people, they were making a great success of the council.

The Army observers were tired of coming every day, but they persisted even if their presence was not needed, or wanted. They had no real part in the proceedings, and so far had not found out about Mexico's attempt to start a Civil War in Indian Territory. Of course, soldiers like General Federico Guillermo De Almeida would continue to foment rebellion, but soon their attention would be taken away from Indian Territory.

It was a beautiful day when Running Wolf finally located Sasa and drew her aside.

"My daughter, I have been waiting for you. I was afraid that something had happened to you," he said.

"To me? No grandfather, I have been here since the first day of the council. Why were you worried about me?" asked Sasa.

Running Wolf looked around him to see if they were in earshot of anyone who might overhear.

"Daughter, do you remember the present I gave you? You know, the chain bracelet with the scary face and the golden serpent on its head? It is so important that you not wear it. I gave that to you, thinking that I would entrust you with a sacred secret of my people, but I have decided it was too dangerous a responsibility for you to be saddled with it, my daughter," said Running Wolf.

Sasa looked down, not understanding his meaning.

"Grandfather, I am sorry that you felt you could not trust me," she said.

"No, no, my girl. You do not comprehend the danger you are in, at this very moment. I cannot tell you why that image is so important, but it was folly of me to try to pass its history on to some-one not in my own family. I have no wife or children now, and there was no one to pass it to. I am pleading with you that you never wear it. There are very bad men who want the object I modeled the bracelet after, and they might even hurt you for any knowledge you might have about the object. I have made sure no one will find it again, though, so much so I am not even sure exactly where I hid it. I traveled into your country here, I looked day and night for a place. When I found something likely, I went at night to hide it under-ground. I can't even say where that is, because I walked away from it that night. It is as dead to me now, as it should have already been to you," cautioned Running Wolf.

Sasa was startled, but quickly thought about the first time strange things had started to happen. It was when the general danced with me at the ball and demand-ed to know where I got it. Then all of the strangeness on the ship and the steamboat followed, *she thought.*

"Yes, I believe that I have already had contact with some bad people who want my bracelet... I did not under-stand why. I will remain on guard, and Wheezer will, too. Thank you, grandfather, for warning me," she replied, as she waved goodbye.

Far off to the side Mendoza watched the conver-sation, but had no idea what was said. He assumed they were discussing where the Golden Serpent could be found. That was fine with him. Better that the girl be reminded of its location. He strolled away and waited for a better time to grab her.

Sasa went back to her seat behind the platform just as a new speech was about to begin. This time it was the Caddo Chief Cho-wa-wha-na's turn to talk. He said:

I was glad when I received the message to meet my brothers here. I had long heard of my brothers that I had never seen. It makes me glad to meet them all. I have heard the talk, when I get home I will call my people even the women and children; and when I tell them the talk that I heard here, it will be as good as if they were all here and heard it with their own ears. My brothers have made the white path for me to travel on. I will go home on it. Should I take a notion to return at some other time I will travel it again. I have met my older and younger brothers, and my uncles, heard the talk, and will follow it; and I will smoke the pipe and tell all my people what I have heard and seen when I get home. This tobacco that is placed in my hands is for the Comanche Chief with ten strands of beads. I will go and hunt him up and give them to him; and if I get an answer I may come back. That's all.

Next would be the Choctaw Chief, but before he was ready to come up, Sasa overheard a conversation among the observers.

"I don't understand why we have to sit day after day through this repetitive and sometimes incomprehensible parade of Indian speeches, which we mostly don't even understand. So what if the Indians get together to cry for peace? It will never happen, and you know it. Ross has bitten off more than he can chew this time, and Congress will laugh at him on his next trip back to Washington City," said one of the Army Colonels.

"Orders are to be here, translate what we can and make sure our presence is felt. Washington is not so sure that a peace conference is what is really going on here, but here we stay," countered his superior officer.

Sasa would relay that conversation to Ross later. Now Nili-catgah, the Choctaw Chief, was beginning his talk:

All of us that are assembled here, are of different nations and colors.

I am a friend to all. I am glad the Great Spirit has ordered this council for all the Red People and white to meet and talk about peace. We are all brothers from one parent and should not disturb each other at home, or abroad. Whatever we have, we should share agreeably, not take each other's property. You might as well take off one of our legs as rob us. There are some persons of all nations who commit wrongs. and I intend this remark therefore as general. We will all recollect the place in the Muskogee Nation, where the Council Fire is built and where the smoke will ascend to the skies. There are four chiefs in the Choctaw Nation; when we return to our homes all shall hear the talk that has been delivered here. I now close and join with the Osages in wishing to get home, tho' we have been here longer than they have. I am done.

Sasa enjoyed his talk very much, especially since he had included white people as being brothers. She felt that way about Jackson and his family, and she knew of many good white people, but most of the other whites hated Indians or treated them badly. She did not understand the reason for that.

After lunch, Coyote joined her for the next talk.

"Black Dog is going to talk now, and I want to hear what he will say. He is an interesting man. I have been in his camp for many moons now and he has treated me with honor," he explained.

"He is feared by most, I know that. So let's see what he will say," replied Sasa.

Black Dog, Chief of the Osage

Black Dog. the Osage Chief, said:

My brothers: The fire was built, and I was invited here. I have come. I see my brothers want all right. When I saw the broken days (beads) I was in a great hurry to get here and I am now in as great a hurry to get back to carry the news. I want to get to my people before they can go to that tribe at the Salt Plains.

I forgot something you have made the white path to the Pawnee Mahas; now before I get back home some of my young men may have lost horses; shall I pursue them that have stolen them? I will do as you say. Some of my men may be killed. If you say let them alone that have killed my people I will do so. I will now wait your answer. Not only may my people be killed and our horses stolen, but your people served in the same way.

Immediately after Black Dog's speech, Tuckabatchemicco, the Muskogee Chief, although he had already given his talk, stepped up to the podium and said:

I heard my friend Black Dog. I listened to him well, and would advise him to keep near home, and wish he would advise his people not to go out too far; and as soon as we can we will let you know. Advise your women to stay at home and if you must hunt, hunt in some other direction than the Pawnee Mahas.

But a short time since we never heard of such people as the Pawnee Mahas. All should do as our brothers the Osages; bring in all the stolen horses-to the General Council. Hereafter quit stealing horses from one another; all Red men and white men too, mean it for all-this is the first cause of bloodshed. The Cherokees our brothers have straggling men passing through the country-murdering and stealing-this must be put a stop to. I am talking to extend my talk to all under this roof.

I speak as the authorized Chief of the Muskogees - General McIntosh. One thing more, in a Treaty with the United States, we are pledged protection. Troops by agreement are to be stationed at Chateau's Trading House, up the Canadian, and also up the Arkansas, at "Ufosloshago" Town. When we shall all get at peace again with, the different tribes, the troops may be recalled or dispensed with etc. Whenever you meet your friends tell them these troops are placed there for our protection. The Principal Chief of our different brothers must assemble their people when they get home and explain all this; this is the last word I have to say. The next General Council, we will invite our brothers through the different United States Agents, to ensure their safe delivery. Young men sometimes travel in the Dark, and are not enough mindful of this good talk. I am done.

Sasa began to look around the council. She saw so many different types of dress, but all were beautiful to look upon. It gave her joy to know that she was part of such a beautiful people, the Indians of North America. She looked up at Coyote, who stood beside her. He was extremely handsome, but there was no violence in him as she had seen in so many other Indian men. She knew he was destined to be become a Peace Chief, a chief that used diplomacy, rather than force, to effect change or accomplish goals.

"Are we not a beautiful people, Coyote?" she asked, brimming over with emotion.

"We are indeed. But I am afraid that there are terrible times ahead for the Northern and Western plains tribes, like the Lakota. I grieve for them," confessed Coyote.

"Did they not believe you when you told them what had happened here? About all the suffering and death? What about the consequences of strong drink?" Sasa inquired.

"No, not one person—not even my mother—would listen to my talk. They just think that the Lakota and their brother tribes are too powerful to be laid so low as the Cherokee and the Osage. They don't see the need to restrict their young men when it comes to "the drink that makes men crazy", as they put it. I talked until there were no more words to say. And so I left them and I will never return," answered Coyote.

"But, they are your people, Coyote," objected Sasa.

"Yes, they are my people, but they are stiff necked and stubborn headed. I cannot stand by and watch them come to harm when they will do nothing to protect themselves, other than what has worked against the tribes for centuries. They don't believe me when I tell them how numerous the white people are, and that they will not just go home. They will keep coming and coming, and maybe the Lakota will be no more if they are not careful. Maybe they will remember my words when they are coming true for them," replied Coyote, with feeling.

"So what will you do with your life, Coyote," Sasa wanted to know.

"I have been accepted as a blood brother by the Osage. They can now see the peril the tribes are in, and that even the mightiest of us will fall if we do not learn white ways. We have no other choices left. They are a proud people, and they have need of my knowledge and level head. They have many young warriors that want nothing but to go raiding. It will take much to get them to stop this behavior. In the meantime, I had hoped that I could come down from time to time to see you, Sasa. Would you accept my visits? Now that you are educated in the white ways, I am not sure I know how to begin. Do I do it the Lakota way? By the playing of my flute outside your parents lodge until you either tell me to go away or accept the gifts I bring you? You tell me, Sasa. I don't have the education you have, but I do want to learn. Will you teach me more about the white way?" pleaded Coyote.

He looked down on her with soft eyes, ready for her denial.

"Yes, Coyote, I would welcome your visits. Maybe we can find some things in common and maybe I can help you to help your new people, the Osage. Oh look, the Chief of the Winnebagos is getting ready for his talk, let's listen," answered Sasa.

*I am here representing the Chiefs of the Winneba-
goes, Chippewas, Tahwas, and Menawallys.*

*Brothers--Once before we sent you a talk, but have
received no answer. We have concluded. Therefore, to send
you another, as we have been informed that the object for
which the present Council has been called, is that you may
meet all your red brethren in General Council, around the
Great Council We, which you, Muskogees, have kindled
since you came to the West, to renew the friendship that for-
merly existed between your forefathers and other tribes, to
shake hands with one another with the right hand and five
fingers, and to devise the best plan by which our children
shall be trained up in the straight path of peace. The talk
which we send is intended not for the Muskogees alone,
but also for our brethren, the Cherokees, the Choctaws and
Chickasaws. When you receive our talk and beads, and have
explained them to your people, you will, afterwards, please
return them. The beads of different colors, that we send,
will represent the Languages of the tribes that send them.
The Muskogees, and all other tribes, who meet around
your Council Fire, we consider our friends, and wish them
to shake hands with our friends for us. When you return
our beads, send us some of yours, and a talk also, informing us of the proceedings of the council. The talk we send
you, is after the manner of our forefathers. Your friends,
the Tahwas and Menawallys, send some beads, as a token
of their friendship, for the Muskogees, which they wish you
to keep in remembrance of them: so that should they send
any of their people among you, seeing those beads they
will then know that they are from their friends. We hope
the day is not far distant when we shall have the pleasure
to see each other, and when we shall have the opportunity
to shake hands and to talk together.*

Then a group of warriors took the podium:

As our leading chiefs have sent a talk to those of the Cherokees and Muskogees, We, the "warriors" of the four different tribes, the Winnebagoes, Chippewas, Tahwas, and Menawallys, send also a talker and beads of different colors, to our friends, the warriors of the Muskogees, Cherokees, Choctaws, and Chickasaws. The objects we have in sending these beads, are to show that we wish to be friendly with all tribes, and to keep open the White path of peace, that we may train up our children in it, and teach them to be friendly with all men. There are many warriors among us; but we fear there are many calling themselves thus, who are not warriors. According to our old customs, it is our duty to take the talks of our head men, and then follow, they are going ahead, wherever they shall lead, but whenever they fail, we, as warriors take their places, and protect them, our women, and our children. Our friends, we wish to send back a talk in reply to this one.

We, also, along with our talk, send a pipe ornamented with beads and feathers of the eagle. The pipe being painted blue, shows that such is the color of the sky at the time we send it, and which we believe to be a token of friendship. Having received the pipe, fill it with the tobacco attached to it, and let all our friends smoke it for when we shall see the smoke rising up to the sky, then will our hearts feel good. The beads are, also, a token of the friendship which we bear towards our brethren. The Eagle feathers, are intended to keep the White path clean, which has, of late, been stained by blood, you must sweep it out clean with them.

It was a stirring speech. The significance of the eagle feathers was something that Coyote could understand, for his tribe also revered the eagle above all other birds. It was a measure of a young man's hunting prowess to hide himself under a brush blind, with a piece of fresh meat on the top, and when the eagle landed to take the meat, the young man would reach up through the brush to grab its feet. Eagles are strong fighters and it takes all a man can do to hold on to one.

But, even with all of this love going on during this momentous council, Sasa still faced an unknown assailant and Wheezer kept on the watch.

Yellow Eyes

Chapter 38
So, You Saw The Golden Serpent After All

As the talks from the various chiefs continued on, day after day, Sasa never let down her guard, so it was impossible to imagine how the day turned out the way it did.

Sasa and Coyote had just finished lunch while Wheezer and Yellow Eyes frolicked in the sun. One moment the two animals were there playing, and the next they were gone. Sasa thought nothing of it at first, but then she began to be worried.

"Coyote, I don't see either of them. Where do you think they have got to?" she asked.

"I can't think why Yellow Eyes would leave my sight. He usually stays right by my side, no matter what. Tell you what, I will go check out that field over there. I think they may just be in that copse of trees and there may even be a small creek. Maybe they went to get a drink," replied Coyote.

"There are trees in two directions, Coyote. I think I should check out the other side. I will meet you back where they were playing in the field," suggested Sasa.

"All right, but do not go too far in," warned Coyote.

The two young people split up to look for the dog and the coyote. They called, but they received no answer. Coyote continued tracking them further away from the campgrounds. The brush showed signs of their passing and what looked like a person running ahead of them. So he kept going. When he finally found the dogs, they were bewildered and seemed to have lost the scent. Coyote ran up to him and immediately Wheezer looked around for Sasa. Then Coyote found a lump of meat on the ground, which the two had not touched yet, but would have gulped it down if he had not stopped them.

"Something must be wrong with the meat, so keep away from it. Do not eat it, boys," he instructed the pair. "Don't worry, Wheezer, Sasa is waiting for us back at the campgrounds. Come on, both of you. You had us worried," he told the two canines, as they trotted back to the clearing.

Upon reaching the clearing, Coyote called for Sasa.

"Sasa, I have found them. Come on back. They are right here," he cried, but there was no answer.

Now Coyote realized that something was terribly wrong, and so did Wheezer. The three plowed into the trees going as fast as the heavy brush would allow. Coyote looked for signs and found a place where a scuffle had messed up the ground. In the meanwhile, Wheezer and Yellow Eyes sniffed the ground and Wheezer came up growling. Now they searched with a purpose, following the scent that Wheezer knew was Mendoza's.

Sasa had not heard a thing, not even a snap of a twig, before she was taken from behind. She fought, but the man never allowed her a chance to grab her knife. He grabbed it out of its sheath and threw it away while he dragged her further away from the campgrounds and Coyote. His sweaty hand was over her mouth and flies were swarming around his head. The smell of dead flesh was all about him, which disturbed and confused her. He dragged and grappled with her until they were in another copse of trees, out of sight.

"All right now, you filthy squaw, you have evaded me for far too long with your high and mighty ways. You're still just a good for nothing Indian," said Mendoza.

Sasa looked at him and listened to his words, but she could not keep herself from laughing. Her laughter enraged him, and he slapped her hard across the mouth.

She grabbed her cheek.

"Here you are, calling me a filthy Indian. Have you taken a good look at yourself? And what is that you have on your head, you smell like you are dead?" exclaimed Sasa.

As she spoke, however, she realized what she was looking at, since the flies buzzed around his head, and she knew he did not have long hair. She was horrified. He had killed someone just for his hair and clothes.

"What can be so important for you to murder someone for your disguise?" she asked.

"You ought to know by now. You thought you were so clever, wearing that bracelet to the ball. When the general saw it, he knew what it was immediately. I too know that you must know where the artifact is... the Golden Serpent is mine, an Indian should not have it," growled Mendoza.

Sasa tried to let out a yell, but he stopped her with a kick to her knees. She fell hard on the ground.

"Don't think you can call for your trusty, mangy dog and his coyote friend. They are either dead by now, or writhing in pain from the wolf baited meat I used to lure them," said Mendoza with a smile.

Sasa knew the practice of baiting meat with softened bone, curled in a coil, but once the animal ate the meat, the bone would straighten out and the animal would die a horrible death from a punctured stomach or intestines.

"Wheezer, Wheezer, Wheezer," she screamed, and tears began to flow down her face.

Mendoza kicked her in the side, "Get up, and show me where that the Golden Serpent is. Now."

"I have no idea what you are talking about, sir. I never have understood what you men were after. Why don't you leave us alone? I don't have your Golden Serpent and I never did," Sasa sobbed.

Mendoza grabbed her up from the ground with firm hands gripping her arms.

"You must know, otherwise why would you have the charm? You are lying. You must have it, and it is mine," he yelled at her.

Mendoza's eyes became crazed for the want of the object as he shook Sasa with all his strength. Then suddenly, not far away, Mendoza heard the growls of the two canines. He dropped Sasa on the spot and took off running as fast as he could. He reached another clearing with well-worn grass and what looked like cow paddies, which had actually been left there by past runs of buffalo. On he ran with the canines close behind and behind them came Sasa and Coyote.

As Sasa ran she watched to see if Wheezer was minding her to not bite him, but Wheezer did not seem to be listening, for he was biting his feet and legs as he ran.

But, still he ran on and on. Sasa was several yards away when Mendoza disappeared into thin air. The dog stopped running and just stood in the place where Mendoza had vanished.

Mendoza ran for all he was worth and he had not been looking in front of him when all of a sudden the ground was no longer under him and he began to fall. As it is in many cases where tragedy occurs swiftly, the person sees it in slow motion, as did Mendoza at that moment.

He saw the edge of the level ground pass by and he noted small rocks and young trees and looked for purchase on his way down. Then, as if to taunt him before his death, he passed by a small cave where the afternoon sun was shining inside just at the right angle to show Mendoza what he would never have: the Golden Serpent had been propped up at the back of the cave, where no one would ever find it. And as he looked at its grotesque face with the large coiled golden serpent on top, he thought he heard it mocking him. It was at that moment that his fall sped up and the ground and rocks below seemed to shoot up toward him.

It was over quickly. Sasa and Coyote came to the edge of a great rift that ran along past Park Hill. In the past it had been used as a buffalo jump. A place where, many years ago, buffalo were run off the edge to fall to their deaths at the bottom. That is where Mendoza was, laying crumpled among the mounds of bleached white buffalo bones, rocks and young trees that littered the floor of the rift. When they looked down on him, he was actually smiling.

Sasa

Epilogue

It would always be a shining moment in Sasa's life which she would cherish, even though the many unhappy things that had happened that summer of 1843. The first ever Inter-tribal Indian Territory International Peace Conference was held at Park Hill near Tahlequah, the Capitol of the Cherokee Nation. There would be others, through the years, but the first one was an exciting accomplishment for the Cherokee and for Chief John Ross.

She remembered that Chief Ross had thanked her profoundly for her help, while he explained his reasons for calling for the unusual peace conference.

"I don't see that I did all that much. The observers never said anything significant and they did not interfere with the conference. I was just there to listen," said Sasa.

"Don't you realize, Sasa, that so many things could have gone wrong? There were several factions that did not want Indian Territory to find peace among the Indian Nations. The government observers could have taken the speeches they did not understand, and wrongly call the Army out to break up the council, or more whiskey could have made it through. Do you know what would have happened if even one keg of whiskey had been smuggled into the conference? Disaster, plain and simple. Just the fact that it was a success shows us that the Creator answered our prayers. Now if he can help with the fighting between the factions within the Cherokee Nation we could help our people even more," replied Ross.

"I agree that this was an exciting time and we all have reason to be proud of what we've achieved, but I will always remember the sadness and worry I suffered through, over some unseen gold artifact. I will never understand what made that man, Mendoza, go after me for some statue he thought I had hidden. It was incomprehensible to me. It is still a myth that probably never had any basis in fact at all.

"After the council closed, I went looking for Running Wolf to discuss it with him, but he had vanished. I guess he did not want to talk about it. I have asked some who live in his village, but his neighbors don't know where he is," said Sasa.

"So what are your plans, now that the conference is over?" asked the Chief.

"I have agreed to allow Coyote to call on me, and then I plan to learn what I can about running the ranch to help Jackson out. Wheezer will be busy with his new brood of Jack Russell puppies," she said.

"Jack Russells are truly an amazing breed of dog," marveled Chief Ross.

Poison Woman and Medicine Man had walked over from their camp to say they were heading back to their home, and many of the attendees were traveling part of the way home with members of other tribes. It was an encouraging sight. Sasa had no idea how long she would have the benefit of them both; they seemed too tough and stubborn to die.

Now, that wondrous conference was a few years in the past, and things were changing rapidly, but Sasa knew there was still a huge amount of trouble brewing in Indian Territory for the Cherokee. Even though they had had a modicum of peace between the nations, they still faced an almost impossible task, that of trying to bring the various factions within the Cherokee Nation together, under one leadership. On top of that, the promised payment from the U.S. Congress had not been paid. Every few months, Chief Ross would make the trip to Washington City to plead his case. It seemed that no matter what amount the United States agreed to in any treaty with the Indian nations, when it came time to fulfill their part, the Army or the Congress would drag their feet in an effort to whittle the agreed upon amount down. The chief fought hard and long to make sure his people received the payment they were promised.

Sasa and her family now worried about the influx of desperadoes and criminals coming into Indian Territory to hide from the law, but the Cherokee had their own laws, which they would enforce by force if necessary.

Things were changing also in the various states of the American nation. Strife continued to build between the slave owners of the South and the abolitionists of the North. She wondered if it would erupt in bloodshed someday. Only time would tell.

Wheezer was getting older now, but no less committed to his family and Sasa. He had taught her a lot about love and loyalty, for which she was profoundly grateful.

Even though it had been some time since that summer and the 1843 conference, Sasa was aware that the Americans had never figured out the reason why Chief Ross held that council. America never knew how close they had come to a cunning invasion from Mexico. Mexico was unsuccessful in starting a civil war within Indian Territory, and because of that failure, their plan to invade while the U.S. Army was embroiled in an Indian Territory war was a complete and utter failure. And all thanks to the Chief of the Cherokees, Chief John Ross.

And shortly after the conference, Mexico was plunged into war with the United States, and ended up losing New Mexico and California in the process. They should have quit while they were ahead.

Sasa, Wheezer and the rest of her family, both Cherokee and white, successfully bridged the gap of hate and prejudice. She would forever be thankful for that.

As far as the interest that Coyote showed in continuing to call on her, she still had not balanced the feelings of her heart and that of her goal to help her people. Perhaps one day she could allow herself to dream of a normal family life. Until then, she wanted to be wherever her people needed her, even if it were just advising a business owner, or farmer, using her legal expertise. She had no illusions about how women were viewed as far as business was concerned, so she would have to keep working behind the scenes and just be available and willing to help. Let the world continue to underestimate women, she would keep faith that it would not always be so. Maybe, far into the future, there would be a bright horizon for her people and for women in general. She hoped with all her heart and soul that she would be alive to see it.

Wheezer crept up to her side as she sat at her writing desk, while she finished up some overdue letters, and placed his front paws on her seat. Then, while standing on his back legs, he laid his beautiful snout on her lap as his back end wiggled from the furious wagging of his white tail. He buried his face in the folds of her full skirt and snuffled from pure enjoyment. His big brown eyes met her bold brown ones and it was as if they knew each other's heart. Their bond was more than friendship, more than love. It was a bond made up of those qualities, as well as unbreakable loyalty and dedication, plus some other quality Sasa could not name, something which seemed spiritual in nature. It was the bond that the Creator meant for mankind to have with the animal kind of the earth.

Sasa put her hand on top of Wheezer's head and pet it softly. With Wheezer still at her side, she knew she could succeed at anything at all.

The End

The Real Wheezer

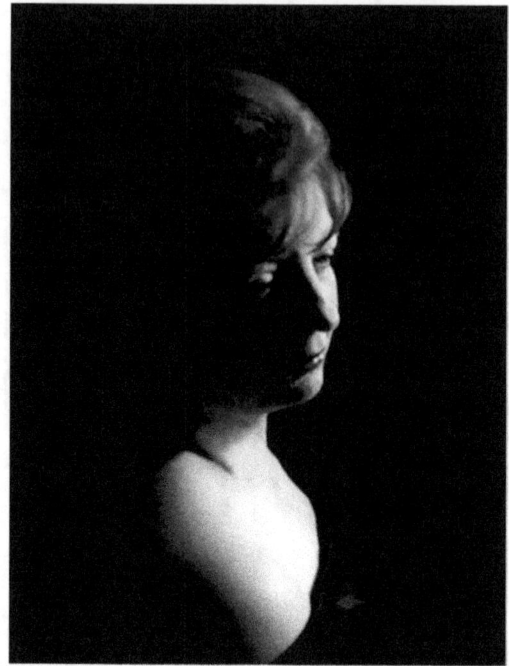

About the Author:

Kitty Sutton was born Kathleen Kelley to a Osage/Irish family. Both sides of her family were from performing families in Kansas City, Missouri and Kitty was trained from an early age in dance, vocal, art and musical instruments. Her father was a Navy Band leader. During the Great Depression, her mother helped to support her family by tap dancing in the speakeasys even though she was just a child; she was very tall for her age but made up like an adult. Kitty had music and art on all sides of her family which ultimately helped to feed her imaginative mind and desire to succeed.

Kitty married a wonderful Cherokee artist from Oklahoma, in fact the very area that she writes about in her Wheezer series of novels. After raising her family, Kitty came to Branson, Missouri and performed in her own one woman show there for twelve years. To honor her father, she performed under the name Kitty

Kelley. She has three music albums and several original songs to her credit and is best known for her comical, feel good song called It Ain't Over Till The Fat Lady Sings. Kitty has been writing for many years and in 2011 we accepted her manuscript of an historical Native American murder mystery. First in a series of stories featuring Wheezer, a Jack Russell Terrier and his Cherokee friend, Sasa, it is called, *Wheezer And The Painted Frog.* Kitty lives in the southwestern corner of Missouri near Branson with her husband of 40 years and her three Jack Russell Terriers, one of which is the real and wonderful Wheezer.

References

Cherokee.org/AboutTheNations/Culture/ About the Nation: Cherokee Medicinal Herbs

About the Nation: Traditional Belief System

About the Nation: Festivals

About the Nation: Hospitality

About the Nation: Clans

American Cookery (1st Ed, 1796, cover)<u>Public Domain</u>

Amelia Simmons, Hudson & Goodwin - Image from Library of Congress. In the Public Domain.

Lovelongears.com/about_mules What is a mule?

Mulemuseum.org/history-of-the-mule History of the Mule & Mule Museum

rootsweb.ancestry.com/-kylchgrs/Business/Livestocktrade

Mule and Horse Trade Between Kentucky and the South

1840-1860, Compiled and Researched By Kym Hitchcock

Chronicles of Oklahoma Pierce Mason Butler By Carolyn Thomas Foreman

wikipedia.org/wiki/Osage_Nation

Wenonah's Stories By **Robin R Gunning** The International Council of 1843

Chronicles of Oklahoma An Indian Territory United Nations:

The Creek Council of 1845 By A. M. Gibson

If you enjoyed *Wheezer and the Shy Coyote,* or if you have questions, or constructive criticism, you may contact Ms. Sutton at kittyandcompany@centurytel.net.

Wheezer and the Painted Frog, Wheezer and the Golden Serpent, and *Wheezer and the Giveaway Child* can be found at Amazon, Barnes & Noble and fine booksellers everywhere.

Also, visit Kitty's website at:
www.kittysutton.weebly.com

Be sure to check out the other books by Kitty Sutton in this series.

Wheezer and the Shy Coyote
Wheezer and the Golden Serpent
Wheezer and the Giveaway Child
And soon to be released
Wheezer and the Road to Gold